THE PRICE OF COURAGE

THE PRICE OF COURAGE

A Korean War Novel

CURT ANDERS

GUILD PRESS OF INDIANA, INC.
Carmel, Indiana

While the major events in this book have had their counterparts in the author's experience, none of the actual incidents occurred as they are set forth here, nor are any of the characters other than completely fictional. Any parallels between any character in this book and any real person, living or dead, are completely coincidental.

THE PRICE OF COURAGE
PRINTING HISTORY:
Sagamore Press Inc., New York, 1957
reprinted by Guild Press of Indiana, Inc., 1999

All rights reserved.
Copyright © 1957 by Curtis L. Anders
No part of this book may be reproduced or copied by any means without express permission from the publisher. For information contact:

GUILD PRESS OF INDIANA, INC.
435 Gradle Drive
Carmel, Indiana 46032

The Guild Press of Indiana Web Site address is
www.guildpress.com

ISBN 1-57860-040-5
Library of Congress Catalog Card Number 57-12432

Printed and bound in the United States of America

Respectfully dedicated
to the officers and men of the combat arms
of the United States army—
especially to those who have known
the terrible loneliness of
being shot at

"The right to command
is no longer a privilege
transmitted by nature, like an inheritance;
it is the fruit of labor,
the price of courage."

VOLTAIRE

The Price of Courage

One

Whenever infantrymen are at war in a hostile month like February, they are certain to spend many of their daylight hours sitting around small campfires, dreading the moment when they must get up, leave their fires, and walk out ahead of the last safe ridge to extend the limits of their government another hilltop or two. While they wait by their fires, they wonder: "Will I get hit this time?" "How bad will it be?" "Is there something else I ought to be doing now, since I might not—?" But they seldom talk about such thoughts. Instead, they sit and watch the flames and soak in warmth, as though it were possible to store up life against the chilling instant when the first enemy soldier aims his weapon at a man and sends death darting across the disputed ground.

There were a number of campfires burning beside a winding road on the backside of a far-away mountain not long ago, and the men of George Company sat huddled around them. The men were waiting, and wondering, and hoping that they would not have to leave their fires to join in the attack that they knew was about to begin. They had been sitting by their fires since the middle of the morning; now it was mid-afternoon, and still the word to move up to the top of the long ridge had not come. The sky was overcast and the wind was sharp, and the men knew that the cold darkness would come up from the riverbottoms early that evening.

Captain Sam Mann shivered as he thought of the danger of attacking so late in the day, but the warmth of the fire he was watching and the hope that the attack would—somehow—be postponed chased his cold fear away.

Like his men, Sam Mann wondered if he ought to be doing something else. He had been up to the top of the long ridge twice—once to hear Major Dahl give the battalion attack order, and once more for a good look down at the rocky riverbed which he would have to lead his men across, and at the ugly, steep hill beyond, which he would have to lead them up. He had long since given his platoon leaders their orders; and only a few minutes before, he had walked through the company area from campfire to campfire talking to the men, checking their weapons and ammunition, and always, as he left, saying something to lift their spirits—as a good company commander should. Now, sitting by Sergeant Gregg's campfire, he wondered if there was something else he should check, something he should do—

The men in George Company had noticed that the traffic along the narrow mountain road which ran by their clearing had been heavy all day. The Third Battalion, which held the long ridge above George Company's campfires, had moved its jeeps and trucks past the clearing around noon. Then five tanks had rumbled up toward the pass at the top of the sharp ridge—the pass which marked the end of friendly territory.

Captain Mann and Sergeant Gregg looked up from their fire as a jeep turned off the road, drove into the clearing, and parked beside Captain Mann's jeep. A tall young man, dressed in dark green fatigue trousers and a field jacket and wearing a steel helmet, got out of the jeep and walked toward the fire.

"It's Lieutenant Holloway," Sergeant Gregg said. "Wonder if he's got the bad news?"

Holloway heard Gregg's question.

"No, Top," he said, "I'm just looking for some drinkin' whiskey."

Holloway sat down beside Gregg's fire.

"See if there's a jug in the jeep, Top," the company commander told Gregg.

4

The first sergeant, a broad grin on his bearded, round face, got up and walked over to the captain's jeep, fished around inside a bulky green bag until he found a fifth, then brought the bottle back to the fire and sat down.

The big captain took the bottle, opened it, and handed it to the guest, who took a long pull.

"Oh, that helps," Eric Holloway said.

Holloway handed the bottle to Gregg.

"What's doing up at battalion?" Mann asked.

Holloway took off his steel helmet and roughed-up his blond hair.

"Nothing much. I've been standing in that damned pass all day looking for signs of the enema, but they're pretty hard come-by."

"Intelligence business ain't so good, huh?"

"Not today. But I don't think I'll be in this job much longer, anyway."

"How come?"

Gregg passed the bottle to the company commander, and Mann took a heroic swig.

"Oh, I don't know. I've been thinking of trying to transfer to another battalion. Staff jobs are dead-end propositions."

"Hell, you'll get promoted to captain sooner or later," Gregg said.

Gregg had been around the Army long enough to know about such things.

"You lookin' for a company?" Mann asked.

"Sure."

"Think one of the other battalions might have one for you, huh?"

"Think I'll find out."

"What have you got against that big fat rear-echelon job you've got now?" Sergeant Gregg asked.

"Oh, it'll do. Not much to it, though. Been dull as hell lately. And I ought to have some company command experience in my record. That'd come in handy after this thing's over. Some of the people who came over when I did have companies."

"Well, what's the talk up at the pass?" Mann asked.

"Everybody's getting restless. Major Dahl and some rear-echelon operations officer—a Major Merlin—have been going round and round about whether or not to attack. The General's on his way up here now, so I don't think there'll be much more delay."

"We might stay, you think?" Gregg asked hopefully.

"Might. Depends on what the General says when he gets here for his look-see."

"That bastard Merlin's the one that ought to come, so's I could put a forty-five slug right between his eyes."

Lieutenant Holloway frowned.

Mann asked, "You think there's much across the river?"

"Hard to say," Eric Holloway answered. "Could be loaded. It's a good place for them to defend, with the river and all. Still, it might be a walk-in."

Mann was nettled by the answer, for it told him nothing. Best change the subject, he thought.

"Want another drink?"

"Yes, thanks."

Holloway took the bottle, took another long pull, then handed it to Gregg.

"How's Wayne Hyde making out up there at battalion?" Sam Mann asked.

Hyde was another young officer who had recently been a platoon leader in George Company.

"All right, I guess."

"Wayne getting restless, too?"

"I don't know."

"I don't reckon he is," Gregg said. "After what he's been through, I don't reckon he'll want no part of a comp'ny this side of the end of the war."

"Yep," Mann said, "and I figure he had plenty of time to think about it when he was a prisoner, last time."

Eric Holloway looked directly at Mann.

6

"You saying I ought to forget about wanting a chance to command a company?"

"No," Mann answered, putting the cork back in the whiskey bottle. "I was just thinking—you've got your hands pretty full right now."

Mann almost went on to say, "I'd get back up there and find out what's out there on that mountain waiting for us," but he figured that Holloway would realize that, himself.

Holloway was feeling a bit embarrassed. I shouldn't have talked about wanting a company to Mann, he thought. Mann might think I want something to happen to him, so that I can get George Company. I mustn't talk about this any more.

Eric rose to go.

"Well, you're right, sir. I ought to be getting back up there."

"Yep."

"Many thanks for the grog."

"You're welcome. Tell Wayne to come see us."

Eric nodded.

Captain Mann and the first sergeant watched the young officer walk back over to his jeep and get in. Holloway waved, and they waved back, and then he drove back up the road to battalion.

Mann and Gregg looked back at their fire, and waited, and wondered.

2

The staff officers at the top of the long ridge called the enemy's mountain the Shark, because on the map its shape resembled the head of a shark with his jaws wide open, swimming west. George Company's mission was to move up along the Shark's lower jaw toward the eye, which was the highest point on the enemy's mountain. To get to the Shark's lower jaw, George Company had to move across several hundred yards of level ground, wade the river, then cross an east-west road that hugged the riverbank. The climb to the top would not take very long, and once the attackers had the high ground, Major Dahl could order his other two rifle companies to cross the concrete bridge that spanned the river on the right side of his zone of action, below the Shark's neck.

In all, George Company would have to move about one mile—but a very long, hard mile.

There were two great dangers that worried the Second Battalion's staff officers: the coming of night, and the unpredictable enemy. Darkness was the enemy's ally; nothing could be done to delay it, but the men in the narrow pass had planned to unload hell itself on the Shark's defenders. The Second Battalion's heavy weapons company had machine guns, recoilless rifles, and mortars aimed out across the valley and the river at the Shark; the forward observers from the artillery battalion that supported the regiment had already registered concentrations on the Shark's peak, where the enemy was supposed to be; and if all this proved insufficient, the Third Battalion, dug-in along the long ridge on both sides of the pass, could turn loose its firepower. But unless the attack took place right away, very few of the supporting weapons would be able to shift or concentrate their fire if necessary—and darkness was stealing a little more visibility with every passing minute. Soon it would be too late to go at all, or prohibitively expensive in casualties; and in either case, Lawrence Dahl rather expected to be relieved of his command by the irate division commander who came thundering up the narrow path which led from the pass to the top of the knob Dahl was using for an observation post.

"Get off your hind-end, Dahl!" the General bellowed. "I've seen all I need to see. By God, Merlin was right. You listen here, Dahl. I want that piece of real estate, and I want it within two hours."

Dahl saluted.

"Very well, sir."

He turned to his operations officer, Captain Harry Hamilton.

"All right, Harry," he said quietly.

Harry Hamilton began giving orders: he told the men who controlled the fire of the supporting weapons to turn loose their hell; called Sam Mann on the radio and told him to "Move your people up the road a-piece," meaning across the long ridge, down the forward slope into the valley, across the river, and up the Shark; and finally he called regimental headquarters to report that the attack had jumped off.

The race with darkness was on, with darkness heavily favored to beat George Company to the top of the Shark.

Sergeant Trent, down on the road, called "Lieutenant Holloway!" several times, as though something terribly urgent had come up.

"What's the trouble, Trent?" Holloway answered when he joined the sergeant on the road.

"A native just came running in from over on the Shark, sir. Says the enemy's not on top, at all. He's dug-in on both flanks—and this guy says they're really loaded."

"Hell, Trent," Holloway replied. "You know we don't trust spies' reports. Besides, I've got a life-size picture of what would happen if Dahl changed the plan of attack and sent people over to the flanks—they'd just get creamed by the fire from the top."

"But the native's been over there," Trent said earnestly, pointing toward the Shark. "He risked getting knocked off by both sides to come tell us."

The artillery liaison officer, Lieutenant Granger, stood a few feet away, watching the two men argue. Giles Granger was a bitter skeleton, five-times wounded, wired together with hate—hate for war, and hate for stupidity. Granger wanted to walk over and intervene, but instead he turned away and watched George Company's men fan out over the open ground between the ridge they had just left behind them and the river bank.

"Okay, Trent, you've told me," Holloway said as he watched the first few men in George Company's leading platoon plunge into the icy water.

Granger grabbed his radio's microphone and told the artillery fire direction center to get ready for a sudden shift. Round after round had slammed into the top of the Shark, and the machine guns and recoilless rifles from How Company were working over the near slopes of the Shark's lower jaw, moving their fire along the path that George Company's men would probably have to follow to the top.

When ten or twelve of George Company's men had emerged on the far bank of the river, the enemy cut loose at them with machine guns and rifle fire—from both flanks. The men dropped, and their screams and shouts were soon joined by cries of surprise and agony which came up from the rocky, almost frozen river where the rest of the company was pinned down.

Granger yelled the commands for shifting the artillery fire into his radio. Captain Hamilton ran down to shift the fire of How Company's supporting weapons, cursing as he ran.

Sergeant Trent turned to Holloway.

"That's where the native said they'd be—right at the Goddam bottom!"

Eric nodded.

"Looks like I goofed, Sergeant."

Holloway ran up to Major Dahl's observation post.

"Sir, a native reports that the enemy's defending at the base of the Shark," he shouted.

The General turned and stared at Eric.

"Lieutenant," he said, "I'd say that was pretty Goddam obvious."

Out on the Shark, George Company got up under Granger's artillery fire and slugged it out with the enemy defenders at the left tip of the Shark's lower jaw in a sharp, bitter fire-fight. Granger was putting artillery fire onto the defenses at the right, too, but the smoke and dust of the explosions was floating across the scene to the right, obscuring his vision.

Darkness had gained a tremendous lead over George Company.

The General fretted and fumed.

"By God, Dahl, the way this thing's going, George Company's not going to get to the top of that damned hill any time today. Are you going to get me that Goddam mountain, or aren't you?"

Dahl turned to the General and answered him in a calm voice.

"General, you'll have that mountain."

Then Dahl left the division commander and walked down to the pass.

"Call Easy Company," Dahl told Harry Hamilton. "Have John Heath move Easy Company down from their assembly area to the riverbank to the right of the concrete bridge as quickly as he can. Tell him I'll meet them there. I'm going to take them up to the top of the Shark from the right. Then call Sam Mann and tell him to get on up the Shark's ridge—the left end, just above where he is now—if he can. And tell Mann to look out for us."

"Yes, sir."

Hamilton began calling orders into the radio, using vague terms and double-talk to confuse any enemy monitor who might be listening on a captured set.

Lawrence Dahl pulled out the forty-five he had never fired in anger and checked the ammunition clip to make sure it was fully loaded. He put the pistol on safety and slipped it back into the holster, then he closed his eyes and prayed. Then he was ready: he called his radioman to him, and together they started down the road to meet Easy Company.

After Dahl left, Eric stayed by the radio and overheard Dahl's transmissions to Hamilton.

"We're about to cross the river. . . ."

Then, about ten minutes later: "They must have pulled out on this side. Haven't hit a thing yet."

Still later: "Climbing, now. . . ."

At six-fifteen, in complete darkness: "Harry, tell the General we're on top. Then bring the rest of the battalion across, but keep everybody off the bridge—it's mined."

Dahl's voice sounded strained, as though he were very tired.

Captain Hamilton told the General that the objective was secured.

The General grunted, then got into his jeep and drove back to division headquarters.

Captain Hamilton walked over and stood directly in front of Eric.

"Well, that hot news about the native's report really impressed the General."

"It would have, if I'd told him when I should have."

"You mean you knew—?"

Eric nodded.

"Eric, dammit, don't you know that an intelligence officer has the duty to pass along everything he picks up in the way of information of the enemy?"

"Of course I do," Eric said shortly, turning away to look at the dark mass called the Shark.

"All right, then. How come you sat on that native's report?"

"I didn't believe it. You can't trust spies—"

"That's not for you to decide. That's Major Dahl's problem. You're not commanding this battalion—you're not responsible for these eight hundred lives. He is. And he needs all the help we can give him. You tell him what you find out, and let him decide what to do about it. And it's about time you began using your common sense, if you've got any, and quit—"

"Yes, but that's what I—"

"Shut up, Holloway. Now let's get this thing straightened out right now. You better by God start paying some attention to what you're supposed to be doing around here. Do you understand, or must I draw pictures?"

"Certainly I understand."

12

"Tack a 'sir' onto that and stand at attention when I'm talking to you."

Hamilton leaned over and picked up the radio handset to call out the orders for the movement of the rest of the battalion across to the Shark. When he had finished, he gave Holloway an order:

"You go over to the Shark and make sure the left end of George Company's line is tied in with the right end of the First Battalion."

"But I've got to—"

"You've got nothing to do but do as you're told. Now get out of here before I cream you!"

Holloway told Trent he was going over to George Company.

"You're taking the radio operator, aren't you, sir?" Sergeant Trent asked.

"No, I won't need him. I'll see you at the battalion command post when I've gotten George and the First Battalion tied in."

Then Eric Holloway headed down the road in the dark toward the river and the Shark. He wasn't quite sure where the First Battalion was—he thought it was supposed to be on the left of the Shark someplace, near the creekbed, probably. If Hamilton wants me to be his errand-boy, Eric thought, the least he can do is tell me exactly where these people are and what he wants me to do. This isn't fair.

When Eric was about half-way across the bridge, he remembered having heard Major Dahl say that the bridge was mined. He stopped, terrified. He dared not move. He stood there in the dark for fully a minute, scarcely breathing.

There were three things he could do: he could turn around and walk back the way he had come, or he could wait there until the engineers came up to clear the bridge, or—or he could keep going.

Eric took another step, and felt a tight wire give slightly as his stomach touched it. He froze.

He had walked into a booby-trap.

He listened for the explosion he knew was coming, but nothing happened. Then he sucked in his breath, gently pulling his stomach back from the wire. Safe! But he was dizzy and afraid of falling into the wire, so he took a step backward, and squatted down to rest.

He took a few deep breaths and tried to think. Then he decided to try to disconnect the wire. God, how I wish I could see, he thought. He reached out—slowly, slowly, until his fingertips found the deadly wire, then he slid his fingertips along the wire, gently, slowly, seeking the pin on the explosive charge and yet trying to keep from touching it.

I'm trembling too damned much, he thought.

His fingers came to a knot in the wire, and then felt a ring. Holding his breath, he slid a finger around the ring until he felt the corrugated surface of a hand grenade, then he put his finger inside the ring while he closed the rest of his fingers around the grenade. Then he slid a finger of his other hand along the wire until he came to the knot in the trip wire. Carefully, very carefully, he untied the knot, and the wire dropped free.

That's that, he thought, and he let out a long sigh.

Holloway stood up and took a step forward. Nothing. Then another step. Nothing. Then another. He thought he might be on the road again, so he knelt down and felt for the ground. His fingers found cold dirt: he was off the bridge.

3

When Eric Holloway came to the left end of George Company's line, at the tip of the Shark's lower jaw, he heard men talking on the other side of a narrow creek—just where he figured the First Battalion ought to be.

"Are you people in Red?" Holloway called.

Red was the code-word for the First Battalion.

"Yes, and for Christ's sake shut up!"

"This is White over here," Lieutenant Holloway replied.

"Okay—now get the hell out of here and quit that Goddam yelling."

Eric Holloway bristled at that.

Eric looked for Captain Mann for the better part of the next hour, since he knew he ought to tell him where the First Battalion's people were, but he couldn't find Sam Mann, or his command post, or any of the men in George Company. Finally he gave up, and headed back down the road to battalion.

As he neared the bridge, Eric heard Hamilton talking to someone.

"Who's that?" Hamilton snapped.

"Holloway."

"Where'n the living hell have you been? Did you get George Company tied in?"

"I found Red, but I couldn't find Captain Mann."

"Well, I knew something was cockeyed. Red's been cussin' me out over the phone for the last fifteen minutes. They say they're not tied in. Now, dammit, what gives? Did you cross over and get the location of their machine guns? Did you arrange to tie in the phone wire when it gets there? Did you get the location of their C. P. foxholes?"

There was an awkward pause, then Eric answered, "No, sir."

"Well, you didn't tie them in, did you?"

Holloway couldn't frame an answer.

"Just what did you do over there, Holloway?"

"I talked with some of their people. They said they understood where we were. They were satisfied."

"Well, by God I'm not. Do you know who you talked to?"

"No, sir. Said they were in Red—that's all."

"They were the battalion headquarters jeep drivers, that's who they were. Their battalion commander told me some clown was back there yelling his head off. He just couldn't believe an officer in the United States Army could be such a Goddam fool, and I told him I was sure that you wouldn't do such a damnably foolish thing. See? Do you see, Holloway?"

Eric was too stunned to answer.

Well, he thought, I'd better go fix it. He turned back toward the road to the tie-in point.

"Where do you think you're going?"

"Back down there to fix it like you want it. I'd have done it to suit you the first time if you'd told me what you wanted instead of—"

"God damn it, shut up!"

A moment later, Hamilton said, "Eric, the best thing you can do to please me is to find your sleeping bag and get the hell inside it and stay there until the Goddam war's over."

"But the tie-in—"

"Forget about the tie-in and do as you're told. I'm going to send Wayne Hyde to do it."

4

A battalion command post in combat is not very glamorous: no teletypes clattering, no "war room" for briefings, no gaily-painted signs proclaiming "We Came To Fight!" A telephone, a map, and Major Dahl—these constituted the Second Battalion's C. P., and by nine o'clock that night all three had been brought together in the one usable room of a ruined farmhouse about a hundred yards west of the concrete bridge.

Harry Hamilton, the operations officer, dozed in one corner of the room. Hamilton was a fairly short man, but he was chunky, and people remembered him when they met him because his hair was almost white. Holloway sat in another corner, sleepy but unable to sleep. Major Dahl, dead tired from the climb to the Shark's peak and the strain of the whole long day, slept in the third corner of the small room. The map and the phone were on the floor. It was cold in the little room, but not so cold as it was in the shallow foxholes up on the Shark.

Eric tried to pretend that the candle was a campfire: it was silly, he knew, but it helped him stay awake. His short visit at George Company that afternoon had been the only part of the day in which he had been comfortable. I don't belong here at battalion, he thought. And after tonight, I'll never be able to ask for a company. Eric tried to imagine what would happen to him next, but he couldn't foresee anything but more bickering with Hamilton. I was wrong in not passing that spy's report on, Eric admitted. But Hamilton—

Wayne Hyde came through the narrow door a few minutes later. He had just returned from tying in George Company and the First Battalion, and his boots and green field trousers were sopping wet from wading the creek.

"You look like a drowned cat," Hamilton said, waking up. "Our sleeping bags are outside in the jeep. Go find yours and get in it before you catch pneumonia and die."

"Thanks. I'll dry out pretty soon. Who's duty officer?"

"Nobody," Hamilton answered. "We're sweating out a counter-attack."

"Has Eric heard something?"

"No. But if we get through the night without one, I'll be mighty surprised."

"I see."

Wayne Hyde sat down in the last corner.

"You hear any gossip over at Red?"

"Negative. But they want us to put our tanks in by the creek in the morning. They're pretty worried about getting hit there tonight. I said I'd tell you."

"Good. Sure you don't want some sleep?"

"Nope. I'm good for a long time yet."

5

Shortly after the companies up on the Shark had called in their midnight reports, Eric stood up and stretched. He was cramped from sitting in the corner, and he was bored. He hadn't been able to drop off to sleep, and his sense of a staff officer's duty wouldn't let him do as Hamilton had told him —to get in his sleeping bag and stay there.

This is madness, he thought as he settled back into his corner. This is no way for officers to be acting. I never dreamed combat would be like this—silly, petty, wasteful sniping. Brother officers! What crap!

Then Eric dozed off.

About two o'clock, Wayne Hyde woke him.

"Phone call for you, Eric. Sergeant Gregg."

Eric took the handset.

"Yes, Gregg," he said wearily.

"Lieutenant, some of the men in Digger Dolan's squad hear jabberin' out in front of 'em. Think it might be somethin'?"

"It could be. I'll be right up there."

Holloway handed Hyde the phone.

"I'm going up to George Company," he said. "I'll send Sergeant Trent in to spell you."

As he walked along the road toward George Company in the dark, Eric Holloway decided he was in luck. Now he was functioning again, doing the job he was supposed to be doing. If there is anything at all to this report of Gregg's, he thought, I can show Hamilton—and Major Dahl, too.

Above the road the ground was rocky and overgrown, and Holloway slipped several times and took some rather clumsy falls as he climbed. Once, when he had stopped to catch his breath from the steep climb, it occurred to him that he might have made another serious mistake.

"Oh, hell!" he said.

I should have told Dahl, he thought. I've got to get to a phone—if anything happens before I do—

The nearest phone was at George Company's command post, but Eric had no idea where that was.

He scrambled up to the top of the Shark's lower jaw, but when he reached the top, no one was there. Just a gap in the line, he thought, so he walked on down the jaw to the left, thinking that surely he'd find someone soon.

But George Company wasn't there. Mann had moved his men one more ridgeline forward—to the Shark's upper jaw.

When Eric came to the end of the ridge Mann had moved from, he stepped out onto the road that curled around it. He was at the same place he had been earlier that night, when he had been trying to tie in George Company and the First Battalion.

Eric knew he couldn't be in front of George Company, so he started walking up the road toward the tip of the Shark's upper jaw. He would run into the line sooner or later, then get to a phone and tell Dahl.

"Halt!" someone ordered in a hoarse whisper. "Who's that?"

Holloway heard the *snap* of a safety being pushed off.

The password, he thought frantically. What's the damned password?

"Business," Holloway said.

His heart was beating furiously, and his breath was coming in short gasps.

"Machine," the hoarse voice answered.

The safety *snapped* again, and a soldier stood up about five feet away from the officer. Eric could see that the soldier's rifle was pointed at him.

"I don't know who you are, Bud," the hoarse voice drawled, "but you sure like to got drilled just now."

"I'm Lieutenant Holloway, and I'm looking for the company C. P."

"Up the ridge a-ways."

The soldier shifted his grip on the rifle, but he kept it pointed at the officer.

"Is this the line?"

"It is."

Holloway left the soldier standing there and blundered his way on up the Shark's upper jaw. He stumbled over two or three sleeping men, and once he fell into a foxhole on top of a man.

Finally he found Sergeant Dolan.

"Gregg said you heard something out in front of the line," Holloway said.

"Yessir, I did," Dolan answered. "But they didn't make as much noise as you did comin' up here from Towson's hole down on the road."

"Could you tell how many were out there? Or what they were up to?"

"Nope."

When he left Dolan and started on up toward the company C. P., Eric worked his way along the backside of the ridge to avoid bumping into any more men, but he bumped into a number of treetrunks and boulders in the blackness and made very poor time.

It would have been so easy, he thought, if I'd just stayed there at battalion. All I needed to do was wake Dahl and tell him what Gregg told me, and everything would have been fine. But this—this is no damned good.

Holloway decided to give up and go back to battalion.

Eric was almost at the bottom of the backside of the ridge when the sound of heavy machine gun fire made him drop awkwardly on the rocky slope. A real fire-fight broke out then, with rifle fire and burp-gun bursts and an occasional *crunch* of a hand grenade. When Eric dared look up, he saw bright yellow streaks—tracers—arching over the ridge, and the sharp cracking of enemy small-arms fire passing nearby deafened him.

Holloway hugged the frozen ground, shaking with fright.

6

Thirty minutes later, the firing stopped: George Company had beaten off the attack.

A few minutes after Eric got up and started up the line again, he found George Company's command post.

"Where's Captain Mann?" he asked Sergeant Gregg.

"He's over in the First Platoon helping Digger and Sergeant Hicks straighten out the mess you caused."

"Wait a minute, Sergeant. Cut that out right now. I didn't cause any mess."

"Lieutenant, you got your Goddam nerve comin' here to my C.P. after the way you goofed things up. You know who just got kilt out there?"

"No."

"Towson did. You know why he's deader'n hell right now?"

"No."

" 'Cause he stood out there and yakked with you instead of slicing your Goddam throat! And the enema must have been praying for some stupid son of a bitch to make some noise—"

The first sergeant paused a moment. Though it was too dark for him to see Gregg's dirty, bearded face, Eric sensed that Gregg was crying and trying to conceal it.

"You better be glad the company commander isn't here. He'd kill you with his bare hands."

"Where's the phone, Top?"

"Tied to that there tree."

Lieutenant Holloway called battalion. Major Dahl ordered him to get back to battalion as soon as he could.

7

Hamilton saw Eric and stopped him before he got to Major Dahl's room in the ruined farmhouse.

"Eric, you really excelled," Hamilton said. "Not only did you leave here without telling anyone what was up, you gave away the positions out there and got some of the men in your old platoon killed. Not only did you get this battalion shot up, but the enemy got in behind Red and raised hell with their battalion C.P. Colonel Wright's over there right now in a damned foxhole, with half his staff officers runnin' around trying to mop up, and the other half dying or dead."

"That'll do, Harry," Major Dahl said from the doorway of the house. "Come in here, please, Eric."

Eric Holloway went inside.

"Eric, we all have bad days. But you've had just about the worst I've ever heard of. One hell of a bad day. One hell of a lot of bad luck."

"It isn't luck, sir."

"Then what is it?"

"I don't know, sir. Captain Hamilton and I have had a few misunderstandings, for one thing."

A look of surprise came over the battalion commander's square-cut features.

"Surely you don't think that's an excuse—"

"Well, Major, he's had me doing things that aren't my job. He's blaming me for things that really aren't my fault."

"Just whose fault is it, Eric, that these things have happened?"

Eric looked down at the candle on the floor.

"Mine, sir."

"That will be all, Eric. Go get some sleep. Wayne Hyde will call you if you're needed."

"Very well, sir."

Outside, in the cold darkness, Eric pulled his sleeping bag out of the jeep trailer and spread the bag on the ground. He took off his steel helmet and his pistol belt and put them on the frozen ground near the place where his head would be, then he crawled into the bag with all of his clothes—and his boots—on. He zipped up the bag and tried to relax, but he couldn't relax—

I'm finished, he thought. *And I wanted a company!*

Two

An army on the offensive is high-ground hungry. As soon as infantrymen have slugged and bled their way up one miserable mountain, there's always another one on the skyline up ahead, and the men know that sooner or later someone back in the rear will pass the order forward for them to "Go get it."

The Second Battalion had seized the Shark after dark, but Major Dahl and Captain Hamilton knew quite a bit about the next mountain—the Octopus—before the sun came up the next morning. They knew from the hours they had spent staring at the map that the Octopus was going to be theirs to get, for it was due north of the Shark. Their only question was, "When will they tell us to go?"

The Octopus' peak was two or three miles from the Shark. One tentacle hooked northeast from the Octopus' peak, another ran due east; both of these would belong to the enemy until the fight neared its end, for the three long tentacles that reached southward were the most likely approaches for the attackers. Of these three tentacles, the one on the left ran west of the peak for several hundred yards, then turned south; just before it turned, the center tentacle branched south toward the Shark's upper jaw; and the third tentacle, the one on the right, ran due south from the Octopus' peak. The ugly mountain dominated the countryside, and the dread of having to fight for it dominated the thinking of the men who would have to do the climbing, and the shooting, and maybe the dying, to get it.

The men in the shallow foxholes on the Shark saw the Octopus, half-waiting, half-grasping, as daylight filtered down to them from the gray overcast. Later they would learn that someone had named the three tentacles Lion, Cougar, and Rhino—for left, center, and right. But in those early minutes of the morning, all that the men in the line knew about the Octopus was aptly summed up by Digger Dolan: "That is the meanest son of a bitch I ever hope to see." And then, curiously, Timothy Dolan crossed himself.

Back of the Shark, not far from the farmhouse that had served as the Second Battalion's command post overnight, Eric Holloway crawled out of his sleeping bag. He was possibly the only man in the battalion who was not yet bothered by the Octopus, but he had worries of his own. He was muddy, he ached all over, he was miserable.

When he went down to the river to get some water for shaving, Eric noticed that the bridge he had crossed last night had been blown up. Downstream from the bridge ten or twelve yards, a gutted, grotesquely misshapen jeep lay belly-up in the water. On the far bank, Eric saw four bodies stretched out on the white pebbles, waiting for someone to start them on their way home.

What happened? he wondered. Then he knew: there had been another booby-trap on the bridge.

While Holloway was shaving, Trent walked up and saluted.

"Sir, I've got our part of the operations tent all fixed up," he said.

"Operations tent?"

"Yes, sir. Over there."

Trent pointed to an area about two hundred yards east of the ruined bridge. Holloway was surprised to see that a number of large, mud-splotched tents had been pitched there.

"Battalion's all set up," Trent said.

And it was. There was a tent for battalion's kitchen, another for the Headquarters Company command post, another for operations, another for Major Dahl. Jeeps were dispersed throughout the area, and parked very near the operations tent Eric saw a jeep that bore a red plate with two large silver stars—the General's.

Trent noticed that Holloway was hurrying to finish shaving.

"I wouldn't go in there if I were you, sir. Captain Hamilton's after your scalp. Of course, it's none of my business—"

Holloway went on shaving.

"You're damned right, Sergeant. It is none of your business."

Eric Holloway did not approve of enlisted men concerning themselves with officers' problems.

Trent was amazed. All right, Hollow Head, he thought. Stew in your own juice. I'll just let you find out the hard way.

Sergeant Trent saluted and started to walk away, but he changed his mind and turned back to the officer.

"If it was me and I had anyplace to go, I'd go," Trent said.

And I haven't anyplace to go, Eric thought, except George Company, and they're mad at me, too.

A moment later he asked Trent, "What's going on in there?"

"They're talking about the next objective—a mountain called the Octopus. Blue's supposed to attack sometime this morning. They're late, though. The bridge. That's why the wheels are bitter."

"No word about us attacking?"

"Not while I was in there."

Eric sensed an opportunity to hang on a little longer.

"Trent," he said, "when you go back, tell anyone who asks about me that I've gone up to have a look at the next objective."

2

So Eric went back to George Company.

He climbed the Shark slowly, turning now and then to look back at the countryside his regiment had won in the last few days. There were barren and dead fields in the valley below, brown and yellow and tired of being fought over, and Eric wondered if they would ever be green with crops again. He saw the road winding up to the pass where he had spent most of the day before, and he thought of the campfires that George Company had built in their assembly area over behind the pass.

When he was about half-way up the Shark, the overcast broke up and warm sunlight flooded patches of the mountainsides. Eric took this to be a good omen, and he quickened his pace. He was almost happy again. He had almost forgotten the damning and confusing events of the cold, tragic night before. He thought about how good it was to be alone, to be free.

When he came to George Company's command post, Sergeant Gregg was heating a can of C-ration hamburgers in the coals of an old fire. Gregg looked up at Holloway, but he didn't speak. He just looked.

"Is the company commander around?" Holloway asked.

Gregg looked back at the swelling can. He picked up a stick and poked the can out of the coals, then he threw the stick away and fished into his pocket for a can-opener.

"I said, is the company commander around?"

"If you had a lick of sense, you'd get the hell back down to battalion where you belong, and leave us alone. We got troubles enough without you—"

Gregg abruptly stopped talking and opened the can. He tasted the hamburgers—too hot.

"Cap'n Mann's up on top."

Holloway fumed as he climbed the narrow path that led to the Shark's peak. He had always been a little bit afraid of

Gregg—he didn't know why—and he was angry with himself for being unable to think of a reply. He was ashamed of meekly walking away, and he punished himself by composing retorts which he could use on Gregg next time.

Gregg looked up from his hamburger patties to watch Holloway go, and just a moment after the officer left, Gregg was joined by Sergeant Hicks, Digger Dolan, and the Mouse.

"I thought you said you was gonna kill the bastard," Dolan said, easing his stocky body down beside Gregg.

"You heered the gossip wrong," Gregg replied, his mouth full of hot hamburger. "It was the company commander said he'd shoot him down like a dog if he ever came around George Company again."

The other soldiers sat down around Gregg's fire.

"He's the nearest nothin' I ever saw," Sergeant Dolan said. "I swear I hate him worse'n any enema in this whole damned country."

"'Cept for last night, what have you got against him, Digger?" the Mouse asked.

"If you hadn't dodged the draft *quite* so long, you'd know. Son of a bitch just about got me kilt," Dolan said, spitting the words in the Mouse's face. "He was platoon leader afore Sergeant Hicks. Hell, ol' Hollow Head just about got us all kilt."

"That ain't a bit fair," Sergeant Hicks drawled. "If you're just snowin' the Mouse, okay. But if you ain't, just remember that you were pretty Goddam green yourself, not so long ago."

"Listen, Sergeant, that bastard's a criminal. What he did—"

"If you mean the first day, shut up. He got his that day, too."

"When was that?" asked the Mouse.

"When we first got into this country," Hicks replied. "Th' Lieutenant got us into a fix and had a lot of trouble getting us out. Matter of fact, he didn't get us out—th' enema just got tired first. Lots of people got shot up. Holloway, too. Digger's bitter at him 'cause Holloway had Digger's squad in the hottest spot and didn't move 'em. They caught everything in the book while th' Lieutenant was runnin' around tryin'—"

"Running is right!" Digger injected. "The eager bastard couldn't get it into his stupid head that it was the enema shootin' at us. He thought it was Lieutenant Hyde's platoon, and he hollered—hollered!—at the enema to stop shootin' at us."

"Geez!" exclaimed the Mouse, impressed.

"Then he bugged out."

"Didn't, either," Hicks countered.

"Hell yes, he did, Sergeant! The yellow son of a bitch was runnin' back to Captain Mann to tell him how brave he was and to get his medal, that's all. He never cared about us. He was just lookin' out for ol' Number One, same as he is now."

"You can't tell what he was up to," Hicks said evenly. "It ain't easy, 'specially at first. That was the first time for him. He didn't do so bad."

Gregg crushed the hamburger can and threw it into the brush.

"Wonder if the company commander *will* shoot him?" Gregg asked.

The Mouse, who hadn't been in combat long, was eager to hear more about the first day.

"What d'ye mean, Sergeant?" he asked Hicks.

"Well, we'd just gotten here. Not much opposition. Orders to go get all the ground we could. It was kinda like yesterday, except in those days we was so far out in front, we was all alone. Even the company commander couldn't see us, we was so far out in front. And Holloway wanted us to go even faster."

Hicks paused to light a cigarette.

"Lead scouts—came from Digger's squad, as I recollect—lead scouts wouldn't go fast enough to suit him, so he got out in front."

"Eager bastard," Digger muttered.

"Hell, it wasn't his idea. He was just doing as he'd been

told. Anyway, he was up there in front, a-hollerin' and a-cussin' at us to catch up. Well, we caught up, and soon as we did, th' enema let loose with machine guns."

"Damn!"

"Well, they had us right where they wanted us."

"In a damned trap, he means," Digger added.

"Digger, if you knowed it was gonna be a trap, why didn't you tell him aforehand?" Hicks asked.

Digger didn't reply.

"Now, shut up and let me tell the Mouse his war story for the day so's he can sit still."

"They was shootin' at you, Sergeant," the Mouse prompted.

"Yes, they was. Well, Holloway was layin' on his belly right by me, and we was talkin' over what to do. Then two of our own airplanes come strafin' at us."

"The hell they did!"

"And I'll have to give th' Lieutenant credit, there. In between passes he stood up and waved his steel at them pilots to try to show 'em we was Americans."

"Did that stop 'em?"

"Naw, there wasn't no stoppin' 'em. They quit when their ammo was all gone. They didn't hit any of us, but while they had us pinned down, th' enema got his mortars a-goin'. Them mortars cut up Digger's squad worst of all, and because Holloway didn't pull off no miracle, Digger's bitter."

"Damn! Then what happened?"

"Well, a bullet passed between my back and a pack I had on—cut the suspenders, it did—and Holloway figured he was goin' to get kilt if he didn't move, I guess. Anyway, he got up, and they started in to shootin' at him with a machine gun. Got him, after a while."

"How'd you get out of it?"

"I just stayed there. I figure if Holloway was wrong in getting up, if he was wrong for runnin', I was just as wrong for not doin' anything, you see, Digger."

"Hollow Head ran. He was yellow, and he ran."

Hicks ignored the Digger and went on.

"We got all the wounded out after a while, when th' enema fire died down a little. Lieutenant Hyde and some of his people came over and helped. Towson told me that the night was the worst part, though."

"That's right," Gregg broke in. "Towson was hit that day, too. Poor old Towson."

"Hollow Head finally got him," Digger said.

"What did Towson mean, the night was the worst part, Sergeant?" the Mouse asked.

"That night the company had to move out and leave the wounded without a guard. Medics wouldn't come up to get 'em, you see. Oh, it wasn't the Medics' fault, exactly. But all them wounded people had to stay there in that open field and sweat out getting their throats cut by enema we'd by-passed. Towson said everybody there that night was pooped —th' Lieutenant was the only one awake, and all he had to shoot with was a rusty old forty-five with mud in the bore. But nothin' happened, and they got picked up the next morning."

"Damn!"

"So you see why the Digger's bitter at Holloway. Me, I don't like the guy, but sometimes I don't think so much of myself, either."

3

Holloway found Sam Mann seated on a small knob that was about a hundred yards north of the Shark's peak. Mann was watching the right tentacle of the Octopus when Eric walked up.

Mann was surprised to see him.

"Mind if I join you?" Eric asked.

"No, guess not."

Mann picked up his pipe and paid a great deal of attention to lighting it, then he picked up his fieldglasses and resumed his scanning of the Octopus' long tentacle.

"What's up?" Eric asked.

"Blue's attacking."

"Are they going up that finger?"

"I heered from Hamilton they are."

Mann's pronunciation of certain words revealed his hillbilly background. But many things in his manner indicated his deeply-felt pity of a humanity that had spent most of his lifetime killing or getting ready to kill again.

Actually, the two men were about to witness a modern battle. The Third Battalion, Blue, had been ordered by Major Merlin, who was only the division operations officer, through the mouths of General Sutliff and Colonel Hobbs to move around the Shark's eastern slope, then to attack the long tentacle named Rhino. The order had long since been given to Major Stace, Blue's commander; and as Mann and Eric Holloway waited high on the Shark, Major Stace stood talking to his company commanders beside a road.

Later, the two observers saw the results of Merlin's plans and Stace's commands.

Mann knew, when he heard the first muted rustle of artillery rounds overhead, that the men of some rifle company were tensing up, waiting for the word to "Get goin'!" He knew that for some of those men, time was running out. An hour, maybe a day—but for those who were to die, the time would be frightening, violent, painful, no matter how long or how short that time might be.

Mann asked Eric what was on his mind.

Eric wanted to tell him, but the words hung in his throat. I'm no good, he wanted to say. I'm a menace. I want out. I can't fight this thing any more. I've wasted my time getting trained for this—now that I'm here, I can't function. I'm just no good. Everything I touch, I ruin. I'm a killer—

"Oh, nothing much," he said.

I ought to apologize, he thought. I ought to tell him I'm sorry I ever came to this battalion, I'm sorry I got this damned commission, I'm sorry I was born. I—

"Well, there they go," Mann said, sadly. "God help 'em."

Eric watched the thin line of men in baggy, dark green uniforms move up from the valley onto the tip of the tentacle. Artillery rounds still pounded the ridgeline about a hundred yards in front of the men, moving up the tentacle toward the first prominent knob.

That artillery didn't do 'em a bit of good, Mann thought. He kept his eyes on the first man in the file, waiting for the man to drop, ashamed of himself for his morbid fascination.

Out on the Octopus' long tentacle, the one that led due south from the peak, the tiny green figures dropped out of Mann's sight. Then Mann and Eric heard the cracks and thumps of machine gun fire.

"What's happening?" Eric asked.

"Some of them folks got shot at, I'd say. Wouldn't you?"

Eric didn't answer.

"Seems like that big rock is what's givin' 'em trouble."

Mann scanned the ridgeline through his fieldglasses, trying to catch some sight of the enemy, but all he could see was the thin green line of infantrymen from the Third Battalion, stretched out on the brown earth, not moving. Machine gun fire cut loose every time anyone tried to crawl forward.

Mann handed the fieldglasses to Eric.

"You see the rock I mean?"

"Yes."

"See how sharp the ridgeline is right there in front of it?"

"Uh-huh."

"Looks to me like only one man at a time can get by that there rock."

The artillery stopped firing.

"That's odd," Eric said. "Blue's backing up."

He handed the glasses back to Mann.

The dust from the last artillery burst floated off to the east, and a strange silence settled over the whole area. Mann watched the men scramble back down the ridgeline, but he couldn't understand what he saw.

"Something's really wrong," Mann said. "That just ain't natural, that backing up."

Eric spotted the reason.

"See that air panel down there?"

Mann did.

"I guess they're going to try an air strike."

For nearly an hour, nothing at all happened out on the enemy-held tentacle. Eric and the captain sat and watched the disputed finger, seldom speaking. The company commander was deep in thought, and Eric was pretty sure that the captain's thoughts, whatever they might be, did not include him.

Eric was right. Sam Mann was thinking about the lonely man whose duty it would soon be to try to get around that rock again. He frowned as he thought of the irony of it all —a complete infantry battalion was attacking on a one-man front! And if this was the only battalion attacking that morning, then that lonely man was *the* war effort! Nothing—not artillery, not air power, nor even armor—nothing could relieve that man of his awful burden. As long as that rock was there, he would have to try to get around it, so that the battalion could follow him, one man at a time. Mann pitied that soldier, and admired him, and prayed for him.

Eric was sleepy. He was tired from the climb, and the warmth of the day added to his drowsiness.

A droning sound in the southern sky made him perk up. Eric and Sam Mann turned to look for the airplanes, but they saw only one—an old training plane, left over from an earlier war.

"Well, I'll be damned!" Eric said as the little plane slipped directly over their heads. "He hasn't even got a slingshot on that thing."

After the plane had passed the knob Eric and Captain Mann were on, it dipped a wing into a tight turn and circled back, as though the pilot wanted a better look at them.

"God!" Eric cried. "You reckon he thinks we're the target?"

"I sure hope not," Mann said, getting up. Like Eric, he was completely fascinated by the little plane.

As the pilot came over them again, he banked sharply so that he could look directly at them. Mann and Eric waved their steel helmets at the pilot, and the pilot waved back as he turned his old trainer back toward the Octopus.

"Did you see the baseball cap that clown was wearing?"

"Gentleman's war," Mann replied. "Thought he was going to put his airplanes on us, did you?"

"Yes, I did. I'm airplane-shy, you know."

Mann would know. He had been Eric's company commander when Eric's platoon had been strafed.

4

At the Second Battalion's command post, the topic of discussion all morning had been Eric Holloway.

"I don't know what you're waiting for, sir," Captain Hamilton argued. "I'd ship him the hell out of here right now."

"Harry, I think we've got enough to worry about without this," Major Dahl replied. "We ought to be worrying about the Octopus."

"Very well, sir. Let's worry about the Octopus. What patrols have we got out there this morning? What observation posts have we got in operation? What information of the enemy have we got?"

Hamilton paced up and down the tent as he spoke.

"In other words, Major, just what the hell is Holloway doing to earn his pay?"

It was not Dahl's nature to get excited, especially over personalities. Dahl had learned in his thirty-five years that he was not a popular man, a little too cool, perhaps even colorless, possibly timid. He disliked judging other men. Lawrence Dahl preferred to take up the young lieutenant's case after the current operation was completed, when the battalion was in reserve.

"Calm down, Harry," Dahl said. "Those are my problems, not yours."

Hamilton left the tent.

The battalion commander called Sergeant Trent to him. Dahl was sitting on an empty ammunition box near the oil stove, not far from the north tent pole. He motioned for Trent to sit down on the other box.

"Where is Lieutenant Holloway, Sergeant?" he asked.

"He went up on top for a look at the Octopus, sir."

"Has he planned any patrols?"

"Not that I know of, sir. I think he wanted to see the ground, first."

Dahl realized that Trent was covering for Holloway, but he didn't say anything about it. Someone, some wise sergeant, had covered for him, years before, too. It wasn't always reprehensible.

"Did the General say when we'll have to attack the Octopus, sir?" Trent asked.

"No. Blue's trying to get Rhino now. If they have any luck at all, we may not have to attack. We'll just move up Lion or Cougar and fill in part of the regimental line."

"I see, sir."

"Pray for Blue."

"I will."

Dahl got up and walked back to the corner of the tent where the maps were located. He looked at the grasping hillmass called the Octopus, and he, too, prayed for Blue. Then he thought of Holloway. What can I do about him? Lawrence Dahl wondered.

A few minutes later, Trent called Sergeant Gregg at George Company.

"Is Lieutenant Holloway up there?" Trent asked.

"He's with the Old Man. I'll send for him and have him call you back."

Gregg sent Gipp, the captain's radio operator, to get Lieutenant Holloway. Gipp scrambled up the path to the knob, and arrived there, out of breath, a few minutes later.

"Battalion—" he gasped, "battalion—wants you—to call 'em—on the phone—Lieutenant Holloway—sir."

"All right, Gipp. I'll be there in a minute."

But Eric didn't leave: the Corsairs were arriving.

The old trainer had been circling the peak and the tentacle called Rhino, trying to spot the defenders. When the fighters arrived, the trainer climbed very high above the mountain and continued its circling.

"Look at those bullies!" Eric shouted as the leader of the flight of fighters peeled-off for a dry run at the target. "Looks like they're going after that damned rock."

The three other planes followed their leader through and circled back to the left after pulling out of their shallow dives at the target.

"Hadn't you better see what battalion wants?" Mann asked Eric.

"Probably Hamilton telling me to go find a job as a general's aide."

"That's what the trouble is, huh?"

"Yeah. Look—there he goes!"

The leader dipped his left wing and turned into a long glide toward the tentacle. The plane seemed to hang there, spitting streams of fifty-caliber slugs at the rock and spewing rockets from under its wings. Then, at the last possible moment, the leader pulled his plane out of the run into a steep climb to the left. For a brief moment, the plane seemed to hang from its prop.

As the leader reentered the slow circle, the second plane began spraying the target and shedding its load of rockets. Out on the tentacle, each rocket exploded in an orange fireball; Eric and Captain Mann heard a *shish-ing* sound after each bright burst—the delayed sound of the rocket in flight—followed by an unusually sharp *crunch*. The other two planes put their loads slightly to the right of the smoky area where the first rockets had hit. The flight was gradually and systematically working down the tentacle toward the panels which Eric and the company commander could see a hundred yards or so ahead of Blue's platoon.

Every time a Corsair rippled out a stream of machine gun fire, Eric caught his breath. He could understand the horror the enemy defenders were experiencing, for the memory of the pounding he had taken on that certain miserable afternoon was still fresh in his mind.

"You sure they're going to relieve you?" Mann asked Eric.

"No. But maybe they ought to. For the good of the battalion."

The leader made his second wet pass at the target. This time he fired neither rockets nor machine guns, but dropped an awkward-looking blob. The elongated tear-drop fell end-over-end and hit the mountain well below the rock. As soon as it disappeared into the trees, a gigantic ball of flame shot up, and burning streams of jellied gasoline flamed out in all directions, setting fire to everything within an area the size of a football field.

"What a way to die!" Mann said.

Eric looked at the captain. True, he thought, it is. He was grateful, now that he thought of it, that the planes which had strafed him had not dropped napalm. He would have been roasted—

"It was low, though," Eric said, referring to the napalm bomb. "I doubt if anyone could have been that far down the slope."

The second plane's bomb hit squarely on the rock, making the mountain look like an erupting volcano. After the bright orange fireball had burned out, a thick black cloud drifted away to the northeast.

Mann wondered how many souls drifted with that cloud.

The third and fourth fireballs hit the ridgeline between the rock and the line of Blue's panels. It was an expert performance—terrible, beautiful, horrible.

After the last plane had pulled up to join the flight as it orbited around the smoking mountain, the old trainer came down to look over the results of the strike. The plane passed over the rock several times, then circled quite low, as though the pilot were looking for survivors. Suddenly he pulled up and climbed high above the fighters' orbit, and a few seconds later the leader went down in another long pass, spraying the portion of the finger which ran back toward the head of the Octopus.

Apparently some of the defenders were trying to escape by running off toward the north and home.

Each of the Corsairs made one pass from the old direction, then the leader swung wide around to the right and made a strafing pass along the ridgeline, hitting the enemy's peak from the same direction as Blue's attack.

Eric supposed that those machine guns must be firing directly over the heads of the attackers; he could picture the rain of brass cartridge cases that must be falling on the steel helmets of the men as they crouched behind rocks and in folds in the ground for protection against the rather good chance that the pilot's thumb might slip and hit the firing button a split second too soon.

Once again the fighters circled the punished rock in a wide orbit while the old trainer came down for a look. After a few passes over the target area, the controller plane pulled away sharply and started to climb.

Just as the old plane's nose was coming around to the south, the engine sputtered a few times, then it caught again.

Holloway and Mann stood up.

"Damn!" Mann said. "Do you reckon he's hit?"

"Don't know."

The trainer's engine sputtered and coughed several more times, then the old plane's nose dipped as the power failed completely.

"He's going down, he's going down—" Eric said under his breath.

"Behind their lines, too."

"Looks like he's trying to stretch his glide, though."

"Yep."

38

Eric's eyes were glued to the falling plane, and he was conscious of the fact that he simply could not have looked away under any circumstances.

The fighters had noticed the plight of their lumbering companion and had turned back to cover him. The four Corsairs flew around the crippled plane in a wide circle.

"What good can they do?" Eric asked. "They've probably run out of ammo."

"It's hard to tell—but I'm thinking that the pilot's mighty glad to have them there. Why, they're almost holding him up."

"Yes—he might make it."

The plane's glide was very shallow; with luck he might make it to the northern slope of the Shark, and if the pilot could just do that, a patrol from George or Easy Company could go down to protect him until he could be pulled out of the wreckage and evacuated.

Eric's face broke into a smile. The engine had caught!

"By damn he's got it going again!"

"Thank God!"

It seemed to Eric that the pilot was applying power to the sick engine gently.

"He must have been holding that thing up with his fingertips!" Eric said as the plane and its swarm of protectors passed over the Shark, heading for home.

"They've got their troubles, too," Mann said. "That guy in the baseball cap would have been in mighty bad shape if he'd gone down."

Behind and below Holloway and Mann, Sergeant Trent waited at battalion for the telephone to ring. He had figured out a good patrol plan, but the plan couldn't do any good unless the patrols it called for left at once. Every minute that passed while Trent sat waiting for the phone to ring reduced the patrols' chances of success, and Trent's chances of helping Holloway.

I'll give him another fifteen minutes, Trent decided.

The sound of artillery rounds passing over their heads

caused Holloway and Mann to turn back toward the scarred tentacle. Just as they heard the muted *swish-swish-swish*, the target erupted. Round after round crunched into the ground; splinters of hot steel tore through the gray dust into the bodies of men and the trunks of trees, killing, ripping, shattering—

"Blue'll have a walk-in now," Eric predicted. "They've thrown everything in the book at the people on that damned mountain."

Mann didn't reply.

"Stace sure knows what he's doing. With that kind of softening-up, nothing could possibly be there to stop them."

"I hope you're right, Eric, but I wouldn't want to be the man who has to go around that there rock."

Then Mann exploded.

"God damn it, Eric, you think this is just a big show, don't you? Something for your entertainment, maybe? Well, it isn't! It's the saddest thing that's happening anywhere on the face of the earth right now. You wanted a company—all right, just suppose that one was yours. You watch that lead man out there. Just suppose you was him. You watch that poor bastard—he's dead and don't know it. You think he can get around that rock? You think you'd have a better chance than he has? Just you watch!"

Eric frowned.

"Well, there they go again," Mann said. "God help 'em."

The green-clad men of the Third Battalion moved along the razorback ridgeline rapidly at first, but their aggressiveness slackened as they neared the big rock. There were about ten men in the leading group, Mann noticed; probably a reinforced rifle squad. When the men were within fifty yards or so of the rock, most of the men took cover behind boulders or tree trunks while two scouts kept moving toward the ugly barrier. The scouts walked at a crouch, almost sneaking up to the dangerous spot. The artillery was falling on the Octopus itself, well away from the squad. Mann supposed that the battalion commander's idea was to isolate that rock

40

—to keep the enemy from moving in additional defenders.

"Yep," Mann said, "it's just a matter of getting one man around one rock. If he don't make it, nobody else can, either."

"He's up there now."

"Either he makes it—"

Suddenly the scout doubled up and dropped, and a moment later the sound of machine gun fire reached the Shark.

"He didn't."

The other scout was down, too. The rest of the squad shot at the rock, and two men crawled out to recover the body of the first scout. A fierce firefight raged as the men snaked their way forward.

"Sounds to me like they've got more guns goin' than we have," Mann said.

"How could anybody have lived through that airstrike? And all of that artillery?" Eric asked.

"God knows."

The crawling men stopped, yards short of the scout's body.

"Damn!" Mann said. "I think they got those two."

The green figures were very still, as though they might have been ripped by the streams of hot lead that were being exchanged over them.

"That's the worst way I know of to get hit," Mann said.

"What?"

"To be hit lying down. Bullet goes all the way down a man's body—all the way down. Only thing that stops it is a bone or something. Hell of a way to get hit."

A chill ran through Eric as he listened to the captain.

"Trouble is, a man's usually down like that when he's being shot at. He's almost bound to catch a bad one, unless he's lucky enough to get his while he's standing up."

"Even then, he needs a lot of luck. Like I had."

"Yes, like you had. You don't know how lucky you were."

Mann put the fieldglasses to his eyes once more. The other

men in the squad were moving forward. The four men who were already down had not moved.

"They're going to rush the rock! Oh, no!"

Eric could see without the glasses: one by one, the green figures dropped, and after a few seconds they were all down. One man had been able to throw a hand grenade, but it had fallen far short of the rock. The firing stopped for a moment, but then more green figures rushed the rock and the fury of the firing increased.

"This is a hell of a thing," Eric said. "And after all that preparation, too."

Mann looked at Eric and said nothing. Eric wasn't sure, but he thought the captain was almost smiling. At any rate, there was a strange new gleam in his eyes.

"I don't see why that company commander keeps sending people out there like that," Mann said, finally. "He's not going to get in by that door."

Another green-clad group appeared far down the near slope from the rock.

"Oh, I see. He's trying to keep the people at the rock busy while he hits them from this side."

"They've got a long way to go," Eric said. "Even after they get even with the rock, they've got to climb up to it. That'll be like dog-paddlin' up a waterfall."

For the next few minutes the two men watched without speaking as the drama developed. The men on the ridgeline took cover and fired their rifles and machine guns at the rock, keeping a steady stream of small-arms fire on the defenders while the group below them moved along the side of the finger. Holloway and Mann could tell that the moving men were having hard going, for the slope was quite steep; several of the men slipped off the narrow ledge.

"They'll be better off when they get to that cleared place," Eric said, pointing to an open part of the mountainside that had been under cultivation once, years before.

The artillery bursts were being walked toward the rock, the two men noticed. The rounds were slamming into the mountain one at a time, each one crunching closer to the place where the defenders were holed up. Eric wondered what more the Third Battalion could possibly do to help. Mortars? Possibly, but the ridgeline was too sharp. There wouldn't be a single place level enough for the baseplates, and digging out a firing platform would take too much time. Another air strike? No, for if the previous one had not been able to kill off all of the defenders, the chances of another one doing any better were slim, indeed.

"It's all up to those men," Mann said. "If they can clean out the people around that rock, somehow, Blue might get that mountain."

The lower group of men reached the cleared field and moved rapidly into the area, for the slope was gentle there and the climbing was easier.

Suddenly there were three gray blossoms among the men in the clearing.

"Mortar fire!" Mann groaned. "Look at that!"

When the dust blew away, only three of the men were still moving, and one of the three was obviously out of his mind in pain, running in wild circles, trying to dash himself into a merciful death against a rock he could not find. The other two were trying to catch him. A few of the others crawled away from the spots where they had been hit, seeking shelter. The rest remained motionless in the places where they had fallen.

"That's awful!"

Mann put the fieldglasses down.

"Just plain awful."

"How can one company be so unlucky?"

"It just shows how feeble we really are, Eric. We do all we can, but sometimes it isn't near enough. Sometimes nothing we try works. The book is fine, as far as it goes, but there's something about this kind of thing that's beyond the scope of any book I've ever seen. I guess Stace's done everything he knows to do, and he still hasn't got that there thing."

"What else can he do?"

"Pray."

"And then?"

"Keep trying every damned thing he can think of that might help get the mountain without the loss of any more men than he can help."

Mann took off his steel helmet and scratched his head.

"That's all any of us can do, when you get right down to it. Work, and pray, and work some more. And never give up. Never quit."

Out on the mountain, another squad moved along the narrow path, down the slope from the rock, edging toward the open field where the survivors of the first flanking attempt were gathering for the long, painful walk back.

The man who had been running in circles was not running any more. He had found a rock.

"You know," Eric said, "it's funny that they didn't drop any more rounds out there."

"No. They may be waiting for more people to shoot them at. They've stopped this outfit cold. No need wasting any more ammo on them."

Mann was right, of course. It was a crude way of putting it, but now the whole business seemed to Eric more cruel than it ever had before.

Cruel—that was the word for it.

"Looks like they're going to try to rush that God damned rock again."

"Maybe it's just to get the wounded back," Mann said. "I can't believe that company commander could keep throwing men away trying to get that thing."

"Stace's probably pushing him."

"Yeah, and somebody's probably behind Stace pushing him. Getting that mountain looks mighty easy on one of them rear-echelon maps."

Once again, sharp firing broke out around the rock. There were more green-clad figures moving this time, possibly twenty-five or thirty. Eric looked down at the green line that was working its way toward the open field. The men were almost running, trying to take full advantage of the fire that the others were placing on the rock. As before, one artillery round after another crunched into the mountain, a little behind the ridgeline now, as though the blind rounds were trying to feel out the location of the enemy's mortar tubes.

Most of the men in the large group that was moving toward the rock were down, or behind such cover as they could find, moving only when someone else fired, and always moving to some other boulder, or tree, or dip in the ground.

Eric picked up the fieldglasses and watched these men as they moved closer and closer to the bodies of the scouts who had been hit in the first attempt. Finally seven or eight men were quite close to the rock; Eric's heart beat rapidly as he watched one of the green figures crawl from one man to another, probably passing some order for rushing the rock. He was the platoon leader, Eric supposed. Some lieutenant of infantry who hoped to be given a job on battalion staff soon, so that he might be promoted to captain; someone who wanted a command of a company, perhaps; someone like— someone like himself.

Eric shivered as he realized that but for a lucky accident, months before, when he had just joined the regiment, he might have been the leader of that platoon out there. That might have been *his* rock to get. If he had been assigned to the Third Battalion instead of the Second, he might—

All of the green figures were up and running, rushing the rock.

There was a burst of machine gun fire.

The platoon leader's body rolled down the side of the mountain.

Eric watched, horrified, until the body was stopped by the trunks of some scrubby pines, then he looked back up at the rock.

The machine gun had stopped firing. All of the men were stretched out along the path, quite still.

Eric put down the glasses.

"Here, sir. I can't look any more."

It was all so wrong, Eric thought. He felt guilty, but he couldn't understand just why. Why, he wondered, should those men die—those men who had been out there trying, fighting, those men who had not given up—and why should I be living, looking at a sight like this, a sight that may be too intimate for the eyes of people like me, people who aren't worth killing? He knew there could be no answer to such a question. The fact was, they were dead, and he was alive. He was alive—and there was still some time.

Eric stood up.

"I'll see you later, sir. I'm going to call battalion."

"Eric," Mann said, "don't take the short view."

Eric nodded, then he walked away.

Three

Sergeant Gregg walked away from the command post as Lieutenant Holloway entered. Holloway went over to the phone and called battalion.

When he had Trent, he asked him what was up.

"I've got a patrol plan made up, sir," Trent replied. "I thought you'd want something to report about the country in front of us, just in case we're ordered to attack. But now it's so late—"

"Fine, Trent, fine. What have you got?"

"You have a map?"

Eric dug into his fieldjacket pocket and pulled out a clumsily-folded map of the area.

"Yes. Go ahead."

"You know what the Octopus is?"

"I do."

"You know what Rhino is?"

"Yes, I've been watching Blue trying to get it."

"The finger in the center is called Cougar, and the next one over is Lion."

"Yes, I know."

"Now, my idea is to send a patrol about half-way up Cougar."

"Good. We'll do it."

"Sir, hadn't you better clear this with Major Dahl?"

"Is he there?"

"No sir, he's gone to regiment. He ought to be back in a few minutes, but even now it's too late. An hour ago—"

"Never mind, Sergeant. I'll take over now."

Holloway hung up.

Gregg wasn't far away, Eric knew, so he yelled for him to come back to the C. P. Gregg ambled up the path a minute later, and Dolan came with him.

"I'm glad to see you, Sergeant Dolan," Holloway said. "I was just going to have Sergeant Gregg get you."

"*You* think," Gregg muttered.

"Dolan, get your squad assembled here. We're going on a patrol," Holloway ordered.

"We are like hell going on a patrol, Lieutenant."

"Sergeant, do you know what you're saying? Do you know you're refusing to obey an order? Don't you know you can be tried for that?"

"No, you can't have me tried, Lieutenant. I didn't say I wouldn't go. I said *we* wouldn't go—meaning you and my squad. I'll be damned if I'll go anywhere with you again."

Captain Mann walked up.

"What's the problem, Top?" he asked Gregg.

"Lieutenant Holloway wants Digger'n his squad to go with him on a patrol. Digger'll take 'em if you tell him to, but not with Hollow Head."

"Major Dahl order this patrol, Eric?"

"No, but—"

"Then by what right do you come into my company and order my men out on patrols?"

"Sir, it's getting late, and—"

"And why didn't you call me? Don't you know you can't just order people out on patrols? I'm the company commander—and I'm the one to say who goes, if the patrol's got to come from George Company. And I don't send anybody unless Major Dahl's ordered the patrol to come from George Company. You haven't got any command authority, Eric. You ought to know that. You're just abusing Dahl's. What the hell are you up to, Eric?"

"Sir, this patrol has *got* to go. We may have to attack out there tomorrow. We ought to know what's out there. If we don't find out, we might wind up like Blue."

"I couldn't agree with you more, Eric. A patrol ought to have been out there all day. But why did you wait till the sun's almost down to think this up? Why didn't you take care of this early this morning, instead of sitting up there on your hind-end watching Blue?"

Mann paused.

"Hell, if a patrol goes out there now, it'll be midnight getting back. You know better than to pull something like this, Eric."

Holloway was angry. "Dammit," he wanted to say, "don't you see I'm trying?"

Holloway picked up the phone.

"All right, sir. I'll call the battalion commander."

Trent answered the phone at battalion.

"Has Major Dahl come in yet?" Eric asked.

"No, sir. He's on the way, though. He called just before he left regiment and said to hold off on the patrol plan."

"I see."

"Sir, you'd better get back down here as soon as you can. Lieutenant Hyde's turned up something that's too hot to talk about over the phone."

"All right, Trent."

Eric put the phone down slowly. He looked at Captain Mann, but Mann was poking up the fire, getting ready to heat a can of beans for supper.

"Get on back to battalion where you belong!" Gregg said.

"Sergeant—" Eric began, but embarrassment choked him off.

"Yes, Lieutenant?"

Holloway left.

2

Holloway was tired. He pulled an ammunition box over in front of the map board and sat down.

"What's the big secret, Trent?" he asked.

Trent handed the officer a canteen cup full of coffee.

"Lieutenant Hyde has been back at regiment. He heard that some of the planes that flew the airstrike on Rhino saw a big build-up of enemy soldiers here."

Trent pointed to a spot just north of the Octopus on the map.

Holloway leaned forward to look at the spot.

"It's in our zone. Does Major Dahl know about this?"

"Yes, sir. Lieutenant Hyde told him."

"What was Lieutenant Hyde doing at regiment?"

"Captain Hamilton sent him back there to spy on the regimental operations officer. He wanted Lieutenant Hyde to call him if Major Owens even looked like he planned on using us. This report is something the Lieutenant overheard, so he called it in."

"I see."

Eric stared at the red circle Trent had drawn on the map to indicate the pocket of enemy soldiers. He wondered what those soldiers might do. He imagined he was the enemy commander. *I can reinforce the people who are keeping Blue from getting around that rock on Rhino*, he thought. *Or I can build up the defenses on Cougar, or Lion, or both. Or I can move my men down Cougar and attack the Shark tonight. Or I can stay put, or for that matter, I can pull out and go home. I can quit.*

"Coffee's good," Holloway said.

Trent smiled.

But what would I do if I were the enemy commander? I'd play it cool and build up a good defense on the Octopus. That, or attack the Shark tonight.

"You had supper, sir?"

"No."

Eric hadn't had anything to eat all day.

"The other officers are eating now, I think. I'll watch things if you want me to."

"Thanks—I think I'll take you up on that."

50

3

Eric noticed that the sky was cloudy as he walked toward the battalion headquarters kitchen tent. More bad weather, he thought. Who the hell cares?

Eric walked around the end of a long line of soldiers who were standing in the chow line outside the kitchen tent. He knew that some of those men resented his being able to walk right into a tent, sit down at a table, and be served—but then, none of these men was worrying about that red circle out there in the darkness. They wouldn't begrudge me this privilege if they only knew, he thought. Matter of fact, I'd swap places with any of them, if I could. And if they knew what's probably waiting inside for me, they wouldn't swap.

He lifted the door flap and went into the tent. The mess sergeant had formed a table by placing some wide planks across ration boxes, and the officers were sitting on other ration boxes or water cans. Eric saw two empty places—one next to Major Dahl, one at the other end of the table, next to Wayne Hyde. He took off his steel helmet and his pistol belt, then he sat down on a water can beside Wayne Hyde.

The other officers watched him get settled, then Major Dahl spoke to him.

"Good evening, Eric."

"Evening, sir."

Hamilton asked him about Blue's attack on Cougar.

"They got a bloody nose," Eric replied.

"Could you see why?"

"I could see everything there was to see, I guess, but I don't understand why they couldn't get that finger. I sat up there and I watched it all happen, and I'm damned if I understand what I saw."

One of the cooks brought Eric a plate of hot food. Ham and lima beans—steaming hot. Eric picked up his fork and began eating.

51

"Eric, did you know Fred Matthews?" Wayne Hyde asked him.

"Yes, slightly. We were in the same plane on the trip out here from the States. He's in the Third Battalion somewhere, I think."

Eric ate a chunk of ham, then he added:

"I used to see him with his wife at the swimming pool last year at Fort Benning. Good looking woman he married."

"He was killed this afternoon."

Eric swallowed hard. It must have been Matthews I was watching, he thought. He put down his fork and took a sip of coffee.

"Did Trent tell you about the report?" Hamilton asked Eric.

"Yes, sir," Eric replied, still thinking about Fred and his wife, sitting in the warm Georgia sun together, laughing.

"What do you think about it?"

"Sir?"

"What do you think it means—or did you think about it?"

"I'll say this. There are certain things the enemy *can* do. He can reinforce his defenses on the Octopus. Or he can attack us anytime—especially tonight. He can also do nothing, just stay put. Or he can go home."

"What do you predict?"

"It isn't my business to predict, sir. I've told you what he *can* do."

"Good."

First Granger, then Hyde, and finally Hamilton finished eating and left. Major Dahl finished, but instead of leaving, he pulled out an old oilskin tobacco pouch and filled his pipe.

"You were up at George Company today?"

"Yes, sir."

"What's the talk up there?"

"Nothing much, sir. I'm not very popular up there, any more."

"Have you noticed, Eric, that once you leave an outfit, you never can really go back to it?"

"I hadn't noticed that until today. But it is true."

"I'll tell you something you probably don't know. Sam Mann didn't want me to bring you up here back in December. He wanted to keep you, even though he knew you couldn't walk well enough to take one of his platoons."

Eric finished his ham and lima beans and pushed his plate aside. He wondered if this could be Major Dahl's way of telling him he was through at battalion.

"Mann didn't want to let Wayne Hyde go, either. But Wayne has pushed his luck mighty far, mighty far. He was a prisoner in the last one, you know. And he's been wounded several times."

And Hyde's going to replace me, Eric thought.

"Take Granger—wounded five times, or maybe it's six, I forget. Sometimes I wonder what keeps him going."

"Granger's had more than his share of punishment."

"You and I have had a little, too. Well, no use feeling sorry for ourselves. What do you think I ought to do about the people the pilots said they saw?"

"I haven't thought about it, sir."

"I'm glad to hear you admit that, Eric. I prefer for people to level with me."

"I plan to call the companies and warn them that they may get jumped."

"Good."

"And I may suggest putting artillery on the place—but not until I've had a better look at the map and talked to Granger."

The mess sergeant came in and filled the officers' cups from a fresh pot of coffee.

"Sit down a minute, Sergeant," Major Dahl said. "How's business been with you, lately?"

"Not so good, sir. Losing too many of these here plates and cups."

"Is that so?"

"Yessir. We started the war with a full set—twelve plates, twelve cups. But now we're down to five plates and six cups, and not a chance of getting any replacements."

53

"Well, don't worry about it. We'll make do, all right."

"Oh, no sir. I'm not gonna worry none. I guess you're bound to lose plates and cups in a war like this here one. Just have to get used to the idea."

"Yes, Sergeant, I guess so."

4

When Wayne Hyde returned to the operations tent after supper, he saw Giles Granger down on all fours by his cot.

"What the hell are you doing, Giles?" Wayne asked.

"Damn phone," Granger muttered. He was tampering with the knobs. "I think one of these wires isn't hooked up right, or something."

Wayne pulled an ammunition box alongside the artilleryman's cot and watched him work.

"You want me to see if I can fix that thing?"

"I'd appreciate it. I'm damned if I can do anything with it."

Granger grasped the side of his cot with his bony hands and stood up, slowly, awkwardly.

"Fixing phones is a little out of my line, though," Granger said. "Like this whole business is."

Wayne picked up the phone and began examining it. He checked the wiring, the operation of the crank, the butterfly switch. Then he put the phone down on the straw floor and reached inside the phone to get the batteries.

"What did you do before the war?" Wayne asked.

"I taught English in a college."

"The hell you did!"

"Not for long. Only two and a half years."

"Are you going to teach again after the war?"

"I suppose so. If I'm not too bitter."

Wayne pulled the two small batteries out of the phone and held them up to the light.

"I'll bet these caused the trouble. They look shot to me. Have you got any new ones?"

"Sergeant Printz has, I'm sure."

Granger went outside to find Sergeant Printz. He returned a few minutes later with two new batteries.

"These do?"

"I think so."

Wayne slipped the fresh batteries into the phone, then he turned the crank.

"Just testing, Concrete," he said into the phone.

"That's odd," he said to Granger, putting the phone back under Granger's cot. "That was the artillery switchboard that answered."

"That's right. It's a direct line they put in for me."

"I see."

"Much obliged for fixing that thing. I don't get along too well with scientific matters, you see. I can tell you all about Euripides' *Medea*, but I can't spot a burned-out flashlight battery."

Granger sat down on his cot and lit a cigarette.

"Are you going to stay in the army after the war, Wayne?"

"Yes, I guess so. I might even try for a regular commission."

"Yeah, I thought about that last time. But never again. If I live through this one, I'll head for some stateside university and bury myself in its library, and I won't come out till I'm Doctor Granger."

"And I'll come be a student of yours."

"I guess I ought to have stayed out of this one—stayed home and worked on that damned degree."

"Could you have stayed out?"

"I suppose so."

"Why didn't you?"

"I don't know. When the trouble started, I figured I'd be needed. I mean, I've been kicked around by these people so much, there isn't much more they can do to me except kill me. And I heard so much moaning back there from people who were called to go. I guess I just got disgusted, or something. Anyway, I told sixteen lies and got back on active duty."

Eric Holloway came into the tent, nodded to the two officers, and walked on down to the other end of the tent.

"Funny what war does to the way a man thinks," Granger said, looking at Eric.

"What do you mean?" Wayne asked.

"Well, I've got a pretty good brain. I know I have. But sometimes—sometimes I get the idea that war is something that's personal—something that's out to kill me an arm or a leg at a time."

"That doesn't make much sense."

"I know. That's the damnable part of it. I see somebody doing something that is stupid, or mean, and the idea hits me, and I damn near go mad. I see somebody acting like this is all a great big adventure, something thrilling, and I could—I could do 'most anything."

"Better stick to your adverbs."

"You're right."

Harry Hamilton walked into the tent.

"Wayne," Hamilton asked, "have the companies called in their eight o'clock reports yet?"

"No, sir. It's not quite time."

"When they do, be sure to tell them to keep half their people awake all night."

"Yes, sir."

Hamilton sat down on his cot and began unlacing his boots.

"What time am I supposed to go on duty officer?" he asked.

"Midnight, sir. Eric's to go on at eight and two, I go on at ten and four."

"I'm gonna get some sleep, then."

"I might as well stay up," Wayne said. "Think I'll write a letter."

He got up and walked over to his cot, which was the next

one down the tentwall from Hamilton's. He picked up a brown leather notebook and took out his fountain pen and several sheets of paper, then he sat down on his cot. The light wasn't good there, so he moved over to an ammunition box near the electric light at the center of the tent. He sat down and began writing.

Two sergeants came in about ten minutes later and began working on a report having to do with the numerical strength of the battalion. They sat on ammo boxes near Lieutenant Hyde, one sergeant dictating while the other wrote.

Hamilton, in his sleeping bag, rolled over and went to sleep.

5

Eric imagined that the enemy group out there in the darkness was beginning to stir. Perhaps the men were being fed, or resupplied with ammunition. Maybe there weren't any people out there at all. Or maybe they were already creeping their way along the valley floor, about to begin climbing the northern slope of the Shark. Maybe—

Something's got to be done about those people, Eric thought. Something.

Suddenly Holloway got up and went over to Granger's cot. Granger was lying on his back, reading a paperback copy of Plutarch's *Lives*.

"May I bother you a minute?" Eric asked.

Granger put the book down, then he sat up and rolled his long legs over the side of the cot.

"Certainly."

Eric sat down and placed the map board on his knees.

"I've been thinking about this pocket that regiment reported. I've been wondering what can be done about them."

"You have?"

"Yes. What about putting a time-on-target on them?"

"Do you know what a time-on-target is, Holloway?"

"Yes, I think so. Heavy, massed concentration of artillery fire, timed so that all the rounds in each volley will explode at the same instant in the same general area."

"So saith the book. But do you know what one is really like? I do. I got this scar on my arm from one. A T. O. T. is pure hell on earth. It is diabolical. The people caught in one who aren't killed outright go crazy. If the steel doesn't shred them, the shock does. And you want to put a T. O. T. on them."

"I'd rather do that than have to sit up on top of the Shark and throw rocks at them."

"All right. If you're sure you know what you're talking about, we'll see."

Granger studied the map carefully. He examined the target area, the trails that led into it, the roll of the ground in front of it, the size of it. Then he wrote the coordinates of the target area in a small notebook.

"You know this is Hamilton's job—laying on a thing like this."

"Yes, but he's asleep," Eric answered.

"Have you cleared this with Dahl?"

"No. I'll go do that."

"I would."

Eric rose and left. While he was gone, Granger put his head in his slender, scarred hands. Don't let them do it, don't let them do it. . . .

Eric returned, smiling. Granger knew that his prayer had not been answered.

"The Old Man okayed the idea. Nine o'clock."

"You know it's eight-twenty now?"

"Can't you do it?"

Granger frowned. He wanted to say "No, we can't." But they could, or he thought they could. He leaned down and picked up the phone and turned the crank.

"I'll see."

The artillery battalion answered a moment later.

"White wants us to set up a time-on-target for nine tonight. Target is 913850—that area. The intelligence officer here at White thinks there may be a hundred or so around there."

The conversation continued for several minutes, then Granger put down the phone and looked wearily at the other officer.

"You got it. Four battalions at nine o'clock."

"Good. Thanks."

"For Christ's sake don't thank me!" Granger shouted. "You think I'm proud of what I've just done? I'm ashamed, Holloway. Downright ashamed."

Holloway didn't know what to say.

"Hell, you wouldn't understand," Granger said, putting on his steel helmet. "I'm going over to get me a cup of rotgut. I'll be there, if anybody calls me."

Granger left.

Strange man, Eric thought. I guess I seem just as strange to him, though. I wonder what I'd have to do—to be like—to please him. Maybe I'm not cut out for an army career, at that. I peeve too damned many people. Maybe this is a good warning to me—I hope I can remember this when the time comes for me to decide whether to stay in or get the hell out.

6

It was almost dark in the kitchen tent. One cook stood by the oven, baking peach cobbler. Granger exchanged a few words with the cook while he was getting his coffee, then he sat down on a crate near the oven and stared into the blue gas flame, and thought.

Holloway just may be right, after all, he thought. That would be the crowning irony. Of course he's right—those people out there have to be stopped, and it really doesn't matter how we do it. It's senseless for me to sit here and grieve, but—but—I just wish Holloway didn't seem to enjoy it all so God damned much!

"More coffee, sir?"

"No, guess not, thank you."

Granger sat there for a long time, holding the empty cup. Why do I have to worry about these things? he wondered.

"Want some of this here cobbler, sir? It's just about done."

"Nope, thanks."

"Mighty fine cobbler. Got plenty, too."

The cook took a large spoon and dipped a steaming sample out of the tray, then he turned to offer the sample to the officer.

How 'bout that? the cook thought. He's gone.

The cook tasted the cobbler.

Not bad. Not bad a-tall.

Four

Giles Granger had been back on his cot only a few minutes when Eric Holloway interrupted his reading a second time.

"I was just wondering," Holloway said, "how it would be if we followed that time-on-target up with another one—say ten minutes later?"

"How would it be?"

"Yes. I figure they ought to be recovering about that time, and we might catch a lot of them milling around."

"If you are thinking up these schemes to prevent them from attacking us, I don't think your idea's worth a good God-damn."

"Oh?"

"The load we dump on them will make complete pacifists out of them—that is, if there's anybody out there. Holloway, aren't you being a little bit sadistic?"

"Then so is the battalion commander. He's already approved the idea. Now—are you going to lay it on, or aren't you?"

"Dammit, Holloway, let's get this thing straightened out right now!" Granger said, rolling out of the cot. "You'd best keep this in mind, too. Artillery isn't here for you to order around. You *ask* for artillery fire. You get it if we can possibly put it out. You don't get it by asking what I think, when you've already sewed this thing up. And you sure as hell don't get it by pulling your battalion commander's rank."

"You're absolutely right, and I'm sorry. I was off base."

Granger's mouth dropped open. He started to add something to what he had already said, but the words wouldn't come.

"Will you please see what you can do about this?"

"Yes, I will."

Granger picked up his phone and called the artillery battalion.

Eric walked back to his end of the tent and sat down. He picked up his map board and began tracing possible patrol routes with a blue grease pencil on the acetate sheet that covered the map. Three patrols, he thought. One from each rifle company. In the margin of the map he made notes of the details of each patrol—objective, size, weapons, radio, times of departure and return. Soon the plan was complete.

Sergeant Trent came into the tent and sat down near the officer.

"What are you doing, sir?" he asked Holloway.

"Doodling. Tomorrow's patrol plan. Want to have a look?"

Holloway handed Trent the board. The sergeant read the notes, looked at the routes, checked the distance each patrol would have to cover. Then he handed the map board back to Holloway.

"Looks good, sir."

"Well, I think I'll take it in to Major Dahl and get his approval."

The officer got up and started toward the battalion commander's tent. As he passed Granger's cot, the artilleryman stopped him.

"Fandango will shoot the follow-up. They didn't think it was worth another four-battalion creaming. I'll guarantee you—one battalion will be plenty."

Fandango was the radio call-sign for Granger's battalion.

"That'll be fine. I'll tell Major Dahl."

Granger stretched out on his cot again as soon as Holloway was gone. Remember that guy, he thought. And quit being so God damned absolute!

2

About fifteen minutes before nine, Eric came back into the operations tent and went directly to the telephone. He called Easy Company first.

"Captain Heath," he began, "Major Dahl has approved a patrol plan for tomorrow, and I want to pass on your part of it tonight."

"Well," Heath drawled, "I don't know as any of my braves up here wants to go on any patrol. But I am glad to get the word this early, if it's got to be. Shoot."

Eric gave him the details of the mission he had for Easy Company's patrol. Then he called Fox, and then George.

Granger couldn't concentrate on Plutarch, so he put the book down and listened to Holloway talk to the company commanders. Once he looked at his watch: five minutes till nine. He thought of the activity down the road, miles to the south, where the tubes of eighteen medium howitzers and fifty-four light howitzers were being pointed toward the same spot on the Octopus' northern slope. Within a few seconds the gunners would call "Up!" and grasp their lanyards; then, a few seconds before nine, the executive officers in each of the twelve firing batteries would scream "Fire!" and the gunners would yank. The evening calm would be shattered as the howitzers barked and sent their rounds spinning through the cold night air. Seventy-two rounds—all spinning blindly toward one point, timed to reach that point at exactly the same instant, catching the enemy completely by surprise, saturating the area with splinters of hot steel and punishing the air with sound. Then, as soon as each howitzer could be reloaded and fired, seventy-two more rounds would arch out over the fields and hills, over the Shark, over the heads of the cold men in foxholes, to the target. Then seventy-two more, and more, until each gun had fired six rounds. The normal dispersion of each gun would insure that an area about the size of an ordinary city block was completely covered by its six rounds; the officers in the artillery fire direction centers had planned this fire mission and computed the firing data so that each gun would have its own city block to clobber. The enemy soldiers who might survive the flying splinters would be so stunned by the shock and concussion of the shelling that they would almost prefer death; and because there was so much artillery fire coming in, there was no place a man could run to escape it. As soon as a man's mind could shake off the shock of one blast, another would smash at him: six blows—six such blows—

Granger shook his head and sat up. He wished that the whole mess were over and done with. He looked at his hands: they were trembling. Then he looked down the tent at Wayne, who was still writing.

"Yes, I know it's a long one," he heard Eric say to Mann. What mischief are you conjuring up now, Granger wondered.

"Dammit, Eric, have you forgotten what it's like to go on a patrol?" the company commander said. "Don't you remember what a man goes through out there on a thing like that? It looks mighty easy on one of them maps, I know, but—"

There was a booming in the south. Everyone heard it.

There they go, Granger thought. God forgive me.

The execs were yelling "Fire!" and the gunners and loaders were jerking and slamming round after round into the night.

3

Suddenly there was a shh-shh-SHH and a loud *crack!*
Granger leaped up and cried "Incoming mail!"
Someone else yelled "Get down!"
Granger flattened himself in the straw, scratching furiously for the telephone.
Eric ran for his cot, grabbed his steel helmet, and tried to crawl under the cot.

Hamilton woke up and merely rolled off his cot onto the ground.

An instant later there was another muffled booming off to the south—the sound of the second rounds being fired. Again, a split second later, the screaming swish-swish-*swish-crack!*

The light went out. Rocks and chunks of frozen earth pelted the tent roof, where there was tent roof left.

Eric heard a low moan, then a hoarse cry.

"Medic! Medic!" someone wailed in the darkness.

Eric tried to burrow under the cot, then he realized that that was foolish. He was being raked by chill after chill—he tucked his arms under his chest and cringed.

Vroom-vroom-vroom. Silence, darkness—shh-*shh-crack!*

"Concrete!" Granger screamed into the phone. "Concrete! Cease firing, for God's sake cease firing!"

Suddenly the light came back on and Eric looked out from under his steel helmet. The tent was shredded. The south tent pole was shattered. The men were all down, some of them badly hit. He caught a glimpse of something red, then he ducked: he heard the base booming again. I can't stand it, he thought. I'm going to get killed! He raised his head and started to get up, to run, to escape, to die, anything—

Something smacked him back into the straw. Someone screamed, and Eric knew he was still alive. He opened his eyes and saw his steel helmet about a yard away in the straw. He reached for it, and as he reached he heard someone yell "My foot's gone—somebody, anybody, help! My foot's—" And then a wet scream.

Eric's hand felt the rough surface of the steel helmet, but just then he saw Wayne Hyde. Wayne was on his back only a few feet away, threshing his arms and legs about wildly. He was trying to speak, but he couldn't. His face was the color of milk, and his eyes rolled in terror.

Granger threw down the dead phone and scrambled to his feet. He jumped through a gaping hole that had been blown in the tent wall near his cot, and disappeared.

Vroom-vroom. Vroom-vroom-boom.

A blinding flash, then complete darkness, screams, the rain of clods and rocks, quiet, sobs.

Eric heard Granger yell "Fandango! Fandango! Cease firing!" and he knew that Granger must have made it to the radio jeep. Eric felt his way over to Wayne's body.

"Take it easy, fella," he said.

"Fandango—Fandango! Turn it off, for Christ's sake turn it off!" Granger shouted into the microphone.

Eric heard the guns again. He picked up his steel helmet and put it over Wayne's face, then he crawled over Wayne's body and covered it with his own. He held Wayne's shoulders to the ground.

"Be still, Wayne!" he whispered hoarsely.

There was a stunning, deafening crash outside, beyond the tent.

Funny, Eric thought, I didn't hear that one coming.

Someone got up and ran, then stumbled over Eric and fell to the ground, sobbing hysterically. A moment later the man got up and ran out. Then a man came into the tent carrying a Coleman lantern.

"Bring that light here!" Eric ordered. "Lieutenant Hyde's hit!"

The man with the lantern stepped over the wreckage toward Eric.

Then he saw the two sergeants who had been sitting near Wayne. "My God!" the man said. He put the lantern down and ran out of the tent to get the medics.

Eric rose to a kneeling position, still holding Wayne's shoulders to the ground. Wayne's face was white, his voice a faint whine.

"I can't breathe," he said as though he were surprised. "I can't breathe!"

Eric looked for wounds, but he couldn't see any. He figured that Wayne had been torn up internally or that he had caught a fragment in his back.

The time-on-target must be over, Holloway thought. We'd have caught the next one by now if it weren't. Then he wondered about Major Dahl. That last round must have been a direct hit on his tent, he thought. And Granger—

The man who had brought the lantern returned with the medics.

"Take the sergeants first," he said.

Eric wanted to protest, to have them take Hyde, instead; but when he saw what the rounds had done to the two sergeants, he had to turn aside and hold his breath. The horrible thing about it was that they were both still alive.

"The medics will be back for you in just a minute," Eric told Wayne. "Just keep still. It'll be all right."

Then Eric felt very foolish, for he knew that the man he was holding was dying.

A minute or two later the litter bearers returned and carefully lifted Wayne onto the bloody litter.

Hamilton walked up to the place where Eric stood watching the medics carry Hyde away.

"You okay, Eric?"

"Yes, I think so. How about you?"

"I'm all right. Where's Trent?"

"I don't know. Was he in here?"

A booming noise came from the south.

Eric was down in the straw before he realized what he was doing. He ducked his head and shivered, then he saw Hamilton's boot.

Hamilton helped him get up.

"What's the matter?"

"Nothing. That gave me a bad time for a second."

"You sure you're all right?"

"Yeah. Just dizzy."

"I'm going to see about Major Dahl," Hamilton said, and left.

Eric remembered he was duty officer. Phone, he thought. I've got to get to a phone and turn off that follow-up. He stumbled out of the wreckage of the tent into the clear, dark air, and his head cleared. He looked up at the stars for a moment, then he heard Granger's voice.

Granger was sitting on the ground, his back against the jeep's right rear wheel. He was holding the microphone in his hand, and he was crying.

"I couldn't stop it," he kept saying over and over. "I couldn't turn it off."

4

Eric finally found a phone that worked in the battalion commander's tent. Dahl was gone, but Hamilton sat on his cot, waiting for him to return from the hospital tent.

"You surprised as I was to see this tent standing?" Hamilton asked.

"Yes. That last one was right by here—air burst, too."

"Damned lucky, or something."

Major Owens answered the phone at regiment.

"My God, Holloway," he said, "I'm glad to hear from you. Just what the hell happened?"

"We don't rightly know. We do know we caught six of our own rounds. They hit mostly around the operations tent —got two sergeants and Lieutenant Hyde, all of them pretty bad."

"Damn, I'm sorry. You need anything?"

"Yes—we have a follow-up concentration laid on for nine-ten. After what happened around here, I think we'd better cancel that. Our phones are out except for this one, so will you get the word to Concrete to stop that fire mission?"

"Certainly. Anything else?"

"Yes. Better have the switchboard operator back there restrict all calls out this way until we have more phones in operation. That'll keep this phone open for Major Dahl until the other phones are repaired. I'll let you know when to stop screening."

"All right. Were any of your companies hit?"

"Not that I know of. You're the first person I've called. We sure as hell don't want anything else dropped on us, so please get that follow-up mission turned off right away."

"Will do."

Eric rang off that call, then he called each of the rifle companies and asked if any of the rounds had landed near them. None had, but Eric had considerable difficulty in finishing his calls because each of the company commanders wanted to know all about the tragedy. Eric's conversation with Sam Mann was somewhat different, however.

"We were talking about patrols for tomorrow when the trouble started," Eric said. "I haven't got my map board—it's in the mess in there—but let's do it this way. I'll start the other two patrols, then I'll come up to George Company. If I need a patrol from you, I'll lead it myself—that is, if you'll give me a few men to go along. And if anyone up there will go with me."

"That's fair enough, I guess. You be sure and call me about Wayne, hear?"

"Yes, sir."

Then Eric called regiment again and told Owens that the rest of the battalion was safe. After that call he put the phone down and sat on the cot beside Hamilton.

"You handled all that pretty well," Hamilton said.

"Having something to do helps."

Granger came into the tent and sat down on the ground. He took off his steel helmet and ran his fingers through his hair.

"I had 'em turn off the follow-up," Eric said.

Granger paid him no attention.

"You heard anything?" Hamilton asked him.

"Hyde's having a hell of a hard time."

"You have any idea what caused it?"

"One gun must have been laid wrong."

"And seventy-two were shooting."

"It won't be so hard to find which one it was, though. It

was a medium. That narrows it down to one out of eighteen."

Major Dahl entered and the three officers stood up.

"Wayne's dead," he said. "His last words were, 'Tell my wife I love her.'"

5

Hamilton turned and walked out into the night.

"I'll keep the duty," Eric called after him, but Hamilton didn't answer.

It was cold in the tent. The men felt tired and old as they gradually realized the full horror of what had happened. Minutes passed in silence, then Granger spoke.

"Why couldn't it have been me?"

"Why should it have been you?" Dahl asked him.

Granger did not answer.

"Wayne Hyde was one of the finest people I've ever known," Granger said finally, "and we've killed him. The three of us. Just as surely as if we'd stood him up against a stone wall and—"

"Stop that!" the major said sharply. "I'm about as cut up over losing Hyde as any man alive could be. Look here, Granger. There is only one fact about life, and that is that it must end. That all men must die. That's the only thing Hyde's parents could predict about his future—that Wayne would die. They could hope that he'd be president, or rich, or good—but they knew he would die, sometime. And he did. And so will we. Maybe a lot sooner than we think."

Lawrence Dahl paused to light a cigarette.

"A good man is gone—and that's tragic. But would it be any less tragic if he had caught pneumonia wading the creek last night, and died of that tonight? And don't forget how lucky he was."

"Lucky?"

"Yes. He didn't suffer much, or long. The shock was so great he couldn't feel the pain. And he got to say what was foremost on his mind. Notice he didn't call down curses on us, or on war, or on anybody. He spoke of love."

"It's still rotten—"

"Yes, it is, but we didn't lay on that time-on-target to kill Wayne. We laid it on to help protect him, and all the battalion. I don't know whether it killed any of the enemy or not, but if it did, it may have shortened the war by a day or an hour, or even five minutes."

The companies began calling in their ten o'clock reports. Eric took the calls, then he called regiment and told Major Owens of Hyde's death.

Dahl turned to Eric.

"Will you find out if Harry has the new operations tent set up yet?"

Eric nodded, got up, and left. Granger followed him.

Alone in the cold tent, Lawrence Dahl wept.

6

At midnight Harry Hamilton took over as duty officer, and Eric took a Coleman lantern and went back to the ruined tent to see if anything of his could be salvaged. He didn't own much—a sleeping bag, an air mattress, a change of baggy, green fatigues, a notebook. But even these were worth seeing about.

When he got to the tent, he looked at Wayne's cot, first. Wayne's air mattress had been punctured in dozens of places, and his sleeping bag had jagged rips in it from one end to the other. Wayne's steel helmet was lying on the edge of the cot. A steel splinter had passed all the way through the helmet's visor, leaving a clean hole.

Eric then looked at his own cot, only a few feet down the tent wall from Wayne's. Nothing of his had been hit, although the tent wall had been slashed to ribbons just over the cot. He looked at the ground where he had been during the shelling. Large rocks, clods, and sharp pieces of the shattered tent pole were scattered all around the spot; but somehow, none of them had hit him.

Eric walked over to the place where Wayne had been writing. He imagined that Wayne must have been a moment too late in getting to the ground—probably too absorbed in what he had been writing to pay any attention to the first round or to the shouts. Wayne must have been up and moving when the second round hit.

Eric picked up the sheets of paper that Wayne had dropped. He folded them carefully without reading them, then he put them in his pocket. I know what's proper, but what is the kind thing to do in a case like this? he wondered.

Then he stepped over the riddled stove pipe near what had been the south tent pole. He was cold and strangely frightened, for the violence and the tragedy of war and death had suddenly become real, and intimate. His gaze swung up to the shredded roof and along the broken ridge pole, and stopped at a place where a large steel splinter had lodged itself in the thick beam. Eric walked over to the pole and worked the splinter loose. He took it back to his cot with him and sat down, looking intently at the scrap.

A fragment like this had killed Wayne. Others like it had cut through the bodies of the two sergeants. Smaller splinters had punctured the tent and demolished the map boards over on the other wall. Eric held the warm piece of steel in his hand and looked at it carefully. It was about the size of an ordinary envelope, warped and distorted by the blast; there were ridges and grooves along one flat side, marks the rifling of the howitzer's tube had made as the round had been pushed out. Eric thought of that gun. He thought of the man who had pointed it, and he wondered what that man was thinking.

Somewhere to the south, a battery of howitzers fired. A chill went through Eric. He ducked his head slightly as he heard the rounds swish by overhead.

I'll be a long time getting over this, he thought. One hell of a long time.

Five

Outside in the night, snow was falling. It had started shortly after midnight, and by four o'clock about six inches of snow covered the ground. Up in the line, men shivered under their ponchos; the snow brightened up the landscape, making the job of peering out along the pathways the enemy might take seem just a bit easier. Still, snow was on the enemy's side, for the white curtain permitted him to move to within a few hundred yards of the line without being seen.

"Had you rather it'd rain or snow?" the Mouse asked Sergeant Hicks as they sat in the hole that was the command post of George Company's First Platoon.

"I dunno—," Hicks replied slowly. "I used to think it was pretty, the snow. Now, if I never see any more snow I'll be just as happy."

"Yeah. I used to wonder what the animals what lived in the woods did when it snowed. I used to wonder how it'd be to just live out, like that, never being under a shelter of any kind, 'cept maybe a tree."

"This here poncho ain't much of a shelter."

The rubberized sheet had been staked down along the highest edge of the hole. Two poles supported the opposite edge, making a sort of lean-to covering the hole and yet leaving enough room for the men to keep their eyes on the finger of the Shark that led directly to their hole.

"What time you got?"

The Mouse pushed the cuff of his snow mitten down and looked at his watch.

"Quarter to five. Get some sleep, Sergeant. I can take it from here on in to morning."

"Okay, Mouse, I think everything'll be all right, now."

The sergeant fumbled around in the darkness for the upper part of his sleeping bag. When he found it he shook out some snow that had blown in around the edges of the poncho, then he wrapped the bag around his shoulders and ducked his head inside. He did not zip the bag up, for he had learned a long time before that the quick-release zipper was far from quick enough when there was trouble along the ridgeline.

The Mouse stared out at the finger. He wondered if the enemy was as miserable as he was; he wondered if the nights were just as long and cold and frightening, the war just as tiring. Hell, he thought, they ain't got ponchos, 'cept the ones they've captured from us.

Out on the finger, the snow fell in wide spirals. The Mouse watched the fat flakes falling, catching them with his eyes about midway up the trees and following them to earth, or losing them in the white mass. So much white—

A hundred yards up the ridgeline, at the company command post hole, Sergeant Gregg whispered hoarsely into the sound-power telephone: "First Platoon! First Platoon! Dammit, Hicks, answer!"

There was no answer.

Gregg had been trying to get an answer from the First Platoon for the past five minutes, but the line was dead. He got up, crawled out from under the poncho that protected the hole, and went over to another hole where Mercer, he knew, was sleeping.

"Mercer?" Gregg asked, punching a body.

"Naw. I'm Collins."

"You'll do. Get up and come over to the C. P. hole."

Gregg started back to the command post. When he was almost there he stopped and looked back to see if Collins was stirring. There was no motion inside the hole that he could see, so he went back. He lifted the poncho once more.

Collins had gone back to sleep. Gregg grabbed the bag and shook it.

"Goddammit, Sergeant, leave me alone!" Collins mumbled, still half asleep.

"I said get up, dammit. Now move!"

Collins sat up, still in the bag. The First Sergeant waited, making sure Collins did not go back to sleep. This is a hell of a note, he thought.

"Damn, Sergeant. I just got to bed an hour ago. Why you pick on me all the time?"

Gregg wanted to kick the whining man: instead, he grabbed the front of Collins' jacket and held his fist under Collins' nose.

"Either the wire's cut to the First Platoon or they're all asleep. I want you to get the hell down there and find out. Now, get up or I'll beat you to a bloody pulp! You hear me?"

"All right, Sergeant, all right. I'll go."

"You God damned well better."

Gregg released the man and turned and walked back to the C. P. hole. A few moments later, Collins shuffled past, his eyes following the thin telephone wire that linked the company C. P. with that of the First Platoon.

Captain Mann stirred when Gregg got back into the hole.

"What's wrong, Top?" he asked.

"Nothing, sir. I can't get the First Platoon to answer the phone, that's all. I just sent Collins to check the wire."

Collins ambled along the path that had been worn in the ridgeline, still half asleep. Suddenly he stopped: there were footprints in the snow in front of him. Collins looked up in time to see two white-clad figures on the path just a few yards ahead of him. There was a flash, as though one of them had struck a match, then Collins fell in the snow, dead before he hit the ground.

The sound of the burp gun carried up and down the Shark's ridgeline, frightening the two figures in white. One of them broke into a run, and the other followed.

75

The shots startled the Mouse. Damn, he thought, I've been sleeping. He turned around to see if Sergeant Hicks had noticed. Then a crushing weight fell into the hole, mixing the snow and the poncho and the men. The weight was another man, kicking and squirming and flailing his arms about wildly, grunting and squealing in his panic. Then the man was gone: the Mouse saw him running down the finger toward the Octopus, closely followed by another man. Before the Mouse could raise his rifle to fire, or shout, or do anything at all, concussion slammed him into the forward wall of the foxhole. Something burned his back, and there was an awful ringing in his ears. He fell to his knees and rolled around to lean his back against the wall of the foxhole to keep from falling over backward. The poncho was gone, he noticed. Then he looked down.

Somebody in the second hole down from the platoon C. P. was firing his rifle as fast as he could squeeze off the shots. Panic firing, the Mouse thought. God, poor old Sergeant Hicks. Then he passed out.

Digger ran up to the hole.

"I stopped Shaw from shootin'," he said, then stopped short, realizing that no one in the hole could hear him. "Damn," he said, horrified.

Digger heard a sharp explosion down the finger, followed by a high scream. He felt the flesh on the back of his neck crawl. Someone was coming down the path from the company C. P., he noticed. Digger snapped the safety off and wrapped his finger around the trigger of his rifle. He drew it up to fire. He relaxed a moment later, for it was Captain Mann that Digger saw.

"That you, sir?"

"Hell, yes. Where's Sergeant Hicks?"

Digger pointed at the hole. The captain knelt down, watching the snowflakes settle on the two bodies.

"Are they both dead?"

"I don't know."

Digger jumped into the hole and felt inside the Mouse's jacket for a heartbeat.

"Ol' Mouse is still alive."

Captain Mann reached into the hole and took the Mouse's arms as Digger held them up. The captain pulled the Mouse out of the hole and held him for a moment, then he turned to his messenger and said, "Simpson, go get the medics."

Digger was looking over Hicks' body.

"Hicks is dead. Looks like he caught a hand grenade inside his sleeping bag."

The captain held the Mouse's body up with one hand while he spread a tattered remnant of the poncho in the snow with the other. Then he eased the Mouse down so that his face rested on the scrap of poncho. He covered the bloody wounds in the soldier's back with another large scrap, then he stood up.

"You take over the platoon, Digger. Better get everybody up."

"Very well, sir."

"Can't tell what'll happen next tonight. You heard about battalion catching six rounds of big stuff, didn't you?"

"Yes, sir. I sure was sorry to hear about Lieutenant Hyde getting it."

"Well, keep everybody awake from now on. Sun'll be up before long."

"I think they hit our booby trap, Cap'n. I heard one blow a few minutes ago."

"Well, don't do anything about it before daylight. It might have been people coming up to hit us that ran into it, and if it was, we'd best get ready. If we don't get jumped before long, though, take a patrol down the finger a ways after the sun comes up and find out."

"Yes, sir."

Sam Mann walked back up the snow-covered ridgeline toward his command post. He was sick at heart. He had felt very close to Hicks, mainly because in Hicks he saw what he himself had been like, seven or eight years before—an oversize, bumbling farm boy.

The captain noticed that a poncho had been spread over Collins' body. He stopped beside the hump that was almost covered with snow; he felt as though there was something he should say, but he couldn't think of words to express how he really felt, and for that matter, it seemed pretty pointless to be mumbling over a dead man. Collins couldn't hear, and God knew.

Mann walked on, feeling very old and very tired.

Gregg was sitting in the hole with his head resting on his knees, his arms folded around them. He did not look up as the company commander slid into the hole.

"Battalion know?"

Gregg looked up.

"Yessir. But the battalion commander wants you to call him."

He handed the phone to the captain. Mann twisted the crank.

"Get me White Six," he said to the operator.

2

Dahl sat beside the oil stove in the semi-darkness of his tent. Hamilton and Holloway were there with him.

Major Dahl listened quietly as Sam Mann told him of the hit and run raid on his line, and of its tragic results.

"All right, Sam. Keep your eyes peeled. They may not let us off this easy."

Dahl felt like a fool telling Mann what to do, and yet that was his function—command. It would have been different, and better, if he had said what he had to say from a hole, out in the snow and darkness; as it was, Mann had a right to a certain amount of bitterness. Dahl's sympathy went out to him, for he remembered how shredded a company commander's heart is at the sight of the dead bodies of his men, and how natural it is for the men in the line to resent encouraging platitudes that come from the comfortable, secure rear-echelon.

"Sam," he added, "we're going to make them pay for this. Regiment has laid on a company-size patrol out in front of your area. I don't know much about it yet—the colonel just called to alert me—but we're going to clobber hell out of 'em."

"Very well, sir. Is George Company going?"

"I don't know yet, Sam. Do you want to?"

Dahl realized as soon as he said it that the question had put Mann in an awkward spot. If Mann said yes, he might feel that he had been forced into risking more lives; if he said no, it might seem that George Company wasn't George Company any more.

Before Mann could answer, Dahl cut back in: "Never mind, Sam. I'll let you know as soon as I can."

He hung up.

"Come here, Eric," he said.

Dahl picked up a map board and studied the ridgelines and valleys of the Octopus in front of George Company. Then he handed the board to Holloway.

"Can tanks get very far up this valley?" the major asked, indicating the draw between Lion and Cougar.

"Yes, sir, they should—" Eric began. "To tell you the truth, sir, I don't know. We ought to have patrolled out there yesterday, but we didn't."

"All right, Eric. Harry, have George Company stretch down their ridge to cover Fox's area. Fox will go on the patrol, and we'll run a couple of tanks along the valley floor as far as we can. Objective—the junction of Lion and Cougar. Can you work it out from that?"

"Yes, sir."

"Sir, if the weather clears, would you mind if I took an airplane ride?" Eric asked. "I might be able to see something that way that would help."

Dahl was irritated by Eric's request. The shelling, the trouble with George Company, and now the certainty of having to fight again soon had left him almost limp. He was tired of problems. But this problem could be solved easily.

"All right," he said, not caring.

3

Once again Harry Hamilton began the task of planning an operation. There was a peculiar feeling in his mind; he was excited by the power with which he was working, and yet he regretted the necessity for its use. Hamilton was proud that he was qualified to do the kind of thinking and acting that was required of him, and yet he was keenly aware of what the consequences of his plans might be to the men who must carry those plans out. It was a strange way to be fighting a war: clean, almost academic, seldom dangerous. Sharp analysis, imagination, and all sorts of knowledge were the weapons he had to employ at times like this, when a decision had been made, an objective announced, and the command "Write up the order, Harry," given. Humility, and calm, considerate recollection of the miseries and fear, as well as the strength and gallantries of the men, added to the depth of all the doing and hoping that was the awful responsibility of this man.

Before he sat down to write out the order, Harry went back to the wreckage of the operations tent and fumbled around in his barracks bag for a box of cigars his wife had sent him a week or so before. When he found the box he opened it, took out three cigars, then put the box away again. He put two of the cigars in his breast pocket; the other he lit, taking long, almost ceremonial puffs.

He took a quick, horrified look at the debris, then he walked hurriedly over to the kitchen tent to write the order.

Harry Hamilton sat alone at the makeshift, officers'-mess table, leaning forward so that he could work by the light of a Coleman lantern that was hanging near the oven. As soon as his cigar was well chomped, he crammed it into one corner of his mouth and smoked in short, thoughtful puffs. One hand held the tablet: the other held a pencil which had already doodled the deaths of any number of the enemy—and, Harry Hamilton knew, all too many of our own men. His mind ranged back over the years he had spent in preparation for this moment; back through the years he had spent as an enlisted man; his miserable three months in Officer Candidate School; the frightening loneliness of a parachute jump one cold night into the heart of an enemy-held continent; a cold night spent in the water, his fingers clawing the mud of a river bottom to keep his body from being swept even six inches farther downstream into the machine gun fire which peppered intermittently all night, and somehow always came that far and stopped. He thought about all of the other times he had stared at a blank tablet, warming up his mind for the order he knew he must write. And from all this, he drew the courage to begin his task.

He wrote "1 Rifle Company" and stopped: about two hundred men, all of them men who had been shot at; about seventy rifles, half a dozen automatic rifles, a scattering of carbines and a few machine guns, three small mortars with enough ammunition to fight for an hour, if they had to; a body of men organized and armed for flexibility, but hampered by an almost complete lack of reliable radio communication. Then under "1 Rifle Company" he wrote "1 section of tanks," and again he stopped. Two tanks, left over from a previous war; a good cannon on each, and three light machine guns to boot; blind, lumbering, awkward beasts, but good to have on our side. Again he wrote: "Artillery F. O. Party." He knew that the artillery could reach out and paste anything on the forward slope of Lion or Cougar, but could they cover the back slopes adequately? He picked up his map and found the ridge; he studied the contours and folds in the earth, judging how each finger would look to the forward observer whose job it would be to bring the rounds down on the enemy in a few hours. There were several potential trouble spots which he thought might be safe from our artillery, so he added "1 Mortar F. O. Party" to the list.

Again, just a few men and a radio, but good to have because they could bring mortar rounds in on targets which the artillery could not hit.

He picked up the map once more and studied it. This time he followed the valley floor from its beginning, to the left of the Shark's upper jaw, out toward the enemy. On each side, sharp ridges—Lion and Cougar—guided the valley in a long, gentle curve to the north. Hamilton guessed that the tanks could go nearly all the way up the valley, although they would not be able to elevate their guns enough to shoot at the ridgetops if they went too far. The men would have hard going along those ridgelines, he knew. There would be no room for maneuver; it would be like climbing a rope.

Major Dahl came into the kitchen tent.

"Hold up on the order, Harry. The colonel's on his way down here. There may be a change."

"All right, sir."

"He may want us to help the Third Battalion."

"Yes, he might."

Hamilton weighed the merits of such an operation in his mind. A real attack would be far better, because whatever ground the men might gain would be kept. He had never liked the idea of combat patrols because of the necessity of risking so much for ground that would be given back almost as soon as it had been won. If he had to fight, he wanted the gain to be permanent; sometimes he felt that no amount of information of the enemy was worth turning men into shooting-gallery ducks. He knew that his was a dangerous and somewhat unsoldierly attitude, but he couldn't help it.

A few minutes later, Colonel Hobbs arrived. Colonel Hobbs was a heavy-set man of forty-four, balding, with a reddish complexion and green eyes.

Major Dahl met him as he climbed out of his jeep and escorted him into the kitchen tent. The colonel nodded to Hamilton, then he sat down. A cook brought a pot of hot coffee and several cups. Colonel Hobbs took off his gloves, stuffed them inside his steel helmet, then put the helmet on the ground. He poured himself a cup of coffee, and he looked intently at the map, getting his bearings.

"Now, Dahl, here's what's up."

The battalion commander pulled a C-ration crate up to the table and sat down. Hamilton stood behind the colonel.

"Stace tried to get this finger yesterday and couldn't make it. He's going to try again today, and I want you to help him."

"All right, Colonel."

"Stace is going up the finger he's on now."

He pointed to Rhino—the long ridge that extended due south from the Octopus' peak.

"His objective is to clear the whole Goddam mountain, but I'm worried about these."

Colonel Hobbs pointed to the long, curving fingers that Hamilton had been studying.

"We've got to get some people working up toward the top from another direction, or Stace'll never make it. Now, here's what I want you to do. Lion is going to be yours after this clambake is over, so I want you to go get it. That means you have to clear the center one, too."

"Very well, sir."

"Stace is going at nine. It's late, I know, but we want an airstrike if the weather will clear, and they tell me it will by then if it's ever going to. After Stace gets the peak, you'll tie in with him here." Hobbs pointed to a knob just down Lion from the peak. "You'll have to watch shooting into Stace. I'll tell him to keep panels out your way and you keep a radio on his channel, whatever the hell it is."

"All right, sir."

"You got any questions?"

"No, sir."

"How about you, Hamilton?"

"I've got it, sir."

"Well, I'm going over to Stace's, then. Anything you want me to tell him?"

"Just that we hope he makes it all right."

"Too bad about Hyde."

"We're pretty upset over losing him."

"I know you are, and I'd rather not have to use you again so soon, but you're in position to get off in a hurry. Besides, sometimes it works out better if you have plenty to do—you know what I mean?"

"Yes, Colonel."

The colonel rose to go. Hamilton stood up as the two commanders went out, then he sat back down at the table and lit his second cigar. A moment later, Major Dahl returned and sat down beside him.

"What do you think?"

"Fox and a couple of tanks. Same as before, except they stay."

"What about the rest of the battalion?"

"They can follow the lead company up Lion. They'll have to—there isn't any room for anything else."

"All right. It'll be Fox. Then Easy behind them, up Lion. George Company last. Easy will have to provide security for the tanks."

"Sir, I'd leave that to Fox."

"Why?"

"Control. It'll be York's show, anyway. If he wants the tanks to move, all he has to do is radio his platoon leader to pass the word."

"You're assuming two things—that he can afford a platoon to stay down in the valley with the tanks, and that the radios will work when the shooting starts."

"He can't use but one man at a time up the damned ridgeline. And the radios haven't been working since the war started, anyway."

"All right, Harry. Write it up that way." Dahl got up. "I'll be in my tent. Bring the order in when you're done."

Harry Hamilton nodded and watched the major go out, then he turned back to his tablet and began writing the order. He had already thought it out pretty well, so the words came easily. Corporal Mayes would put it in proper form

84

later, he knew, so he wrote quickly, omitting all but the essential points, concentrating on details of paramount importance.

Soon it was finished. He took the tablet to Major Dahl, got his approval, then listened as Dahl phoned the order out to the company commanders. Then he went back to the kitchen tent to eat breakfast.

Hamilton always felt uneasy during the time between the completion of an order and its execution, for until it passed completely out of his hands he was always tempted to make changes; and these, he had learned, often led to tragedy. Now he simply wrote orders and tried to get them as nearly perfect as he could the first time; he did not allow himself to tamper with a completed order, and experience was proving this to be a wise policy. Sometimes he felt that he would prefer to be a company commander again, receiving and executing orders instead of framing them. But he felt pretty certain that this order was a good one. There had been only one possible way of carrying out Colonel Hobbs' instructions, and besides, the real order had been given by Major Dahl verbally. The company commanders would be guided by what Dahl had told them; the written order, which Mayes would type out later, merely made the operation official, a matter of record.

Earlier in the war there had never been time for writing orders. When the rear echelon had screamed for records, Hamilton had been forced to dream up detailed plans for fights that had taken place months before; now he made it a point to write something about each action so that he could keep the paper-shufflers off his neck. A smile came to Hamilton's lips as he thought of the harrassed and befuddled nit-pickers he had seen in staff sections in rear-echelon headquarters, grown men almost in a panic lest the chief of section find a dangling participle in a front-line battalion operations order. Harry Hamilton hated war in every form, shape, and fashion; yet there are worse ways to fight a war than being shot at, he mused.

4

The artillery battalion's airstrip was located on a small, blocklike island in the middle of the frozen river about ten miles south of the Shark. Eric had called to arrange the flight as soon as Major Dahl had okayed the idea, and he had been told that he could fly if the weather cleared.

The clouds were still too low to allow any of the small planes to fly when Eric arrived at the airstrip. While he was waiting, he went inside the operations tent and called Captain Hamilton to see if there was anything new he should know about.

"You're damn tootin'," Hamilton said, then he gave Eric a quick run-down on the operation that was to get underway at nine.

"Is George going?" Eric asked.

"Fox. Say, keep your eye on the Third Battalion's panels if you get anywhere near us. We don't want to shoot 'em up by mistake. Also, you might have a look at the results of the time-on-target, if you can find any."

Eric's fingers clenched the telephone he was holding until his knuckles were white. When his anger had passed, he said, "Very well, sir," and hung up. Later he realized that Captain Hamilton might not have meant any offense: his request was legitimate, and it wouldn't have occurred to Eric to look for the results of the shelling.

A major came in a few minutes later and asked, "Lieutenant Holloway in here?"

"Here, sir," Eric said, getting his field jacket back on.

"Let's go."

The major was short, stocky, and had a small mustache. Somehow he matched Eric's idea of what a rear echelon pilot should look like. I've been in the line too long, he thought. A man looks downright queer if his face isn't dirty.

Outside, the sky was clear and the glare of the sun on the

snow was blinding. As Eric and the pilot walked across the frozen strip to the plane, a helicopter was being started; several of the light planes' engines were being warmed-up, making a terrific racket and blowing snow out over the frozen river.

Eric noticed that there were only two approaches to the strip: up-river or down-river. Middle-sized hills blocked side approaches, and besides, the island was too narrow to allow any sort of strip but the one it had. It was a fairly level island, with sheer cliffs on all sides. Eric estimated that the strip was about fifty feet above the level of the river.

Eric climbed into the rear seat of the little airplane. The pilot got in, shut the door, and fussed with his earphones for fully a minute before he waved to a mechanic, started the engine, and opened the throttle. The engine accelerated smoothly and pulled the little plane out of the line and onto the runway.

God, Eric thought. This clown's taking off without a run-up! He was even more horrified to notice that the throttle had been pushed all the way forward. The plane was taking off from half-way up the runway with a cold engine!

To his immense relief, the jarring caused by the wheels' crossing the ruts in the runway ceased, and the plane lifted from the frozen earth as though taking off like that were the most natural thing in the world. The plane climbed steadily to the level of the hilltops and followed the river bed northward toward the battle line.

Eric relaxed and enjoyed the sensation of flight. Maybe he knows what he's doing, Eric thought. He probably doesn't want to die any more than I do. The snow-covered mountains were lovely in the morning sunlight, making it seem incredible that so much pain and misery and death could take place on them.

Suddenly the landscape looked familiar. Eric made out the low hills on which the battalion had spent a wet, frightening night a short time before. Then he saw battalion: it went by below them so rapidly that he didn't have time to look for the craters the artillery rounds had made.

All at once he realized that they had passed over the Shark and were above the Octopus. The plane had picked up a few hundred more feet of altitude, and Eric was grateful for that. He was coming to respect the pilot more and more. Then the left wing dropped and the nose went down in a long swoop that carried them far behind the Octopus, almost into a pass. When they had regained their altitude, the pilot shouted something, but Eric couldn't hear it. He leaned forward and cupped his ear.

"Tracks!" the pilot yelled.

Eric remembered: there had been tracks in the snow. But which way had they been going—toward the Shark, or away from it?

He tapped the pilot on the back and yelled "Let's go back."

The pilot nodded, and once more the plane dipped into the pass. Eric saw the tracks clearly this time: hundreds of them, all going toward the line. Eric wanted to follow them, to spot the exact location of the enemy troops, but the pilot shook his head. Eric soon saw why. Artillery was falling on the finger where Love Company had been attacking. The pilot swung around to the west and passed over the Shark once more.

Down below, Eric could see the men of his own battalion moving down from their old line, preparing to fight for a new one on the Octopus. The tracks—my God, Eric thought. Major Dahl has to know about those tracks!

He tapped the pilot's back again. "Let's go home!" he yelled.

The pilot nodded, then he eased the plane back over the river bed. When he was still several miles north of the island, he went down so low that the wheels were barely off the ice. Eric didn't like that: a gust of wind coming from the hilltops might slam them into the ice. Still, it was quite a thrill, and Eric wished that he could quit worrying and enjoy the ride.

There was a pontoon bridge just ahead, and a truck carrying about a dozen men was passing over it just as the plane reached it. Eric instinctively braced himself for the crash, but instead he felt his weight pressed into the seat as the pilot eased the plane over the truck.

Eric looked back: the truck was still moving, but most of the men were on the floor.

The pilot pulled up and circled the airstrip, and when he was a mile or so south of the island he turned back upwind and let the plane glide toward the runway.

Eric finally relaxed. It was almost over, and he was very thankful that none of the foolish chances the pilot had taken had clobbered them. He felt very contented as he watched the landscape take on its familiar perspective. You never have to sweat out landings, he thought. Besides, he's been careful on this landing. Eric wondered if carrier landings were something like this.

Suddenly the propeller stopped dead still: the plane settled rapidly toward the cliff.

Eric looked to the right of the island, thinking that they might go down on the ice. To his horror he saw a helicopter there, parked squarely in the way. And the pilot couldn't stretch his glide enough to reach the runway. It had to be the cliff!

No, not like this! he thought frantically. He braced himself for the crash.

The plane slammed into the earth, but bounded up and over the edge of the runway and came down on one wheel and the left wing. It skidded for ten yards or so, then came to a stop. Eric looked up. He was still alive, and so was the pilot.

"Damn!" the major said, his face white with fear. "You hurt?"

"No."

"Let's get out of this bastard before it burns!"

People were running toward the plane from all over the tiny island.

Eric and the pilot scrambled out, brushed themselves off, and walked over to the edge of the cliff to see the place where the plane had hit first. There was a beveled slope, perhaps ten feet wide, just at the place where the wheels had hit and crumpled; everywhere else along the edge of the island there was a thin cover of scrubby pines, any one of which would have prevented the life-saving bounce. Moreover, the level of the island seemed to dip slightly at the beveled spot. Eric took a long look at the scarred places in the snow where the plane had skidded, then he remembered the tracks he had seen in the snowy pass behind the Octopus. He ran to the operations tent to call Major Dahl.

Once inside, he looked at his watch: nine thirty-five. The attack had already started!

He couldn't get Major Dahl, but he gave the word to Trent.

"I'll tell him, sir. But you've got a hot deal brewing."

"What do you mean, Sergeant?"

"Division chief of staff called here about an hour ago. They want you to be aide to the new assistant division commander."

"The hell you say!"

"They want to see you as soon as you can get back there."

"Does Major Dahl know?"

"Yes, sir. Said tell you to go get interviewed, then come back to the west end of the Shark if you don't take the rear echelon job."

"How's the scrap going, Trent?"

"Poorly. They just made contact, and that was when Fox got ambushed. They're pretty badly cut up, and can't move."

"You think Dahl needs me there?"

"He said for you to go talk to the man at division."

"All right. I'll be back there after a while."

"You mean you aren't going to take the job?"

90

"I didn't say that—I'll be back there in any case."
Eric hung up the phone. General's aide—

5

Division headquarters was the most glorious sight Eric's eyes had beheld in months. At the entrance, a large gate had been formed by a masterpiece of sign-painting: division shoulder patches on either side, an arch bearing the division's code-name in two-foot letters. Military Police guarded the splendid entrance, but these were no ordinary MPs: these wore steel helmets which had been chromium plated. Both soldiers wore immaculate uniforms, spit-and-polished boots, and light blue scarves around their necks, ascot-fashion.

The guardians did not recognize Eric as an officer.

"Where do you think you're going, Bud?" one of them asked him.

Eric laughed.

The MP, furious, shouted, "Shut up!" The other MP started yelling orders at the driver to turn the jeep around.

"Not so fast," the first defender countered. "This jeep's a disgrace to the service. And both of you are out of uniform. You—what's your name?"

The businesslike MP took out a neat black notepad and a short yellow pencil and prepared to make a report.

"Holloway, Eric J., First Lieutenant, Infantry. And if you and your playmate here don't put your toys away and let us pass, we'll shanghai you back to the line with us when we're done with the chief of staff."

The redfaced MP put his notebook away and executed a snappy rifle salute, which Eric returned.

"Your stacking swivel is rusty," Eric said to the MP as the driver cranked the jeep's motor. "In a line outfit you'd dig a latrine for less than that."

Division was using an abandoned highschool building. Eric entered the center doorway, then paused before a carefully lettered sign which served as a building directory. Eric saw that the chief of staff's office was to the left, so he walked down a long hall until he came to a former classroom which was marked "C/S."

Eric opened the door and went into the office. One officer was seated behind a desk, another stood nearby. The seated officer was heavy-set, dark, dumb-looking. The standing officer was short, lean, wiry, nervous; he squinted at Eric through pink-rimmed glasses. Both officers looked at Eric as though he had intruded at a most inopportune moment.

"Well?" the dumb-looking man asked.

"I'm Lieutenant Holloway, sir. I was told to report here. Something about becoming a general's aide."

"Is that the way you report in your regiment?" the nervous one asked. He turned toward Eric so that Eric could read a nameplate on his shirt: "Maj. Merlin."

"Major, we don't do a hell of a lot of reporting where I come from. I'm here because I was sent for. Am I at the wrong place?"

"No, Lieutenant," the stupid-looking man said. "I'm the assistant chief. You can wait for Colonel Sprague outside."

Eric turned to go.

"Not so fast, Lieutenant," the jittery major said in a high voice. "If you're going to be a general's aide, the first thing you have to learn is to take your hat off when you're indoors."

Eric almost lost his temper. He knew that it was technically correct for him to have his steel helmet on, for he was wearing his forty-five; still, it had never occurred to him to remove his steel. He wasn't used to being indoors, and removing one's hat, he had always been taught, was a mark of respect.

Eric was tempted to say what was on his mind. Instead, he said simply, "Please tell the chief of staff that I would not care to be a general's aide. I appreciate the consideration, but prefer to stay where I am."

Outside in the hall, Eric smiled. Real men, these—he thought.

Colonel Sprague came striding up the hall just as Eric was about to leave the building.

"You Holloway?" he asked in a booming voice.

"Yes, sir," Eric said, saluting.

Sprague had a wise look in his eyes. A heavily eroded face told Eric much.

"They tell me I'm about to make general," Sprague said. "They're rushing things a bit, I guess, but they want me to have an aide. Now, son, don't answer me yet. I had 'em call you because you've been wounded once, and then that business last night. I don't know how you feel about the duty you're pulling in your battalion, or how you feel about general's aides, but the job's yours if you want it. I can't guarantee you anything, but you'll probably live. If an airplane doesn't crash, or somethin' like that. Leastways, you won't get shot at."

Eric looked out the doorway into the schoolyard. He saw the great entrance signs, the chromium-plated steels, the elegant MPs. He also saw his jeep—muddy, a bullet hole through the windshield, a five-gallon gas can tied in front of the radiator. And he saw the driver.

There is your choice, he told himself. You can get away from Hamilton, from death, from Granger, from being blamed with every tragedy that happens. Here, you can get in on real high-level doings. You can make contacts. You can be clean, eat well, sleep on a cot in a warm tent, really live. Really be an officer. Here's your choice.

"You won't hurt my feelings if you say no. Either way, it's all right—I'll understand. Had to make up my mind myself, once. Guess that's why I'm alive today."

Eric wanted to ask him what he meant, but he happened to see another rear echelon MP come up to his driver and begin giving him hell over something.

"I warn't doin' nothin'," he heard his driver protest, but the MP's pencil was poised over the little black book.

"Colonel, thanks very much for giving me this chance. I appreciate it, and if I were going to be anybody's aide, I'd be yours. But I'd be about as far out of place here as a man can get. I'd better stay where I am. I'd like to think I belong there—I know I wouldn't get along back here."

"Fine, boy, fine! I wouldn't have the God damned job, myself. Now go get your driver out of here before these draft-dodgers draw and quarter him."

Eric threw Sprague one of the smartest salutes he had ever given.

Six

Eric's jeep arrived at the foot of the hill where the battalion command group was situated just after Colonel Hobbs' jeep pulled up. He saluted the colonel, then broke into a run up the Shark's slope. He reached the top almost completely out of breath and looked back: the colonel was far behind, puffing up the trail as fast as he could climb.

"Sir, Colonel Hobbs is coming," he told Major Dahl, pointing down the backside of the hill. "I saw a lot of fresh tracks in the snow over behind the Octopus—they're loaded up there. They must have reinforced during the snowfall last night, or even after it stopped this morning."

"How many of the enemy did you see?"

"None, sir. Just tracks. We couldn't get a good look because of the artillery."

"You didn't see their mortar positions?"

"No, sir."

Eric realized that his flight had been a failure.

"You going to stay with us?"

"Yes."

"How's it going, Dahl?" the colonel said, coming up behind them.

"Hard to tell just now, sir."

"Well, fill me in from the beginning."

The colonel sat down on a large rock and spread a map at his feet.

"Fox Company jumped off at nine and began climbing Lion. York had all but one platoon up there, but the climbing was pretty difficult, and he was having a hard time keeping his column moving, so he left his lead platoon up there —told them to keep going up the ridge. York took the rest of his company down to follow the tanks up the valley floor."

"I see."

"That lead platoon got pretty well along Lion, and the tanks were getting into the valley without any trouble, then all hell broke loose."

"How?"

"They were fired on from ambush positions on both sides of the valley."

"Didn't the platoon on Lion take care of that?"

"No, sir. The firing wasn't coming from the top, you see. The platoon up there ran ahead to take care of it, but they didn't find anybody on top. The people down below with the tanks were pinned down by the fire from the ambush positions."

"Dammit, Dahl, couldn't the tanks break up the firing? Isn't that what we carry them around for?"

"The tanks shot up every round they had, sir, but they didn't get it stopped. When they tried to turn around to come back for more ammo, one of them hit a mine and blew a track. The other one ran over one of our men who was hiding under it. I think the mine got three or four of Fox's men, too."

"Damn!"

"The tank that could still move got back and loaded up, and he's gone back out there. York's following the tank in with the rest of his company now. He's going to try to clean out the ambush and get his wounded out. We haven't heard any shooting down there yet, so he must be doing all right."

"Well, why aren't you putting artillery on Lion?"

"York wanted it turned off, sir."

"Why?"

"The enemy's too close to his wounded people."

Dahl didn't want to talk about it, but he was desperately

96

afraid that some of his men had been hit by the few rounds that had already been put on the ambush area.

"It'll be up to the tank, then," Colonel Hobbs said.

"Yes, it will. But the tankers are afraid of running over somebody else, and the infantry's having to lead it in."

"Afraid—afraid—everybody's afraid. York's afraid of a little artillery, tankers are afraid of running over people—"

"Colonel, we're a little touchy about killing our own people today."

"Yes, Dahl. I forgot. I'm sorry. Well, what's the other tank doing?"

"It's all right. The enemy's kept it under fire, but only with machine guns. They can't hurt the tank, but we've got to get it out of there before long. I've already asked regiment for another tank platoon and the tank retriever."

"They sending it?"

"Colonel Marvin said he'd let me know, sir."

"Well, what are you going to do to get this attack going?"

"As soon as Fox gets the ambush cleaned up, and York gets his wounded out, I'm going to have him slip over to the right side of the valley and secure Cougar. We got shot at from there, too."

"The hell you did! Was it part of the outfit that hit George Company last night?"

"We don't know, sir. The two bodies that George Company found were no help in finding out. Lieutenant Holloway thinks they moved a lot of new people in here during the night."

"No kidding?"

"I've got Easy Company alerted to take Lion. I'm going to paste the whole ridgeline with artillery before they go. And that'll be after York is clear."

"Gimme a phone."

Mayes brought one and handed it to the colonel. Major Dahl told Eric to check the radio to see how Fox was doing, and Eric left.

The colonel got Major Stace on the phone and asked him

how his attack was proceeding. "I see, I see," he kept saying as he listened to the report.

"All right, Stace. I'll be here with Dahl a little while longer. He's got a real mess on his hands and won't be much help to you. Call me here if anything breaks."

Hobbs hung up and handed the phone back to Mayes.

Machine gun firing broke out in the valley.

Eric was talking to York on the radio when it started. York must have been hit, Eric thought, for the radio went dead in the middle of a transmission. Eric tried to regain contact, but there was no response. He switched the radio over to the tank's channel and called the tank platoon leader.

"This is Gasoline Two," he said. "What's happening?"

"Caboose One, here. We're getting it from both sides. It's higher up, this time. I can't elevate the damn main armament enough to get it."

"This is Gasoline Two. Can you adjust artillery? Over."

"Caboose One. Affirmative, but they're liable to splatter the infantry. People are down all around here."

"Stand by, Caboose."

Eric handed the set back to Saxon, and walked over to Major Dahl.

"Sir, Captain York's radio went out while I was talking to him. I got the tank platoon leader, though, and he says he can shoot artillery on the place the shooting's coming from."

"Why doesn't he go ahead and shoot, for God's sake?" the colonel asked.

"He can't elevate his own gun high enough. They're higher up this time, sir."

"Does the tank platoon leader have communication with anybody in Fox Company?" Dahl asked Eric.

"No, sir. He said the Fox Company people are all down. He's afraid some of them might get hit with artillery, but he's willing to try."

"Ask Lieutenant Granger to come over here, please."

Eric left to go get Granger.

98

"Dahl, I hate like the very devil to have to do this, but we've got to get this thing going. Get Fox out of there the best way you can, but Lion has got to be secure by noon—or the Third Battalion might just as well quit and go home now. You understand?"

"Yes, sir."

"I sure as hell hope you do, Dahl. I haven't got time to be a gentleman about this thing. Division's riding me—you know. Now, quit worrying so much about accidents and get aggressive about this thing, or—well, get going."

"Very well, sir."

"I'm going over to Stace's now. I'd like for you to call me at eleven and tell me how it's working out."

Colonel Hobbs got up and started down the hill toward his jeep.

2

Major Dahl called Eric and Granger over to him.

"Are you laying on the artillery, Giles?"

"Yes, sir. I've been talking to Lieutenant Jamison, the forward observer with Fox. He says York is badly hit. Nearly everybody down there is. Nobody can move. Jamison says he can adjust artillery, but he's not sure where the platoon on the ridge is."

"All right, tell him to start shooting. We'll just have to hope that platoon isn't in the way."

"What if it is?"

"Remember that there are a lot of people down there that need that fire—and if Jamison can shoot to help them, I think that's what he ought to do. See what you can do about it, please, Granger."

Granger went back to his radio and got Jamison's fire mission laid on.

Eric and the battalion commander walked slowly back to the spot which the major had been using as his observation post all morning. Eric felt sorry for Major Dahl, but he couldn't think of anything to say that wouldn't sound hollow or dramatic.

As they sat on the Shark watching the artillery feel its way cautiously along Lion, Mayes brought a phone to the major.

"It's Captain Heath, sir."

"White Six," Dahl said into the phone.

"Captain Heath, sir. The platoon from Fox Company is back here with me. They ran out." Heath sounded angry.

"They did?" Dahl was both thankful and astonished. "Are they all right?"

"Yes, sir, but scared green."

"Well, here's what I want you to do." This is the first real break in the whole operation, Dahl thought. "Have the platoon take over the ground you're on now. Then move your company out as soon as you can and get on Lion and go as far as you can. In other words, you're taking over York's mission, except for the valley. You understand so far?"

"Yes, sir."

"Now, this is very important. We're having trouble with communication, as usual, so keep your radio operator talking to mine. And keep your forward observer's radio going, too, if you can. Granger will be monitoring him. Fox's F. O. is putting fire on Lion now, so have your F. O. take over the mission. You have all this?"

"I do, sir."

"One more thing. Keep a panel out our way, if you can. Now let me speak to the platoon leader from Fox."

There was a pause, then a new voice came onto the line.

"This is Lieutenant O'Connor, sir."

"What happened out there, O'Connor?"

"We were overrun, sir."

"Overrun? That shouldn't happen to an attacking platoon. What do you mean?"

"We got hit from both sides—and in front, too. They

were all over the place—shootin' and hollerin' and raising all kinds of hell."

"Well, how many men did you lose?"

"None, sir."

Dahl was glad of that.

"How many of the enemy did you get?"

"I don't think we got any, sir. We concentrated on getting out of there."

"All right. How far up the ridge did you get? Can you give me the coordinates of the place where you think the enemy was?"

"Yes, sir, just a minute while I get my map out."

Dahl waited impatiently.

"Major, it was at Dog Sugar 542661. I've already told Captain Heath."

The battalion commander repeated the numbers to make sure he had them correctly, then he found the spot on his own map.

"O'Connor, are you sure of those coordinates?"

"Yessir. Positive."

"Well, according to my map, you've got the enemy in the middle of the creekbed!"

"Gee, Major, that's wrong."

"I haven't got time to mess with you any longer, O'Connor. Heath has orders for you, and I want to see you when this operation is over. By the way, pick out a good man from your platoon and send him with Heath as a guide."

"All right, sir."

Eric had watched all this, fascinated. This, he thought, is what they ought to teach for leadership: how to operate with a telephone in one hand and a map in the other. Eric had been impressed by the calm, even manner in which Major Dahl had handled all of these complex situations. Dahl's voice had never been raised, his face had not betrayed a single emotion. He was not angry at the platoon's apparent cowardice, nor was he wishy-washy in dealing with the problem. He was not unduly distressed over what amounted to the loss of Fox Company; rather, he was pushing his attack as hard as he could, hoping that Easy would be able to do the job that Fox had botched. Eric also knew that Dahl was grieving inwardly over the fact that so many of his men were casualties, but he also knew that Dahl's primary concern was winning so that the shooting, and the danger, could be stopped for good.

Another thing about this attack that had impressed Eric was the vital importance of communication. There had been some very bad moments before the exact location of Fox's floating platoon had been determined; and if it weren't for the tank's radio, the battalion commander might still have been in the dark about the situation down below. As it was, Fox's predicament was severe—but something was being done about it, and done because the artillery radios worked.

The battalion command group on the Shark reminded Eric of a picture he had seen of some Civil War generals and their staffs standing on top of small hills slightly in the rear of the fighting, commanding divisions and regiments and waving whiskey bottles at their opposite numbers on a distant hilltop. Here, there were no whiskey bottles; and if there were any opposite numbers for this battalion staff around, they couldn't be seen.

Through his fieldglasses, Eric could see the men of Easy Company moving up the long finger called Lion. A panel was visible now and then, whenever there was a break in the woods that covered the ridge; the men were climbing rapidly, steadily, as though the end of the war depended on their getting control of that ridge. Easy's a good company, Eric thought. So's George. But Fox—

He walked over to Granger's radio and listened to the forward observer's transmissions. The place on the Shark where the battalion command group was working was directly under the high, arched path of the rounds that were pounding the base of Lion: every time the swish-swish-swish passed over, Eric ducked. Then he remembered that theoretically the rounds are already over and gone when the people on the ground hear their muted rustle. I heard them swish last night, he thought. He was very uneasy, but he tried to think of the good those rounds were doing Fox Company, and that helped.

"They're not shooting at us any more," Eric heard Fox's F. O. say over the radio.

Now would be a good time to get the wounded out, Eric thought.

He dog-trotted over to the rock where Major Dahl was sitting.

"Jamison says the artillery's stopped the enemy from shooting at them, sir. Now might be a good time to get Fox out of there."

Eric was glad to be bringing good news.

"Yes, it might be."

"Sir, could I take O'Connor's platoon in to get the wounded out?"

Eric felt that he might as well do that; he knew that he was doing little or no good as things were, and that Dahl's confidence in O'Connor was badly shaken.

"No, Eric."

"Then may I go along? We could sure use a prisoner, and there's a chance the artillery left us one."

"No. I'll tell O'Connor to get you one, if he can."

"Very well, sir."

Eric couldn't think of anything else to say, so he went back to Granger's radio, embarrassed and hurt. He was sorry that he had added to Dahl's problems, and surprised that Dahl apparently had so little confidence in him. I wouldn't have mentioned my taking that platoon, he thought, if I hadn't believed that he trusted me more than he did O'Connor. But I guess he's still thinking about the way I goofed things up the other night.

3

Harry Hamilton walked up to the rock where Dahl was sitting.

"Anything new?" he asked.

"Fox Company's F. O. thinks he's silenced the enemy ambush out there."

"Do you have any contact with York?"

"No. He's hit. Eric wanted to take O'Connor's platoon in to get a prisoner and to get the Fox people out, but I think O'Connor can do it."

"Holloway's still too eager for his own good, isn't he?"

"Well, he's got to learn that he can't do it all by himself. I guess that's something we all have to learn sooner or later. He's trying mighty hard—too hard. But he'll learn."

"I couldn't disagree with you more, but it doesn't matter, I guess. Has O'Connor started moving yet?"

Major Dahl shook his head.

"Not that I know of."

Mayes handed the battalion commander the phone.

"White Six," Dahl said.

It was Captain Webb, the heavy weapons company commander.

"Major, I'm taking O'Connor's bunch in there to get York and his people out."

"No, Webb. I want O'Connor to do it."

Dahl was frankly tired of denying requests to take the platoon in. Everyone but O'Connor wanted to go, it seemed.

"Sir, York's my best friend. Our wives live together back in the States. I can't sit back here any longer. I want to get him out!"

"Listen, Webb. I need you up here. We may need some mortar fire on the objective. I'm not at all satisfied with the support How Company's giving, and I want you to come up here so we can get this thing straightened out."

"Dammit, Major, you don't understand—"

"Yes, I understand, Webb. I'll take care of York. You come up here. Do as I ask you."

"Major—"

"I said come up here, please, Captain Webb."

"All right."

Webb hung up.

Dahl turned to Hamilton.

"I'm going to change my mind, Harry. Fox won't be able to do any more fighting today, even if we get them out within the next hour."

"You're right—they've had it."

"I'm going to have George move along Cougar, abreast of Easy."

"Sounds good," Hamilton replied. "Those ridges meet up ahead. If George beats Easy to the junction, we may whip this thing after all."

"Yes. And when Mann gets by the ambush position, he can have some of his people mop it up. The medics can go in and get Fox Company's wounded out. Will you give the word to Mann for me?"

"Yes, sir."

Hamilton took the phone and called George Company.

As he was talking to Sam Mann, giving him the battalion commander's order, mortar fire started falling in the valley where Fox Company was.

"Oh, hell!" Hamilton said as he saw the smoke rise from the bursts.

Mann heard the explosions, too.

"Harry, even when we get up on that there ridge, we can't see to shoot at them mortars. Can you people do something about them?" Mann asked.

"Yeah, Sam. We'll put artillery on 'em, or mortars. We're waiting on Webb to come up, now."

"No—no. Webb just went by down in the valley. Had O'Connor's platoon with him."

"God's teeth!" Hamilton said. "Well, wait a minute, Sam."

Hamilton turned to Major Dahl.

"Webb's taken O'Connor's platoon into the valley."

Dahl seemed to Hamilton as though he hadn't heard, or didn't understand what Hamilton just said. Finally he spoke.

"Very well. Get Granger on those mortars. And get Sam moving."

How cool can you be? Hamilton wondered.

"Sir, do you want me to do anything to get Webb back? Call him, or something?"

"No, I don't think we can do anything about that, Harry. Webb'd disregard anything we might try. We'll just have to pray that he gets away with it."

Hamilton thought differently.

"Sir, I'd try to stop it. We—"

"All right, Harry. Just how would you stop it?"

Hamilton suddenly realized how far ahead of him in his thinking Dahl was.

"I'm sorry, sir."

"Now do as I asked you, please."

While he was alone, Lawrence Dahl closed his eyes and prayed.

4

"Yes, sir?" Granger said, sitting down near the battalion commander.

"Get after those mortars, if you can. Eric might be able to tell you a little about where they are. Also, you might tell Fox Company's F. O. that Captain Webb's bringing in some help. Jamison might pass the word. Also, see that Jamison turns his fire mission over to Easy's F. O. as soon as the Easy man can shoot."

"Very well, sir."

Granger went back to his radio.

"Time to call the colonel, Major," Mayes said, handing Dahl the phone.

"Get me a report on Easy, please, Mayes," Dahl answered, then he called the regimental commander.

"What's the story over there, Dahl?" Colonel Hobbs asked.

"Well, sir, we're moving. Easy's up on Lion. Fox is still down in the valley, but their Third Platoon is moving in there now to clean up the ambush and to get that situation under control. Captain Webb is in charge of that."

Dahl hoped the regimental commander wouldn't question him about that, but it had to be said.

"George Company is going to attack up Cougar right away. Right now we're bothered by enemy mortar fire falling on Fox, but we're putting artillery on the backside of the ridge, and that ought to do it."

"Easy and George attacking abreast, huh?"

"That's right, sir."

"Why in the hell didn't you do that to begin with, Dahl?"

"No excuse, sir."

"Don't hand me that crap, Dahl. Why?"

"Because I believed that Fox could do the job. I was wrong."

"Well, push Heath and Mann all you can."

"Very well, sir."

"What projects you have going on besides the mission I gave you is your own business. Just be damned sure you get that ridge cleared by noon. Hear?"

"Yes, Colonel. How is Stace making out?"

"Well as can be expected until you folks get off your butts. Most of their trouble is coming from the upper end of your ridge. Cougar, that is."

"We'll get up there as soon as we can, sir."

"You do that."

Colonel Hobbs hung up.

Granger returned.

"Fire mission's on the way, Major. But that enemy fire's shifted. It's falling on George, I think."

"Keep raking the backside of the ridge where you think their mortars are, then."

Dahl wished for Webb: this was a job for him. Instead, there he was, off on an adventure that might cost him a court-martial, if not his life; and for what? a code of friendship that for Webb justified the risking of the lives of a whole platoon to get York out. Dahl knew that Webb might also have been thinking about the others who were wounded; still, he had the strong conviction that Webb wouldn't have done this if it had not been for his close friendship with the Fox company commander. Friendship—

A moment after Granger had gone back to his radio, Dahl got up and went over there, too. He stood watching the artillery officer direct the fire that was feeling out the reverse slope of the ridge, groping for the draw where the enemy mortars were coughing out the rounds that were falling deep inside George Company.

Mayes walked up.

"Sir," he said, "Captain Mann's command group was just hit."

"My God!"

"How bad is it?" Granger asked.

"Lieutenant Frost was killed instantly, sir. Captain Mann isn't hit bad, but he'll have to be evacuated. They were the worst hit. A few others caught fragments."

"All right, Mayes, thank you," Dahl said, then he returned to his rock and sat down.

Cracks and thumps of rifle and machine gun fire from up the draw made Dahl wince. Could that be Webb mopping up the ambush? he wondered. He got up and went back to the artillery radio.

"When you can, Giles, please find out who's doing the shooting down there."

Dahl was afraid his ears had already given him the answer: the cracks and thumps he heard told him that the ambush was far from silenced.

"Fandango Five-Six, this is Fandango Two-Zero, over."

"This is Five-Six, over."

"This is Two-Zero. Who's doing the shooting? Over."

"This is Five-Six. Who the hell do you think? They just

opened up on the platoon coming in here. I saw them drill Captain Webb. He was way out in front—never knew what hit him. Over."

"Did you hear that, sir?" Granger asked.

"Yes, I did."

Dahl turned away from the radio and walked back to his rock. He told Harry Hamilton about Webb, then he turned and looked at Eric.

"You know, Harry," he said, "I'm going to give George Company to Holloway."

"Now wait a minute, Major. He can't—"

"Eric!" Dahl called. "Come over here, please."

Holloway walked over, a quizzical look on his face.

"Yes, sir?"

"Eric, I'm placing you in command of George Company."

Holloway drew a deep breath.

"As you know, they're short a company commander, an executive officer, and a platoon leader. We've also lost the commanders of Fox and How Companies. Easy and George have to be my fighting companies, so they have to have fighting leadership."

Eric wanted to stop the major, to tell him he didn't feel he could command a company—but he was too shocked to do anything. He was trembling, and he felt his heart beating somewhere in the middle of his throat.

"Your first mission will be to attack up Cougar, and I mean attack. Eric! Are you listening to me?"

"Yes, sir."

"I don't know how your company is fixed for radios, but somehow you've got to keep in constant contact with me."

Dahl paused.

"Don't take anything for granted. Go up there to get that ambush position cleaned up—we'll get the wounded out. Get that ambush cleaned up, then keep going to the place where Lion and Cougar meet. Dig in there.

"Now, you'll be responsible for both Cougar and the valley. Try to keep abreast of Heath. And get going as soon as you can get your company organized and your orders issued. You have all this?"

Now, Eric thought, tell him! But he couldn't. He knew he would have to take George Company. He had to.

Eric stood up.

"And Eric, be careful. Use firepower wherever you can. Don't expose yourself any more than you absolutely have to."

Eric nodded, still unable to speak. Then he ran over to Granger's radio, told Sergeant Trent to keep the battalion commander informed of anything that turned up, and went down to join George Company.

5

Eric saw a litter up ahead, so he ran to catch up with it. Captain Mann was in the litter, conscious, but in great pain.

"Sir," Eric said, "Major Dahl sent me down to take the company."

"Okay, Eric. Do as you're told, but always take good care of the men. Don't get 'em kilt if you can help it. They're mighty fine men."

"Sir, I—" Eric began, but he couldn't talk. Besides, the medics lifted the litter and carried the wounded captain on down the trail.

Eric stood there for nearly a minute, thinking, watching the figures grow smaller as they moved along the narrow, winding path that followed a rocky creekbed down the draw.

Seven

Sergeant Gregg and a number of other soldiers were huddled in a group not far from the spot where the mortar round had landed. Lieutenant Frost's body was lying where he had fallen, although someone had rolled him over onto his back and placed his fieldjacket over his face. The wounded, except for Captain Mann, had been moved to a gulley about twenty-five yards away.

Holloway noticed Lieutenant Frost's body as he passed, then he called Sergeant Gregg over to him.

"Top, I'm taking command of the company," he said.

Gregg was astonished. This can't be, he thought. Dahl would never do a thing like that to George Company.

"Get the platoon leaders up here, please."

Gregg looked away.

"Lieutenant," he said in a grave voice, "if this thing has got to be, all right. I don't like the idea. But I'll soldier for you, because that's what my book tells me to do. Just one thing, though, Lieutenant. Please, for Christ's sake, don't goof."

"Get the platoon leaders, please, Top."

"Very well, sir."

Gregg passed the word to each of the platoon leaders, then he returned and began shouting orders at the command group.

"Gipp, you get that Goddam radio on your back and keep with Lieutenant Holloway. Tolbert, you break up that mob over there. And scatter! All you bastards get spread out, or you might as well go check in over to the gulley right now. Scatter!"

Holloway watched Gregg get his house in order, then he decided to find a spot from which he could see Cougar better.

"I'll be over yonder, Top," he said when he spotted a small clearing not far off the path.

"Watch out for your hind-end."

"I will, Top."

Lieutenant Schaefer joined the company commander first. Eric hadn't known Schaefer very well, for Schaefer had joined George Company after Holloway had gone to battalion.

Eric learned a few things about Schaefer from looking at him as he walked into the clearing. Schaefer was five or six inches shorter than Holloway, and his face was beginning to show age—about ten more years of it than Holloway had. His hair was short and half-gray, and there was a certain grayness around his deep-set eyes that told Eric that Schaefer was very tired.

"Hello, Holloway," Schaefer said, extending his hand. "Congratulations."

Eric thought he detected a touch of sarcasm in Schaefer's greeting, for he knew that Schaefer ranked him by three full years. But he took Schaefer's hand, and he thanked him.

Sergeant Dolan passed Holloway and Schaefer, but instead of stopping he went on along the ridgeline to speak to Gregg.

"Top, what the hell gives?" Digger asked.

"Huh?"

"Why don't we just line up and shoot ourselves, and be done with it?"

"Shut up, Digger. The company commander'll hear you."

"I don't give a good God damn if he does."

"Digger, I said for you to shut up, and you'd better by God do it."

"God help this poor company," Dolan said.

"Amen," Eric muttered.

"What'd you say?" Schaefer asked.

"Nothing," Eric replied. You heard it all, he thought.

Dolan walked into the clearing and sat down without speaking or waiting to be told he could sit. Eric ignored the gesture, but he watched the dark, bearded man intently, wondering how in the world he was going to be able to get along with Digger.

The other two officers, Dan Felty and Peter Cannon, arrived together, spoke casually to the new company commander, and sat down. Eric had met Felty and Cannon, but that was all. He knew nothing whatever about them.

Dan Felty was tall and thin, and very young—twenty-two at most. His uniform was dirty, like the others, but the new hadn't worn off. Cannon looked very much like Felty from a distance, but he was blond—almost as blond as Holloway. And he seemed to be more sure of himself than Felty did. If Cannon was older than Felty, it was in experience only—but Cannon did seem older.

Sergeant Gregg joined the group, and then Holloway began giving his first order.

"I'm going to have to do some hasty reorganizing first. It may not take, but it'll have to do for today.

"Major Dahl has given me command of this company. For how long, I don't know, but that doesn't matter. We have an order—to attack—and we'll do as we're told as a company until I'm either shot or pulled out of this job. You may as well know that I'm not happy to have gotten the company under the circumstances, but I've got it, and it behooves me to function—to soldier—as effectively as I can. I think that's the way Captain Mann would want it. This is no apology. I just want you to have this thing straight.

"Now. Schaefer, you turn your platoon over to your platoon sergeant, and take over as executive officer."

"Very well, sir."

"You have the holes in the command group filled, Top?"

"Yes, sir. Ready to go."

"All right. Now, as you know, the enemy isn't giving away any of his real estate these days."

"We know," Digger said bitterly.

"This regiment has the mission of getting that mountain—the Octopus. Blue is going up that finger over there, the one called Rhino. Our battalion has to get Lion and Cougar.

"That's where we come in. Easy's up on Lion now. We are supposed to get going up Cougar as soon as we finish here. Our mission is to clear the finger, which includes the ambush position—wherever the ambush is."

"Are we responsible for the valley?" Felty asked.

"Yes, but we're not to worry about Fox Company or their wounded. There are two tanks down there, but they're under battalion control. Besides, they can't elevate their gun tubes enough to shoot for us. The valley's too deep there where they are."

"I see."

"We're going to keep abreast of Easy, after we catch up with them, but our first concern is getting up on the ridge and cleaning up the ambush. When we get to the ambush, we'll hold up there long enough to send a platoon down for the clean-up job, then we'll continue the attack up the ridgeline."

Eric turned to Lieutenant Felty.

"Your platoon will lead, initially. If you run into anything, clobber it. We've got to stay on the ridgeline, and there won't be any room for maneuver. Figure on going straight ahead all the time."

"All right."

"The company command group will be right behind Felty's platoon. Cannon, you follow the command group, and be ready to take your platoon down this side of the ridge to take care of the ambush. You go on my order. And stay up in front of your platoon where you can see and hear me. I'll tell you exactly what I want done when we hit the thing."

"Okay."

"Schaefer, have the mortars follow the Second Platoon. You have the recoilless rifles farmed out, I suppose."

"The Third Platoon—that's Felty's—has one. The other two are busted."

"Have they been sent back for repair?"

"Yes, but a hell of a lot of good that does us."

"What do you mean by that?"

"Those guns have been back there three months. If anybody back there gave a damn, they'd have been returned or replaced months ago. But nobody back there cares. And memorandum receipts don't shoot so good."

"All right. Have the mortar people ready to shoot on a moment's notice, because we haven't got any other direct support. Maybe you'd better stay with them in the column."

Schaefer nodded.

"Digger, your platoon will have two things to do. Look out for our rear end in case we get ambushed, and give the mortars local security when they set up to shoot. By the way, how'd the Mouse make out?"

"They took him out a couple of hours ago. He'll live."

"Good. You understand what I want you to do?"

"I do."

"Do the rest of you have any questions?"

Cannon asked, "Are you going to redistribute the radios?"

"We ain't got but three that work out of the twelve we got, sir," Sergeant Wood broke in.

Eric hadn't noticed Wood, who was the company's communications sergeant, but he was glad he was there.

"The rest is no good, and the three we got usually go out as soon as the first shot's fired."

"Thanks, Sergeant. Felty, you take one. Cannon, another. I'll keep the third one with me. Schaefer, I'll call you on the spare Three-Hundred, if I need you."

The company commander turned back to Sergeant Wood.

"Did the mortar round get both of the Three-Hundreds, or are they still working?"

"They're both working now."

"All right. If anything happens to mine, get the exec's set forward to me, Sergeant."

"Very well, sir."

"We getting any artillery support?" Schaefer asked.

"Not at first. Maybe later. If we need it before we get an observer, I can relay it over my radio to Granger at battalion. You get that, Felty and Cannon?"

Both officers nodded.

"Let me know if you need artillery, and we'll handle it that way. Anything else?"

Nothing.

"All right. Get moving, Felty. We'll pull in behind you."

The platoon leaders got up and returned to their platoons. Gregg and Wood went back to get the company command group on its feet and ready to follow Felty's platoon.

The company commander raised his hand to shield his eyes from the glare of the sun on the snow and looked across the narrow valley at the long, sharp finger called Cougar, the objective his company—*his* company—had to win. He was afraid, and he was lonely, and he knew that the fear and the loneliness had just begun.

2

Gregg came to get Holloway when the command group was ready to go.

When Eric turned to go with Sergeant Gregg, he sensed that something was wrong.

"Wait a minute, Top. I haven't got a shootin' iron."

Gregg had the sniper rifle that Captain Mann had been carrying all through the war. It was a superb weapon: the stock was polished, and the rifle was equipped with a telescopic sight, cheek pad, and flash hider.

"Your old M-1 around here anywhere?" Eric asked.

Sergeant Gregg grinned.

"Sure is. Tolbert, you go get that M-1 I gave Joe and give it to the Lieutenant."

Tolbert returned a minute or two later with Gregg's old M-1 and a bandolier of ammunition. Holloway threw the bandolier over his shoulder, slung the rifle, and started walking along the trail. Gregg, Wood, and the company command group followed him.

Most of the men in George Company were lying along the Shark's ridgeline, resting. Eric supposed that they were all giving him the once-over. Some of the men would remember him from his days as a platoon leader in George Company, he figured; others might have been on patrols he had ordered since he had become battalion intelligence officer. Now the lives of all the men were in his hands, he realized; and he knew that all of them would be judging his every move from then on. That frightened him, for he didn't know what he could do to keep those men fighting if they judged him a failure, if it turned out that they had no confidence in him. What will I do, he wondered, if they won't go?

When Eric and his command group reached the Third Platoon, Holloway stopped and sent for Lieutenant Felty.

"Call the battalion commander, please, Gipp," he said.

When Gipp had Major Dahl on the radio, he handed the handset to Eric.

"George is moving out now. Over."

"This is Gasoline Six. Roger, Eric. Good luck. Out."

Felty and his radio operator walked up as Eric was giving the handset back to Gipp.

"Ready to go, Felty?" Holloway asked.

"Yes."

"All right. I'll be right behind you."

Felty called out "On your feet!" and his men got up and fell into a single file, with intervals of about five or ten yards between men.

Felty's men grumbled a bit, as soldiers always do in a good outfit; then they headed down the side of the ridge with a let's-get-it-the-hell-over-with attitude. Nobody was pushing them or urging them on with platitudes: nobody had to. These men knew that the route home ran down the northern slope of the Shark, over Cougar, over the Octopus, the way they were moving; and they knew that unless they moved together, as a company, none of them would ever see home again. Felty had told them what needed to be done, and that was all that was necessary. They had a good deal of experience in doing jobs like the one they now faced. They had faith in their weapons, and they had faith in their own ability to fight. They didn't worry about causes, or war aims, or high-sounding phrases: they did as they were told, and they prayed that the men who had established the war aims and had uttered the pious phrases knew what they were doing. If there was anything that worried them, it was their immediate leadership: Lieutenant Felty tried hard, but he had been known to clutch; and Lieutenant Holloway had just come from battalion.

As the last man in Felty's platoon passed, Holloway swung in behind him. The command group followed.

There was something of a path that led down the sunny side of the ridge. Some snow-covered rocks and brush were in the way, but it was easy to step around them and keep going down. Eric looked back every minute or two to see how the rest of the company was doing. He could see well back into Cannon's platoon, but that was all. He couldn't see Schaefer, but he imagined that he was trying to keep the mortar section moving. Since the mortars are the heaviest loads in a rifle company, the men who must carry them determine the company's speed.

Felty was moving a bit too fast for the mortars, Holloway thought, but the lead rifleman would have to slow down as soon as he reached the valley floor and started to climb the enemy's ridge. Eric decided that he would halt the column on the first good knob on Cougar that Felty reached so that he could make sure the company wasn't getting too strung out. Then, too, the men would need a short breather.

Holloway looked to his left to see if the panel in Easy Company was visible. If it was out, he couldn't find it.

"Gipp, do we still have radio contact with battalion?" he asked.

"Yes, sir. You got something for them?"

"Not now. If you lose contact, be sure you tell me."

"Will do, sir."

Eric felt terribly proud of his company. He was just beginning to realize that it really was his, that he was George Six, the company commander. He thought of the peculiar boastfulness of Captain Mann, and for the first time, he understood it. It was pardonable pride: George Company was something to be proud of. But he also knew that George Company had been proud of Captain Mann.

3

When the Third Platoon reached a point on Cougar that was roughly opposite Fox Company's position in the valley below, Holloway called Felty on the radio and told him to hold what he had for a few minutes. Eric knew that Felty's men would soon hit opposition, if the ridge was defended at all, and he wanted the men to be ready for anything that might happen to them.

"Felty, have your people fix bayonets," he ordered.

"What?" Felty asked over the radio.

"I said, have your people fix bayonets. Now."

"Isn't that being kinda Hollywood?"

"Have your men fix bayonets. Out."

Eric looked up ahead to see if the order was being carried out. It was. One by one, Felty's men were taking their rifles from their shoulders and reaching for their seldom-used bayonets. There was some joking as the order was being passed from man to man, but the joking stopped as soon as the soldiers thought it over for a moment.

Then Holloway ordered Felty to go again.

The climb continued for another four or five minutes. When Holloway's command group was even with Fox Company, Holloway stopped Felty again.

"George Three this is George Six. Hold where you are. Set up a blocking position facing in the direction of the attack. Do you understand? Over."

Felty replied that he understood.

"Come here, Cannon," he called, then he turned to the first sergeant. "Hold the command group here, Top."

Cannon dog-trotted up to Holloway.

"Come with me," Holloway said. The two officers moved down the west side of Cougar to a spot from which they could see the valley clearly. Gipp followed the officers.

"We're mighty lucky, so far," Eric said. "I don't know whether they've seen us or not. Assume that they have."

"That's always safe."

"Can you see Easy Company's panel?"

"No, but I see some people up there on Easy Company's ridge."

"Where?"

"On the ridgeline—right on the skyline—right above the tank."

"I'll call Easy Company on the radio to make sure where they are."

Gipp came over and handed the handset to the company commander. Holloway called Captain Heath, Easy's company commander, while Cannon kept his eyes on the figures on the ridgeline.

"Wonder who those folks are?" Cannon asked himself. "They're too brazen about exposing themselves to be the enemy, but I'm damned if I can say for sure."

"Heath said he'd mark the position of their lead people with a panel," Holloway said. "Look for it."

"The people are gone now," Cannon said.

"There it is, sir," Gipp said, pointing back down Lion from the place where Cannon had seen the figures.

A long, narrow patch of red fabric caught the glint of the early afternoon sun as two men spread it in the snow near the top of Lion.

"Oh hell!" Holloway said. "We're way ahead."

"Yeah, and that was the enema we saw a minute ago."

Holloway called Heath and warned him of the figures up ahead of him. Then he called the battalion commander.

120

"George Six here. We're ahead of Easy, about even with Fox. Everything is quiet down below at the moment, and we've hit nothing up here. We saw about six strangers ahead of Easy about a minute ago—Easy's been warned. Over."

"Gasoline Six here. That's good. Anything else? Over."

"This is George Six. I am going to hold up here while somebody goes hunting, unless you want me to keep going. Over."

"You say you're ahead of Easy? Over."

"Yes. Affirmative. Over."

"This is Gasoline Six. Better wait until I talk to Easy Six. I'd like to have him even with you before you turn your hunters loose. Wait."

Holloway listened as the battalion commander called Heath. When Dahl asked why Heath's people were behind Holloway's, Heath replied that his lead people were moving slowly because they were in the same general area where O'Connor's guide said the ambush had been.

"I hate to tell you to hurry, because I know you're trying to be careful, and I want you to be careful," Eric heard Dahl tell Heath, "but George can't wait. Just make the most of any breaks up there you may get. I'm going to have George send out the hunters. Out."

Then Dahl called Eric and told him to proceed with the mission, which meant to go clean out the positions from which Fox Company had been ambushed. Eric acknowledged the instructions.

"Cannon," Holloway told his Second Platoon leader, "I'd like for you to pull your platoon out of the line and get them ready to go hunting. I don't know any more than you do about the whereabouts of that ambush position, but I'll be surprised if we go much longer without their shooting at us—and then we'll know."

"Damned if we won't."

"Now, move right down the slope to the valley floor, and don't let the men show themselves any more than they can help."

"All right."

"Figure on finding people between here and the bottom. If you don't, then they might be on the bottom, or on the other ridge, part way down."

"I've got it."

"One more thing. If you hit anything, let me know. I'll have the rest of the company in positions from which they can cover you. If you need us, holler, and we'll open up."

"Sounds good."

"Take off."

Holloway watched as Cannon pulled his platoon out of the column and down the slope to the left of the path that led up the ridge to the Octopus' peak. He was pleased by the way Cannon's men spread out as they moved down the slope. And Cannon had ordered the men in his platoon to fix bayonets.

As soon as Cannon's people were clear of the ridgeline, Eric went back to the command group and sent word to Lieutenant Schaefer to close the gap Cannon's platoon had left. As soon as Schaefer reached the command group, leading the mortar section, Holloway went forward to see how Felty's platoon was getting along.

Holloway was not pleased by what he saw of Felty's platoon's blocking position. Fully half of the men were flat on their backs, apparently asleep. The others were anything but alert.

Eric finally found Felty. He had to resist the temptation to kick the platoon leader.

"Lieutenant Felty," he said, "get up."

Felty scrambled to his feet.

"Felty, I'll give you fifteen seconds flat to get this platoon off their butts and into positions from which they can kill somebody besides themselves."

"I was just giving them a break. What's wrong with that?"

"You see Fox Company down there?"

"No, but—"

"They're taking a break, too. Felty, you're all wet if you think you're doing your men a favor. You're liable to get them jumped by such foolishness as this. Now get them set up, and get it done right now!"

Holloway was speaking through firmly set teeth; his fists were clenched.

"And come back here as soon as you've done it!"

Felty went from man to man, getting his platoon awake and ready to fight. When he had pointed defenders in all the threatening directions, he returned to the company commander.

"They're set, sir."

"Felty, why didn't you just call your four squad leaders and tell them to get their people in place?"

Felty shrugged his shoulders.

"Well, I got the job done."

"But you did it the wrong way. That's what sergeants are for. When you do something yourself that is really their job, you undermine their authority and ignore them. It makes them look useless, and if you live long enough you'll sure as hell learn that they're not. Has Captain Mann been letting you get away with this?"

A hurt look came over Felty's boyish features.

"I just got here from the States. I've only had this platoon three days, and the only time we've moved was crossing the river the other day."

"Well, didn't you learn better in training?"

"I've never had any training in infantry tactics."

"What?" Holloway was astonished.

"I've never been in an infantry outfit before."

"Ye Gods! Where in the name of God did you get your commission?"

Felty was about to answer when both officers heard several shots crack below.

"Felty, get this—quick. Cannon may need your people to cover him. Have your squad leaders ready to have their squads fire at that ridge over there. Don't have them shoot until I give you the word. You got that?"

"Yes, sir."

"Then do it just like I told you."

Then Eric ran back to find out about the shooting.

Cannon was in trouble: that was certain.

Eric sensed that the firefight was fairly even, for only about half of the shots had the sharp *crack* and dull *thump* characteristic of incoming fire. He looked down into the valley to see if he could make out what was happening, but the action was too far down.

The firing subsided after another thirty seconds or so, and then Cannon called Holloway on the radio.

"This is George Two," Cannon said, almost out of breath. "We hit a whole nest of them by surprise. We killed two and ran the rest up the valley."

"Damned good!"

"You want me to chase 'em?"

"Negative. Hold what you've got. Are any of your people hit?"

"Negative."

"I'll call you in a minute. Out."

Eric put the little radio down, then he took Gipp's handset and called Major Dahl. While he was waiting for the battalion commander to answer, he looked for Easy Company's panel. He knew that his platoon was in a dangerous position, and he hoped that he could move it before the enemy had time enough to zero their mortars or bring fire on the platoon from a new direction. It'll help if Easy has caught up, Eric thought. But Easy's panel was nowhere to be seen.

"This is Gasoline Six," Eric heard the battalion commander say.

"This is George Six. My people flushed a covey and killed two birds. No hunters hurt. Over."

"That's fine."

"This is George Six. I'd like to either send them on or bring them back home. They're sitting ducks, now that they've made noise. Over."

"Send them on to check the other side. Then they can

come back up to where you are now. Easy is almost abreast of you now. Can you see their panel? Over."

"Negative. Over."

Eric listened as Major Dahl called Heath and asked him to drop a panel in George Company's direction. A minute or two later, Eric saw a patch of yellow in the snow, almost directly across the valley from him. Easy made good time, he thought.

Holloway called Cannon on the small radio and told him to start on across, but to holler if anything bothered him. Then he turned to Gregg.

"Top, get the rest of the company alerted to be ready to fire across at Lion in case Cannon says he needs it."

"Right, sir."

Some of the men in the company had to move in order to get a clear shot at the other ridge. The range, most of them estimated, was about five hundred yards. The men were loaded and ready, but they all hoped that there would be no need for any more shooting. They had all had enough, no matter how little that had been.

Heavy firing broke out across the way, in front of Easy Company. Eric saw at once that the firing was all on top of the ridge, not on the side. Too, the firing was at Easy Company, not at Cannon's platoon. Eric was sorry that Easy was in trouble, but the diversion would help Cannon move up the side of Lion to finish his mission.

Holloway's eyes worked all over the side of Lion, watching first one thing and then another. While he was looking for signs of Cannon's progress, the enemy ambush he had been seeking opened up on Cannon's men. Eric saw one man drop.

"Did you see where that firing was coming from?" Holloway yelled at Felty's machine gunner.

"Sure did, Lieutenant."

"Cut loose!"

The gunner took quick but careful aim, then let go a burst of half a dozen rounds. Then he fired another burst, and then

125

another. He raked back and forth across a small finger that jutted out from Lion. The gunner could tell nothing about the effectiveness of his fire, but he could tell from his stream of tracers that his rounds were hitting where he wanted them to hit.

"Hold it!" Eric called.

The gunner ceased firing.

Holloway called Cannon.

"This is George Six. Did that do any good?"

"George Two here. Affirmative. Better than a back-scratching. Over."

"Anybody hurt down there? Over."

"Yes. Over."

"How many?"

"Only one, as far as I know. You want me to leave him here, or bring him out when we come? Over."

"This is George Six. Bring him out. I'll have the medics here ready for him. Are you almost to where you're going? Over."

"Affirmative."

"All right. Keep going, and let me know if you want any more goodies. Out."

Up on Lion's ridgeline, Easy Company was having a bad time. The firing was sharp and steady, and from time to time Eric thought he heard the muffled *crunch* of a hand grenade. Holloway wondered if there was anything he could do to help Easy, but he knew Heath wouldn't want to be bothered by a radio call at such a time. Eric scanned the ridgeline, looking for the enemy, but in vain.

"Anything on the radio, Gipp?" he asked.

"No, sir. Not a damned thing."

"Major Dahl been talking to Easy Six at all?"

"No, sir."

Cannon called in about ten minutes later.

"This is George Two. We're up here where we're supposed to be. The enemy's cleared out, but they left a hell of a lot of blood in the snow. Over."

"George Six here. Fine! You see anything of Fox Company lately?"

"No. I think they're farther down the valley toward the Shark than we thought they were. Over."

"Is any of the stuff up on top bothering you?"

"Negative. Over."

"Well, you wait there, and keep your eyes peeled. I'll call you back in a minute. Out."

Then Eric called the battalion commander on the other radio.

"Gasoline Six, this is George Six. My hunters are in the nest, and the birds are all gone. The Foxes may be safe, now. I've left the hunters at the nest, but I'd like to have them back as soon as I can. Over."

"This is Gasoline Six. That's good work, Eric. But hold the hunters where they are a while longer. You move on up the road with your people, and I'll tell you when you can pull your hunters back. They can follow you, you see. Over."

"George Six here. Roger, out."

Holloway didn't like the idea of moving on without his best platoon, but he figured that the battalion commander would give him the word to call them back by the time the tail of the company passed the spot from which Cannon's platoon had gone down. If it worked out that way, Cannon's people could have it easy for a while—and they deserved a break. They had accomplished the first part of George Company's mission, and Holloway was very proud of them.

Holloway said so when he called Cannon a moment later.

"You stay put until I give you the word, then come back and be caboose for a change. You understand? Over."

"Roger. Out."

"George Three, move out. Move out. You have it? Over."

"This is Felty—I mean George Three. Roger, we're going. Out."

Then Holloway passed the word to get going again back through the mortar section to Digger Dolan's platoon.

There was the usual grumbling—perhaps a bit more than

usual, for it was past noon, and the habits of a lifetime had not taken notice of the tactical situation: most of the men were about half-way through their C-ration meals. Eric hadn't noticed, since he had been somewhat busy and too excited to be hungry. Anyway, he had no food. As the company started moving again, some of the men were still dipping their plastic spoons into small green cans of ham and lima beans, or hash, or frankfurters and beans, or hamburgers, or pork and beans. Others were stuffing dog biscuits or cans of fruit cocktail into their pockets. The rest, not caring greatly, went on their way with a smile or a curse, hopeful of eating decent food once more before death robbed them forever of the luxury of hunger.

Eight

Cougar, the ridge George Company was climbing, ran into Lion a few hundred yards north of the place where the company had halted while Cannon's platoon cleared the ambushes. Eric Holloway knew that if George Company could reach that junction, and capture it, before the enemy had time to set up strong defenses, or to reinforce whatever forces were already in place, then the battalion's mission could be accomplished rather quickly. But Eric realized that the enemy commander must be equally aware of that, and so he expected to have to fight for that knob, and possibly for the rest of Cougar. I'd better warn Felty, he thought. He's got to keep going, but he'd better be careful.

"Top, I'm going up ahead," he called to Gregg.

The first sergeant nodded.

Eric had passed three or four men on his way forward when shots cut the air over his head.

That's it, he thought. We'll have to fight for it.

Eric hit the ground, as did the rest of the column. He reasoned that the shots might be coming from the survivors of the ambushes Cannon's platoon had gone after; on the other hand, Felty might have hit the enemy's main defense line. Either way, Felty was in a spot.

Holloway looked ahead to see what was happening. A rise in the ridgeline blocked his view, so he crawled forward. Shots still cracked over his head, but the firing was intermittent and not well-aimed.

Eric noticed that Felty's men were waiting for orders;

none of them showed the least inclination to do anything about the threat to their lives. Eric was surprised by this at first, but then he understood: there was nothing visible to shoot at.

When he reached the spot where Felty and his radioman were down, Holloway took cover behind a rock and peered ahead. He could see several prone figures, men from Felty's lead squad, but that was all.

"Felty, crawl over here," he ordered.

"Yes?"

"Anybody get hit?"

"No, but we're pinned down."

"What do you mean, 'pinned down'?"

"Every time anybody moves, he gets shot at."

"What have you tried to do so far?"

"Nothing. Nobody can move."

"Listen. I crawled all the way up here. Nothing touched me. You crawled over here, nothing got you. It's all overhead. Can't you hear the cracking? Hell, we can't even see where the trouble's coming from."

"Yes, but—"

"Now, what are you going to do about this thing?"

"I don't know."

"You have a good squad up in front?"

"Yes."

"All right. Tell that squad leader to have his squad inch up toward the trouble. Have him get them in position so they can kill somebody."

"Okay."

The platoon leader slid away, crawling up toward his lead squad leader. A moment later, Eric saw the squad leader crawl up to the man ahead of him, and in less than a minute the whole squad had moved forward.

Felty's not yellow, Eric thought. He's just ignorant. I've got to teach him what I can, when I get the time.

Two or three minutes passed. Then a sharp firing broke out ahead. Dull explosions: hand grenades!

Felty came running back, out of breath and greatly upset. "They're just rolling those hand grenades down!"
"What—"
"We're pinned down again."
"Look, Felty—"
"We can't move!"
"Shut up and listen to me! Cut out this 'pinned down' business. You come with me."

Eric ran forward, crouching. There were a few shots over his head, but he stayed close to the ground and kept moving. Soon he reached a position from which he could see the whole show. There was a small, rocky knob about a hundred yards ahead and towering above him. He saw that no one could rush the knob, for the rocks were large and almost cubical. And as long as the enemy's hand grenades held out, Eric knew, Felty's men would have one hell of a time taking that knob.

Eric looked to his left to see if this could be the knob where Lion ran into Cougar: it wasn't. Lion was several hundred yards away and still roughly parallel to Cougar. The junction knob, Holloway knew, would be a long, bloody way off.

"Okay, Felty. Let's get something going. You have the Fifty-Seven, don't you?"
"Yes."
"Get it forward."
"Pass the word back for the Fifty-Seven to come forward!" Felty called to a soldier near him, and the soldier passed the word.
"You see, if the men can't move, the thing to do is to put supporting fire on the enemy. Then the men can move forward while the enemy's hiding from the covering fire. You get the idea?"
"Yes, sir."
"All right. No more of this 'pinned down' foolishness?"
Felty hesitated a moment, then he said, "Okay."

The leader of the Fifty-Seven squad crawled in between the officers.

"You got that recoilless rifle back there?" Eric asked.

"Yessir."

"We want some fire put on that knob up ahead."

"Loo-tenant, you're nuts. If we shoot that thing it'll give away our location!"

"Bring me the gun, Sergeant."

The squad leader went back for the gun.

A minute or two later, Eric crawled into the open and took the Fifty-Seven from the men who had lugged it forward.

"This thing loaded?" he asked.

"Ready."

Eric moved around a bit in order to get a stable rest. Then he took careful aim, placing the telescopic sight's crosshairs directly on the knob. He squeezed the pistol grip, and the gun fired with a deafening roar.

The round hit the left side of a large rock at the top of the knob.

"Load another one!" Eric yelled.

The soldier behind him opened the recoilless rifle's breech and slammed another round into the tube. When the breech was closed and locked, the loader looked behind the gun to make sure that no one had moved into the backblast area, then he slapped Eric's back and yelled "Up!"

Holloway aimed at the right side of the knob and fired. Again the blast and the ringing noise in his ears.

The round cleared the rocks and landed on top of the knob, causing a flurry of snow as it exploded.

If this is killing, Eric thought, it is damned impersonal. If it has to be, this way is best.

A rifle shot glanced off a rock very near Eric's head.

"Enough of this!" the company commander said, scrambling behind the rock. "Sergeant, get your gunner to plaster that knob with this thing. Pick out a better position than that, and move after every couple of rounds."

132

"Very well, sir."

"Felty, you get ready to move out as soon as the boomstick people get set up and start shooting. Have your machine gun come up here and spray the target between rounds from the Fifty-Seven."

"All right."

Felty hurried to get the orders passed while the Fifty-Seven crew was seeking a good firing position.

Holloway noticed that Felty's edginess was beginning to wear off. He was glad, but he knew that Felty would still need a lot of help.

A messenger from the company command group crawled to within a few yards of the company commander and called him.

"Sir, Captain Hamilton's on the phone raising hell. Wants to talk to you right now."

"Thanks. I'll be right back there."

Holloway yelled to Felty. "You think you can handle this now?"

"Sure."

"Get going, then. And keep punching till you get the knob."

Eric didn't want to leave just as the critical part of the action was about to start, but he remembered all the trouble he had had with Hamilton. He took a deep breath and ran back down the trail to take the call.

2

"Where'd this phone line come from?" Eric asked Sergeant Wood.

"Battalion put it in, sir."

"You know what Captain Hamilton wants?"

"No, sir. Wants you to call him pronto, though."

So Holloway called.

"This is Lieutenant Holloway, sir."

"Well you better by God cut out this movie-star stuff and

look out for that comp'ny of yours or all hell's gonna break loose. That kinda showing-off may be big stuff here at battalion, but you aren't much good to those braves of yours dead. Now stay there where you belong and leave squad leading to the people who're getting paid to do that."

"Yes, sir."

"Damned if I wouldn't relieve you for that! You're a company commander, Holloway. Now start behaving like one, or Major Dahl will sure as hell jerk you out of there."

"Yes sir."

"Now. What's going on out in front of you?"

"My Third Platoon's being held up by some people who can't shoot very good. They're trying to get the knob the enemy's on right now."

"Knob? Are you already at the junction?"

"No. It's still a long way ahead. But this one's a bitch!"

"They gonna make it?"

Eric didn't know how to answer that.

"Yes, they'll make it," he said, "but it may be messy. I'll call you back as soon as we're up there."

"Well, let's don't have any drawn-saber charges. We've lost enough company commanders for one day."

"Are they getting Fox out?"

"Yep, and by the way, you can call your platoon back in now. York's dead. So's Webb."

"I'm sorry to hear that. How many other men did we lose?"

"It looks like twenty-one dead and sixteen badly wounded."

"Is the tank still functioning?"

"No. We're pulling it out. Why?"

"I thought it might be able to shoot at this thing that's bothering us."

"Use your Goddam bayonets. Wait a minute. Here's Major Dahl."

"Eric, I want you to stay with this phone from now on."

"Very well, sir."

"Did Harry tell you about pulling in your platoon?"

"Yes sir, he did."

"We didn't make it to the top of the mountain by noon, and Colonel Hobbs is pretty upset about that. But we've got to keep trying. Now, I don't know how soon Easy's going to get going again, but it looks like you're going to have to carry the ball. Can you get to that junction pretty soon?"

The perplexing question again.

"I'll try, sir."

"I know that, Eric. Answer my question!"

"Yes, sir."

"All right."

"I'll call you as soon as we have some progress to report, sir."

"That'll do. And you be careful!"

The conversation ended with that.

Holloway called Cannon on the radio and told him to rejoin the company. Then he sent for the executive officer, and while he was waiting for him he looked around for some place to set up the mortars.

"What's up?" Schaefer asked.

"Felty's got troubles with a big knob."

"I see."

"It'll be like climbing a tree, except this tree's dripping with hand grenades."

"That do make a difference."

"I got off a shot or two with the Fifty-Seven, but it just rearranged the snow. Felty may need the mortars, so I wish you'd get them ready to shoot for him."

"All right."

"There's a good place—as good a place as I can find, that is—right over there."

"Okay."

Schaefer went back to get the mortar section leader.

A few minutes later, Eric noticed that the men from the mortar section were hacking away at the side of the ridgeline, trying to prepare platforms for the mortar baseplates.

When the mortars were ready to fire, Schaefer climbed back to the top of the ridge and found the company commander.

"All set. You want them to register?"

"No, but send a forward observer up with Felty. He can use Felty's radio and talk to my radio operator if Felty needs help."

"Will do."

Then Eric turned to Sergeant Gregg.

"Top, we can't do any good from back here. We've got to move the command group far enough forward to see what gives."

"All right, sir. Don't like the idea of getting shot at, myself, but maybe the enema'll see me coming and give up."

"Maybe."

Eric turned to lead the command group forward, but a muffled crunching sound stopped him cold. He turned and looked back down at the valley, where his Second Platoon was, and he saw two gray clouds of smoke drift above the bare trees. As he watched, two more clouds blossomed. Then he heard two more crunches, and a loud scream.

3

Eric closed his eyes. Dear God, he prayed, help them!

When he looked down into the valley again, he saw several men running toward the base of Cougar, trying to get out of the enemy's mortar fire. Eric wanted to reach down to them, to pull them out, to get his men clear of the danger, but for the moment he could do nothing but pray, and hope.

God, please lead them out of there! I'll settle for half of them—just half.

But as he bargained with God, it occurred to him that

getting those men out of there was his job. There was still something he could do.

Holloway picked up the radio and tried to contact Cannon, but there was no answer. He thought about sending a messenger down to lead the scattered platoon out, but that seemed to him to be too much to ask: any man who went down into that valley would have practically no chance of surviving the mortar fire that was systematically stabbing both sides of the valley.

All at once, Holloway knew that he would have to go.

"Schaefer!" he called. "Look after things until I get back."

Holloway ran down the side of Cougar, slipping in the snow most of the way, breaking his descent by grabbing the trunks of small trees; he heard three rounds crunch near him as he ran, but he paid them little attention.

As soon as he reached the bottom, Eric began yelling.

"Come over here! Second Platoon, over here!"

Right away, two men appeared. Holloway pointed up the ridgeline toward the command group and told the men to get up there as fast as they could climb.

As the men scrambled past, Eric asked, "Where's Lieutenant Cannon?"

"Damned if I know," one man said.

"Down that-a-way," said the other, pointing down the creek line.

Eric called "Cannon!" and "Second Platoon!" several more times, and another soldier appeared.

"You stay here. Yell for people to come to you. You got it?"

The man nodded. A moment later he began yelling, as Eric had been.

The company commander ran down the creekbed, meeting other men on the narrow path that followed the water's edge.

"Up the way," he panted to each man as he passed. "Keep moving!"

God, help me to get them out! he prayed as he ran.

Suddenly he heard a cry from the other side of the stream. "Lieutenant!" Then again, faintly, "For Christ's sake, somebody—"

Eric jumped into the creek and waded across. Several shots thumped into the water behind him, but he kept moving. Once across, he looked for a rock or a tree to hide behind.

Damned sniper, he thought.

When he had caught his breath, he began looking for the man who had called him. He yelled "Hey!" and "Where are you?" several times, but the man didn't answer. Holloway was about to give up and continue his search for Cannon when he almost stumbled over the wounded soldier's body.

Eric knelt beside the man and felt for a heartbeat. The pale face and tightly clenched fist made Holloway think that the soldier was dead, but a moment later the soldier opened his eyes and looked at Holloway.

"I'd given up," the boy said. "I thought sure I'd die here."

"You'll be all right. Where are the others?"

"Just—just a little—bit farther down."

Eric reckoned that he was almost as far down the creekbed as Fox Company had been earlier in the day. The distance back up to George Company was so great that Eric, too, was tempted to give up.

Give up and do what? he asked himself. Give up and die, came the answer. No, not yet. Not yet.

"Look. I'll come back for you in just a minute. Or somebody will come. Don't give up, and don't worry about being left. All right?"

"Yessir."

The man tried awfully hard to smile.

Holloway left the man and ran on down the creekline. When he had gone about fifty yards, a mortar round landed directly in front of him, rocking him back, dropping him on a pile of sharp rocks. His ears were ringing when the echoes of the blast died away: I'm still alive, he thought. He had difficulty in breathing, and he thought of Wayne Hyde's white face and wild eyes, the yellow lips that whispered "I can't breathe! . . ."

Slowly, painfully, Eric got up. When he saw that he was not really hurt, he stumbled on. After he passed the crater, he saw about a dozen men coming toward him, and Cannon was among them.

"Cannon! Over here!" Holloway yelled.

The group dog-trotted toward him.

"Damn!" Cannon said. "Am I glad to see you!"

"Let's get these people out of here. Are you all right?"

"Yes, but where's the company?"

"Up on top."

"How'll we get out of here? They've got the upper end of this damned valley covered with mortar fire."

"You'll just have to keep scratching and run through it. By the way, they've got a sniper with some kind of automatic weapon covering the creek. Anybody who stops is dead. Oh, yes: you've got a wounded man up ahead. Have you got everybody else with you?"

"Yes, I think so. I've sent a bunch of people up ahead, and we can't think of anybody who hasn't been seen. That's Kelsey that's wounded, isn't it? We can't find him."

"I don't know. Find out, and if it isn't, we'll have to find Kelsey."

Cannon ran on up ahead.

Another mortar round landed nearby, and everyone got down.

"Man, we've got to get out of here!" one soldier yelled.

"Cut that out!" Holloway shouted. "You'll be out of here in nothing flat!"

Cannon returned, smiling.

"That's Kelsey."

"All right, then. I've put one of your men up the creek about a hundred yards. By that big bare tree—you see the one I mean?"

"Yep."

"When you get there, go straight up the side of the finger. Gregg will show you where to reassemble. You may have to fight again before long, so get your breath as soon as you can. And count noses!"

"What are you going to do?"

"I'm going up from here. I just saw Dolan's people up yonder, and I'm going to try to get that sniper before your folks have to cross that stream. Now get going—and be careful."

"Be careful yourself," Cannon called after him.

Holloway ran directly to the shallow creek and plunged in. He was almost across before the sniper got a wild shot at him. Once out of the water, he ran up the snow-covered slope and climbed as rapidly as he could.

He hit the ridgeline in the middle of Digger Dolan's platoon. He fell on his face on the path, completely worn out.

Dolan ran over to see about the officer.

"You hit?"

Holloway got to his knees.

"No. Where's your machine gun?"

"Over yonder."

"Haul it over here."

Digger, puzzled, trotted up the path a few yards and picked up the platoon's machine gun. The gunner threw a belt of ammunition around Digger's neck, and then Digger returned to the company commander.

Holloway was on his feet again, looking up the valley to see how Cannon was making out. The sniper opened up on the creek as Eric saw a couple of Cannon's men try to cross.

"You see that, Digger?"

Digger nodded.

"Cut loose!"

Digger had the gun in place and firing in five seconds. He raked the area where he and Holloway had seen the flashes of the weapon the enemy sniper was using, then he stopped to see if his firing had had any effect.

It had. Cannon's men were wading across, and they were not being fired on.

"Phillips!" Digger yelled. "You come here and shoot this damned thing. You see where I was shootin'?"

"Yes, Sergeant."

"All right. They open up again, you paste 'em."

Digger turned to tell Holloway that everything was under control, but Holloway was gone.

4

When he reached the command group, Eric Holloway sat down, exhausted.

"How's Felty making out?" he asked Gregg.

"He's nearly up there. He's tried everything in the book, and a few things that ain't."

"Good. Battalion call?"

"No sir, they haven't. And it's strange. I think the wire's cut, or something."

Gregg was grinning.

"Better get it fixed, Top," Eric said. "And thanks."

"We been havin' trouble with the radio, too. We can hear, but we can't send. Ain't that too bad?"

"Yes it is, Top. I have an idea it'll clear up pretty soon, though."

"Morris, you can go fix that wire now," Gregg called. Then, to the company commander, "We've got the Second Platoon over here, sir."

"Fine."

Eric got up and went with the first sergeant to see about the Second Platoon. Gregg had told them to reassemble near the mortar crews, on the eastern slope of Cougar—the safe side.

"They made good time," Holloway said.

"They was goosed, sort of."

A medic was working on the man Eric had found in the

valley. Holloway walked over to see how the man was feeling.

"Hi, Lieutenant," the soldier said. "You was right. I got out."

Eric got down on one knee beside the man and said, "You've got it made, now. All the way home. The war's over, for you."

Kelsey smiled, and then he said, "I hate to leave the comp'ny, though. I just wish they was all going, too."

"So do I."

"You don't remember me, do you, Lieutenant?"

Eric tried hard to think, but he couldn't remember having seen the man before that day.

"No, I'm sorry, but I don't."

"You drove an old green Buick, and you used to buy gas at my dad's filling station."

"Of course. You're Noah Kelsey—well, I'm—I'll be damned."

"Noah Junior, sir."

"How's your dad?"

"He's fine, sir."

"Give him my best regards when you get home."

"I will."

"And tell him—"

"Yes, sir?"

Eric wanted Noah, Senior, to know how sorry he was to be sending his boy home flat on his back, to know how hard he had tried—

"Nothing, Noah. Just tell him hello. I'll be by to see you when I get back."

Litter bearers from battalion arrived to start Kelsey home. Eric stood up as they lifted the man, and as he watched them carry him down the path, he thought of all the responsibility that was his—awful responsibility.

As he looked around the assembly area at the men of the Second Platoon, sitting in the snow, laughing and joking, glad to be alive, he realized that his awkward, hurried prayers had been answered: the platoon was back, and Kelsey was the only man who had been hit. Another man had broken a finger in falling, but that might have happened in his own home. Eric had been able to get them out, just as he had prayed, and for that he was very grateful.

·As he thought back over the experience, he was shocked, in a way, that any of the men had survived. Mortar fire is deadly, he knew; and yet the mortar round that had landed ahead of him had not touched him. There was no logical reason for the survival of the Second Platoon that Eric could think of; and his own survival was just as remarkable, just as inexplicable.

Eric listened to the men swapping stories about their experience like members of a winning football team in the locker room after an especially close game. Dirty, miserable, tired, but more alive, more animated than ever before.

And Eric Holloway knew that he would have to use all the energy, and skill, and intellect that he had to protect those men; not simply because of men like Noah Kelsey, Senior, whom he would have to face someday, but because of a feeling of even deeper obligation which he sensed but could not fully understand—a feeling that was bound up with the words "Company Commander."

Nine

When Eric returned to the command group, he asked Sergeant Gregg if Lieutenant Felty had reported any progress.

"No sir, he hasn't made it yet, but he's still trying," Gregg said.

"Well, I guess I'll go see if there's anything else he can try," the company commander began, but Gipp handed him the telephone.

"Battalion wants to speak to you, sir."

Eric took the phone.

"How's your show getting along?" Major Dahl asked.

"Felty's still trying to get the knob that's holding him back, sir. My Second Platoon is here with us again—only two men wounded, and they've been evacuated. I was just about to go see what Felty needs."

"All right. I'm sending Jamison up to you. Frankly, I think you're going to have to get this whole mountain for the battalion, so I want you to have all the help I can give you."

"Very well, sir. We'll be glad to have some artillery. That ought to help Felty a lot."

Major Dahl hung up.

"Bad news, sir?" Gregg asked.

"No, Top. Lieutenant Jamison's coming up here to shoot artillery for us."

"Fine—fine."

"I'm going up to the Third Platoon now, Sergeant. If Jamison gets here before I get back, please ask him to come up."

Holloway started up the path.

"Did he say Fandango's coming?" Gipp asked the first sergeant.

Holloway turned around and listened.

"Yep."

"Sergeant," Holloway asked Gregg, "who's Fandango?"

"Lieutenant Jamison, sir. You know him."

Eric remembered Granger's voice screaming "Fandango —turn it off, for Christ's sake. . . ."

"That's the artillery's call-sign, sir. Last time Lieutenant Jamison was with us, that's about all we heard. He was shootin' all the time."

"I'm sure glad it's him that's coming," Gipp said. "He sure does shoot that artillery good."

Eric smiled.

"He's a very good man," the company commander said, turning back toward the Third Platoon.

When he reached the rock Felty was using as his observation post, Eric crawled in beside Felty and asked him what was happening.

"Well, I got a squad on each side of this bastard," Felty replied. "They're trying to set up cross-fire on the enemy up yonder on the knob."

"I can't see either squad. Have they had any luck?"

"Well, no. You see, neither one can climb without getting shot at."

"Have they been able to kill any of the people on the knob?"

"No."

"I see. Well, it'll be all right, though. We've got an artillery forward observer party on the way up here now."

"Good."

"I guess you'd better leave those people out there until Jamison gets here, then we'll pull them in and plaster the place."

Felty nodded.

Steve Jamison and his radio operator arrived a few min-

145

utes later. Jamison was short, but solid; he had something like a strut in his walk, as if to say "move over, men—here comes the best damned artilleryman in the whole bleedin' world."

When Holloway saw them coming, he told Felty to get his squads in; Felty sent the word to the left squad by messenger, but he went out to get the right squad himself.

"What the hell is this—a Sunday School picnic?" Jamison asked as he sat down beside the company commander.

"It is now. Glad to have you with us."

"Got something for me to do?"

"We sure as hell have."

Eric jerked his thumb in the direction of the knob.

"Felty's getting his people backed up now. As soon as he tells us it's clear, I'd appreciate a good creaming job."

Jamison studied the knob while Eric talked.

"Felty's tried everything he could, except rushing the thing. You can see that rushing it would be murder. We tried Fifty-Seven fire on it, but we still haven't got the knob. I don't want to force Felty to risk his people—"

"Give me that microphone," Jamison said to his radioman. "The man wants some goodies put out yonder. I'll get the clobber party set up, then you can give me the word when you're ready."

"Fine."

Jamison spread his map on the ground in front of him and began figuring the coordinates of the knob. Then he took out his compass and looked through a peep-sight to determine the magnetic azimuth from the rock to the target. This done, he pressed a button on the microphone and called the fire direction center.

"Fandango Seven, this is Fandango Five-Seven. George Six will have a fire mission shortly. Azimuth, one-five. Dog Sugar five-four-four-six niner-six. Enemy strong point. How-Easy. Will adjust. At my command. Over."

The voice on the artillery radio read back the data, and Jamison answered.

"Seven, this is Five-Seven. Roger. Wait."

Then he turned to Holloway, who had been fascinated by the cocky little artilleryman's seemingly complicated procedure.

"We're ready when you are."

Holloway nodded, then he got up to look for Felty. He could see the left squad—they were clear—but he couldn't find Felty.

"Wait just a minute," he said, then he moved down the trail to look for the platoon leader. Holloway was vexed with Felty: this shouldn't be necessary, he thought.

Holloway saw Felty climbing back up the slope about a minute later.

"Don't do this again," the company commander said shortly when Felty reached him.

"Don't do what?"

"Don't take off like that—send somebody else to do things like getting your squads in."

"Oh. Okay."

Holloway waved back to Jamison as soon as he was within Jamison's view. Jamison nodded and picked up the mike again.

"Seven, this is Five-Seven. Fire. Over."

"Five-Seven, this is Seven. On the way. Over."

"This is Five-Seven. On the way, wait."

Holloway and Jamison ducked in behind the rock just as the first round rustled overhead. There was a flash, then an explosion out on the knob. The round was exactly where Jamison wanted it to be.

"Fire for effect," he said into the microphone.

"Damn!" Felty said. "That gives me the creeps! First round."

The radio repeated Jamison's command, and a few seconds later six rounds crunched into the knob, covering the entire area. Then there was another flight of six rounds on the way, and six more gray blossoms out on the knob. It was beautiful and deadly and frightening.

Holloway noticed that there was very little wind: the gray

147

smoke and dust seemed to hang over the knob, and that gave him an idea.

"Can we get some white phosphorus up there?"

"Sure. You want some?"

"Yes. Felty, get your people ready to move up under this."

"All right, sir."

"Wait until the rounds have landed, then go like hell while the white smoke has 'em blinded."

Jamison called the order back to the fire direction center. "Willie Peter, repeat fire for effect. Over."

The F. D. C. echoed the order, and Jamison nodded to Felty.

"Better go, huh?"

"Better go," Eric answered.

"This is Seven. On the way—over."

"Five-Seven. On the way—wait."

The rounds came crashing in, flashing into six brilliant orange fireballs for an instant, then casting burning fragments of phosphorus in long, graceful arcs; a dazzling white mushroom-shaped cloud towered above each burst, lingering and blinding all those who had been caught near it. The white smoke hung over the knob, obscuring everything but the rock face nearest the Third Platoon. The next six rounds glowed briefly in the great white cloud, then their smoke made the blanket even thicker. Six more orange bursts, barely visible to Eric and Jamison because of the cloud, fell behind the knob, cutting off any of the defenders who might have tried to escape by climbing higher on Cougar toward the Octopus' peak.

"That was damned fine," Eric said to Jamison. "Much obliged."

Jamison nodded.

"Seven, this is Five-Seven. Cease firing, end of mission. Out."

Holloway stood up to see how Felty's platoon was making out. He could see a single file of men climbing the rock face; he was glad that the men were moving quickly, so that they

148

could take full advantage of the shock and blindness the shelling had inflicted on the enemy defenders. The head of Felty's column was already in the smoke, and Eric could hear muffled explosions as the lead scouts threw hand grenades at everything within throwing range that might have concealed an enemy soldier.

Soon the whole platoon was inside the white pall. Eric sent a runner back to tell Gregg to move the rest of the company up: this might be just the break he needed, and he wanted to make the most of it.

Felty called in on the radio.

"This is George Three," he said. "We're up here. Can't see much, but I think we've got this thing all to ourselves. Over."

"Fine," Eric replied. "Keep going. Over."

"This is George Three calling George Six. We're on top. What do you want us to do? Answer please. Over."

Eric pressed the sending switch on his radio and repeated his order, but Felty called back that he was on top and wanted instructions, as though he hadn't heard the company commander at all.

"Damn," Holloway said to Jamison. "I guess my radio's out."

"Better yours than his."

"Maybe so. Well, things are normal again. These radios always get the battle-rattles precisely when we need them most."

When Eric looked back over his shoulder, he saw Gipp and Gregg leading the command group and the rest of the company up the finger.

"Better get packed up," he told the artilleryman. "I think we better get up there with him."

Gipp brought the Three-Hundred radio to Holloway so that he could call the battalion commander. When Eric had Major Dahl, he told him of Felty's success.

Major Dahl said he was glad to hear of it.

"Just keep him going. Push him as hard as you can."

2

Felty met Holloway at the top of the knob.

"My lead squad's out in front of the smoke," he said. "You want us to go on?"

Eric nodded.

"Yes, but tell your people to expect trouble."

"Will do."

Felty ran forward into the smoke to pass the order.

Eric stopped to think. He was bushed from the climb up the rock face, and he wanted to be sure he was clear in his own mind as to what he should do next.

Gregg joined him.

"Top, are Cannon's people pretty well rested?" the company commander asked.

"Yep."

"I wish I could let them take over from Felty."

"Want me to get Lieutenant Cannon?"

Eric knew that Felty's men must be tired from the strain of being shot at, but he couldn't afford to take the time to pass Cannon through them.

"No. Felty'll have to keep going, I guess. Keep Lieutenant Cannon right behind the command group, though."

"Very well, sir."

"And have Sergeant Wood bring me Cannon's radio. Mine went out."

Holloway and Jamison started on up Cougar, following Felty's last man. Holloway saw three or four bodies, enemy soldiers who had been burned to death. Several rifles were scattered around in the dirty snow, and Eric saw a good many tracks leading down both sides of the finger, indicating that some survivors had fled the knob in panic, dropping their weapons in their haste.

Funny, Eric thought, I'm glad they got away. I only hope they're gone for good. I'd better pass the word for people to watch the flanks as they go up, just in case we cross trails with them again.

When he looked back at the blackened bodies he found himself wishing that they, too, had made it off the knob. He found little satisfaction in their deaths: he was glad that they were no longer shooting at his men, but that was all. He wished that they and all their kind could have realized that they couldn't win, that sooner or later they would have no more hills to defend. He wished that the enemy would just pull out of the whole wretched country. That would end the war without any more killing, and that would be a good thing—too good to be true. I am a hell of a soldier, he thought, standing here feeling sorry because these people got killed when we've finally got what we risked a hell of a lot of life to win. But—what I really want is safety for these braves of mine, and that means the top of this damned thing.

The sound of shooting—cracks and thumps—up ahead told him that the top wasn't his yet.

Felty's platoon had moved up Cougar as quickly as the trail would allow, but the lead scouts were still hundreds of yards short of the junction of Cougar and Lion when a machine gun opened up, and both scouts dropped.

The rest of the men in that squad dropped back, stunned by the sharp resistance.

Somebody yelled "Start shootin'!" and one or two men began firing timidly.

Felty crawled up to see what was wrong. Holloway was not far behind him.

"Can you see anything?" Felty asked one of his men.

"Naw, th' damn sun's right in my eyes. Sun and th' snow."

Holloway couldn't see any movement on the knob, but the thumps that followed the cracks overhead told him what he needed to know. He crawled back to get Jamison and to get set for a hard fight, for he knew that Felty's people were tired, and tired of being the company's battering ram.

"Here we go again," he said wearily when he found Jamison. "Let's us find us a good place to shoot from and blow that damned knob off the map."

Eric led the artilleryman down the side of the ridgeline, off the path, so that the enemy couldn't get a shot at them while they were moving. Gregg and the radio carriers followed a few yards behind. The going was rough, for the sun had melted the snow on that side of the ridge, but in less than a minute Holloway reached a place that would do.

"Over there, Fandango," he said, pointing. "Behind that rock. Gipp, bring me the radio."

Jamison had his radioman set up the artillery radio while Eric called Major Dahl on the infantry radio.

"This is George Six. George Three's people are—" Eric almost said "pinned down" but he caught himself in time— "trying to get the knob where Lion and Cougar meet. They've met resistance, so I'm going to put artillery on that place. Over."

"This is White Six. Does it look as though you'll have much trouble?"

"George Six here. Affirmative. Two of George Three's people have been hit. The knob looks pretty mean, and the sun's behind it. But maybe if Easy could come in at the same time, we could get it. Over."

"This is White Six. No, that's out. Easy is too far behind you. Wait."

Eric wondered why Dahl didn't tell him to go ahead. He looked at his watch: only three-thirty. Late, but not as late as the fight for the Shark.

"This is White Six. Hold what you've got. Get ready for tonight. Shoot the artillery if you want to, but you'll be registering defensive fires pretty soon anyway. Over."

"This is George Six," Eric answered, surprised. "Roger."

Eric didn't like the idea, now that it was an order. He could hold what he had of Cougar, all right, but he would feel much more secure if he could go into a perimeter defensive position on the junction knob.

Major Dahl's voice came back on the radio: "White Three

will be up there in a few minutes to show you what we will do overnight. Over."

"This is George Six. Sir, I'd feel better about this if we were on that knob. Could we have one try at getting it? Over."

As soon as the words were out, Eric regretted them. He remembered the friction between Dahl and the General, and he knew that the decision to stop short of the objective must have been a hard one for Dahl to make.

"Eric, just do as I told you. Out."

"Somethin' wrong, sir?" Gregg asked as Eric passed the handset back to Gipp.

"Nothing that a forty-five slug between my eyes wouldn't cure, Top."

Holloway walked over to Fandango's rock and sat down.

"Major Dahl just ordered me to hold up here for tonight. I'm going to pull Felty back a bit, then I'd appreciate some creaming from your people."

"Okay. Just tell me where and when."

"It'll be that knob up ahead. And pretty soon."

"All right."

"Hamilton's on the way up here to give us the full order. And I just goofed but good."

"What do you mean?" Jamison asked.

"I crossed Dahl about stopping."

"For good reasons?"

"I don't know. Maybe they weren't. I thought we'd be able to kill people better from up there. But then there's the problem of getting up there, and I guess Dahl figures it would cost us too much."

"What do you really think?"

"I think we'd better make the best of what we've got, and I'd better just do as I'm told."

Eric crawled up ahead to tell Felty to get his wounded people out, and to pull the rest of his platoon back. Then he returned to his command group and began giving orders for the defense.

"Top, find us a home," Holloway said.

"Back here?" Gregg asked. "I thought we was supposed to keep on goin'."

"Set up our command post somewhere this side of the knob. The one behind us, I mean. I'm going to look around for the right place to put the line."

"Very well, sir."

Gregg went back down the finger to find a good spot for the C. P. When he found a fairly level area about fifty yards behind what he supposed would be the line, he told Sergeant Wood to get the phones wired in. Then he had a native ammunition bearer dig a hole for the company commander.

"Wood," Gregg said, "be sure your clowns dig holes. And Acker, you dig a hole for Fandangle and his people."

Up ahead, at Fandangle's rock, the company commander watched Felty move his platoon back. Felty was carrying one of the wounded men on his back.

Jamison noticed, too.

"Felty's a good human being," Eric said. "I just wish he knew a little more about how to run a platoon."

"Felty'll be all right."

The platoon leader gave the wounded man to a medic when he could, and a minute or two later he plopped wearily behind the rock.

"We're clear," he said.

"All right. When you get your breath, tell your people to go easy on their ammo. Have them set up a good blocking position. I'll give you the order for tonight later."

"Okay."

"Are your wounded men going to make it?"

"I think so. One's hit in the leg—the other one in the gut."

"You want me to start shooting now?" Fandango asked Holloway.

"The knob, yes. We'll register the defensive fires after I get the word from Hamilton about how we're to go in for the night."

"Sounds good."

Gipp came up from the ridgeline and called the company commander.

"Cap'n Hamilton's back at the C. P., sir. Wants you to come see him."

3

"Have a see-gar," Hamilton said as Eric walked into the command post.

Eric took the cigar and lit it. He wondered, as he puffed, if the gesture could be one of reconciliation. Surely Hamilton had seen a great deal on his way up to George Company, and it was just possible that having seen, he understood why Eric had to take a personal hand in the day's fighting.

"Have a seat," Eric said, pointing to the rim of a crater the artillery had dug. The ground was still warm, and the odor of phosphorus was still in the air.

"You did pretty good to get up here," Hamilton began, "first day with the company, and all."

"It's a good company."

"Easy didn't make out so good. And Fox is all cut up. The Third Battalion didn't get their ridge, either."

Eric had heard firing over on Lion and to his right on Rhino off and on all day, but he had been so engrossed in his own attack he had paid the other firefights little attention.

"Colonel Hobbs has been raising hell all day, but it hasn't done anybody any good. He's just made everybody feel like hell."

"That's too bad."

"Yeah. He's taking it out on Dahl, especially. Thinks Dahl isn't aggressive enough. Thinks he isn't pushing you fast enough."

Eric recalled the radio conversation he had had with Dahl only a few minutes before. If Hobbs was pushing Dahl, it would seem logical from Dahl to permit—even to order—

George Company to take the junction knob. So Dahl must have had a strong reason for holding off. One hell of a strong reason. And what could it be?

"While you were on your way up here, we had a little discussion about whether to stop here for tonight or to try to get the knob," Eric said.

"Well, he'd already made his mind up about that."

"Why did he have me stop?"

"He wants you to have plenty of time to get set up for tonight. And he wants Easy to pull up even with you, and that'll take time. Besides, he's tired. He figures your people are, too."

"I see."

"That kind of caution—or consideration—will probably cost him his promotion."

"You know, I was off base when I tried to talk him into letting me go on. I should have kept my mouth shut."

"Yes, you should have. He can be a little more flexible about these things than you can. A company commander had better do as he's told. He can fight City Hall when he gets to be a battalion commander, if he's got it in him to rebel."

"And whether a battalion commander is right or wrong makes little difference to the God damned rear echelon."

"Well, Dahl had rather do this thing his own way, no matter what division thinks. Doing what's right makes one hell of a big difference to him—he knows he's got to live with himself for the rest of his life. I admire hell out of the guy."

"So do I."

"Now, you—when he tells you to go, you go like hell, see? Get him every inch you can. But when he tells you to hold up, just do it."

"All right."

"I guess we'll wind this thing up tomorrow. But tonight may not be good sleeping weather. You want to see the line for tonight?"

"Yep."

The two officers got up and walked over to a cleared space on the western slope of the ridge from which they could see across the deep valley to Lion, the long finger on which Easy Company had been slugging it out with the enemy all day.

"Easy's going to straddle that ridge yonder. They'll come down that little nose and stop just short of the bottom."

"I see."

"They aren't quite up that far yet, but they'll make it all right. Heath'll call you on the radio when he's ready to tie in. You've got the valley, you understand."

"I understand."

"Now, I may be able to get a tank up to you."

"No, there's a creek down there, and it's too rocky. It's hard enough for a man to move. I'm sure a tank couldn't get up that far."

Hamilton took his cigar out of his mouth and looked directly at Eric.

"You been down there?"

"Yes."

Hamilton put the cigar back in his mouth.

"Well, no tank. You tie in with Heath, then come across this here ridge."

Hamilton motioned for Holloway to follow him over to the other side of the ridge so that he could show him the rest of the line's trace. When he reached the eastern slope, he looked over at Rhino, nearly a mile away.

"No hope of tying in with Blue. I 'spect they'll send out contact patrols over this way, though. Have your people look out for them, and tell 'em to go easy on shootin' at 'em."

"We won't pull any patrols to Blue, will we?"

"Shouldn't have to. They've only got that one finger to defend. We'll use people out of Fox to patrol, if we have to send anybody. Just box-in the right end of your line, and we'll see about patrolling later."

Eric nodded.

"How are you going to put your platoons in?" Hamilton asked.

"I think I'll have Digger Dolan tie in with Easy. Felty's got a blocking position in the center now, and I'll probably leave him there. That leaves Cannon for the right—the open flank. Mortars below the cliff, back there."

"That sounds pretty good. You like this job?"

"Yes, I do. Very much."

"Well, I'm glad to see you have it, and I want to see you keep it. But everything I said before still goes—you'd better quit taking chances and settle down."

Hamilton shot Eric a knowing glance.

"Yes, sir."

The captain turned to go.

"You reckon I could get to Easy Company by crossing the valley?"

"I suppose you could, but I wouldn't risk it."

"It's a long way around."

"Safe, though."

Captain Hamilton motioned for his two bodyguards to join him. Then he started down Cougar's narrow ridgeline toward battalion, taking the long, safe way around.

About ten minutes after Hamilton left, Corporal Mayes called Eric from the battalion C. P. and gave him more information about the battalion's plans for living through the night.

"We're going to move the C. P. up the valley, sir," Mayes said. "Fox Company will go in around us for security, 'cause we won't be too far behind you folks. Major Dahl's gone back to regiment, too. Maybe to get more orders for tomorrow. That's about all we know, sir."

"Fine, Mayes. Thanks for calling."

"That's all right, sir. It's going to be a hell of a long night."

"Sure is, Mayes."

4

Eric called his platoon leaders and Lieutenant Schaefer together and gave them the order for the night's defense, then he went forward to watch Jamison register the defensive concentrations.

When Holloway reached Fandango's rock, he stood up and looked across his company's front, looking for approach routes which the enemy might use in attacking during the night, and wondering how he could stop the enemy out there before he could get close enough to endanger the men of George Company. Some of the approaches, he decided, could be blocked off by artillery fire; Fandango could register concentrations on them, and if trouble came from one of those directions, he could simply call for that concentration by number and cream the attackers. But there were other routes the enemy might take—routes which the artillery could not hit because of the ridgelines. Holloway decided to have his forward observer from the mortar section register on them.

He sent Gipp back to get the mortar forward observer, then he turned to Jamison.

"Want to start shooting?"

"All set."

"Well, here's what I figure. I'll have my mortars cover the threats in the valley. If you will, I'd appreciate your covering the junction knob, then put a concentration down there to the right of the Second Platoon. I may ask for one or two more later, but that ought to do for a starter."

"All right."

Jamison got out his pocket compass and began the curiously technical task of calculating the data he would have to furnish the fire direction center.

Eric watched him, fascinated.

Later, when Sergeant Brook from the mortar section arrived and began his registration, Fandango helped him. Holloway noticed that Fandango was making a sketch of the whole company front; every time a concentration was established, the artilleryman got the concentration number from the F. D. C. and wrote it on the sketch.

Within the hour, the registration of the defensive fires was completed. The artillery had left the junction knob shattered and smoking, and Fandango had even walked single rounds right up to the top of the Octopus' peak. He had also pounded the valley between Rhino and Cougar, as if to tell the enemy, "You come in here tonight and we'll clobber you."

Easy and Blue were registering, too. All of the firing was calculated to discourage enemy soldiers as well as their commanders, to force them to think it over before launching an attack on the feeble regimental line.

The sun went down behind the enemy-held junction knob about five o'clock, sending darkness up from the valley floor before anyone in George Company was ready for it or expecting it. The sky was getting cloudy; a chilly wind was blowing out of the north, and the men were depressed and tired. There was nothing left to eat, but that wasn't important; the night would be long and dangerous, and the longer it lasted the more dangerous it would become. Some of the men were thinking of Sergeant Hicks and the Mouse and Collins. Others were thinking of their own close calls, wondering just how long their luck would last. As the daylight faded, the men dug holes, or tried their best to. The ground was rocky and hard, and in many places on the steep slope a little scraping and filling was all that could be done.

Night fell suddenly, and the long wait was on.

5

At the company C. P., Eric Holloway and Alex Schaefer got into the hole that Sergeant Gregg had made a native dig for them. The hole was large enough for both of the officers to stretch out in, and yet small enough to be covered by one poncho.

Eric placed his pistol near his head, then he put his steel helmet over it. He unloaded his rifle and placed it between the two sleeping bags.

"Alex, do me a favor tomorrow," Eric said.

"What is it?"

"Sergeant Trent sent my sleeping bag up here from battalion. Remind me to thank him."

"I sure will."

Eric crawled into his sleeping bag, then Schaefer began getting settled for the night.

"By the way," Schaefer said, "we've got some C-rations and a basic load of ammo on the way up here. It'll be pretty late getting here, but we'll have it for tomorrow. We didn't use a hell of a lot of ammo today, so we'll be in good shape."

"That's fine. Can we get water from the creek?"

"Yeah."

"Good. God, I'm tired."

Holloway was very glad that Alex had taken care of those matters.

It will be good, he thought, if we can get this thing over with tomorrow. We're all so tired, so damned tired.

"What are you writing?" Eric asked a few minutes later. He was reminded of Wayne Hyde, who used to write long into the night.

"Letter to my wife. Tomorrow's our wedding anniversary."

"Oh."

"That makes all this pretty tough, you know. If anything should happen to me on that day, of all days—it would be too ironic."

"Oh, you'll be all right."

"There's always a temptation to write one of those letters-to-be-read-after-my-death on nights like this one. I've never written such a letter, and I hope I never do. Maybe that'll keep my doom away from me."

"Maybe."

"You used up about six lives today, Eric. You know that?"

Holloway thought for a moment.

"Three to go, then," he said.

"Are you a fatalist, or something?"

"No."

"I wondered. You seemed oblivious to danger."

"Well, I sure as hell wasn't. I was scared, all right. It's just that—"

"Yes?"

"Sometimes it doesn't matter what you *want* to do. There are some things that have to be done, regardless. Today I ran into an awful lot of that sort of thing. That's all."

"You better get some sleep. I'll watch things for awhile."

"Think I will," Eric said, settling into his sleeping bag.

"I've got to stay awake until the stuff gets up here, anyway."

"Okay. Be sure to goose me if anything happens."

Eric was worn out. His last climb over the ridgeline had been especially fatiguing: he had walked the company line from one end to the other, making sure that the company was securely tied in with Easy Company, and that every man was in a position from which he could kill an attacker. Holloway had been surprised to find that most of the men had to be moved: for some reason or another, it had occurred neither to them nor to their leaders to check that. I'll have to work on that when we get back into reserve, Eric thought.

Holloway looked at Alex, scratching away at the letter to his wife, then he fell asleep.

6

When Alex finished the letter, he snuffed out the candle and climbed out of the hole. He walked over to Sergeant Gregg's hole, which was open and quite large.

"You awake?" he asked.

"Yessir. I sent Acker down to guide the ration party up, so I'm takin' his phone guard. Couldn't sleep, anyway."

"Company commander's asleep. He was pooped. It's good he can sleep."

"Yep. He really had hisself a day."

"Well, if he can hang on, he'll make captain and maybe go places in the army."

"He's more than I can figure out, sometimes."

"What do you mean?" Schaefer asked.

"Well, sometimes I think he's one of the best officers I've ever seen, and sometimes I want to kill him. I never know when he's going to change from one to the other, so I don't feel right about him. Time was when he was full of talk about getting out, then he got eager. Now, I don't know what he's up to."

"Why was he talking about getting out? That doesn't sound like him."

"When he was hit, they told him he wouldn't be able to walk very far again. It worried him for a long time—I know he used to go down to the ocean and exercise his leg in the surf to try to get it to heal."

"It must have healed pretty well. He can outwalk anybody over here."

"Yessir, but he sure worried about it. Talked about what he'd do after he got out, and stuff like that."

"What snapped him out of it?"

"I don't know for sure. One day he and I were back in the rear echelon, and he got mighty upset over somethin' he saw. We were back at a hospital to see about some of our people who'd been hit, and the place was running over with civilians who'd been caught in airstrikes, or artillery, or somethin' like that. Hell of a mess. We was about to go when Holloway says, 'Top, look at that,' and he pointed to a man and a woman who'd been clobbered. Both of 'em had bandages over their heads. Just slits for their eyes and mouths. He made me stop the jeep, and he just sat there, staring, for a good minute. Then he said, 'Gregg, that's a good thing.'

I asked him what he meant, and he said, 'They'll always have a good marriage. Neither one will be jealous of the other, because they'll both be too horrible for anyone else to look at.' "

"That's a strange attitude."

"Yessir, it is."

"Was he serious?"

"I guess he was. Anyway, after that he quit feeling sorry for himself. He got real eager, just like he had been before he got hit. Most of us were sorry to see him get eager again. I'm scared of eager people, 'specially officers."

"What do you mean, 'eager'?"

"Well, all the time showing off. Trying to be a big hero when some general's around. Trying to get ahead no matter what he has to do or who gets killed. Or making a mess of things, and trying to cover it up or blame it on somebody else, so his precious career wouldn't get spoilt. You know the type."

"You think he was being eager today?"

Gregg thought about that for a moment.

"No, I don't think he was. I liked the way he worked today. I just wish I knew he'd stay that way."

In his foxhole, Eric Holloway turned over in his sleeping bag and went back to sleep.

Ten

Eric stirred in his sleeping bag when Schaefer returned to the foxhole.

"Everything all right?" he asked, still half-asleep.

"Yep. All quiet."

"What time is it?"

"Twelve-thirty. It's foggy outside."

"The witching hour."

"I just walked the line to make sure the rations and ammo got out. The men are pretty jumpy. Almost got shot a couple of times, myself."

"They remember last night."

"That's it, especially in Digger's platoon. Digger's got all his people awake."

"Good. That's where the trouble will be, if there is any trouble."

"Why do you think so?" Schaefer asked.

"I think they'd like to get into the valley. They could shoot up battalion, for one thing. And they might even be able to get all the way back to the river. Then they could raise hell with trucks back on the road."

"I see. You know, I've never thought of it before, but if it weren't for us, they could go all the way to Washington."

"I think I'll get up for awhile. Why don't you get some sleep?"

"Thanks, I will."

Eric wiggled out of his bag and fumbled around for his boots. When he had slipped them on, he got out of the hole and finished dressing, for there was very little room in the hole, and every time anyone moved, dirt and snow crumbled and fell on the sleeping bags.

Holloway was stiff from sleeping in a cramped position, but the brief rest had refreshed him. He looked at the fog that had closed in during his nap, and he thought of the anxiety the men in the First Platoon must be feeling: the fog was the best cover the enemy could ask for.

When he had laced his boots and strapped on his pistol, he put on his steel helmet and walked over to the phone guard's hole.

"Hand me the phone, please," he said.

Gipp passed him the phone, then twisted the crank on the side of the phone box, alerting each of the platoon phone guards.

As each phone guard answered, Eric said, "Stand by." Finally, when they were all in the net, he gave the guards a message for the platoon leaders:

"This fog is going to bother the enemy, too. He'll probably blunder into us, if he comes. Tell your platoon leaders to have everybody get low—as low as possible—so that he won't see us. That way, maybe we can get the first shot. Get everybody ready to open up on anything that moves. And one more thing—no more walking the line. As soon as this word's passed, I want everybody to stay put. Any questions?"

"First Platoon. No questions, sir."

"Second Platoon. You looking for something?" Cannon asked.

"Yes, I am. If I were the enemy, I'd sure as hell use this fog."

"All right. I got it."

"Third Platoon. No questions, sir."

"Fourth Platoon. No questions."

"All right. That's all I have. Let me know if you hear anything out there and we'll try to put some big stuff on it."

Holloway handed the phone back to Gipp. He was chilled

through and through; he waved his arms about, trying to get warm.

A few minutes later, Holloway heard rifle fire over on the right. His first thought was that Cannon's platoon had been hit, but he soon remembered that the fog made all noises sound differently. It's over at the Third Battalion, he decided.

The firing continued for several minutes. When Sergeant Trent called to get the one o'clock report, Holloway asked him about the firefight.

"Is that Blue that's getting hit?"

"Yes, sir. But we don't know any more about it than that. Everything quiet on your knob?"

"So far. Anything out on tomorrow's business?"

"No, sir, not yet. Captain Hamilton and the battalion commander are working on something, but I don't know what it is."

"Okay, thanks. See you tomorrow."

"Goodnight, sir."

"Oh, Trent—I almost forgot. Many thanks for sending my sleeping bag up here."

"That's all right, sir."

"Goodnight."

Eric looked at his watch: a little after one. The firing over on the right was heavy, as though the enemy didn't intend to be content with merely probing the line to feel out its strength for a later attack. Holloway wondered if the enemy had patrols out seeking the line between the Third Battalion and his own Second Platoon—the line that wasn't there. If the enemy happened to be pouring people through that half-mile-wide hole, he could make it extremely tough on the regiment; and if he didn't find that hole, it would be a stroke of almost incredible luck. Such thoughts frightened Eric, making him even colder.

Holloway asked for the phone again, then he called the Second Platoon.

"Cannon," he said, "better pass the word in your platoon

that it's just as possible they'll get jumped from behind as from in front."

"Yeah, I know. I've already turned every other man around."

"That's good. I'm going to have the mortar section people get set up that way, too."

"Anything happen over on Digger's side of this thing yet?"

"No. That shooting over in Blue is the only thing I know of that's going on, and I can't find out anything about it. Have any of your people heard anything out there in your valley?"

"Nothing. The artillery's been laying eggs out there all night. A few of 'em have been damned close, too. I've been about to call you a time or two to get it turned off."

"Well, you do that if they get too close. Otherwise, they may be keeping prowlers out."

"Yeah. See you later."

Eric handed the phone back and sat down on a ration box. His feet were cold, and his old wound was beginning to ache. His mind was quick and alert, stimulated, perhaps, by the night's fears and discomforts. He fed his mind questions to keep it nimble:

How long is it until morning? Answer, too damned long. Four hours. Five, maybe. But it'll take six for us to notice any warmth.

How long does the average fight last? Answer, about ten minutes. Perhaps thirty, or five, but usually ten.

How many fights could take place before daylight? Answer, that's too complicated. It would take calculus to do it right—but six times six, God! thirty-six possible fights!

What day is this? Answer—

A sharp fire fight broke out just below Holloway.

"The First Platoon's getting hit," Gipp yelled.

Eric ran over to Gipp's hole and jerked the phone out of his hand.

"Gipp, get everybody in the headquarters group up and

tell 'em to go into a perimeter. Tell Sergeant Gregg to put 'em in!"

"Yessir."

Gipp put on his steel helmet and scrambled out of the hole.

Holloway wanted to call Digger, to find out what was happening, but he resisted the temptation. He remembered how he resented being bothered at a time like that, so he relaxed and waited for Digger to call him. Holloway hoped that battalion, too, would be patient, but he had an idea they wouldn't be. Any minute now, he thought, they'll call and ask what the situation is, and I'll have to say 'I don't know,' and they'll think I don't care, or something.

The firing was sharp and steady, and it seemed to be coming from the very bottom of the valley. Once or twice Holloway heard muffled explosions: concussion grenades, he thought.

Finally, the phone rang. It was Digger.

"Sir, they're hitting the squad in the creek bed. We got the drop on 'em, though, and we roughed 'em up."

"That's good, Digger."

"You want us to chase 'em any?"

"No. Don't. Hold what you've got. Would a flare help you any?"

"I don't think so, sir. It'd just blind us. This fog's thick as goose grease down here."

"Well, you might rearrange your people down there so the enemy can't pinpoint them if he tries it again, but stay low and keep your people awake."

"All right, sir."

"You're doing fine down there, Digger. Be sure to let me know if there's anything we can do up here to help you."

"Very well, sir."

Eric called battalion as soon as Digger left the line. Harry Hamilton answered.

"What's the matter with you people down there?" Holloway asked, jokingly. "You didn't call me."

"Hell, we couldn't. We had to go out and wake up Fox Company. Did any of the enemy get through?"

"No, Digger's people got the drop on them, and they ran back up the draw."

"You figure they'll try it again?"

"Yes sir, I do."

"That's safe. Well, if they do, for Christ's sake don't let any of them get through. Fox is in a perimeter around us, but I'd just as soon be alone. We'll have to turn out the cooks and jeep drivers to defend Fox Company, I imagine. Heard anything on your right up there?"

"No, not a thing."

"Three cheers for our side. See you in the morning."

Eric put the phone down, then he walked over to the hole where Jamison and his radioman were supposed to be sleeping.

"Hey, Fandango," he said softly, shaking a sleeping bag.

"Huh?"

"Jamison, get up, please."

"You want th' Lieutenant?"

"Yes. Where is he?"

"Damn if I know. Said he was going up to the Third Platoon about an hour or two ago."

"All right."

I might have known that, Holloway thought.

The company commander called Felty's phone guard and told him to pass the word that he was coming up the ridgeline. "Tell them not to shoot me," he added.

Before he left, he told Schaefer where he was going.

"Keep an eye on things, please, Alex. And by the way, Digger Dolan might want some mortar fire out in front of him."

"I'll see about it. You watch yourself up there."

"I'll do that."

2

As Holloway approached the knob where Fandango was working, he heard him talking into his radio. From what he could hear, it seemed that the artilleryman was setting up a fire mission for use in case Felty's platoon was hit.

"What are you up to?" Holloway asked him.

"Hello. I'm just getting ready, in case we get some callers up here."

"Good. Everything been quiet, so far?"

"Yep. Blue's having a lot of trouble, though."

"I heard the shooting."

"I've been monitoring them on the radio. They think a full battalion hit them, but Blue didn't budge. Heavy casualties on both sides."

"That's too bad. Blue's been taking a bloody nose all the way through this little adventure."

The two men sat there on the bare rock in the darkness, staring up the path toward the enemy, for a long time, neither of them speaking. It was as though they were storing up energy for the rest of their long wait. Up the way, Eric saw the irregular shapes of poncho-covered holes with rifles pointing up toward the place where the fog permitted vision. Every now and then the rifles would move slightly, as the men shifted their sitting positions in the holes.

"Nearly two," Fandango said.

"Night moves damned slow."

"Have you heard anything about tomorrow—or today—or whatever?"

"Not yet. I imagine we'll be told to go on up, though."

"How do you feel about that?" Jamison asked.

"I don't know. I don't like to think about my braves having to take the punishment, but if it'll help end the war, I guess the thing to do is get busy and quit bitching."

"You aren't interested in 'having the honor to charge,' as they used to say?"

"No. If Dahl tells us to go, I'll know why. We're up here within spitting distance of the knob, so we go. And we've got you with us—that's another reason."

"You make it sound like a business. Don't you have a sense of dash, or adventure, or whoop-la? Has all of the romance gone out of this thing?"

"As far as I'm concerned, it has. I don't know whether this makes me a poor company commander or not, but I've grown tremendously fond of these men. When I think about all the things I have to order them to do, and when I see how gallantly they respond, I feel mighty humble. There sure as hell isn't any romance in this for them. Why they keep going, how they can endure, why they don't just throw up their hands and die—all that is beyond me. But I do know this: they've set me a hell of an example. For me to do what I have to do even as well as the weakest and most miserable of them will be one hell of a tough job."

"You're getting quite an education."

"Am I?"

"You've learned something important. Humility."

The radio interrupted them.

"Eight, this is Six-Five. Fire mission! Over!"

The voice was frantic. And a moment after that transmission, Eric and Fandango heard heavy rifle and machine gun fire from across the valley to their right: the Third Battalion was being hit again.

"Item Company's forward observer is Six-Five. And they're on this end of Blue's line."

The fire direction center, Eight, answered Item Company's forward observer, then Six-Five's voice came back on the radio.

"You know who Six-Five is?" Holloway asked Jamison.

"No. Sounds like Norton, though. Norton's new over here."

Six-Five's nervous voice went on: "Azimuth, two-seven. Coordinates Dog Sugar—no, wait—azimuth, two-seven-FIVE, coordinates Dog Sugar—"

"Poor bastard," Fandango said. "He's rattled. That won't do."

The F. D. C. came on the radio almost as soon as Six-Five's transmission had stopped.

"This is Eight. I have 'azimuth, two-seven-five, coordinates Dog Sugar.' Say again all after Dog Sugar. Over."

"That's the Old Man—Eight. He works fire missions now and then."

Six-Five came on again: "This is Norton—I mean, Six-Five. We're about to get cut off—"

Jamison and Holloway looked at each other: a chill ran up Eric's spine.

The voice went on: "For God's sake, get something on the way. Shoot for the west end of the line. Over!"

This last had almost been a panic-stricken scream.

Eight came on: "Norton, give me the coordinates. Over."

The artillery battalion commander's voice was steady, demanding. Eric wondered if the colonel hoped to snap Norton out of his panic through the firmness of his words.

"This is Six-Five. Dog Sugar five-five-one—they're all over the place—shoot, please, shoot!"

"Damn!" Fandango said. "Those coordinates are nonsense. The colonel can't shoot on suspicion."

"What can he do?"

"Not a hell of a lot, right now. Put another F. O. in for Norton later, but that thing will be over by the time another man can get there. I'd better get this thing back on my channel. He might have something in mind that I could do to help."

Jamison got down from the rock and flicked the switch on his radio.

Although he was intensely interested in the plight of Item Company, Eric was relieved when Jamison switched channels. Listening to the horror in Norton's voice reminded him of the curious feeling of shame he had sensed as he had watched Fred Matthews and his men die, only a day or two before. He was frightened by the thought that Item's troubles might be a prelude to an attack on his own company, but he was more than frightened by something else: he was upset by the fear he had heard in Norton's voice, a fear that he knew he would have to fight down in his own handling of his company's destiny. He hoped he wouldn't ever sound like Norton, and a moment later he was flooded with shame for having forgotten that Norton was fighting for his life.

"I'm glad you turned that off," Eric said.

"Yes. It makes me feel pretty helpless. It's hard to listen."

"What do you mean, helpless?"

"Just that with all our firepower, there's nothing that can be done until somebody who can play it cool gets on that radio."

Fandango walked around, waving his arms in wide circles to warm up his body.

"It makes me mad as hell."

"If you were the colonel, would you shoot on suspicion?" Eric asked.

"I don't know. I could say, 'Hell no' from here, now, but it's easy to decide these things when you're not involved. He's damned if he shoots and kills a bunch of our people, and he's damned if he holds off and lets that company get chopped up."

Jamison switched back to Eight's channel.

"Let's see about this thing."

A transmission was underway: "—then work closer to the line. Maybe that'll pull 'em off Six-Five. Over."

A moment later the colonel's calm voice came on: "Fandango Three-Zero, this is Fandango Eight. On the way. Over."

Eric and Jamison looked eastward into the fog that covered the valley between Cougar and Rhino and listened for the rustle of the artillery round. A few seconds later they heard the swishing and the sharp ka-*runch*.

"Well, they're doing something," Jamison said, relieved.

"Who's Three-Zero?"

"Captain Mollett. He's the liaison officer with Blue. Must be shooting from the battalion C. P."

Three-Zero and the colonel gradually walked rounds in toward the line. When they were as close as they dared come, the colonel began adding more guns to the firing, and within five minutes a terrific bombardment was being placed on Rhino.

"What happens to Norton?" Eric asked.

"I don't know."

"I feel sorry as hell for him."

"Oh, they won't do much. He's some general's son. They'll cover for him, maybe give him a job in supply. That is, if he lives."

"That isn't what I meant."

"Good."

3

Gipp came running up the path.

"Lieutenant Holloway, sir. The battalion commander wants to talk to you on the phone. Right now!"

"Thanks, Gipp. I'll be right there."

"Tomorrow's order?"

"I expect it is. See you later."

Holloway picked up the phone as soon as he reached the company command post.

"This is Lieutenant Holloway, sir," he said, almost out of breath from dog-trotting along the path.

"This is Major Dahl, Eric. I have the order for tomorrow —or rather today—and I imagine you can guess what it is."

"Yes, sir, I think I can."

"Well, the powers that be are pretty unhappy with me because we aren't on top now. They want us to get up there as soon as we can. Division is particularly upset."

"Yes, sir."

"Now, here's the way I want to do it. A little before six

o'clock, I want you to pull in your flank platoons. Fox Company will move up the valley and take up the positions your people are in there now. We won't worry about the people on the other side. I want you to move out as soon as possible after six, preferably right on the button at six. I know that all this will depend on how quickly you can get your flank people in, of course, but I think the sooner we get started the better off we'll be."

"Very well, sir."

"You already have some artillery concentrations registered on the knob, haven't you?"

"Yes, we have."

"Then you can check them anytime after five-thirty, if you wish."

"All right, I'll do that."

"Now, when you get to the junction, you'd better put some people in a blocking position facing down toward Heath. That's going to be tricky, because I'm having him move up his ridge, too. Better keep your radio in contact with Heath so you don't shoot each other up. I figure there might be a few enemy stragglers caught between you and Heath, and they might try to shoot their way out, so have your people keep on the lookout for anything."

"We'll do that, sir. I'll set that up as soon as we have that junction."

"Good. Now, as soon as you have that knob and we know what's doing, I'll have Heath pull in behind you and follow you on to the top."

"Sir, do you want me to keep going after I get the knob, or wait?"

"I want you to keep going, but you'll have to leave some people—a platoon, I'd say—at the knob to hold it until Heath gets there. Blue has taken such a beating tonight that they can't possibly make it. Get the peak, go into a perimeter, and as soon as I can move Heath in we'll add him to the perimeter. Fox will go in from the peak down toward the knob you're going for at six. I doubt if Fox can stretch very far, but they ought to be able to keep a path for supplies open, if they have to supply us from that direction.

"I've got it, sir."

"Blue will move up after we have the top, and they'll clear that finger that runs east from the peak. Can you make that one out on your map?"

Eric had all but memorized the map of the Octopus.

"Yes, sir. I'm sure I know the one you mean."

"Good. It'll be a matter of your getting started and getting up on top as soon as you can. If you can get this objective for us, Eric, you'll really have done something."

"I'll do the best I can, sir."

"Fine. I've heard a rumor that the First Battalion will relieve us all, either later this afternoon or tomorrow morning. Of course, it's just a rumor, and even if it's true it will depend on the luck we have."

"That'll be fine, sir."

"Don't put too much hope in it, and for God's sake don't shoot up all the ammo. If you aren't relieved you may need it, if the enemy counterattacks, and if you are relieved, Red might need it."

"All right, sir."

"Everything's been pretty quiet in front of us, so far. If you're in trouble at six, we'll just have to go anyhow. If you get hit, call me first thing, and we'll try to work something out. Maybe I can use Heath, but I'd rather do it the way I've outlined to you."

"Very well, sir, I'll call you on the radio at a quarter to six in any case. Is there anything else?"

"No, Eric. You've been doing very well up there. I hope this attack winds it up for awhile so I can give your people some rest."

"So do I, sir. They surely do need it."

"Well, see you on top."

"Yes, sir."

Eric gave the phone back to Gipp and sat down on a ration box to think out the order he would give his platoon leaders.

After a few minutes of deep thought, Eric asked for the phone again and called battalion. Harry Hamilton answered.

"Sir, I'd like to have my First Platoon up here before six because I want to use them in the lead, initially. I can jump off right at six if you can have Fox relieve Dolan earlier than that—five-thirty would do."

"Wait a minute, Holloway. I'll ask the old man."

There was a long pause.

"All right," Hamilton said finally. "We'll get Fox up there in time for Dolan to start climbing by five-thirty. That make you happy?"

"Yes, thanks. That'll do it."

Holloway handed the phone back to Gipp.

"Call all the platoon leaders, please, Gipp, and tell them to come up here as soon as possible."

He looked at his watch: four-fifteen.

"Ask the F. O.'s to come, too."

Gipp went about the familiar business of calling in the platoon leaders and forward observers. In a hole not far away, Sergeant Gregg, who had been pretending to sleep, began to get up, raising an enormous fuss because snow was in his boots.

4

The platoon leaders arrived one-by-one, the mortar platoon leader first because he was right down the path from the company command post. Then came Felty, whose platoon was just a few yards up the ridge. Fandango was with him. Sergeant Dolan was next, puffing from the long climb up from his hole near the floor of the valley. Lieutenant Cannon was last.

Sergeant Gregg had spread cardboard from the ration boxes on the snow, giving the platoon leaders a place to sit. Cannon and the Digger were particularly in need of a place to plop, and plop they did. The others sat down near them.

Eric took off his gloves and raked up enough snow to mold

a small representation of the Octopus and its finger-system. When he had finished, he wiped his hands on his trousers and slipped his gloves back on.

"Here's where we are now," he began, dragging a small twig across one of the snowmounds—the one representing Cougar. "Up the way from us a few hundred yards, this ridge runs into another one, the one over there on the left, where Easy Company is. Then one big ridge runs on up to the peak of the mountain. You all know about the other ridge, the one the Third Battalion's been trying to get."

"Getting creamed on, too," Cannon said.

"Well, there are two others, this one that runs east from the peak, and this one button-hooking out to the north."

Eric pointed to the ridges on his snow model. The platoon leaders watched intently.

"Blue was hit by a whole battalion. They're pretty well blocked, it seems, so our battalion has the mission of getting the top. Blue will come up their finger after we're on top, then they'll clear this finger, the one that runs east from the top.

"Now, here's where we come in. Before five-thirty, Digger, Fox Company will come up the valley behind you. They'll take over your positions. Have your platoon move right up the side of this finger, and assemble them over there."

Holloway pointed back to an open space near the C. P.

"At six o'clock, Digger, you'll move through the Third Platoon, and attack up this ridgeline to seize the knob where this ridge runs into Lion. When you have that knob, set up a perimeter defense that will hold the knob no matter where you get a counter-attack from."

"Very well, sir."

"Be careful about Easy Company. They'll be coming up their ridge toward you. We'll try to keep in touch with them on the radio, but you may get some business from the people Easy'll be pushing in front of them. And your main threat might well be from the defenders of the ridge that runs on to the top—so be ready in all those directions."

"We will, sir."

"Now, I'll have the command group right behind the First Platoon. We'll go at six sharp. Cannon, I want the Second Platoon to start moving up the finger at six. Fall in behind the command group, and follow us on up. When Digger gets the knob and goes into his perimeter, you'll pass through him and continue the attack, your mission being to seize the peak itself."

"Okay."

"Go as fast as you can up that ridge. I'll be right behind you with the command group. As soon as you've got the peak, we'll go into a company perimeter—but you go into a platoon perimeter as soon as you get up there. You'll be vulnerable as hell for a few minutes."

"All right."

"Felty, you stay where you are until the junction knob is secure. Then I'm going to move the mortars up to the knob so that they'll be in positions from which they can support Cannon. You'll follow them to the knob, then pass through Digger's platoon and follow me and the command group up after Cannon."

"Roger," Felty answered.

"Digger, you'll give the mortar people security inside your perimeter. Easy Company will come up that ridge behind you as soon as they can, and they'll relieve you. When they do, come right up the ridge behind Lieutenant Felty's platoon."

"Very well, sir."

"Sir, what about my mortar people after Digger moves out?" the leader of the mortar section asked.

"Unless you're in a fire mission when Digger moves, follow them up. If you're shooting, continue your mission and I'll move you when you're done. Digger will move anyway, but not until Easy's people get there, so you'll be protected all the time. That answer it?"

"Yessir, it does. But what about the Fifty-Seven?"

"It goes with the First Platoon until they're on their objective, then with Lieutenant Cannon's platoon to the top."

"Right, sir."

"Now, as soon as we get the peak, we'll go into a perimeter with the Second Platoon from ten o'clock to two, First Platoon from six to ten, and Third Platoon two to six. I'll have to show you what I mean by twelve o'clock after I get up there. I can't tell a hell of a lot from this map—I've heard it's wrong—and I'm not sure where the maximum threat will be. But that's how I want the rifle platoons to go in. Mortars and company headquarters will be inside. Any questions?"

There were none.

"I've got twenty-three minutes before five."

The others checked their watches.

"One last thing: be as aggressive as you can whenever you get a break. When you've pushed them off one knob, follow them so fast they won't have a chance to stop and set up again. That way, we'll get this thing over with faster and with fewer chances for our people getting hurt. Watch your ammo supply, and if any of you get low, let Lieutenant Schaefer know. Or me. We'll redistribute, or something. Anything else?"

"Preparation?" Fandango asked.

"Thanks, I had forgotten it. You may start checking the concentrations you've already registered at five-thirty. By the time we have the junction knob, we ought to have enough daylight to see the top, and we may want to do some more shooting then. No mortar preparation, but I want the Sixties to be ready to fire on the concentrations they registered yesterday until I give you the word to pull up and come forward."

"All right," Fandango replied. "I'll check 'em all, and rough up the knob a bit."

"That'll be fine. Now, Digger, in case you're being hit at five-thirty, we'll have to do something tricky. That goes for you, too, Cannon, at six. Be sure to let me know the minute anything happens that might put the kibosh on this attack."

"We'll be damned glad to be getting out of that valley, sir. Fox Company's welcome to it."

"Good. If you have any booby traps out, better take them in—no, be sure you get them all in."

"All right, sir."

"That's all I have, and all I can think of right now. I'll see you up here at six."

The platoon leaders got up stiffly, adjusted their equipment, and walked away.

"Well," Holloway said to Gregg, "here it goes. Think we'll get away with it?"

"It sounded good to me, sir."

Holloway suddenly realized that he was tired.

"Think I'll take a cat-nap, Top," he said, crawling back into his foxhole. He kept his jacket and boots on, but he wadded the upper part of his sleeping bag into a crude pillow and laid his bare head upon it. He fell asleep immediately.

5

Eric Holloway's cat-nap was shattered by the *crunches* of two mortar rounds which fell within a hundred yards of his hole. He woke up instantly, and pressed down against the cold earth as hard as he could, shivering with fear. The sounds of clods of earth falling recalled the horror of the almost forgotten night in the operations tent, and Eric was all the more frightened. He listened carefully, as though he thought he could hear the rounds coming; he did hear a faint "chump-chump"—the sound of the mortar being fired—and he cringed again and held his breath, expecting to die. Seconds later, the two rounds fell far below him, behind the Second Platoon. They're wild, he thought. Maybe that'll save us.

Holloway jumped out of his hole and ran over to the phone. He called the Second Platoon and asked if the rounds had hit anyone.

"Hell no, sir," the phone guard said. "They was 'way back."

"Thanks," Holloway replied, putting down the phone.

"Gipp, you listen carefully for the sound of that damned mortar firing. When you hear it, make sure everybody back here gets down. Got it?"

"Yessir."

"I'm going up to the Third Platoon. Call me there if anybody wants me."

Eric ran up the path, crouching at first. This is silly, he thought, and then he straightened up to his full height and walked the rest of the way. That's what fear does to a man, he thought. I wonder if I'll ever get over being afraid?

"Greetings," he heard Fandango call from up the path. "Mortar rounds shoo you out?"

"Damn right, they did! Do you have any idea of where they're shooting from?"

"No, but I'm thinking about pasting the whole ridge up there anyway. It's ten after five, and there's no limitation on our shooting back there, is there?"

"No, shoot anywhere you please except on our concentrations."

The artilleryman began calling data into his radio.

Holloway walked on up to Felty's hole. Felty, he noticed, had just finished giving the order to his squad leaders, who were returning to their squads as Eric walked up.

"Everything still quiet?" the company commander asked.

"Yes, so far. I've got everybody up and ready."

"Good."

"What do you think that mortar fire means?"

"I don't know. Could be a preparation, but it isn't observed fire and there wasn't much of it. Could be they're shooting up their spare ammo so they won't have to lug it back with them. I doubt if they have any to spare, though, so that isn't likely. Maybe it's just to let us know they've got mortars. Jamison's going to tickle 'em a bit with our artillery. Maybe that'll keep 'em out of action."

"I'd just as soon they left us alone. I'm allergic to lead poisoning."

"I am, too. Well, it won't be long before we'll be up there on top, and then we won't have quite so much to worry about. This has been one hell of a long night."

"It sure has."

Overhead, flights of artillery rounds rustled toward the dark ridge where the enemy sat, waiting for sunrise and the attack they knew would come. Down below, in the valley to Eric's left, Fox Company was stumbling along beside the rocky creek, fumbling up toward the thin line the First Platoon had held all night. Major Dahl and his command group had left the valley and were climbing Cougar behind George Company's line to get into position to watch and to control the attack, which was to begin in less than an hour. All up and down the line, men were rolling their bulky sleeping bags into awkward bundles, checking their weapons to see that no mud or snow would interfere with their functioning, and generally getting squared away, first for the climb to the top of the ridgeline, then for the long and perhaps bloody walk to the peak.

There had been plenty of time for preparation: each platoon leader had gone from man to man, passing the word, giving last-minute tips on how the attack was to be made. The men of George Company were as ready for that attack as they could ever get, and because of this, they were impatient and anxious to get started. Time seemed to be hardly moving, and yet each man in that company realized that this might be his last day, or even hour, of life. Standing or sitting in the cold, pre-dawn darkness was a poor way to be spending it, but the sun would be up soon, they knew, and the fog would be burned off, and there might not be many more mountains after this one before the war would end, and then they could go home and spend the rest of their nights in a warm bed beside the soft body of a woman.

Holloway, too, was impatient. He had performed his part in the drama of the attack, and now he had nothing to do but wait. If everything went well, all he would have to do would be to walk up the ridgeline behind his lead platoon until there was no more ridgeline to climb, then call back to Major Dahl that "George Company is on the objective." If anything did show up to oppose his company, he might have to go up to see if he could influence the elimination of the trouble. He hoped—and prayed—that all would go well.

In thinking back over his own order, he could see nothing in it that could have been different, or better. Funny, he thought, that the solution had been so simple, so obvious. What he had ordered had been the only possible approach. When he thought about the problem that Major Dahl had faced in preparing his order, it occurred to him that the battalion commander's order had been the only possible solution. What had been the regimental commander's choices? Blue was cut up from the long night's fighting. There was no place to employ Red, except in relief of Blue, and that would have been risky and time-consuming. It had to be White, and White had been given the mission. Simple, really. Eric supposed that the division commander had been given a slice of the country to take, and he had been faced with similar choices. And so it goes, right on up to the lonely man whose awful responsibility it is to run this war. God be with him!

Back at the command post, the first men from Dolan's platoon were coming up from the valley. Eric returned just as they reached the top of the ridgeline.

"Gipp, lead them over yonder," he directed. He pointed to the cleared area, not far from the mortars, where the platoon was to rest and prepare for the attack.

A few minutes later, Major Dahl and his command group came out of the fog. Dahl was leading. Then came Hamilton, and then Major Dahl's radio operator. In all, about ten people followed Dahl up the path. All of them were tired from the climb, and all but the two leading officers sat down on rocks or bare spots beside the path as soon as Dahl motioned for a halt.

Holloway met them.

"Eric, I hope we get this over with pronto," Dahl said.
"So do I, Major."
"You have your orders out?"
"Yes, sir."
"You'll be ready to go at six, then?"
"Yes, sir. The assault platoon's coming up the ridge now."
"That's fine."
"Lieutenant Jamison's checking the concentrations now. Better keep your ears tucked in—some of the rounds were pretty close yesterday afternoon."

Dahl and Hamilton sat down on the cardboard strips Gregg had provided for the platoon leaders. Holloway was too excited to sit down with them, and his excitement mounted as each additional man came up the path from the valley and turned toward the gathering place. Soon they would all be there, soon it would be six o'clock, soon the attack would be on.

Up ahead of the Third Platoon, artillery rounds crashed into the treetops on the junction knob. Fandango was pounding the First Platoon's objective, trying as hard as he could to soften it up for Dolan.

And time—time was running out for them all, friend and foe, those who would die that day on that mountain, those who would live only to die on another mountain, those who would live on and on and die—where?

Jamison walked up to Holloway a few minutes later.

"I've broken down my radio and I'm ready to go with you."

"Fine. It's almost time to go."

"If you need anything while we're on the way up, just tell me."

"I'll do that."

Holloway went down to the crowded assembly area and found Sergeant Dolan.

"Are you all set, Digger?" he asked.

"Yes, sir. You give us the word, and we're on our way."

"Good. Now, don't let anybody get caught in an ambush

if you can help it. Have your lead people move carefully, and have them check everything that looks like it might give cover to even one man. When you get to the knob, figure it's defended. Make sure your people keep low. And ask for mortar or artillery fire if you want it."

"I will, sir."

"Okay. Let's get this thing over with."

When he returned to the company command post, he waved to Gregg.

"Get the headquarters group ready, Top," he called. "Same people we had yesterday. The rest and Lieutenant Schaefer with the mortars."

Holloway went over to his hole to see about his poncho and his sleeping bag, but they were gone.

"I done had him get it," Gregg said, pointing to a native who was grinning and bowing not far away. "I'll keep my eye on him. He's got mine and Lieutenant Schaefer's, too."

"All right, Top," Eric said, looking at his watch.

Half a minute to go.

Eleven

Digger Dolan saw the company commander's signal. He turned to the soldiers who would be the First Platoon's lead scouts and said, "Now."

The line of men in the First Platoon started to move past the seven or eight men in the battalion command group, and headed on up the ridgeline toward the Third Platoon's line.

As the lead scout passed through the Third Platoon, Eric Holloway looked at his watch: six o'clock on the button.

"George Company's off on time, sir," he told Major Dahl.

"Fine, Eric. Good luck."

Then Holloway gathered his own command group and followed the last of Dolan's squads up the trail. Fandango and his radioman joined them at Fandango's rock, as Eric had come to think of the place.

The company command group had not gone very far past Felty's line when Dolan's men stopped moving. Eric didn't mind that, in a way, for the delay would give Cannon's men a little more time in which to climb the sharp slope to the top of the ridge. Still, the delay might mean that there was trouble up ahead. Everything in combat is a mixed blessing, Holloway thought.

Holloway looked back: Cannon and his messenger were coming up the path. He looked forward: Dolan's men were moving again. Holloway felt more confident now that his company was moving as a unit again, not as a brave but tentative feeler.

A few minutes later, the command group halted again.

Up ahead, Eric could hear Digger's voice ordering his men into a new formation. Eric knew that Dolan hated his guts, but he admired the man for being big enough to forget the feud and pay attention to his men. As for the bitterness he knew Digger felt toward him, Eric supposed that time would work the whole difference out; he was prepared to forget the icy stares, the half-whispered curses, the intentional discourtesies, and perhaps Dolan would get over whatever was eating him.

When he saw what Dolan was trying to do, Holloway motioned for his command group to settle down for awhile. Holloway walked a few yards forward of the rest of the group so that he could get a better look at the platoon's maneuvering.

To his astonishment, Eric saw the junction knob almost directly in front of Dolan's lead squad. And it was not so much of a physical obstacle as he had imagined it would be; in fact, it was hardly defensible.

Five minutes later, Dolan's lead squad was on top, and the men were standing up. They had won the first objective for the day without a fight!

Suddenly it occurred to Eric that this might not be the real junction knob at all, but a false one. He looked to the left to see if Lion was still some distance away, but he could not tell for the fog.

"Top, hold the command group here," he yelled to Gregg, then he ran forward to the place where Digger was setting up an all-around defense of the knob.

"I'm not sure this is the right one, Digger," he said. "What do you think?"

"I don't rightly know, sir. But I'm making sure we've got this much, anyway. I'm gonna send my point squad up to feel out the ground ahead, to make sure."

"All right. I'm going to hold the Second Platoon back until we're sure we know where we are."

Dolan looked behind the company commander: Gregg was coming up the path. Digger walked down to meet Gregg.

"What is this," Dolan asked Gregg, "Grand Central Station?"

"Jus' checkin'," Gregg replied. "I heered you had some alky up here."

Holloway ran on up the finger behind Dolan's probing squad, trying to find some evidence that this was the junction knob.

"Gettin' cautious in his old age, ain't he?" the Digger said.

"You better believe it. And I'm damned glad of it, too." Holloway returned.

"If it isn't the junction knob," he said, "it'll sure as hell do. There are craters all over the place from the artillery's preparation, and I can't see anything on the other side but fog. Digger, you keep what you've got. I'm going to send Lieutenant Cannon's platoon on through you."

"Very well, sir."

Eric ran back to his command group and told Cannon to pick up his attack formation and to pass on through the First Platoon.

Cannon's lead scouts moved out at once, and the rest of the platoon followed in a long single file, with intervals of five or ten yards between men. Their bayonets clanked faintly on the rifles, reminding some of the men of the days long ago when those same bayonets, perhaps, had clanked their way through parades.

Holloway called the battalion commander on the radio and reported that the junction knob had been secured by the First Platoon without a fight, and that Cannon was on the way up to the peak. Next, Holloway called Heath, the commander of Easy Company, and told him that the knob was secure. Heath promised to warn his lead people, and also to hurry on up the ridge.

When Heath and Holloway had finished their conversation, Major Dahl gave Holloway a call.

"I'm moving the battalion command group on up to the knob," he said.

Holloway acknowledged the message, then he turned to Gregg and said, "Let's go."

The command group followed Cannon's platoon out of Dolan's perimeter on the knob, and began what Holloway devoutly hoped would be the last part of the long climb.

Although it was still foggy, enough light had come upon the mountain to allow Holloway a glimpse, now and then, of Cannon's lead scouts. The two soldiers were walking cautiously up the path toward the peak, stopping now and then to throw hand grenades or to probe with their bayonets. The men were working as a team, one covering while the other investigated; they were being extremely careful, and yet they were moving steadily up the ugly ridgeline. Holloway admired their manner of movement tremendously, for he saw in it the right mixture of prudence and aggressiveness, the kind of mixture that wins objectives with minimum casualties.

The rest of the lead squad followed the two scouts in rather loose and spread-out formation, for the nose was broad and the tree cover was sparse. Lieutenant Cannon and his radio operator were pretty far forward, moving within the lead squad. Cannon's radioman was really a rifleman, for none of the company's platoon radios was working. Behind the lead squad there was another rifle squad, and then the Fifty-Seven squad. In all, Cannon's attacking force numbered about forty men.

Cannon can do a lot with that number, Holloway thought as he watched the platoon climb. He might have to.

The company moved steadily up the ridgeline, feeling more alive with each added foot of altitude, each appreciable increase in warmth and light. No schedule had been set for the attack, but all of the men sensed the fact that they were doing far better than anyone had expected.

If things could only stay this way, Eric wished. I'd give anything for a walk-in! And yet, he knew, a walk-in on a mountain such as the Octopus was extremely unlikely. He had noticed in his brief airplane ride that the Octopus dominated the area for miles around, especially to the north. He remembered a wide river up there, a river that someone would have to wade, someday soon. If the enemy lost the Octopus, he would have to pull back across that river; and so, Holloway realized, any enemy commander would be a fool to give away so valuable a piece of real-estate. The seizure of the peak would be no walk-in.

Up ahead, the scouts were moving more cautiously than ever, now. They had come within the range of the machine guns and rifles that the enemy was almost sure to have around the peak, and the scouts were taking advantage of every bit of cover they could find. Eric could see Cannon moving among the men, directing them, and he was glad to see that Cannon was not forcing his men to expose themselves needlessly.

Holloway decided to set up a temporary command-observation post on a small knob that overlooked the part of the finger that led to the peak.

"Better get set up," he said to Jamison. "Cannon might want some goodies dropped on the top before he goes up."

"All right. Might be some good classical music on, anyway."

Fandango and his radio operator assembled the set, then checked into the net.

"Artillery's open for business," he said.

"Fine, thank you," Eric replied.

Holloway sat on the path, watching Cannon's scouts through his fieldglasses. The fog had lifted, but the sky was cloudy, and the day would never be very warm. Holloway estimated the distance the lead man had to go at two hundred and fifty yards, but the last fifty would be almost straight up the face of a cliff. The cliff was something new: it wasn't represented on the map, and he hadn't noticed it the day before. The enemy might have trouble firing at people just at the base of the cliff, but in that case hand grenades could be dropped, and that could be mean. It might be necessary to send people around both sides of the cliff, if the hand grenade problem became too great. Or, again, it might be a walk-in, at that. The enemy might be putting too much faith in the ruggedness of the cliff.

The two scouts made it to the base of the cliff, but no one else did. Machine gun fire and all hell itself opened up on the rest of the platoon as the men crossed the last patch of open ground short of the base.

Eric saw several of Cannon's men go down, but as he watched, other men crawled out and got them and pulled them clear of danger. Soon all of the platoon was behind some sort of cover, but Eric saw to his horror that the two lead men were cut off, taking cover at the base of the cliff.

2

"You ready for some goodies now?" Jamison asked.

"No, I don't think so. I've got two people right up under the damned cliff, and that complicates hell out of this thing."

"Can't you get them back up?"

"I'll sure try, but if I can't, we've got trouble. I don't want to cream them, much as I'd appreciate artillery support."

"I can shoot better than that."

"I know it—I'm sorry—but if they think we don't care, they might be better off dead. Let me see what I can do to get them out, first."

"All right."

"If I don't have any luck, I may ask you to plaster the flanks of the cliff. Or something 'way on top. You might get ready for that."

Holloway called a messenger over.

"Go tell Lieutenant Cannon to concentrate on getting those two scouts back out of there. Then I want him to pull his platoon back. Understand?"

"Yessir."

"Go."

"Eric, we may find this shooting thing pretty tough, at that," Fandango said.

"Why?"

"The map's wrong. Doesn't even show the cliff. The first round may land anywhere. I can adjust from it, but by then the damage may have been done."

"Oh, hell."

Eric looked back at the two men under the cliff, and realized how tragically limited he really was: commander? well, command, then, if you can.

"We'll wait on Cannon as long as we can," he said. "In the meantime, I'd better go see if there's any other way to take care of this."

Holloway turned to Gregg.

"Top, stall battalion if they get uneasy."

Then Holloway walked down the path toward his Second Platoon.

Battalion was getting uneasy, but both Major Dahl and Captain Hamilton had resolved to wait for Holloway to call them. Regiment had insisted on progress reports every half-hour, and so far they had been delighted with what had been reported. But division operations was riding regiment, and presumably, someone else was riding division, and so on, all the way back to Washington.

Holloway passed through the rear squads of the Second Platoon on his way to find Cannon. When he saw his messenger standing behind a large rock talking to another soldier, Holloway called him over.

"Did you find Lieutenant Cannon?" he asked.

"No, sir."

"Why the hell not?"

"Sir, he's up there," the messenger replied, pointing to the base of the cliff.

"You mean he's one of—"

"Yessir."

"Oh, no!"

Eric felt as though he had been kicked by a mule.

"Why did he do that?" he asked of no one in particular. "What made him do that?"

Then Holloway realized that he himself had done almost exactly the same thing one day, and he had a bullet hole in his leg to show for it. Riding up in front is a temptation that few platoon leaders can resist, he remembered, but that doesn't make it right, nor does it bring the mountain any closer to being captured.

"You wait here," he said to the messenger, then he told the other soldier to find the platoon sergeant and bring him forward. Holloway started forward again.

A minute later he was as far forward as he could get, out of breath and uncomfortably crouching behind a large tree-trunk about fifty yards from the base of the cliff where Cannon and the scout were. Holloway had passed the bodies of two badly wounded men. He did not want to lose any more.

He called over to Cannon: "Can you get back over here?"

"Hell no," Cannon replied. "Every time they catch us moving, they cut loose. I think they're moving, too! Watch yourself!"

"Where are they?"

"Mostly on the left. They've got a machine gun there. In a bunker, I think."

Fifty-Seven, Eric thought.

The platoon sergeant crawled up behind Holloway. It was Sergeant Graves—not a top-flight non-com, but he'd have to do.

"Graves, you're in command of the platoon until Lieutenant Cannon's out of there."

"Very well, sir."

"He says a bunker's bothering him from over on the left. It sounds like a job for the Fifty-Seven. Have the squad leader get that thing up here."

A burst of machine gun fire cracked over their heads. The thumps confirmed the location of the enemy bunker.

"Hurry!"

Holloway looked around him, seeking a good firing position for the recoilless rifle. He figured that a machine gun would help keep the enemy in the bunker quiet while the gunner got ready, so he selected a place for the platoon's machine gun, too. A squad could assault the bunker while the Fifty-Seven and the machine gun were keeping it covered, he thought. And that might do it.

God, he prayed, let me be right. Keep me from making a mess of this—this has got to be right!

Within a minute, Graves and the Fifty-Seven squad leader were on the ground beside him. Holloway explained his plan to them, then they crawled away to get the weapons in place.

Holloway called over to Cannon: "Something's about to happen. When you can, get back over here. Run for it."

"We'll try, but it's a hell of a base to have to steal."

"Is there any place else that's bothering you?"

"There may be another one about half-way up—same side."

"All right. We'll cover it, too. Keep your head down."

"Roger."

Graves returned.

"We're ready to try it, sir. Thornton's squad will assault the damned thing if the Fifty-Seven doesn't get it."

"All right, Sergeant. Lieutenant Cannon says there might be some more of them about half-way up the cliff, up there somewhere."

"Right, sir."

"Better put an automatic rifle on that whole area."

"Want us to start shooting now?"

"Yes. Let's get those people out of there."

"Fire!" Graves yelled.

The Fifty-Seven's backblast rocked Holloway, and the noise from the machine gun and the automatic rifles deafened him.

Holloway crawled out in front of the tree to see if the bunker was knocked out, but he could see nothing. He didn't dare stand.

He heard Graves' voice: "I think we got 'em!"

"One more round," the gunner answered.

Once again the gun fired.

Holloway looked up again. This time he could see a great deal of smoke coming from the place where the round had hit.

"Try a smoke round, or white phosphorus," Holloway yelled.

"We ain't got any, sir," someone answered.

"One more round, then get Thornton's people going."

Once more the recoilless rifle punched at the bunker.

"Now!" Holloway called to Cannon. "Come now!"

Thornton's squad was pouring rifle fire into the blasted bunker.

"Run, dammit!"

Cannon and the scout ran out from the base of the cliff, heading straight for Holloway. Two grenades dropped just behind them; one exploded before it hit the ground. The scout made it to Holloway's tree, his back full of fragments. Cannon was stretched on the ground, in the open, not halfway from the cliff.

Hands reached out and grabbed the screaming scout and pulled him down the path.

Holloway looked back at Cannon's body and wondered what to do. As he watched, another hand grenade dropped and bounced right beside Cannon's head, coming to a stop about a foot in front of his face.

Cannon opened his eyes, looked at the thing, then reached out to grab it. He clutched it and threw it as far away from him as he could. The grenade exploded as it hit the ground near the base of the cliff.

Cannon crawled, painfully, slowly, back toward the shelter of the cliff, as though he despaired of ever getting back to his platoon again alive. Rifle shots pinged all around him.

Holloway watched, horrified, as the wounded lieutenant winced from nicks in his neck and in his hip, but somehow

Cannon made it back to the relatively safe place from which he and the scout had started.

Cannon slumped, unconscious, or dead.

Holloway called to him, but Cannon gave no sign of having heard.

"Cannon! Cannon—"

I am so sorry, Lord! he thought.

3

Holloway looked over to see how Thornton's squad was getting along, hoping that some of them might work their way under the cliff by hooking around to the left. But he couldn't see Thornton's men: they were all down, seeking cover from sniper fire.

One of the men crawled by Holloway, almost in a panic.

"What's going on?" Holloway asked.

"They got us trapped!"

"Sergeant Graves!" Holloway shouted. "Get over here!"

"What is it, sir?"

"Listen. You've got to get that squad of Thornton's back out of there, and do something to kick the panic out of 'em. Then I want you to back your people up—all the way back."

"What about the Lieutenant, sir?"

Suddenly the clock stopped: the question hung in the air, screaming for an answer. Eric realized that it was a choice between Cannon and getting the Octopus, one man's life versus the safety of the whole company. But it wasn't a black-and-white choice, and maybe—maybe there was a way out, yet.

I could go in and get him myself, Holloway thought. Graves could have the platoon fire while I'm up and running, and it might just work. But he remembered Captain Webb's gallant, foolish gesture.

What should I do? he asked himself. It made him angry and ashamed to concede, I don't know.

"Sir, are we gonna leave th' Lieutenant?"

Holloway turned and looked at the cliff, trying frantically to think of an answer other than "yes." Is there any other way? he wondered. I've tried to knock out the bunker, but that didn't work. I've tried to move people around to the left, but that didn't work. Cannon tried to run for it, but he couldn't make it. So just what the hell do I do now? I go get him myself.

"Graves, have the platoon—" he began, but the words died on his lips. "Have the platoon back up. We can't do any more for him here."

Holloway got up and ran back toward his command group, completely whipped. As he ran he heard sniper fire cutting the air around him, but he kept moving. He ran as fast as his bad leg would let him, realizing that artillery had to be put on that cliff at once, even if the platoon wasn't completely clear.

"Cannon's at the bottom of the cliff," he gasped as he reached the command group. "He's badly wounded, dead, maybe. Fandango, we've got to shoot anyway."

Jamison nodded.

"Fire mission!" Fandango cried into the microphone.

Gipp ran up.

"Battalion commander wants to talk to you, sir."

Holloway took the handset from Gipp's hand.

"This is George Six, over."

"This is Gasoline Six. What's going on up there? Over."

"George Six."

Eric paused, thinking: I've botched things up, as usual. I couldn't do anything right when I was at battalion, and I'm killing my own company up here now. For God's sake, relieve me and get it over with.

"We're held up by some enemy around the cliff, just short

of the peak. We just roughed up a bunker at the base, and I'm putting artillery fire on top right now. Over."

"This is Gasoline Six. Well, they're putting all kinds of pressure on me to get going, Eric. I hate to say this, but you're going to have to forget about casualties and get going. Division is taking this thing out of our hands. But that's the order. Over."

Eric wondered if he should tell Dahl about Cannon, but he felt that it would only add to Dahl's misery, and it wouldn't help Cannon. This is something I'll have to keep on my own conscience, Eric thought. Division can't take the responsibility for this. Or anything. It's all mine.

"This is George Six. Pray for us, Major. Out."

Holloway sat down in the snow. There were tears in his eyes.

He heard a swish-swish-swish as the first round went by overhead, then the sharp *crunch*.

4

The round was well up on top.

"This is Fandango Five-Seven. Right, five. One gun. One round. Over."

"Fandango Five-Seven, this is Seven," the radio called back. "Right, five. One gun, one round." There was a pause, then, "On the way, over."

"Five-Seven. On the way, wait."

Again, the round was on top.

Jamison walked a series of rounds closer and closer to the near edge of the cliff, then he started moving the rounds along the edge, working gently, carefully, with extreme precision, from right to left.

When about twenty single rounds had been put on the top edge, Steve Jamison turned to Holloway.

"Are you sure you want to go on with this?" he asked.

He doesn't know what Dahl said, Holloway thought.

"I don't know how much longer I can hold these things up there."

Eric felt terribly alone, and he was afraid. It was almost as though he were standing at the exact center of a gigantic turntable, or perhaps even the world, for everything seemed to be spinning about him while he and time stood stone still. He knew he would have to answer Jamison, but what could he say? Only yes or no, but which? and why?

He turned and looked at the cliff, groping for the strength to make up his mind. He saw the ugly peak, the rock face, the craters the rounds had dug in the snow. The mountain was the objective, the goal, the mission: it had to be secured. Now. There was no getting around the fact. The Octopus had to be taken. And the enemy had decided that the Octopus had to be held. Now the dispute would have to be bled out. But he could duck the whole problem by quitting, by telling Alex Schaefer to take over; he could dodge the decision, but he knew he could never really escape. He knew that as long as he lived, he would never erase the image of that cliff from his conscience. I brought this company here: I tried like hell to keep this from happening this way, but it's my mountain to get—

The speed of the spinning around him increased. Holloway felt weak, as though he were about to faint. There was so much to think about, so much to weigh—life, family, hope for the future, all that Cannon is and lives to be; the rest of the men, Dahl, division—so much, so much! But time was beginning again.

"Keep shooting. I'm going to start Felty in under the artillery."

Holloway was sick at heart, now that the spinning had stopped. Instead of the peace he had formerly known after having made a hard decision, he felt only anxiety. This can only get worse, he thought. I've got to get out from under this hellish responsibility!

"On the way, wait," he heard Fandango call back to the F. D. C.

"Top, get Felty up here," Holloway yelled to Gregg.

Holloway watched the cliff, holding his breath as the round slid by overhead. Then he saw the gray cloud, still a safe distance away from Cannon.

Felty arrived.

"Look. We have got to get that mountain. I want your platoon to move out right now. Go in under the artillery. You have a flare?"

"Yes, sir. Red star cluster."

"Fire it when you want the artillery turned off."

Gipp interrupted the officers, thrusting the handset at Holloway.

"Major Dahl again, sir."

"This is George Six."

"Eric, I know you're trying a precision adjustment, and I know why. But you've got to get going. Are you moving? Over."

Eric heard the *pop* over Jamison's radio that meant another round was coming, and Fandango's "On the way, wait."

"Steve, this is the last one," Holloway said, unable to stand the strain of the risk any longer.

Holloway pressed the sending switch on his radio and answered the battalion commander: "This is George Six. Felty's going right now. I'm—"

Then, to his horror, he saw the round explode at the base of the cliff.

"We're going. Out."

Holloway dropped the handset in the snow.

"Cease firing—" Fandango began, but Eric stopped him.

"No, Steve, no! Cream the place. Fire for effect!"

Then Holloway turned to Felty: "Go, and don't forget about the flare!"

Jamison called back the order to demolish the cliff. A minute later, the whole mountain top erupted as round after round slammed into it. The artillery fire was vicious, bitter, punishing, and on the small knob that was George Company's command-observation post, Eric Holloway cried "More, Steve, more!" in a new, strange voice.

Felty's men looked at the agonized face of their company commander as they passed, saw the tears streaming down his dirty face, and walked on just a bit faster to capture the punished mountain.

Twelve

Holloway and Jamison remained on the knob, watching for Felty's signal. They couldn't tell if Felty was having to slug it out with rifle and machine gun fire, for the rumble and crashing of the artillery bombardment deafened everyone within miles of the Octopus.

Finally, the red star cluster rose above the thick gray smoke cloud, arching over the valley toward the Third Battalion.

"Fandango Seven, this is Five-Seven. Cease firing. Cease firing, end of mission. Out."

The last volleys crunched into the torn peak, and an eerie silence descended over the Octopus. Gradually, the cloud floated away, and within five minutes Holloway saw Felty waving to him from the top.

The Octopus was captured.

Holloway took the handset from Gipp and called the battalion commander.

"Gasoline Six, this is George Six. George Three is on top. The peak is secure. I am taking the rest of my people up there now. Over."

"This is Gasoline Six. Good work, Eric. Move on up there as fast as you can. We'll be right behind you. Out."

Eric Holloway looked at the snow-covered ground for a moment, then he stood up.

"Get the command group ready to go, Top. Jamison, you can break down your radio now, too."

Holloway noticed Schaefer standing nearby.

"Are the mortars with us?" he asked.

"Yes, sir. So's Digger's platoon."

"All right. Have the mortars follow Graves, and have Digger bring up the rear."

Everyone in the command group could tell from the terse, flat tone in Holloway's voice that he had taken a terrific beating.

"We'll be right behind you," Schaefer said. "Lead the way."

When the command group reached the base of the cliff, Holloway noticed that the medic from Felty's platoon had pulled Cannon's body out of the rubble. Holloway and Jamison stopped for a moment and looked at Cannon, and then they went on up the trail.

Enemy bodies were scattered all along the edge of the cliff, men who had been killed in their firing positions, men who had been killed while trying to run out of the savage bombardment.

Holloway turned and looked down to the tree from which he had directed the assault on the bunker, and to his horror he saw that it would have been possible for any enemy soldier to have killed him simply by dropping rocks over the side. He wondered why he had been spared—but he knew he would never really find the answer.

When the command group reached the top, Holloway put George Company into a perimeter defense and had Jamison register defensive fires on the finger that ran northward from the peak for a few hundred yards. Behind him, Holloway saw the Third Battalion coming up Rhino—the ridgeline they bled themselves out on, but could not win.

Major Dahl brought his command group into Eric's defense perimeter a few minutes later. Easy and Fox Companies followed him, and went into position on the ridgeline George Company had won.

"God bless you, Eric!" Dahl said when he found Holloway. "You got it! Sam Mann would be mighty proud of you."

Eric nodded, but he couldn't speak.

"I'm glad Cannon's alive. I've sent for a helicopter to pick him up."

"Alive?"

"Yes—barely. Didn't you know?"

"No, no I didn't."

"Helicopter's on the way, sir," the battalion commander's radio operator said. "They want us to put out an air panel to mark this place."

"Sergeant Gregg!" Holloway called. "Get an air panel out."

"Right, sir!"

Almost immediately, a messenger spread the yellow and orange strips on the snow.

Some soldiers brought Cannon to the top of the cliff, and Holloway and Jamison walked over to see if the platoon leader had regained consciousness. He had not.

"I wish I could tell him how sorry I am," Jamison said.

Eric wanted to thank God, but even those words were blocked.

When the helicopter landed, the division commander got out. Major Dahl went over to report as soon as the blades stopped whirling.

"Damn," Holloway said. "That isn't the medics' helicopter."

The General walked over and looked at Cannon.

"Put him in and take him back to the hospital," the General said to the pilot. "Don't worry about me—I'll hitch a ride back."

The General looked at Holloway.

"You the man that took this thing?"

"No, sir. My company took it."

"That's an unorthodox way to report."

Holloway was on the point of saying "So what?" when the General spoke again.

"Your company did a damned fine job. You ought to be proud of them."

206

"I am, sir."

After the General left, Holloway and Jamison sat down on the rim of a crater. Hamilton joined them a few minutes later.

"Well, they got him," Hamilton said.

"What?"

"They got Dahl. He's relieved."

"You taking the battalion?" Fandango asked.

"No, they got me, too. They're sending both of us home, which is fine—but they aren't talking about the reason."

"How soon?" Holloway asked, still dazed by the news.

"Today. Red will relieve the battalion up here, and you'll go into reserve for a while."

"What happened?" Holloway asked. But he thought he knew.

"Division got panicked. Started screaming for us to get going. Dahl told the division operations officer—Merlin's his name—to come take over, if he thought he could do any better. The bastard squealed, and the General took Dahl up on it. Major Merlin is your new battalion commander."

"Merlin?" Holloway asked, remembering the rude, nervous little man at division headquarters.

"Yes."

"We're all dead. You and Dahl are lucky."

"You know the guy?"

"No, but I've seen him."

"You should have heard Dahl talking to him on the radio. Merlin was out of line, ordering Dahl to get going. Hell, he was going around Colonel Hobbs and the General. But that doesn't seem to matter. Dahl said, 'The kindest thing I can think about a rear-echelon son of a bitch like you is that you just don't understand what's going on up here.' I don't know what Merlin said to that, but Dahl—"

"It's my fault," Holloway said.

"What do you mean?"

"Dahl's getting creamed because I was too cautious. He's

taking the beating I've got coming. Every damned thing I touch, I ruin."

"He'd have done exactly the same thing you did, if he'd been you. He's proud of you, Holloway. He'd have let you get Cannon out, if he could have, but division had already started this thing by the time you moved out from the junction knob. It would have happened even if you'd had a walk-in. Something's rotten in this division, and its name is Merlin."

"Dahl told me the thing was out of his hands, but I didn't understand."

"He knew you didn't, and he couldn't explain. He's sorry as you are about Cannon."

But Holloway knew that no man could be.

2

Two hours later, in the afternoon, Major Merlin reached the top of the Octopus. He was met by Major Dahl and escorted by him on a short tour around the battalion perimeter.

When the two majors reached George Company's command post, Holloway walked over to meet them.

"Don't you salute, Lieutenant?" Merlin asked him.

Holloway looked at Major Dahl: Dahl's eyes seemed to say, "do it." Holloway saluted.

"George Company. Lieutenant Holloway commanding, sir."

Merlin did not return the salute.

"That's better," he snapped.

The new battalion commander looked around at the men of George Company, captors of the Octopus, worn out from the strain of being shot at.

"I've already assumed command of this battalion, Lieutenant. And I want your men to get their steel helmets on right away. That is, if they haven't thrown them away."

Holloway looked at Dahl again but instead of assurance

he saw something not entirely new, but extremely acute: pain. Then Holloway's gaze ran around the perimeter, taking in the whole company; some of the men were wearing their steel helmets, but a few were sitting on theirs, or using their helmets as props to keep their rifles out of the snow. Others had found that they could not dig with any degree of gusto with the heavy, awkward steels bobbing about on their heads, and had set their helmets on the ground.

Eric looked back at Major Merlin.

"Very well, sir," he said.

Holloway walked over to Sergeant Gregg.

"Top. Pass the word. The steels stay on. All of them, all the time."

"What?"

Gregg was astonished. Holloway knew he had not seen, much less met the new battalion commander.

"Steels. They stay on. Pass the word. Now."

"Sir—"

"Sergeant, dammit, do as you're told."

I'll be damned, Eric thought, if I'll apologize. Gregg'll understand sooner or later.

"Move."

"All right, sir."

Gregg moved away, muttering to himself.

Major Dahl led the new battalion commander away before Eric returned. Eric was grateful for that.

Holloway returned to the crater and sat down beside Steve Jamison.

"Did you see that?" Holloway asked.

"I did, and I'm sorry I did."

"God."

"I feel sorry as hell for you. But did you notice the beating this thing's given Dahl?"

"Yes, that is pitiful. Having to take that bastard Merlin around is too much."

"Dahl's a hell of a hard man to follow," the artilleryman said. "That alone would make Merlin seem chicken."

"One of my braves is likely to put a speedy end to his career."

"Self-defense."

"Maybe. You can take the man out of the rear-echelon, but you can't take the rear-echelon out of the man."

"Holloway, that's downright corny."

"I'm afraid it's also true."

First Sergeant Gregg came up and saluted with grave formality.

"Sir," he intoned, "the First Sergeant reports to the Company Commander that the steels—are—on."

"Thank you, Sergeant," Eric replied in an equally solemn voice, returning the salute.

Gregg did a snappy about-face and marched off, counting cadence as he went.

"He has the general idea," Jamison said.

"I think he has. The others worry me, though. I hope they catch on as quickly, but I can't expect them to."

"You have got a problem—something we artillerymen never really run into. You're damned if you pass chicken orders along, and you're damned if you don't. We're lucky. All we have to do is shoot."

"That's plenty for any man's conscience to carry."

"What are you going to do about this Merlin?"

"Obey him."

"Even if he's wrong?"

"I hope it won't come to that."

"Do you honestly think it won't?"

"I don't know, I don't know."

A few minutes later, a line of men came into sight: it was the First Battalion, and the relief was on. Eric wanted to whoop for joy, but he was too exhausted. He watched the men come toward him until his eyes filled with tears, and then he got up and walked out to meet the lead company commander.

"I'm glad to see you," he said, extending his hand.

The Able Company commander shook his hand, obviously a bit perplexed.

"You got the battle-rattles from bein' up here in these high altitudes, or somethin'?"

Eric laughed.

"If you do, I reckon we'd better go back down where we come from."

"Come on," Holloway said, "and I'll show you where we've gone in."

Eric led the new company commander all the way around his perimeter, pointing out the locations he had picked out for his machine guns and the Fifty-Seven.

"I'll leave all of our phone wire in, and we'll leave you all of the ammo we've got left."

"Thanks. You think we'll be needin' it?"

"Can't say. They raised hell with Blue all night, and they had to be blasted off this thing. We haven't seen anything of them since we've been up here, but then we've stayed put. Blue's clearing that finger that runs east to the saddle, but nothing's been done about that finger out in front."

"I'd say thanks, but I reckon you understand. I'd just as soon be home as here."

"I can understand that."

3

A half hour or so later, the relief was completed, and Holloway led his weary but elated men down from the mountain they had won. His orders were to go into a temporary assembly area at the base of the Octopus, then to join the rest of the Second Battalion for the march back to the area in which they would spend the next few days as the regiment's reserve.

The men moved down the slick path quickly, laughing and joking and generally letting off the pressure of combat. Soon they reached the bottom, and the first sergeant directed them into platoon areas in a large, open field.

Holloway and Jamison walked across the field, through the men, to the road. Jamison's jeep was waiting for him at the road, and he climbed in, dead tired.

"Well," he said, "I'll see you later. I've got to go back to the battery until you people rest up."

Eric wanted to thank him, but he felt rather awkward about his feeling.

"Come back before you have to, if you can," Eric said, scraping the mud off the edges of his bootsoles on the jeep's front tire.

"I'm scared you people would make me keep my steel on."

Jamison, too, wanted to say more than he was able to.

"See you," he said, and then to the driver, "Let's go."

After Fandango had gone, Eric Holloway walked around the field alone, speaking to the men, stopping now and then to ask or answer a question. They were all muddy and dirty, and there was at least four days' growth of beard on every face, and they were all completely worn out. Still, they were laughing and talking in loud, confident voices, as though nothing had happened, as though they were on their way home instead of to another muddy field where they would exist until another mountain needed to be taken. They were as happy and as contented as they could be—just to be alive, just to realize that the danger was past, just to know that they would not be shot at for a while.

Major Dahl walked into the company's field and found Eric. Dahl was alone, and curiously, he looked as though he had lost twenty or thirty pounds.

"I'm on my way out, Eric," Dahl said. "I don't guess I'll be seeing you again for a while."

"I'm sorry—we're all sorry, sir."

A grin came over Dahl's pale face.

"Sorry to see me leave standing up?"

"No—"

"I know, I was just kidding, or trying to. But Eric, what happens to us isn't the point around here. I think you've learned that in the past few days. These men are important.

I think you've learned that, too—I needn't have said it. You've got to help Major Merlin along. Not for your sake or my sake or his sake, but—you know why."

"Yes, sir."

"Merlin will find it pretty different up here from life at division hindquarters, so you help him get adjusted."

"I'll try, sir."

"I said do it, Eric."

"Yes, sir."

"He won't understand for a long time. New people, and other people, sometimes, have to learn just as you and I had to learn—the hard way. Unless somebody teaches them, and that's a pretty hard thing to teach. But you be patient with him, and he'll be all right in the long run."

"I'd hate to be in his shoes."

"Well, you may be, sooner than you think. Good-bye, Eric. Take good care of this fine company."

"I'll do that, sir."

"God bless you."

Dahl got into his jeep and nodded to the driver.

Eric Holloway saluted.

As he watched the jeep drive away, Eric felt a real loss. He knew he ought to be grateful that Major Dahl had lived, and that he had been with the battalion for as long as he had, but the sense of loss was foremost in his thoughts. We won't see his like again, he thought.

Gregg walked up.

"What'll we do tomorrow, sir?" he asked. "Polish our mess kits?"

"Probably."

Gregg saw that his company commander was not in a mood to appreciate that kind of humor.

"Oh. Uh, anything out on the move yet?"

"No. Tell you what I want, though. While we're back there I want these people left alone. I want them to get some sleep—all they want. Then I want them to get cleaned up. If they want to write letters, you see that they've got all the paper and envelopes they need. If they want a church service, either get hold of a chaplain or prepare to become one. You might tell the platoon sergeants to let these people alone, too. Understand?"

Gregg nodded.

"I done sent Sergeant Wood back to help Lieutenant Schaefer get things set up. I told him not to put us anywhere near battalion."

"That's good, Top. We'll want to get into some rear-echelon unit's showers, if we can, tomorrow. You might send a scouting party out this afternoon to see what's back there these days."

"Very well, sir. Last time I was in one of them places I got chased out nekkid as a jaybird. Some quartermaster bastard said they was reserved for 'service troops only' and run me out."

"What'd you do?"

"Nothin' much. Just picked up a tire tool and took after him."

Eric laughed.

"This time better take a squad with you."

"Damn' if I won't, sir. I wouldn't have minded if he'd said 'officers only.' Hell, that's easy fixed. But 'service troops'—"

"Well, you've got some enemy rifles and stuff for trading material, haven't you?"

"Sure."

"See what you can do, then. I want these people to have showers and clean clothes, if they can be had this side of the beach."

"Them captured rifles ought to do it, if nothin' else does. I heered some of them rifles was bringin' fifty dollars and more apiece back at division."

"Showers, Top."

"Yessir."

There was a commotion up the road from the place where the two men stood talking.

214

"What the devil is this comin'?" Gregg asked. "Looks like the angel Gabriel hisself."

It was a motorcade, led by a jeep from the heavy weapons company. The lead jeep's windshield was down, and a heavy machine gun was mounted at the right end of the dashboard. In the second jeep, a light machine gun had been mounted in the pedestal which was intended to support a fifty-caliber machine gun. A man stood up in the jeep's bed, beside the gun, one hand on the grip, the other steadying his dignity.

Major Merlin sat in the front seat of the second jeep, a light blue scarf around his neck and a prominent gold major's leaf glittering on the front of his helmet.

Another machine gun-equipped jeep followed the new battalion commander.

The procession stopped in the road beside George Company's field.

Most of the men stopped talking and stood up to look at the glorious sight. If they had not been so tired, so very tired, they probably would have laughed.

Eric Holloway went over to the battalion commander's jeep and reported to Merlin.

"Lieutenant Holloway!" Major Merlin roared. "Your company area is a disgrace to the battalion. Your men should be at least five yards apart, not bunched up like they were at a Sunday School tea-sipping convention. Have them get properly dispersed. Do you understand?"

"Very well, sir."

Actually, Eric did not understand. What is this man afraid of? he wondered. Artillery? an airstrike? Could such things happen—? Yes, they could. They could. But—

The battalion commander continued.

"Lieutenant, you are to move your company—as soon as you have dispersed them—you are to move your company down this road to the battalion training area. It's at a mountain called the Shark. Captain Lester will meet you there, and he will show you where to put your company. Vigorous training will get underway first thing in the morning. Captain Lester will have the training schedule ready for you when you get there. However, you can figure on having reveille formation at six o'clock."

"Very well, sir."

"Move on, driver."

The impressive motorcade moved on down the road toward the rear echelon.

"I will be damned!" Eric said through clenched teeth.

"Sir, did I hear right?" Gregg asked.

"I'm afraid so, Top. Can you beat that?"

"No sir, I sure can't."

"Sergeant Gregg. I've only been a company commander for one full day, and I'll freely admit that you've forgotten more about this army than I'll ever know. But—"

"No, sir. I haven't seen anything as chicken as this since I got busted the third—no, 'twas the fourth time. I'm sorry for you, sir, 'cause I'm going home. I'm an old man, and I can hear those boat whistles down at the beach right now. They go 'Tooo-t Toooo-t.'"

"Will you get the company on the road for me before you go?"

"Yessir. What about the dispersal?"

"Get the company on the road."

"Yessir. 'Toooo-t Tooo-t.'"

Gregg walked a few paces into the field, planted his ten-and-a-half double-E boots on the spot squarely in front of the place he wanted the company to form, rocked his head back, and shouted:

"George Com-pin-nay, *fall in!*"

The bedraggled figures in muddy uniforms got stiffly to their feet and shuffled awkwardly toward their places in the formation. It had been so long since the last time they had formed up, many of them had forgotten where they were supposed to stand. It took several minutes for them to get organized, and even then it was one hell of a formation.

Each squad leader counted heads, then rendered a report

to the platoon sergeant. Then, when Sergeant Gregg ordered "Ree-port!" each platoon sergeant saluted Gregg and reported.

"First Platoon, one man killed, one man wounded."
"Second Platoon, five men wounded."
"Third platoon, three men wounded."
"Headquarters, one man dead, six men wounded."
"Weapons Platoon, no casualties."

The first sergeant gave "Post!"

The platoon sergeants moved to the rear of their platoons, and the platoon leaders replaced them in front of each platoon.

First Sergeant Gregg about-faced and saluted the company commander.

"Sir, the company is formed."

Lieutenant Holloway returned the salute.

"Post!"

Sergeant Gregg saluted and marched away.

"Rest!" Holloway shouted.

His gaze swept the company from the First Platoon on his left to the Weapons Platoon on his extreme right. So many were gone! Sergeant Hicks, dead. The Mouse, wounded. Lieutenant Cannon, horribly wounded, possibly dead by now. Captain Mann, wounded. Frost, dead. The man from his home town, wounded and gone. Two and fifteen—the price of one mountain to one company.

Good Lord, remember the price they had to pay, Eric said to himself.

"Turn and look back up there," he said to the company. "Look at that mountain. Turn and get a good look at it. *You* captured it. Nobody else could. But *you* captured it. Remember it."

Holloway paused while the men looked back at the ugly peak.

"Com-pan-nay, Ah-ten-*shun*. Right *face!*"

The company popped-to and executed the command.

"Sling arms."

217

The men slipped their right arms through the slings of their rifles. Those who were carrying the mortars and the other heavy weapons arranged their loads for the march.

"Column of twos from the right. Forward, *march*."

The column of twos moved out, following Holloway and Gipp. Soon George Company was on the road, stretched out for nearly a quarter of a mile, walking wearily away from the Octopus.

4

When the company passed the place south of the Shark where the artillery rounds had shredded the battalion operations tent a few nights before, Schaefer joined Holloway at the head of the column.

"You made pretty good time," Schaefer said.

"Just like basic training," Holloway replied.

"Have you seen the training schedule these people have put out?"

"No, but I'll bet it's enough to rot your socks."

"It sure is. But we've got a hot meal waiting, in spite of them."

"What do you mean, 'in spite of them'?"

"They put out the word that C-rations would be it for tonight. We went back and borrowed some groceries from a Q. M. outfit, and I've got the kitchen set up. I've got a tent set up for a command post, too."

"Fine. But how come they didn't get hot chow for the rest of the battalion?"

"They had it, but the battalion commander had 'em send it all back to the rear echelon. Made 'em get C's, instead."

"The hell he did!"

"He sure did. Wait'll you see where he put the company, too."

"Where?"

"On the ridgeline. Not quite where we started from, but almost."

"Oh, no!"

"That's the new S3's idea of what a rest area's supposed to be."

"He's mad."

"That's not all. Company commanders are to meet at battalion as soon as you get in. More goodies will be passed out then, I suppose."

"I think I'll shoot myself in the foot."

While the company was moving past the new pontoon bridge, where traffic was heavy, Holloway became quite irritated with several rear-echelon jeep drivers who drove between the columns of the company at dangerous speeds. Each time, Holloway stopped the jeeps by standing squarely in their path; then he gave each driver a tail-chewing that was not likely to be forgotten soon.

The sight of the company's destination was the most cruel blow of all. The Shark's lower jaw, from the western tip to a point about half-way to the Shark's top, was to be the company's "training area."

A stocky, blond captain was waiting for Holloway. Schaefer introduced Holloway to the officer.

"This is Captain Lester. He's the new S3."

Eric nodded.

"Lieutenant, you're to put your people in tactical positions. I've already indicated your portion of the line to your executive officer. You may have him put the company in."

"Sir, I'll admit I'm a little stupid, but just why the hell are you people doing this to these men? Don't you realize—"

"Holloway! That's enough!"

Lester looked as though Holloway had blasphemed.

"All right, Captain. I'll take this up with the battalion commander. I just want you to know that I protest this, officially. I think it's about the worst—"

"Lieutenant Holloway, these are Major Merlin's orders. They will be carried out."

Lester left hurriedly.

"Shall we register our mortars that-a-way?" Schaefer asked, jerking his thumb in the direction of battalion.

"Absolutely."

A few minutes after Lester had gone, Eric and Schaefer sat down on a crate of potatoes inside the kitchen tent and had a cup of coffee. Outside the tent the men were going through the chow line, getting their first hot meal in days.

"You wanna eat now, sir?" the first cook asked Holloway.

"No, thanks. I'll eat after I get back. Save me something."

"I bet you wish you were still at battalion," Schaefer said.

"Like hell, I do. What made you say that?"

"You might be going home sooner."

"That's a fact. Won't be long, as it is."

"Anything you want me to do while you're gone?"

"No. Pass the word there's all the coffee they can drink. Gregg told me Mann had a fifth in his barracks bag—I remember having a drink out of that jug, by the way. You and Felty help yourselves. If you aren't plastered when I get back, I'll make you both sleep with your steels on."

"No, not that! Gregg and Wood have already gone off someplace. You know about it?"

"Yes. It's an old habit of Gregg's. He likes to get drunk, but he'll never do it around the men if he can sneak off someplace. Like tonight. He's very conscious of the dignity of the first sergeant—which is a damned good thing—and he has a whole set of professional standards he lives by."

"That's wonderful. I had never heard of that." Schaefer was surprised at how much Eric knew about Gregg. "Where'd you find all that out?"

"From Captain Mann, mostly. Other than that, from experience. He isn't afraid to call things as he sees them—that I learned. Even when he's wrong, he's honest about it. Captain Mann's the same way. He was a first sergeant once, you know. Something like Gregg, I imagine, only younger. Come to think of it, he's like Gregg in a number of ways. I know I've never admired a man as much as I admire old Sam Mann."

"He's a good officer."

"He's that, and more—he's a good human being. Day in, day out. Utterly consistent. Always several cuts above what you'd expect, no matter what standard you were judging him by. And the funny thing, Alex, is that I don't think he'd have seemed so to me any place but here."

"Why?"

"If I'd known him Stateside, served under him, even, I doubt very much if I'd have liked him. Too ignorant, or too crude about things. But here—he's educated me. He taught me what combat command is, and nobody else could have done it the way he did. You see, he never said 'this is how it is done' or 'here's what to do when—' like I've been trying to teach Felty. All Mann did was to be himself, and he was great."

Eric's coffee was gone.

"I'd better be going," he said, and he got up and left.

Thirteen

"Glad you could make it, Lieutenant," Major Merlin said sarcastically as Holloway entered the operations tent.

Holloway noticed that he wasn't the last company commander to arrive; John Heath wasn't there yet. And he recalled that Merlin hadn't set a definite time for the meeting. He was somewhat peeved at Merlin's implication that he had delayed the business of the battalion, but he figured he'd better forget it.

John Heath arrived a few minutes later and sat down on an ammunition box beside Holloway. The two company commanders were both dirty and unshaven, rude contrasts to the dapper major and the new operations officer. Merlin was still wearing his light blue scarf, and Eric noticed that his boots were so highly shined that they might have been used for shaving mirrors.

"Gentlemen," Merlin began, "I have called you together so that I can outline some of my policies. I shall expect complete and cheerful compliance with the points I shall make. If I do not get this cooperation, please be assured that I shall take sharp disciplinary action at once, no matter how fine a combat record you may have. Is that clearly understood?"

The officers, except for Captain Lester who stood behind the major, nodded their assent.

Eric and Heath watched Lester all through the meeting, shocked and disturbed to see how exempt from the lecture he seemed. Both company commanders got the impression that Lester was the real author of the remarks, and that the battalion commander was simply acting as Lester's mouthpiece.

My education is being completed, Eric thought.

"Take notes, gentlemen."

The company commanders fumbled around in their jacket pockets for notebooks and pencils. Eric found a pencil quickly, but the point was broken and he had to chip some wood away from the lead with his fingernail in order to write at all. He had no notebook, so he pulled out some toilet paper and tested it with the pencil to see if it would take a mark.

Holloway happened to look up at Lester as he did this. Lester's face was a study in excited horror: "No, No!" it seemed to be saying.

Merlin had noticed, too, and a look of stern disapproval came over his face.

Eric put the toilet paper back in his pocket and pulled out the old, folded map he had been carrying for days. He found a portion on the backside that was reasonably clean, and he prepared it to receive the battalion commander's message.

"A good officer, Lieutenant Holloway, always carries notebook and pencil."

Eric heard Heath mutter, "Toilet paper, too."

"Captain Heath?"

"Nothing, Major."

"First, I was greatly displeased over the way the relief and march back here were conducted. George Company was the worst-looking unit in the battalion, but Easy Company was but little better. Accordingly, there is a sizable block of close-order drill in the training schedule.

"Next, saluting and reporting. The fact that the battalion is in a combat area does not set aside the usual amenities of military courtesy. There will be classes in this, also, to include officers."

"Sir," John Heath broke in, "the policy has been no saluting in the line. We lose enough officers without asking for it like that."

Merlin raised his eyebrows so high his forehead was a mass of lines.

"I am well aware that no saluting has been carried on before now. I cannot imagine what reason you might have had for such intentional discourtesy, but I can only assume that it is indicative of a gross lack of discipline in this battalion. Your irrelevant interruption, Captain Heath, simply confirms my belief.

"Now, to go on. I watched the progress of this battalion in the operation just concluded, and I was shocked—shocked —at the lack of aggressiveness that was displayed. The division commander ordered that the mountain was to be taken by noon yesterday. You were more than twenty-four hours late. That will not happen again. Moreover, the reasons for the delay were indicative of poor leadership, if not plain cowardice."

Heath could stand it no longer.

"God damn it, Major, I resent that."

"I don't care what you resent, Captain. Remember that I am the battalion commander. I don't expect you to like what I have to say, especially when it seems to strike a tender spot, but I couldn't care less."

Merlin paused for emphasis.

"May I go on, Captain?"

Heath was silent, breathing heavily, a grim look on his face.

"As I was saying, I want this battalion to get its objectives on time regardless of the cost. We have a duty to higher headquarters to carry out their instructions to the letter. That duty has been willfully ignored, I find. It will be vigorously carried out, hereafter. There will be no slack in the execution.

"For an example of what I mean, take what happened in George Company today. When I visited their area, a number of men were not wearing their steel helmets—in direct violation of orders I had given not one hour before. Once an order is given, I mean for it to stand, Lieutenant Holloway. Is that clear?"

"Yes, sir."

"Another thing. I ordered that the training we are about to begin would be under conditions resembling combat as closely as possible. George Company disobeyed my order flagrantly and directly, almost as soon as the words had left my mouth. Their executive officer illegally took a jeep and went begging—begging!—to numerous service units for food!"

"Damn good, Eric," Heath muttered.

"Sir, may I ask a question?" Holloway said with cold formality.

"Yes, Lieutenant."

Eric's eyes were fixed on the small, wiry battalion commander.

"Sir, just how did that violate your order?"

Steady boy, he said to himself. Be little ice water.

"I said combat conditions, Lieutenant! Combat conditions!"

"We feed hot meals whenever we can steal enough groceries from the God damned rear echelon and there's an outside chance of getting the stuff up to the line," Heath shouted.

Major Merlin was blind with rage.

"Captain Heath! Get out of here! Out!"

Heath rose to go. He shot one more long stare at the battalion commander, then he left without saluting.

"See you later, Eric," he said as he went out.

"This meeting is dismissed. Leave. Leave, all of you!"

Woolcott and Ames, the new commanders of Fox and How Companies, saluted. Eric Holloway did too, but only after they had.

Holloway looked to see if Lester had made a move to go. He hadn't.

"Coming, Captain Lester?" he asked, holding the tent flap for him.

"Not just now."

Eric dropped the tent flap and went out into the cold, clean air. On his left he noticed the old tent Major Dahl had used for his sleeping quarters whenever the battalion was in reserve. It had been turned into something else: there was a freshly-painted sign at the entrance that read, "Field Grade Officers' Latrine." Some distance away there was a new tent and another sign: "Battalion Commander's Quarters."

It occurred to Eric that Merlin was the only field grade officer in the battalion, but he was willing to bet that one captain had quartermaster toilet seat privileges.

I must bring Gregg to see this, he thought.

2

It was almost dark when Eric returned. The kitchen tent was being taken down and loaded onto the company's lone truck.

"How was the battalion commander's little sewing bee?" Alex Schaefer asked.

"Great. Just great. What's going on here?"

"It is forbidden."

"Aren't you even going to keep a burner to make coffee with?"

"Nope. The kitchen is to be turned over to battalion as it is. The cooks are to come back here and take the training with the rest of the company. They will be a rifle squad under Sergeant Brady, onetime cook, and leader of men."

"Any volunteers to go back to the line?"

"Not yet, but numerous questions about going home."

"Prepare to receive one more."

Holloway went over to a row of five-gallon water cans and sat down on one.

"This is a hell of a thing," he said.

Sergeant Dolan came over a few minutes later and sat down on a water can beside the company commander.

"You look like you got troubles, Lieutenant," Dolan said.

"We all got troubles, Digger."

Holloway pointed to the cooks, who were loading the last pieces of kitchen equipment onto the already overloaded truck.

"How'd you like to have the cooks' squad in your platoon?"

"Noo-sir! Not those clowns! I've got a good platoon. And we ain't done nothin' to deserve that kind of punishment."

Eric laughed.

"Don't worry," he said.

The two men watched the gypsy wagon drive away, Sergeant Brady perched atop the shapeless mess, holding a double-axe aloft, King of Misrule in a procession quite unlike the Mardi Gras.

"Sir, I feel kinda stupid sayin' this, but—"

"What is it, Digger?"

"I want to take back a lot of things I said and did."

"Forget it."

"No, I mean it. There was a time when I'd have killed you. But the other day, when you come back to the company, I figured I'd leave it up to the braves in my platoon. If they soldiered for you, so would I. If they didn't, I'd have kilt you. They soldiered."

Eric didn't speak, so Digger went on.

"I just wanted to let you know. To square things, sort of. In case we might maybe get called back up on top, and all that."

"Thank you, Digger."

Eric wanted to tell the soldier how deeply moved he was, but the words wouldn't come.

3

The men who worked in a rear-echelon outfit just across the river, on ground George Company had won only the previous Saturday, were not required to wear steel helmets. Instead, they wore soft green caps. Most of the time these men went around unarmed, and their uniforms were not only clean, but pressed. They lived in squad tents, each having a wooden floor, and each man had a cot. There were electric lights in all of the tents, and a snack bar was maintained in the kitchen tent between hot meals.

Around supper time, several of the men from the Third Platoon were thrown out of the neighboring unit's snack bar. The commanding officer of the rear-echelon unit called Holloway about the incident.

"Lieutenant, I'll thank you to keep your men the hell out of my area," the man roared. "It's off-limits. Do you understand?"

"We'll stay on our side of the river, old friend," Holloway replied calmly. "But by the way—where were you folks last Saturday about this time?"

"What's that got to do with it? I just want you to keep your people out of here. This side is off-limits."

"All right. You'd better be glad we left our ammo up on top of the mountain, though."

"Are you threatening me?"

"No, I'm not threatening you. But how'd you rear echelon pansies like to go up with us, next time we attack?"

The line went dead.

Holloway called Schaefer over.

"Better pass the word. The Promised Land over there is off-limits. Their poppa doesn't want any soldiers cluttering up the area. The General might come around."

"That son of a bitch! Dammit, sometimes I wonder if our own people are for us or agin us. Some of these bastards—"

"I said a few words, myself. The river's the limit. Pass the word."

"All right. Have you heard about Heath?"

"No."

"Relieved."

"Can't say I'm surprised. I guess that makes me next."

"Oh. Captain Lester drove by here a few minutes ago.

Passed a few words about our men not wearing steels and not carrying their weapons."

"He picked this area, didn't he?"

"Yes."

"The man's sadistic, in addition to his other accomplishments. I wonder if he noticed that the people across the river don't even own steels?"

"Training. Vigorous training. Good for discipline."

"What?"

"Builds morale. Haven't you heard? A bitter soldier is a good soldier."

Schaefer pretended to vomit.

"Well, pass the word. All the goodies you can think of. Let's get it over with."

Holloway was ashamed to be a part of such a system. He knew that the men would obey the orders and say nothing about them, because it was beneath them to let something so childish and petty get them upset. But there would be a reaction in their minds. They would think, "We do all that they ask us to, and this is what we get for it. They don't care how tired we are. They don't understand that we just want to be left alone. They just don't care about us, except when there's something dangerous and nasty that has to be done."

And yet, Eric thought, nothing that battalion had ordered or done or said had really been unjust or unreasonable—technically. It was possible, highly improbable but still possible, for an enemy guerrilla force to make a raid that far back, and it might be argued that there was some truth in the old saying about bitter soldiers. Training, too, was needed. Holloway had a number of things he wanted to go over with his men, but close-order drill and saluting were not among them. Better, he thought, better they all stay in the sack.

Then he recalled what Major Dahl had said just before he left:

"Give him time, and your help."

I'll do that, Eric decided. I'll do that if it kills me.

4

That night, campfires burned in each platoon area along the backside of the Shark's lower jaw. Around one, in the Second Platoon, three men sat talking, as soldiers have since the first two cavemen ganged up on a neighbor.

A tall soldier with a thin face and long bony hands drawled, "I'd just tell him to go to hell, I would."

Another Southerner spoke up: "Hell you would! You been around here long enough to know better. You know you'd God damn well do what the man says."

"Not when he's wrong. If he's wrong, I tell him to go to hell."

"Well, he'll be a general someday, if he keeps his mouth shut and makes us do what the man says do. He won't get to be no general shootin' his mouth off, that's for God damn sure."

"All right. What'd you do, you're so God damn smart?" the tall soldier asked.

"I'd just go right ahead about my business and play like I don't hear nothin' that's said to me. That's what."

"Hell you would!"

"I would."

"You wouldn't do it long," the third soldier said.

The tall soldier spoke again: "Well, answer me this. If he gets told to make us do somethin', and it turns out to be the wrong thing for us to be doin' to begin with, and a bunch of us get killed or somethin', who's to blame—Holloway, or the dumb bastard what made him do it?"

"Christ, that's easy. Holloway'd be wrong if he didn't carry out the order. He's got no sweat, as long as he does like he's told."

"Even if he knows people are gonna get kilt?"

"Well, he'd sweat, stupid, but not like you think I mean. He wouldn't *like* it but he'd have to do it just the same, or

230

they'd get him for misbehaving before the enemy, or some Goddam thing like that. The order's got to be carried out, right or wrong."

The three soldiers around that campfire took no notice of a tall figure standing close enough to hear, but too far away to be recognized.

"Well, just who the hell *is* to blame in a thing like that?" the tall soldier asked.

"The stupid son-of-a-bitch that thunk the order up in the first place, that's who," the third soldier replied. "Hell, it all goes back to war's being wrong. And if war stinks, why then the whole damn business is lousy."

"Who's to say if'n it's a good war? You?"

"Damn if I know. The ones that win it, I guess. Hell, I don't worry about crap like that. I just do like they tell me and pray to Christ my enlistment runs out soon. I don't know if this kind of thing's right or wrong, this killing and all, but somebody's got to do it, and right now I'm it. I just hope it does some good in the long run."

Eric Holloway walked on down the line.

5

Eric found Captain Lester in the operations tent, writing on a tablet.

"Are you busy?" he asked as he came in. He had already been told that the battalion commander wasn't seeing anyone.

"Writing up some training memos."

Lester did not ask Eric to sit down or otherwise make him welcome.

Eric sat down anyway.

Lester looked over at him indifferently, then went on with his writing.

He looks so clean, Eric thought.

Eric started to get up and leave, but he changed his mind. He had come to offer his help, and the reason he had done so was his concern for the company. He could not allow this personal dislike for Lester to prevent his doing all that he might to take care of his braves.

"Captain Lester, there are a few things that my men need that you don't have on the schedule. Maybe I can help you with that."

"Lieutenant, I know my job. It seems that you don't know yours very well. Suppose you get your company under control before you come up here to battalion presuming to take over my job, too."

Eric got up to go, his face white with anger.

The men, he remembered.

"I'm not going to argue with you, Captain. You can make all the snotty remarks you want to, and it won't bother me a damned bit. I've been in this battalion for a good while, and I think there are a few things about it that I've learned, things that can help you. I'm here to offer them to you for the good of the men. Now, do you want my help, or don't you?"

"I'm not the least bit interested in your war stories, Lieutenant. But I am interested in your maintaining light discipline in your company area. I've already called your executive officer about those bonfires, and I don't want to have to say any more about them. In all your combat experience, you must have learned not to broadcast your position to enemy aircraft."

"Has the light line been moved this far back?"

"No, it hasn't. But that isn't the point, Lieutenant Holloway. This is training."

"Do you know that the rear-echelon bastards have a movie going right across the river, and my men can't go because their faces are dirty? What about their light discipline?"

"I'm not concerned with other units' operations. I'm not the division commander. And please don't refer to service troops as 'rear-echelon bastards.' They play their part—a very vital part. And I wish you'd play yours."

"And you don't want to hear what I came to say?"

232

"For the last time, no. You are dismissed, Lieutenant."

Eric got up and left. He heard the captain mutter something about military courtesy, but Eric was too furious to pay any attention.

When he reached George Company's command post, which was an old foxhole, he spoke to the phone guard.

"Anything new?"

"No, sir. Battalion calls about every fifteen minutes to tell us to quit doing something. That, and wire checks. They've got Gipp's radio going, too. Net control problem, they call it. Damndest thing you ever saw. Code, and stuff like that."

"Okay. I'll be in my hole if anyone wants me. Did you leave plenty of slack in the phone wire so you can bring the phone over there?"

"Sure did, sir."

"Goodnight, then."

"Goodnight, sir."

Eric took off all his clothes but his underwear and his socks, and crawled into his sleeping bag. Schaefer was already sound asleep; Eric tried not to disturb him.

This is a hell of a note, he thought, being in a hole—this far back, and right after a combat operation. But there is this—none of my people will die tonight. And tomorrow—only training, not an attack, not even a patrol.

Maybe this hellish thing will blow over.

Eric dozed off.

Less than an hour later, the phone guard woke him.

"Phone call, sir. It's battalion."

"Thanks," he said, taking the phone down into the hole. "George Six."

"Lieutenant Holloway, this is the battalion commander."

Merlin needn't have said that, Eric thought.

"There is loud singing coming from your area. I want it stopped right now."

Eric listened. He heard some men in the Third Platoon singing negro spirituals very softly, but that was all.

"Loud singing, sir? Are you sure it's in George Company? The rear-echelon people had a movie."

"Dammit, Lieutenant, I said I heard loud singing and I want it stopped! Isn't that clear enough?"

"Very well, sir."

Eric knew that his voice had no enthusiasm in it, but he didn't care. He was tired, and tired of the little man and his peeves.

"And for your information, Lieutenant, Major Dahl left me your promotion papers. I have decided to tear them up. At such time as you display the degree of competence I expect, I may—I may—draw up new ones. There'll be no coasting in the Second Battalion. I expect you to earn your captaincy for me. Do you understand that?"

"Yes, sir."

"Get that bitched tone out of your voice!"

"Is that all, sir?"

Eric wondered if he had called the other company commanders and harassed them the same way. He probably had.

"Yes!"

The line went dead.

"Come get this damned thing," Eric yelled to the phone guard.

"What was all that about?" Alex Schaefer asked, waking up.

"Division hindquarters' gift to the Second Battalion. Raising hell because a few lonely, cold, frightened, mistreated, miserable men are sitting around what used to be a campfire, singing some very beautiful old songs of faith amid misery, and probably relaxing for the first time in a week or a month or God knows how long."

"The bastard."

Eric was tempted to unload his feeling to Schaefer. He wanted to very much; but he expected to be relieved any time, and he knew that Schaefer's troubles would begin soon enough. He wondered if Major Dahl was still at division—but no, he had said all that there·was to say when he left.

Fandango? Maybe tomorrow. Or maybe I'd better just keep it all to myself, he thought. Either it'll blow over, or it won't. If it does, no one need know how close Merlin came to getting me. If it doesn't, they'll relieve me anyway, and that'll be that. Mum's the word—tonight, anyway.

He went back to sleep.

Fourteen

Battalion called at 6:01 the next morning for the reveille report. Holloway had intentionally neglected to issue the order for a formation, so none was held.

"What'll I tell 'em, sir?" the phone guard asked.

"Present or accounted for," Holloway mumbled. "Oh, hell. Is it morning?"

He looked outside. Still dark. Even so, he noticed, he felt pretty good. There had been no more calls to bother him. Even the bastard Merlin sleeps, he thought.

Holloway noticed that a great deal of artillery was being fired, and he wondered if the First Battalion was in trouble. If so, the Second Battalion might be ordered back into the line—and that would solve more problems than it would create, for once. But people would be shot at up there, and a few men were bound to be hit, and in a moment Eric was ashamed of his whole train of thought.

The much-hated training program got underway on schedule after Eric decided to beat battalion at their own game. He called the platoon leaders and the platoon sergeants together and told them that battalion had put out a training schedule that was pleasing to battalion, and that it would be followed to the letter. Then he added that when there were no snoops in the area, he had no objection to training being given in the subjects each leader felt his men needed most.

"Use break time for that if you have to," he said.

To his surprise, the men seemed to get a grim sort of pleasure out of the morning's training. It was so absurd, it was funny; they laughed as they went at their drilling and saluting, just as though it were all a huge joke.

Lester and the battalion commander were in and out of the area all morning, never coming to Holloway to be escorted, but pointedly ignoring him and going right to the training groups. Eric hadn't minded that, except for the fact that he had to ask the men what corrections had been made by the two visitors, and that had made him look a bit foolish in the eyes of the men. That didn't bother him very much—the thing that hurt was the thought that Merlin and Lester were aware of the implications of their discourtesy, that they knew they were undermining the confidence of the men in their company officers.

What a hell of a way to be fighting a war! Eric thought.

Later that morning, Holloway was called to battalion for a resumption of the company commanders' meeting.

Major Merlin presented an elaborate but wholly hypothetical plan for an attack through rolling, not mountainous, terrain.

Lester, as before, stood in the background and said nothing.

Holloway found no fault with Merlin's plan. It was all right for easy country, but it was utterly useless in the kind of fighting Eric had seen ever since he had joined the battalion, many months before. And it was a bit complicated, at that. It would make good reading for the regimental commander, and perhaps the General would be impressed. That, Eric imagined, was the general idea.

As Eric was leaving, he spotted Sergeant Trent and went over to say hello to him.

"Did I thank you for sending my sleeping bag up to the boondocks the other night?"

"Yes, you did, sir. I'm glad you got it."

"It really helped. I didn't get to spend much time in it, though. By the way, how'd Red make out up there last night?"

"They got hit pretty hard. There was first-degree panic around here because Colonel Hobbs alerted us to go help."

"Is that right?"

"I was on phone guard and heard it all. Times sure have changed."

"They sure have, Trent."

"Sir, do you realize where we're standing?"

"No, I hadn't thought about it."

"This is the same place where Lieutenant Hyde was killed when the artillery came in."

"Good Lord!"

"They had a bulldozer to come fill the craters. I don't know, but I kinda think they should have been left here."

"I think I know what you mean. It's funny—it's damnable —how they've changed everything, and in just one day."

"Well, how are things going in your company, sir?"

"Pretty good. Trent, I got the biggest thrill of my life commanding that company. It's more than I can even talk about. But I guess my head'll roll pretty soon, like Heath's."

"I doubt it, sir. There was some talk of it last night, but then the panic came on, and that changed everything."

"You must have had quite a phone guard tour."

"Well, you know how it is. I sit and listen, speak when I'm spoken to. But they're going to keep you. I'm sure of that."

Eric was surprised.

"Thanks for the intelligence. It's going to be a long war, isn't it?"

"I'm afraid it is."

"I'll see you later."

Holloway waved and walked back down the road to his company.

When he reached the C. P., he found that the morning's joviality had given way to sullen resentment. He understood. He had been surprised that any degree of good humor had ever existed.

"Gregg," he said, "cancel the training right now."

"Sir?"

"Stop all that foolishness. What I said yesterday goes. Get them cleaned up if you can, but I don't give a damn if they just flake out. As far as I'm concerned, it's good sleeping weather."

"Lieutenant, you're gonna get creamed."

"You watch."

"What'll I tell 'em if anybody comes around?" Schaefer asked.

"Tell 'em to go to hell, and that we're preparing for a night problem."

Holloway was acting out of confidence rather than sheer boldness. If they plan to keep me, he reasoned, they'll have to ignore this, just as they've been ignoring me when they come snooping around my company. Besides, if anything hits Red tonight, these men may not get any sleep—they'd better get all they can now.

A cheer went up from the men as the cancellation was announced, then there was a mad scramble to get back up to the ridgeline.

Five minutes later, nearly all of them were in their sleeping bags, dead to the world—and battalion.

Another meeting of company commanders was called that afternoon, right after what would have been the noon-day meal, had they not been eating C-rations, which needed only to be opened and eaten. It occurred to Holloway that the frequent meetings were giving the new battalion commander the feeling that he really was commanding—a feeling, Eric supposed, that he found hard to realize between meetings. The company commanders were serving more as sounding-boards for the battalion commander's vanity than as integral links in the chain of command. This seemed pretty infantile to Eric, but he sensed that he was gradually getting used to the strange mannerisms of the man.

The sermon for this meeting was a harangue about tactics. The text was taken from a stack of contact reports which had been received at division headquarters during the fight for the Octopus.

Holloway wondered if Merlin had brought the reports with him for just this purpose. As far as he knew, the man had been no nearer the fighting than the operations room at division's schoolhouse C. P., where messages had been phoned in by regiment.

As before, Lester was standing in the background. Eric was impressed by this sinister man, for he seemed so completely sure of himself. Lester could afford to be spiteful, mean, vindictive, cold, self-confident, Eric guessed, because of some kind of evil control he had over the battalion commander.

But something else is wrong, Eric sensed. Merlin must have considerable influence somewhere in the division to get this battalion. Hell, Owens ought to have gotten it, if Dahl had to go. Or could the General have sent these two down here just to get them out of division?

Holloway knew that it was fairly common for a senior commander to set people up for promotion as expressions of gratitude, or to compensate them for the shock of being kicked out of rear-echelon jobs. He knew that it could almost be said that the men in line outfits are simply those individuals who lacked sufficient pull to get assigned to the rear echelon. He knew that this was not altogether true, but the officers who were in the line because they had felt a strong sense of duty and had asked to be put there were pitifully few in number. The same thing was true, in many cases, of the men in line outfits; nearly all of them were draftees, nearly all of them could name half a dozen friends who had been able to dodge the draft, or, once drafted, had been able to wangle soft jobs Stateside or in the rear echelon. It was cause enough for bitterness; but, Eric thought, much of the glory of the men in infantry rifle companies can be attributed to the fact that those men are the unwanted, the kicked-around, the uninfluential. Because of this, their accomplishments are all the more heroic; their battle is not merely against the cold, or the mud, or death, but against a diseased national attitude, as well. How could it be otherwise, Holloway wondered, in a nation that worshipped technology and looked to the slick-talking Horatio Alger-type hero's success story as a cultural ideal? Why should a man meekly go to the line and suffer for long months in a hole, wondering how soon he would begin his final suffering and then die, when he could—just by saying the right things to the right people—wear a colored scarf around his neck, sport a soft cap, see movies, sleep on a cot in a tent with wooden floors, and never worry about anything but the next promotion and another decoration? The war would get won, anyway—by slobs who haven't wised up.

"I've heard a lot of whining about casualties," he heard Merlin saying, "and I don't want to hear any more."

Eric wondered what whining he had heard.

"When I say 'take that hill,' I want it taken, period. I don't want any long arguments or excuses, I want hills!"

Holloway noticed that the other company commanders were busily taking notes. He had his old map out, but Merlin had said nothing that Holloway considered worth noting.

Am I the one who's out of step? he wondered. If I am, I've misinterpreted an awful lot of supposedly high-caliber training—and what I've learned from all these months of combat.

The other company commanders, he noticed, were all new. He was astonished to realize that he was the senior company commander in the battalion—and he had had his company only two days.

Eric listened to everything Merlin had to say, but try as he might, he couldn't find anything important or coherent in the whole long lecture.

"Take care of your men," he had heard over and over again in lectures elsewhere. Here, an improperly conceived training schedule had denied every humane consideration he had ever been taught to provide.

"Set the example," he had once heard an eminent military historian say, but the two men who stood before him now were certainly misapplying the concept, increasing the comfort of battalion while the men slept in holes along a rocky ridgeline—a ridgeline which they, themselves, had won. They might just as well have been allowed the luxury of sleeping on flat ground.

"When you are faced with a difficult decision, ask yourself, 'am I wasting anything?'" he had heard a beloved chaplain say once, in a sermon. Here, time was being thrown away. Not only the time of those men present at the company commanders' meeting, but the time that had been taken away from the men by the morning's folly. Lester had wasted whatever help Eric might have given him the night before, rejecting not only the offer, but the principle which had inspired it.

How many men, Eric wondered, will have to die before this diabolical pair can learn what Dahl and Hamilton knew even before the damned war started? That's the tragic part—the men will be the ones to pay. Things'll go wrong, but the men will get the blame. They'll always be blamed, because they can't defend themselves against this kind of enemy. My braves are the absolute end of the line—

"Furthermore," he heard Merlin say, "I want it clearly understood that whatever Major Lester says, goes. His orders are to be complied with just as though I issued them personally."

Holloway jumped as though he had been shot. Sure enough, Lester had a gold leaf on his collar. He looked at Merlin's collar and saw that he, too, had been promoted. And both officers were wearing the Combat Infantry Badge, although they had come to the battalion after the shooting had ended. It was possible that they had been shot at before, but Eric hadn't heard of it.

Soon the meeting ended. The company commanders saluted and left.

Eric was glad to be outside again, for he had almost thrown up the cold ham and lima beans he had eaten for lunch. Battalion's kitchen, he noticed, was going full blast, serving hot meals. Holloway didn't begrudge them their good fortune, but the sight convinced him that he should get his own kitchen back if he had to steal it. And he knew he probably would have to do just that.

All through the meeting, Eric had been impressed by the fact that he was really alone, although there were six other men in the tent. He felt as though he had outlived his time, as though he were the last survivor of some other war, long since ended.

What good will it do the men for me to carry on a feud with battalion? Holloway wondered as he walked back to his C. P. They'll suffer. They'll pay, not me. Maybe it'd be better for the men if I get myself relieved. Maybe Merlin's right. Maybe I'm as out of line as Merlin and Lester say I am. Lord knows I have a reputation for messing things up. If I really am a menace, and I stay here, crossing Merlin and Lester, some of my people may get hurt—just because I stayed. . . .

2

Things were quiet at the company; nearly everyone was asleep. Holloway was restless, worried: he knew it would do him no good to try to rest, so he told the phone guard he'd be back after awhile, and walked out.

Eric looked across the river, beyond the rear-echelon unit with the terrible-tempered commander, to the pass, the windy pass where he had stood most of last Saturday, waiting for the attack on the Shark to begin. It was there that Hamilton had chewed him out, but the incident seemed months, not days, ago. Then Eric looked down the river at what was left of the concrete bridge. The jeep was still there, blasted out of shape, a sharp, cruel reminder of the events of that awful night.

In a few minutes Eric reached the end of the Shark's lower jaw, the place where he had tried to tie in the battalions. He realized that the walk he was taking was somewhat like the long, lonely walks he used to take, years ago, in his home town—walks along dark streets on rainy nights. I haven't changed a hell of a lot from the kid I was then, Eric thought.

I'm still alone, still walking, still trying to figure out if I belong anywhere, still wondering if I make any difference to anybody, and if that difference is for good—

Pretty soon he passed the tip of the Shark's upper jaw, the place where Towson had stopped him, the place where Towson had been killed a few minutes later. The ridge was deserted, now. But not even the rear-echelon units would want it—too ugly, too rough. Fit only for infantrymen to spend their time in reserve on. Why Lester hadn't put George Company back on their old line, he couldn't imagine. That would have been even more cruel than putting them where they were, back on the lower jaw.

Funny, he thought. I'm going back to the line. I don't want to, but that's where I'm headed. The same way we went the other day.

He saw the place where he had said good-bye to Sam Mann and had taken his company. Knowing Merlin made Mann seem even greater in Eric's estimation.

Old Man, what would you do about this bastard? Eric wondered.

It was there that Gregg had said, "Don't goof." Just how the hell does a man keep from goofing?

Holloway walked up the narrow path that led up Cougar, the ridge his company had cleared. He noticed the telephone wire that had linked his phone with battalion during the fighting. This was the wire Gregg had cut, the wire that had carried Major Dahl's steady voice. The wire was dead, now. It would lie there forever, he supposed. It had played its part, now it was forgotten. Some native might pick it up, years from now—some native who would come up to cut wood, or to poke around the deserted and forgotten foxholes, hoping to find a can of C-rations, or maybe a field jacket some soldier had thrown away, or even a piece of cardboard for patching a roof.

That wire had carried Major Dahl's voice, saying: "I hope this attack winds it up for awhile so you can give your people some rest. . . ."

Eric climbed the knob that Felty's men had taken. The enemy dead were gone, or buried, and he was glad of that. Strange, he thought, how different fighting men are from the causes that make fighting men of them. These people—the enemy—fought like demons. There wasn't a real coward among them—I even wonder if my braves would have taken the pounding these men took. And for what? For whom? Surely they had even less reason than we have for fighting this war. But when you think about reasons, the mind sickens. Think about men, and you get nobility. Strange!

Holloway walked on up the path to the old command post, to the line on which the company had spent the long night in misery and fear and valor.

Not much of a battleground. Certainly it was different from the mossy banks of the Buffalo Bayou, where Sam Houston had whipped Santa Anna at San Jacinto. Cougar and the Octopus bore no resemblance to the rolling hills east of Vicksburg. Stony Point was rocky and thick with trees, but not like this. And there had been plains for Wolfe and Montcalm, and ordinary farmland for Napoleon and Wellington.

But here—here there had been a world extending maybe twenty feet in any direction, bounded by fog and the rocks and the treetrunks, the cold ground, the slope of the ridge. Into that world, any number of things might have come, dropping suddenly out of the mist, ending that world. A mortar round, blossoming in the bare treetops, spraying hot steel splinters through the cold air and yielding flesh. Or a stream of hot, spinning machine gun rounds, arching through the night and thumping into the earth, or the treetrunks, or a man. Or a grenade, no bigger than an electric razor, bouncing on a rock, blinding and crushing and shredding and killing as it destroyed itself.

And all that a man might do about it was wait for something terrible to happen—wait, sit, endure, hope. If nothing broke through the fog and darkness to shatter that world, perhaps he could live into the sunlight once more. But there was nothing he could do, except, perhaps, to pray. But for what? For a quick, painless death? For a golden chariot to speed him away? No, only, "Lord take away this night—speed this waste of the time you *have* given me so that I may live some useful years of a peaceful sort again before I die."

Eric walked on up to the rock which his good friend, Fandango, had used. He stopped there, and sat down. He took off his steel helmet, and he sat there for a long time, thinking.

3

Gregg met him when he returned.

"Didn't have no luck getting the kitchen back, sir. Wouldn't let us have it. Battalion commander's orders."

"More C-rations, huh?"

"More and more."

"Well, anything else go wrong?"

"No sir, everything's been quiet. Most of us slept all afternoon."

"Did you?"

"No, to tell you the truth, I got into a little hassle up at battalion."

"What'd you do?"

"Well sir, I was still a little bit plastered from last night. And I kept hearing those boat whistles down at the beach. You know, they go 'Tooo-t—'"

"I know."

"Well, I saw them fancy signs they got painted down there, and I broke out laughin'. Some rear-echelon sergeant I never seen before came out an' told me to stop, and I kinda roughed him up a bit."

"I don't blame you."

"Seems you ain't supposed to laugh at their signs."

"Looks that way."

"Some new major took my name. Lots of strange faces

down there. This major said he'd bust me. Then I laughed some more. I should'a told him I been busted by better'n him, but I guess I'm losin' my guts in my old age."

"Well, don't go down there any more than you have to."

"I sure won't, sir. Jus' on my way out, maybe. To punch a few of them rear-echelon bastards in the nose."

About an hour later, Major Lester called Holloway.

"Lieutenant, I was insulted by one of your non-commissioned officers this afternoon. I want you to prefer court-martial charges against him at once."

"You do it, Major. You're the aggrieved party."

"Lieutenant Holloway, I'm giving you a direct order. I want that man court-martialed. Do you understand?"

"No, Major Lester. I don't. I don't court-martial my people that way, and I should think you'd know better than to order me to. What you want isn't legal, sensible, or fair. Now, if any of my braves are out of line, I'll straighten them out. My way. Who did what to you, and why?"

"Lieutenant, I don't have to be lectured by you about military justice. But for your information in preparing the court-martial charge sheets, Sergeant Gregg called me a—quote—rear-echelon son of a bitch—unquote."

"If you want to make a complete ass of yourself, sir, prefer the charges yourself."

"Lieutenant—"

"And for your information, Major, I've already put out the word that no man from George Company will go to battalion except by order. And if you don't want any more of those rear-echelon non-coms you've brought up here with you from division hindquarters punched in the nose, you'd better keep them the hell out of my company area."

The line went dead.

Holloway sent for Gregg.

"Top," he said, "pack. I'm getting you the hell out of here now."

"Yes-sir!"

Gregg ran off to get the remains of a fifth of whiskey and his sleeping bag.

Holloway called the regimental personnel officer, whom he knew, and explained that a fast transfer was the only thing that could save Gregg's stripes. Eric emphasized the time Gregg had been in combat, Gregg's age, and the fact that he had been pushed about as far as a man could be.

The personnel officer had been a company commander in the First Battalion until he had been shot up, so he understood.

"Send him back here to me," he said. "I'll get him out."

"I'll assume all the responsibility—I've got nothing to lose anymore."

"Then get him back here as quick as you can."

Within five minutes, Gregg was in Eric's jeep, ready to go. He was the happiest, and the saddest, man Eric had ever seen.

"Sir, I never thought I'd live to see the day," Gregg said, breaking down. "I sure will miss the comp'ny. I just wish they could come, too."

"So do I, Top."

Holloway had told him nothing about the call to regiment.

"Sir, it was good, soldiering with you. We had some bad times, but there was some good ones, too. The good ones was damn' good. I hope—I hope we cross trails again, some time."

"We will, Top. You play it cool going through the rear echelon. Don't stop to punch anybody in the nose, or you'll be back here after all."

"I'll just follow the sound of them boat whistles, sir. They go 'Toooo-t Tooo-t.'"

4

Holloway realized that Gregg's departure would probably cost him his career. He knew that he had given the battalion commander sufficient grounds for relieving him, if not for court-martialing him. Still, he was glad that Gregg was out of it. It would be mockery, somehow, for one of the last survivors of the once-proud race of first sergeants to be made the victim of Major Lester's vanity. Holloway did not insist, even to himself, that Gregg was justified in what he had done, and yet it was understandable. If Merlin wants to make a big thing of it, Eric thought, let him.

Within an hour after Gregg's departure, the message for Holloway to report to battalion came.

Eric wasn't surprised. In fact, he felt somewhat relieved to know that within the next hour or so the air would be cleared.

"Tell them I'm on my way if they get impatient and call," he told the phone guard as he left the command post hole.

Holloway walked the line—for the last time, he figured. He stopped frequently to talk with some of the men who were awake. And in between these short visits, as he walked along the ridgeline in the darkness, he thought of how much he loved and respected those men—his men. Grand, heroic, noble, great-hearted—corny, inadequate words for these men. It was too dark for him to see their faces, but he remembered—he knew he would always remember—the lines of suffering that were beneath the dirt and the beards. There were reasons for those lines, stories that would never be told, stories which wouldn't be understood or appreciated if they could be told. But now I know, he told himself, now I know. And no matter what happens, ever, all this will have been worthwhile, because of what I've learned. And these men taught me.

When he had finished walking the line, he got into his jeep for the short ride to battalion.

Just as the jeep pulled out onto the road, fires flared up all along the ridgeline, in each of the platoon areas.

"Stop, please," Eric said to the driver.

He looked at those fires for nearly a minute, until tears filled his eyes. They know what's happening, he thought. They understand. Wise men!

5

Colonel Merlin did not admit Holloway when he arrived at battalion. Eric wondered why, but it really made no difference to him. Time, too, had ceased to matter.

Finally, Merlin called him in.

Holloway went into the battalion commander's tent and stood awkwardly for a moment while his eyes became adjusted to the glare of the electric light, then he made out the figure of Merlin seated on the edge of a cot. He couldn't bring himself to salute at first, but he realized that there was no point in being rude. He saluted and reported as carefully and as formally as he could.

Merlin returned the salute as though he were vexed that Eric had observed the formality. When he spoke, it was with extreme agitation in his voice.

"Holloway, I have learned of your insubordination. I intend to take strong action."

"Very well, sir."

"Do you realize that I can have you court-martialed for this?"

"Yes, sir."

"Or I can relieve you?"

"I do."

"How could you have done this?"

"Sir?"

"Don't you know that these mock heroics of yours aren't impressing anyone?"

Eric thought of the fires, and said nothing.

"You've already lost your promotion. Are you trying to throw away your whole career, too?"

"No, sir."

"Are you trying to become a martyr? Don't you know that went out of fashion a long time ago?"

Eric did not answer. A lot of artillery was swishing by overhead, and he was thinking about it.

"Lieutenant Holloway. Since I assumed command of this battalion, you have been systematically—"

The phone rang, interrupting the battalion commander. He took the handset impatiently.

"White Six," he snapped.

Then, in a warm, friendly tone, "Oh, yes-sir!"

Merlin listened, smiling at first, then frowning. He broke each pause with "Yes-sir!" or "Certainly, sir!" never hesitating or indicating any sort of reaction to what was being said to him.

"We must obey the orders of higher headquarters cheerfully," Eric recalled Merlin saying at one of the company commanders' meetings. At least the bastard practices what he preaches, Eric thought.

Finally the one-sided conversation and the "Yes-sir!" punctuations ended.

Merlin held the phone in his hand and stared at the straw on the floor for a long, long time. Then he remembered Eric, and looked up at him with a look that was strange and pitiful, as though Merlin realized how utterly helpless and afraid he really was, in spite of his rank and his authority.

Then Eric Holloway knew that he had been wrong when he had said, "You can take the man out of the rear echelon, but you can't take the rear echelon out of the man." Eric saw in the feverish eyes of the frightened little man the same look he had seen in the eyes of some of his men: in Kelsey's darting eyes, in the creekbed with mortar rounds punching the ground all around him, in Cannon's pain-filled eyes, crawling back, shot and shredded, seeking the shelter of the cliff.

Eric Holloway realized that Merlin's lonely and painful baptism had begun.

"That was the regimental commander," Merlin said in a weak, breaking voice. "Red is being hit. Blue is in serious trouble. We are to get on the road right away."

(God help him, Eric thought.)

"Major Stace has been killed. Major Lester will replace

him in command of Blue immediately. You will replace Lester as my operations officer."

"Very well, sir."

"Call your executive officer and tell him to take command of George Company. You know what to do about getting the battalion on the road, don't you?"

"Yes, sir."

Fifteen

Once inside the operations tent, it took Eric's eyes a long time to become accustomed to the glare of the electric bulb that was hanging on the north tent pole. The oil heater was in the usual place, but everything else in the tent seemed strange and artificial to Eric.

He remembered how the tent had been arranged Sunday night, when the artillery rounds had come crashing out of the darkness behind them. There had been cots along the east tentwall; now there were no cots at all in the tent. The personnel and supply people had used the south end of the tent sometimes, but now they had large tents of their own. There was a new field desk along one wall, and on the desk Eric saw a large, freshly-painted nameplate that someone had fixed for Major Lester.

"Evening, sir," Trent said, getting up from a folding chair near the light. He had been reading a paper-back book and hadn't noticed the officer at first.

"Hello, Trent. Are you duty officer?"

"Underfed and overpaid, but duty officer just the same. Till midnight."

"Well, we've got work to do. Major Lester's going to Blue. I'm replacing him as operations officer—temporarily, I imagine."

"That's fine, sir. Good to have you back in the rear echelon again."

Trent sat back down, but he got up again quickly.

"This is Major Lester's chair. You inherit it, too, I guess."

"No, you keep it. Better hide it, though. He'll be through here before long to get his nameplate."

Holloway walked over to the map board and studied the grease-pencil marks Lester or someone had made on it.

"Poke that light over here, please, Trent," he asked, since the board was some distance from the north tent pole.

Trent swung the cord toward the map board and held the light so that the officer could see. The map board was too heavy to be moved easily because of a large wooden frame that had been built around it. The frame had been painted light blue, and a division shoulder patch had been painted near the top of the thick plexiglass sheet that covered the map.

"Radio crew built that damned thing," Trent said. "It has a light in it, but it won't work."

"I can't make any sense of this mess on the map, anyway. Can you?"

"No, sir. I think Major Lester was planning counter-attacks."

"Maybe so, but these are all in zones that belong to other regiments. None of these masterpieces apply to the place we're going tonight."

"Where's that, sir?"

"Someplace around the Octopus."

"Oh."

Holloway took one last look at the cluttered map board, then walked back over to an ammo box and sat down. He took out his old map and spread it in the straw on the ground.

"This one will do."

Holloway looked intently at the brown lines on the map that represented the Octopus, the star-fish mountain on which he had suffered with George Company. He knew that Red had taken over that portion of the line which ran from the peak west along the finger that eventually split into Cougar and Lion. Blue tied in with Red east of the peak, then ran eastward down the finger that led down to a pass. At the pass, Blue was tied in with a battalion from the other regiment.

Where will White fit? Eric wondered.

He picked up the phone and called the regimental operations officer, Major Owens.

"This is Lieutenant Holloway at White, sir. I'm taking over as operations officer from Major Lester."

"Good," Owens replied. "Glad to have you there."

"I called to ask if you've got anything on our movement."

"Well, the Old Man is on his way down there now to give you folks the order verbally. This is what it amounts to, though. You'll start moving at midnight—it's about ten-thirty now—and we're putting you in around the Octopus' peak. Where Red is now. You know where that is, don't you?"

Eric grinned.

"Yes, I know where it is, Major."

"You folks ought to be in place up there by four. That's when we expect the other fellow to make his big try. You have a map handy?"

"Yes."

Eric spread his old map in the straw once more.

"See the finger that leads into the Octopus from the north? The one that hooks back east a few hundred yards out?"

"Yes."

"It's crawling with visitors. Red has been taking a beating right at the peak, where that damned thing comes in, but that's not all. That finger is broadside to Blue's line, so they've been spraying Blue all night long, too. That damned thing's lower than Blue's finger, so artillery doesn't do a hell of a lot of good. The artillery's had the devil's own time trying to get rounds over Blue's heads to get at the other folks."

"I see."

"They're batting about five-hundred, though. Well, any of this help?"

"Yes, sir. Thanks much."

Eric rang off and walked over to the field desk to hunt for a tablet and a better pencil than the one he had. When he opened the desk, he was astonished: Lester had copies of almost every field manual stuffed into the pigeon holes of the desk.

"Trent, come look at this."

"I know, sir."

"Has he got one on mountain operations in here?"

"I bet he hasn't."

"So do I."

Finally he found a tablet and a fresh pencil, and he sat down to write the order for the move back to the line.

In about five minutes, he was finished. He looked up from the tablet and thought, this isn't how I thought it would be at all. This isn't thrilling, it's brutal. All I'm doing is organizing the misery of the battalion.

Then Eric read back over the order, looking for opportunities for making things easier for the men in the companies. He found that he could move the heavy weapons by having the jeeps start shuttling them to a forward assembly area at the base of the Octopus right away. That would reduce the loads the men would have to carry, he knew, and the men would arrive up there far less worn out by the march.

He found several other details in the order that could be simplified, then when he felt he had done all that he could, he took the tablet into Colonel Merlin's tent for his approval.

"Sir, I talked to Major Owens at regiment. He said the regimental commander is on the way here, and that he would have the complete order for us."

The tent was dark at first, but Merlin switched on a light while Eric was talking.

Merlin was in his sleeping bag. He rolled over and looked angrily at the lieutenant. He had been sound asleep, and it was obvious that he resented the interruption.

Scowling, he said, "Dammit, Lieutenant, do you have to bother me now?"

Before the astonished Holloway could think of anything at all to say, Merlin crawled out of the sleeping bag and rolled his bony legs over the side of the cot. He was wearing yellow silk pajamas.

"Did you say the colonel is coming?"

Merlin was slowly coming out of his drowsiness.

"Yes, sir. Ought to be here any minute."

Holloway could hardly conceal his amusement at Merlin's panic, but then it occurred to him how tragic and pitiful the scene really was. Here is a man, he thought, a man entrusted with the care of over eight hundred lives, sound asleep in yellow silk pajamas at a time when—

Eric heard a jeep motor outside.

"The colonel."

"Go meet him. Hurry!"

"I'll take him to the operations tent."

Holloway stepped outside Merlin's overheated tent and hurried over to the colonel's jeep.

I ought to take him in to see the yellow pajamas, he thought, but I haven't got the guts.

2

"Lieutenant Holloway reporting, sir," Eric said. "I'm White Three."

"Oh yes, Holloway. Is Colonel Merlin here?"

"Yes, sir. He'll join us in the operations tent right away."

"You think you can get on the road by midnight?" Colonel Hobbs asked as they walked toward the tent.

"Yes, sir."

Holloway lifted the tent flap for the colonel, then followed the heavy-set man into the tent.

"Trent, please go get some coffee and as many cups as you can find," Holloway said as they entered.

Trent nodded and left.

The regimental commander plopped down on an ammunition box and took off his steel helmet. He was very tired, and his face gave away the full extent of his concern over the way the night's heavy fighting had been going. He ran a heavy, rough hand over the top of his almost bald head, then he looked up at Eric, his clear, blue eyes squinting slightly.

"Son, we're in trouble."

The phone rang, and Holloway answered it. The General wanted to speak to Colonel Hobbs, so Eric passed the phone to the weary, worried man.

"This is Colonel Hobbs, General."

Then, a bit later, "Yes, White will move at midnight. . . . I know, General. . . . I've just come from there and I'm fully aware—"

Merlin walked in and sat down in Lester's folding chair.

"General, I'll tell you what I'm going to do," Hobbs continued. "I'll put Merlin on the road as soon as he can get out there."

The conversation ended a moment later, and the colonel turned to Merlin.

"We're in a real blind, Jack. Now division wants you up there as soon as you can get there. Here's what I want you to do."

Colonel Hobbs got up and walked over to the elaborate situation map. Holloway and Merlin followed.

"My God, Merlin. This map is a mess!"

Holloway wanted to tell the colonel that he planned to throw the monstrosity away, but he decided to keep his mouth shut.

"Holloway, couldn't you spend less time painting shoulder patches and more time keeping this map up to date?"

"Lieutenant Holloway has a lot to learn about being an S_3, Colonel. But I'll see to it he gets it cleaned up right away," Merlin volunteered.

Eric could think of nothing proper to say, so he simply

looked the battalion commander in the eye as steadily as he could.

Merlin looked away and made a great show of erasing Lester's grease-pencil marks with the palm of his hand.

"You have an order prepared, of course, Merlin," Colonel Hobbs said.

Merlin looked awkwardly toward the end of the tent where Sergeant Trent was having difficulty in getting the coffee pot and a cardboard box full of cups through the heavy canvas flaps. Holloway walked over to help the sergeant.

"Owens told me Holloway called to ask for details," Hobbs added, breaking a silence that was becoming embarrassing to Merlin.

"I have an order drafted, sir," Holloway told Merlin.

"Give it to me."

Merlin read the tablet hurriedly, muttering "uh-huh" and "hum" under his breath as though he were giving the order an extremely close going over.

"This part about jeeps won't do at all, Holloway. The men must learn to be self-sufficient. Every man will carry his own equipment—all of it, all the way."

Eric did not embarrass his commander by arguing the point in front of Colonel Hobbs. Besides, he expected that Hobbs would reverse Merlin anyway; it simply didn't make sense to ignore the advantages offered by the use of the jeeps when time was of the essence, as it was then.

But Colonel Hobbs took a cup of coffee from Trent, thanked him for it, and turned back to the map without asking Merlin what the jeeps had to do with the movement.

"Why didn't you show me this order before now?" Merlin whispered hotly to Eric.

Holloway almost answered, "Because you were asleep in yellow silk pajamas," but there wasn't time.

Colonel Hobbs called Merlin over to the map.

"Lieutenant Holloway," Merlin said, "call the company

commanders and tell them to come up here to get the order."

Eric called each of the company commanders and alerted them for the move. He told each company commander the gist of the order, and added that Merlin wanted to issue the order personally as soon as all of the company commanders were assembled at battalion.

"Hell, you've already given me the meat," Schaefer protested. "Why does the bastard have to waste time repeating it?"

"Do as you're told," Eric replied good-naturedly. "He might want to read you the funnies."

Colonel Hobbs left before the company commanders arrived. Eric was sorry he had not been able to listen to the conversation between Colonel Hobbs and Merlin, for he needed to know what the regimental commander wanted in order to be sure that the plans he was to prepare in Merlin's name dovetailed with those of Colonel Hobbs.

When Eric asked Merlin to fill him in on the conversation, Merlin snapped, "Mind your own business!" and began walking up and down the length of the tent, wringing his hands.

3

At the meeting, Merlin read the order from Eric's tablet.

Holloway noticed that Merlin was extremely nervous—even more so than usual. He wondered if he were afraid of the men before him.

When Merlin finished, he asked if there were any questions.

"Sir," Schaefer asked, "will we get a chance to register any artillery or mortars after we get up on the mountain?"

Merlin was dumbfounded. He looked blankly at Schaefer, opened his mouth once, then closed it and turned to Eric with a glance that was half pleading, half scornful.

"Lieutenant Holloway, you've left that detail out of the order."

Merlin was peeved that Eric had not volunteered an answer.

"Chances are you won't get to register, Alex," Eric said. "Nothing's been said about it. Red may have some numbers to give us, but don't count on a damned thing. I look for it to be a matter of throwing grenades. We'll be arriving up there at a hot time, and they may be too close for anything but grenades and bayonets."

You could have answered that yourself, Eric thought as he turned to speak to Merlin.

"If anything comes out later on this, I'll call the company commanders directly," he said evenly.

"Very well. See that you do."

The meeting broke up a short time later, and the company commanders left to get their companies on the road. Merlin returned to his tent without saying anything further to Holloway.

"Better get a command group together, Trent," Holloway said.

Trent nodded and left. Holloway strapped on his pistol belt and put on his steel helmet, then he followed the sergeant through the tent flaps out into the night. As he went through the tent flaps, he looked at his watch: eleven-thirty.

All over the Shark, the men in the rifle companies were reluctantly getting out of their sleeping bags and lacing up their boots. Others were checking their weapons, or passing out ammunition, stamping out fires, or filling canteens. Hardly any of them spoke, for they were all drowsy, and all of them were depressed and discouraged at the prospect of having to go back up to the line, of being shot at again, of pushing their luck even one night further. But then, there was nothing to say: the Octopus had to be held, and unless they helped hold it, it would be lost. It was simple to understand, but still awfully hard to accept.

Standing in the chilly, wet darkness outside the operations tent at battalion, Eric Holloway thought of those men in the rifle companies. He knew—he remembered—how much they hated to move, once they had stopped anyplace for a day or so. He realized that their hearts were not in what they had to do, and he realized that their glory ought to be even greater because of that. These reluctant, unwilling men would do the killing and the bleeding and the dying for their unknowing and indifferent countrymen with a kind of skill that Eric knew would amaze objective military historians, years hence. Glory ought to be heaped on those gallant infantrymen, but he knew it wouldn't be. The story of those great-hearted men would die in their own breasts, for no one would care to listen, or care at all.

Well, hell, he thought. A man doesn't go around whimpering because he happens to have been born into a generation of clay pigeons: he dies all the harder.

Sixteen

By midnight, the men of the Second Battalion were filing by the battalion command group in a column of twos. It was pitch dark. The only noise came from the road itself, where feet weary of war were squishing through mud, for it had started to rain a few minutes before the first company had moved onto the road. It was a soaking rain, one that would last through the rest of the night.

"The battalion commander is wanted on the radio, sir," a radioman said to Holloway. "It's Honeycomb Three—Major Owens."

"Trent, have you seen Colonel Merlin?" Holloway asked.

"He hasn't showed up yet, sir. Shall I get him? I think he's still in his tent."

"No, I'll talk to Owens."

Holloway took the radio handset and identified himself.

"This is Honeycomb Three, Gasoline Three. Tell Gasoline Six that Honeycomb Six wants him to come up here where we are as soon as he can. Over."

Eric said he'd pass the word. He thought about going to find Colonel Merlin himself, but he decided against it. Just as he was about to send Trent, Holloway heard the colonel's jeep coming out of the field behind the command group.

When the jeep pulled up beside Holloway, he saluted and told the battalion commander that Colonel Hobbs wanted to see him up the road, at the base of the Octopus, where regiment had set up a forward command post.

"Well, that's where I'm going," Merlin growled, "if you'll get these people out of my way."

Holloway broke the column of marching men for a moment while the colonel's jeep pulled up onto the road between the two columns.

"We'll go now," Holloway told Trent.

Trent passed the word to the rest of the members of the command group.

Eric watched the dark bulk of the jeep moving ahead of him. He could tell from the sound of the jeep's engine that the colonel was not making much progress. Once or twice he heard the colonel's voice above the motor and the squishing.

"Dammit, get out of my way. . . . Move over!"

Holloway called the lead company on the radio and told the company commander to halt.

"Move your people off the road until Gasoline Six's jeep is clear and out in front of the column. Pass the word back. Over."

As the word filtered back the men gave way, and the jeep churned on through.

Holloway led the command group between the lines of resting soldiers to the head of the lead company, then he told the company commander to get his people up and moving again, and to follow the command group on forward.

The already tired men got back on the muddy road, and the miserable march continued.

When Merlin reached the forward command post of Colonel Hobbs, which was in a half-ruined native hut near the base of Rhino, Colonel Hobbs brought him up to date on the fighting.

"There's a lull up there right now, and we're lucky to have a breather," the regimental commander said. "If you can get up there and get into place before it gets thick again, maybe we can beat this guy off. Where's Holloway?"

"Bringing the battalion up, sir. Damn slow, too."

"I don't know, Merlin. Holloway's doing pretty well. Tell

you what. Get your recon made so you can tell him what to do with the battalion when it gets here."

The two officers heard heavy firing break out far above them, on the ridgeline.

"Trouble. Sounds like they're hitting Blue again."

Then, a moment later, "Get going, Merlin. You've got a lot of real estate to look over before Holloway gets here."

"Yes-sir," Merlin said, saluting. "White'll rock 'em back."

"Just do what I asked you to do, Merlin," the tired colonel said, turning away to look at the map.

Merlin left.

2

Down the road from the regimental command post, White slogged on in the mud, through the dark rain. Occasionally litter jeeps headed between the columns, loaded with quiet, wounded men on their way back to the regimental aid station.

The men in the battalion who were carrying mortars and recoilless rifles were having a hard time keeping up with the riflemen, but the officers realized this and gave the word for the men to pass the heavy weapons around.

In Fox Company, Lieutenant Marella, who had been a cop before the war, carried a Fifty-Seven nearly all the way. There was no straggling in his platoon.

When Holloway's command group reached the regimental command post, Eric halted the column and went to find Lieutenant Colonel Merlin.

"Damn, Holloway, isn't he out there?" Major Owens asked.

"No, sir. At least I can't find him."

Eric had looked all around the command post area, made inquiries, and had even called Red and Blue to see if he were already up in the line. No one had seen or heard of him.

"Well, we need bodies in the line, and we need them up there right now, Eric. Take the battalion on up to the peak.

You know how to go in up there after you get there, don't you?"

"This will amaze you, Major, but Merlin hasn't told me."

"You're right. It does. Well, here's what Colonel Hobbs told Merlin. Red is going to slide down the ridgeline to the right, toward Blue, to fill the gaps left by Blue's casualties. You defend the peak, tie in with Red on the right, and cover as much of the finger leading west from the peak as you can. That's the finger you people took. You remember."

"All right, sir."

"Take the battalion on up, and consider yourself in command until Merlin gets there or turns up."

The major paused a moment, then he said, "Eric, what's with this guy Merlin, anyway?"

Eric started to answer the question directly. The words were just about to rush out, damning Merlin in detail, but he suddenly realized that it was not for him to judge or criticize his commander.

"Beats me," he said, shrugging his shoulders.

In a way, that was the truth. As mean, as petty, as downright lazy as Merlin seemed, he had done absolutely nothing wrong—according to the theory of combat command as it is taught in professional military schools. The school solution, Eric had noticed, was Merlin's code and his standard. But there was nothing wrong in that. Merlin lacked something, Eric couldn't say just what, but whatever that something was, it made all the difference. For example, Merlin was technically right in laying on a heavy training schedule when the battalion came back into reserve, but there was something in the way he did it that made the whole business wrong. What was it? Lack of experience? No, Merlin had more than ten years of commissioned service, Eric knew. Fear? Maybe. Eric couldn't say for sure. But there definitely was something lacking, and Eric knew that he had to find out what that missing quantity was and supply it, for the sake of the battalion, if for no other reason.

Major Owens had sensed all this, hence his question.

The answer—the real answer—will have to wait, Eric thought.

While he was leading the battalion up the dark, slippery trail that led to the Octopus' peak, Eric thought about the order he would have to give the company commanders shortly. He tried to visualize the important features of the ridgeline so that he could organize the defense in such a way as to take full advantage of the ground around the peak. He wondered how he would attack the peak if he were the enemy commander. That helped, for it focused his attention on exactly those parts of the mountain that might be critical. Gradually his imagination warmed up to the task of making the analysis—an analysis that might determine how many of Eric's men would live and how many would die. There were no absolutes and few facts which he could use, but there were some prejudices, and those prejudices gave him a place from which he could begin.

George Company's the best, he thought. They get the peak. Fox is weakest—put them next to Red on the ridgeline, to the right of George. Easy gets the left end. How Company's heavy weapons in the draw behind the peak—

Putting the battalion into position was a delicate maneuver, for although the enemy was not attacking at the moment Eric arrived on top, there was an excellent chance that all hell would break loose at any time. Artillery was swishing so close as it went over the ridgeline that one man in the command group said he'd feel better if somebody'd cut a groove for the rounds to slide through.

Holloway had his companies line up directly behind Red's companies, so that all that the men of the battered First Battalion had to do was stand up, face to their right, and begin walking. Men from the Second Battalion stepped right into their foxholes, and the relief was complete.

The relief was far less simple for the headquarters groups, for Eric had to get all of the information he could from Red's battalion commander and operations officer before they left, and then he had to check the entire line to make sure it was properly tied in with Red on the right and well button-hooked on the open left flank.

It was nearly five o'clock, nearly morning, when he returned to the oversize foxhole that was the battalion command post.

"What? No painted rocks?" Holloway asked Trent as he slid into the hole.

"No, sir, and no Colonel Merlin, either."

"No word from him at all?"

"Nope."

"Companies all reporting negative?"

"Yes, sir."

Eric took off his steel helmet and rubbed his hand over his short hair. The light drizzle felt good: he began to relax.

"I think I'll just be still for a few minutes."

It was too dark for the dead-tired officer to see Trent smile.

Well, Eric thought, this is what I spent five years getting ready for. All of that schooling seemed like a hell of a waste of time, didn't it? Maybe it was—certainly it was dry, sterile, negative, boring. But right now this battalion is in pretty good shape. Not the best possible shape, maybe, but every man is in a position from which he can kill anybody who tries to get him. That's something. Somebody had to say the words that made that so, and until Merlin gets here, I'm that somebody. So if we hold this mountain, if these men have a fighting chance, or a fair chance to fight, maybe all those years weren't wasted, after all—

3

"Hey, Holloway!" someone called.

Eric woke up. He could see a figure standing near the hole, but he couldn't tell who it might be.

"I heard you had a field grade officers' latrine up here."

It was Steve Jamison—Fandango.

"You people use any artillery-type shooting?"

"Bless your heart, Steve. Crawl in out of the heat."

"Owens told me Merlin's out strolling. Said you're Gasoline Six till he turns up."

"You know what I am? I'm a tired old man, and I keep hearing the boat whistles down at the beach. You know how they go? They go 'Tooo-t Toooo-t.'"

"You *are* ready to flip."

"Well, we're glad to see you."

"You want me to shoot some?"

"Can you guarantee that every other one will clear the ridgeline?"

"That's a fair percentage—fifty-fifty."

"I think we're set for the time being, thanks. Ogilvie left me some hot concentration numbers—said to call him on this private wire if I needed help."

Eric handed Fandango a piece of paper with six numbers on it.

The artilleryman took a flashlight out of his pocket and cupped one hand around the lens, then he crouched down as far into the hole as he could get and turned the light on for a moment.

"Got 'em."

He stood up again and put the flashlight away.

"Just tell me when to pull the chain."

"Will do."

The companies called in their five o'clock reports: all quiet.

Trent called regiment to pass the word, and regiment wanted to know about Colonel Merlin.

"No sign of him," Trent replied.

"What do you think happened to him?" Jamison asked Eric.

"I figure he's walking around on the backside of this mountain, someplace, probably lost."

Eric thought for a moment, then he added, "Of course, he might not be lost at all."

"Hiding, you mean?"

"No. I mean he might be getting the feel of the ground up here. He's never really seen the Octopus before. Maybe he'll turn up when he knows what a bastard of a mountain this thing really is."

"If that's true, it makes him pretty stupid."

"Not entirely. The book says to make a personal reconnaissance."

"Book also says, 'keep in touch.' Did Dahl ever do anything like this?"

"Not that I know of. But I imagine even Dahl was green once. He must have had to get a certain amount of stupidity out of his system. I get a little kicked out of mine every time I turn around."

"Are you taking up for Merlin?"

"In a way, yes. He's got a much harder war to fight than we have. The book's in his way—he knows too much."

"You mean, the book doesn't match the war?"

"No, it matches the war all right, I guess. I haven't seen a hell of a lot of the book, lately. It's just a matter of blending, or reconciling the book and the war, or something. And I guess that's what Merlin has got to do."

The phone rang. Trent answered.

"It's Fox Company, sir," he said to Holloway. "Colonel Merlin's coming up the ridgeline from there."

"Good."

4

Firing broke out in front of the peak, in George Company's part of the line.

The men in the command post hole ducked instinctively, then recovered a moment later when they realized that noise wouldn't kill them.

"Better get ready to pull that chain, Fandango," Holloway said.

"Done."

Jamison cranked the handle of the artillery phone, then

270

he asked for one of the concentrations Red had registered.

"That'll give the guns something to warm up on while I go up to George Company."

Jamison jumped out of the hole and ran up to the peak.

In less than a minute, rounds were slipping overhead, then crashing into the finger that led northward from the peak, the finger where the darkness and the rain and the long, miserable night had teamed up with the attackers who were trying to recapture the peak George Company had taken from them only two days before.

Alex Schaefer called Holloway a few minutes after the shooting started.

"It's a big one," he said quite calmly. "Jamison's up here, and I'm getting ready to throw mortar fire right in front of the Second Platoon."

"Sounds good, Alex. I'll leave you alone as much as I can —you call me, if you need help."

Eric remembered how much he resented battalion's well-intended interference at critical times. Still, this would be Schaefer's first fight as a company commander.

God be with us, Holloway prayed.

Eric waited about five minutes, thinking that Merlin would arrive to take over anytime. But Merlin didn't come, so he called regiment and told Major Owens what he could about the situation.

As soon as he had completed his call, Fox Company's commander called Eric.

"Merlin's been down here raising pure hell," the officer said. "He moved a bunch of my people all to hell and gone. I'm not sure I'm still tied-in with Red—I'm pretty sure I'm not!"

"Merlin's left your area, has he?"

"Yeah, he's gone, headed your way."

"Look. We—"

Sharp machine gun fire interrupted him. He knew that Fox was tied in now—with the enemy.

He tried to get the company commander back on the

phone, but he failed. Eric could imagine what was going on down there: fright, confusion, fumbling, all in the wet darkness. The firing was heavy and violent, but Eric knew that most of it was coming in rather than going out, and he didn't like to think about what that might mean.

"What's happened, sir?" Trent asked.

"Merlin's moved Fox. They're tied in with the enemy, and not with Red."

"Oh, hell!"

The telephone rang, and Holloway picked it up.

It was Fox Company.

"What do you want me to do about this thing?" Fox Six asked. "Hold till we get some light, or try to get 'em out of there now?"

Holloway realized that another critical moment had come. He couldn't speak for a moment, and during that long agony he tried to think his way through the whole problem. Be right, he told himself. People are going to get killed if you goof now.

If he told Fox to hold, it would give the enemy time in which to bring up more men and more ammunition, and it might take all day to clean them out. Or, the enemy might play hell with Red. Or he might just roll over the ridgeline and slide down the gully to shoot up the regimental command post. Hell—he could go all the way to the beach.

But if he told Fox to counter-attack now, Fox would be shooting into Red's nearest company. Too, Fox would be burning up ammo, and they might need just that much to hold off the main event, if it came their way.

This problem, like so many problems combat commanders must face, was not a question of picking the right answer, but the least wrong answer. And the hell of it, Eric thought, is that this really isn't my problem at all—it's Merlin's. Now that I know he's alive, nothing I say will be legal anyway. He's got to show up.

"Hold what you've got, and when Colonel Merlin gets here I'll get a better answer for you."

"Dammit, Holloway, you're going to be talking to one of those bastards if you don't quit being the gutless wonder and make your Goddam mind up. I've got people getting killed out there—"

"I know it, and I'm sorry as hell. This is the way it has to be. Don't give up any more ridgeline—do whatever you can —but wait, wait and we'll get this damned thing straightened out."

"Go to hell, Holloway!"

The Fox Company commander threw down the phone.

Eric handed his phone back to Trent.

"Send somebody to find Colonel Merlin. Have them drag him back bodily if you have to, but get him up here."

Holloway picked up the phone to call regiment. He twisted the crank on the side of the phone a number of times, but there was no sound at all in the line. It's dead, he thought. Now we're really alone.

As soon as Trent returned, Holloway told him about the phone's being out.

"I'll send a man to trace the wire and find the break," Trent said, then he scrambled out of the hole once more.

Just as he got clear of the hole, a shot rang out in the night.

Trent screamed.

His body fell back into the hole and rolled over Holloway. Holloway grabbed the sergeant and turned his body so that he could see how badly he was hit.

"Where is it, Trent?"

Trent opened his eyes and moaned. His hands moved to cover his stomach.

Eric looked and felt for blood, but there wasn't any.

"How'd it get you?"

Trent felt his belt buckle. There was a large, deep dent in the brass, and the buckle was hot. A slug had ruined the belt buckle and given Trent the scare of his life, but except for a severe soreness, he was all right.

"Now let's find out who shot you," Holloway said.

"No, sir. Keep your head down. It was from a long way off—Fox Company, maybe. Been any closer, they'd have had me."

As they were talking, Holloway heard someone coming along the path that ran down to the command post hole from the ridgeline. Whoever it is, Holloway thought, he's making too damned much noise.

A moment later, Lieutenant Colonel Merlin slid into the hole.

"We're mighty glad you're here, sir," Holloway said. He realized he really meant that. "We've got troubles."

"Yes, we have, Holloway. Mostly because of the way you ran headlong up here with my battalion."

"Sir, I was acting under orders from regiment. Until I heard you were at Fox Company, I—"

"I know damned well what you were up to. Now remember that you're just a staff officer, and that's all. You won't even be that as soon as I can get some competent officer replacements."

"Very well, sir. Do you want a report on the situation?"

"I know what's going on, Holloway. Somebody shot at me while I was on the way up here. I want the name of the man who fired that shot."

Eric and Trent exchanged knowing glances.

"What are you going to do with the man if you find him, sir?" Trent asked.

"What do you mean?" Merlin snapped.

"Poor bastard was jerked up out of civilian life by a draft board, kicked around in basic training for too short a time, shipped to the infantry, slapped overseas, and there are a couple o' hundred people out there on that finger who are doing their damndest to kill hell out of him. Now just what difference will taking his name make to a poor son of a bitch like that?"

"Get out of this hole! Out! Get out!"

"See you later, Lieutenant. I'll go see about that line myself."

274

5

"Colonel, Trent was hit by the round that missed you," Eric said.

When he saw Merlin wasn't going to answer, Holloway continued.

"The phone line to regiment is out. So is the radio—that net control problem last night sapped all the batteries. Fox Company has been penetrated at the place where they were tied in with the First Battalion. Fox Six wants a decision about that—do you want them to counter-attack, or hold what they've got left until daylight, and then counter-attack?"

"Counter-attack now."

"We have no way of letting Red know that's what we want to do. They're likely to think it's an attack on them, and shoot Fox up."

"What would you do—wait till they're behind us with their whole army?"

"I'd hold. There'll be some daylight in thirty minutes or so, and we might get our phones back in, in the meantime."

"You think I was wrong to change Fox's line, don't you?"

"I have no opinion, sir, of whether you're right or wrong. I wouldn't have changed the line, if I'd been you."

When Merlin answered, it was in a strange, almost friendly voice.

"I want to protect my battalion. I wanted to make sure Fox was strong enough to hold our flank, so I put that platoon into a perimeter. I'd have put the whole battalion into a perimeter."

Merlin's voice began to betray rising excitement.

"But you—you had them strung out so thin I could hardly find them!"

"My orders were to go into the line and to tie in with Red, sir. Those orders still stand, as far as I know. Until we get contact with Red again, we're off-base."

Merlin was quiet for nearly a minute. Eric knew that Merlin was trying to make up his mind, and he pitied the man. Eric also knew that there was nothing more to be said. Merlin had to fight it out alone—horribly alone.

Finally, Merlin spoke.

"We'll wait."

Holloway sent a runner to Fox Company with the order. Then he sent another runner back to regiment to report the whole situation and his plan for counter-attacking. Regiment, in turn, would get word to Red so that the company nearest Fox would know what the shooting was about.

As Eric listened to the runner slogging down the path, he thought about the irony of it all. Here we have the most expensive, most elaborate system of mechanical communication the world has ever seen, he thought, but the fate of hundreds of men depends on a runner, sliding down a muddy path in the pre-dawn darkness with a message. We've substituted our mechanical inventiveness for effort, but somehow there are still enough guts to save us.

"Holloway, I was lost," Merlin said quite calmly. "But I know we ought to be in a perimeter. Regiment be damned."

Holloway said nothing.

"I want to save this battalion—that's all. And that's the only way. Come daylight, we'll go into a perimeter."

Holloway realized that Merlin was feeling his power. He remembered feeling that way when battalion's control had cramped him in his command of George Company. Eric knew how hard it is to face the fact of higher authority. I may be a gutless wonder at that, he thought, but regiment happens to be right about this. Authority has supported Merlin in the past. Now Merlin must accept authority.

Seventeen

There was scattered firing throughout the rest of the hour, but no really severe attacks developed against the Second Battalion.

As soon as there was enough daylight, Fox Company's First Platoon recovered the ground it had been removed from the night before. There were no casualties; the enemy had pulled out just before the attack. Fox tied in with Red, and both radio and phone communication with regiment were restored. Things were looking up.

About eight o'clock, when the sun was up and the mist had burned away, Merlin woke up from a short nap and announced his intention to walk the line. Before he left the oversize foxhole, he had Eric call each of the companies to order a general police of the line.

"Shaves, too, Lieutenant Holloway. They've all got to shave. Tell them."

Merlin knew that water was being carried up to the ridgeline by a native carrying party.

"Supervision is the essential element of combat command," Merlin said in a sing-song voice as he walked up the path toward George Company.

From what field manual did he get that? Eric wondered.

As soon as Merlin had gone, Trent slid back into the hole to talk to Holloway.

"I shot my mouth off, sir," Trent said. "I know I shouldn't have, but the bastard made me mighty Goddam mad."

"Personally, I don't blame you a bit, Sergeant. He's hard to take, Lord knows. But I wish you could have been here to hear him admit he was lost."

"He did?"

"He sure did."

"Where's he off to now?"

"Walking the line."

Eric stared out toward the land the enemy held, thinking. A thick layer of clouds covered the low ground, and the men on top of the Octopus could look down on that blanket as though they were in an airplane flying over the weather. It was a lovely sight. Off to the north, miles away, another ugly line of sawtooth mountains cut upward through the layer, and beyond that line of mountains there was another line, and another—

"What if the men laugh at him?" Trent asked suddenly.

"What did you say?"

"What if the men laugh at him, like they did at that fat General we used to have. Don't you remember the time he went stomping along the ridgeline—three dog-robbers trying to keep up with him?"

"I don't think Merlin could take laughter."

"That guy couldn't, either. A whole company doubled over in hysterics, and the General roaring at his aides. 'Get those names!' he hollered. It was wonderful."

Trent paused and pointed to the cloud mass.

"God, that's beautiful."

A moment later he went on with his story.

"Anyway, the madder he got, the more they laughed. It broke him. He left the division a week later."

Holloway almost said, "That's good." But he thought for a moment, and he saw that it wasn't good, perhaps; perhaps it was tragic. I'm standing right on the line that separates the two, he thought. I can understand the laughter of men who are miserable, and I can be glad that such a General is no longer commanding them. But I can also understand the basic cruelty of those men, and the destructive effect their laughter had on the General. They killed in a minute the thing he had worked thirty years—thirty years —to build. They killed the good he could do along with the bad they thought they saw. And yet I can't really blame the men. From their holes, he was a menace. And with the unerring instinct of men used to living in a dog-eat-dog world, they used the most devastating weapon they had, and they used it with brutal effect.

Now—would they do the same to Merlin?

2

"Got any drinkin' whiskey in there?" Eric heard someone say.

Eric looked up: it was Sam Mann.

"Lord! Am I glad to see you!"

Holloway jumped out of the hole and shook Mann's hand. Trent followed him out of the hole and greeted the captain.

"What the hell are you doing up here?" Eric asked.

"Well, I heered you-all had some drinkin' whiskey up here, and I come up to help you get rid of it."

"Are you all right, sir?" Trent asked.

"Sure. Just ask them nurses back at the pill-rollers'."

"Damn, I'm glad you're back. We sure need you. Are you for duty, or what?"

"Colonel Hobbs sent me up here. Thought Merlin could use me for something or other."

A moment later, Mann asked.

"Who's got George Company?"

"Lieutenant Schaefer has, since last night. Things have been pretty flexible. I had to grease the skids to get Gregg out of here without a court-martial. Did you hear about the rest of what's been going on?"

"Yes, I did. I heered you done good, Eric."

Mann spoke softly, almost apologetically.

"I heered you did a good job getting these folks up here last night, too."

Holloway smiled. This counts, he thought.
"Got a job for a crippled man up here?"
"Sure, we have. The battalion's been without an executive officer for over a week—or you could take the Three job so I could go back to George Company."
Eric paused, embarrassed. He had been too definite and emphatic on a subject that was beyond his control. Too, George Company was Mann's, and would always be, as long as anyone remained in the company who had known Mann. Other men might command the company with Mann gone, but as long as he was in the battalion, it was his, because of the curious and powerful loyalties which bind violent men forever to the companies in which they shed their blood.
" 'Course, I'm a little beat-up," Mann said as though he, too, realized that Eric had gone too far. "If I could go to George Company, I could kind of rest up, you know."
Eric was troubled by this remark, for somehow—he didn't know why—it occurred to him that Mann was dying, and had come home to die there. It was a wild notion, Eric knew. And yet, for Mann it was not so wild at all.
"Trent, is there a jug anywhere on this mountain?" Eric asked.
If Gregg had been around, he knew—but Gregg was not around, and they were not in George Company any more, but at battalion.
"Hell, I brought one with me," Mann said, recovering the bluster that served to hold men away from his painful lack of education and his earthiness, and at the same time drew men to him.
"Never saw me when I didn't have one, did you?" Mann added.
"Never want to see you when you don't."
Eric took the bottle from Mann. He pulled the tape from around the neck, cut the tax stamp with his fingernail, and took out the cork. He raised the bottle in salute to Mann, then he took a long pull. He handed it back to Mann, and Mann threw his head back and took a lengthy gulp. He of-

fered the jug to Trent, and Trent took two shots before handing the whiskey back to Mann.

" 'Nother one, Eric?"

"Thanks, no."

"Trent?"

"I pass."

The three men sat down on the floor of the foxhole. Mann put the whiskey on the ground within easy reach of the other two.

"To tell you the truth, I went AWOL from the pill-rollers'."

"Better food up here, huh?"

"Too Goddam many war stories back there. They wore me out telling me about Hill 745 or some damned thing. Nurses got upset 'cause I goosed one carryin' a bedpan."

The phone rang. Holloway answered it.

"White Three—yes, I'll be right up there. I got good news. Cap'n Mann's back with us."

When he finished, he stood up and put on his pistol belt and his steel helmet.

"That was Steve Jamison. He says he's glad you're back, and that you're a damned fool."

"I done been told that twenty-five times since I been back on the mountain."

"Colonel Merlin's out inspecting shaves. Fandango wants to do some shooting out in front of George Company—wants me to come look. Like to come?"

Mann thought it over.

"Guess I'd better wait and see the colonel," he said finally. "Besides, I ought to shave, I guess."

Holloway looked at Mann's face. There was about four days' growth of beard on it, but that didn't catch Eric's attention nearly as much as something else did: Mann had aged tremendously. His face was pale, and the lines in his face were etched much deeper. The man looked sick.

"I'll be back in a minute," Eric said, then he crawled out of the hole and left for George Company.

Trent picked up the phone and called Fox Company.

"You got any water down there yet?" he asked.

A moment later he laid the phone aside and turned to the captain.

"Natives poured out the water on the way up here."

"Easier to climb, that way. Well, no shave."

3

A few minutes later, Merlin came trotting down the path that led along the line. He was sweating, and Trent could tell that all hell was about to break loose, for there was a wild look in the battalion commander's eyes.

Merlin stood, breathless, looking down at the two men in the large foxhole.

Mann rolled over onto one hip and slowly, painfully, got up. He was dizzy for a moment. He hadn't realized how weak he still was, but he managed to salute.

"Cap'n Mann reporting for duty, sir."

Merlin did not return the salute.

"Trent, the men aren't shaving. Where's that water?"

Merlin looked steadily at Mann, though he spoke to Trent.

"The natives poured the water out on the way up, sir. They do that every time they think they can get away with it."

"Get more water."

"Very well, sir."

Trent called regiment and asked for another carrying party.

"What are you doing here, Captain?"

"Colonel Hobbs sent me up, sir. Thought you might maybe could use me."

Merlin didn't try to conceal his dislike for Mann. He winced at Mann's grammar, then turned away from Mann and spoke not to Mann but at the cloudbank.

"What does Hobbs think I'm running up here, a hospital?

282

Dammit, I can handle this battalion without any help, thank you, Captain. I don't think we have any openings."

Mann started to speak, to ask for George Company. That was all he wanted. He knew that staff duty was not for him. He had already come as high in the army as he would ever go, and he knew he could command George Company, even though he wasn't in such good shape.

"That's all, Captain," Merlin snapped, obviously anxious for Mann to leave. "And don't forget this!" he added, kicking the bottle of whiskey in Mann's direction.

"Very well, Colonel," Mann said.

Mann stooped painfully and picked up the bottle. He held it for a moment, then he handed it to Sergeant Trent.

"Give this to Lieutenant Holloway, 'cause I don't guess I'll see him again."

Trent took the bottle and nodded.

Mann straightened up and saluted once more.

Merlin flipped a hand to his brow without looking at Mann, then Mann started crawling out of the hole. He gritted his teeth in agony as he got to his feet again, then he walked slowly down the path that led down into the valley behind the Octopus.

4

Eric returned to the battalion command post about five minutes after Mann had gone. Merlin, too, had left again in the meantime.

Trent gave Holloway the whole story.

"Cap'n Mann was down—and th' bastard kicked him!"

Trent was so angry he could hardly talk.

"I could have killed the bastard!"

A moment later, he added: "I should have. I should have!"

Eric caught Mann about halfway down the path. He stopped him and pulled him over beside the trail to a place where they could sit down. Then Holloway realized that there was nothing to say.

Mann spoke first.

"He ain't runnin' no hospital."

"I'm sorry as hell, but he's—"

"He's the battalion commander, Eric. He's king of the damn mountain, and if he doesn't want help, that's all there is to it. I kinda wonder, though, if some of the men couldn't use a little hollerin'-at. That's what I thought I might do, that's all."

Eric looked at the ground, and said nothing.

"Hell, I couldn't get along there, anyway. Never was any good at playin' politics. He and I live in different worlds, Eric. It wouldn't do for us to have to stay in the same hole longer'n five minutes. He knows it. He was man enough to kick me the hell out without making any excuses or thinkin' up any fancy lies—just said 'Git!'"

"But you know he's wrong."

"No, I don't. Maybe he's right. Anyway, it's over and done. Maybe Hobbs'll have me something to do. Never heered of a soldier dyin' for lack of work, did you?"

Eric shook his head.

Mann was right, of course. Merlin was everything that Mann was not. Merlin was trained—not educated, but he'd been to the schools army officers are supposed to attend, and apparently he'd done well. And yet, training was not enough—Merlin proved that. For all his schooling, Merlin lacked the qualities that Mann had in abundance. Somewhere, somehow, Mann had acquired the kind of heroic humanity that made him a real leader of men. Mann was almost primitive; he might have been a caveman-age tribal leader, or Ajax, or Uncas. Eric knew that Mann and Merlin must have sensed these basic differences when they had met. But why hadn't Merlin been big enough or smart enough to sense the good that those very differences might do the battalion?

"Well, you've got work to do up there," Mann said, rising to continue his lonely trip down the mountain. "Oh, I nearly forgot," he said, reaching into his pocket.

He fished around in his pocket for a moment, then he

pulled out a battered set of captain's bars and handed them to Eric.

"You'll be needin' these pretty soon. I got me some new ones back in the rear echelon. I'd kinda like for you to have these. They ain't so good lookin', but—well, there ain't many captains around any more, and you might not get any given to you for awhile. These'll do, till you can get back to get you some new ones."

Then he turned and walked down the trail, before Eric could speak.

Eric looked at the bars for a long time, then he turned and began climbing back up to the ridgeline.

5

When he reached the battalion C. P., Holloway sat down beside Trent.

"What's up?" he asked.

"Plenty," Trent answered, disgusted.

"Battalion commander gone again?"

"Yes, sir."

Trent jerked his thumb in the direction of George Company.

"A little water got up here, so he's gone to make sure George's doggies shave."

Trent shook his head slowly from side to side.

"Regiment wants him to call. They'd probably tell you what they want."

Eric picked up the phone and called Major Owens.

"I'm glad somebody up there cared enough to call," Owens said. "Colonel Hobbs wants you to send a patrol out to clear that finger that leads into George Company. As soon as you can get somebody up and moving."

"How many somebodys?"

"Oh, a platoon ought to do it. Hell, this is for your battalion's own good. It's not exactly any of my business, but why haven't you laid on something like this before now?"

"If I told you, sir," Holloway answered, thinking of Merlin's preoccupation with shaving, "you wouldn't believe me. Well, I'll set this thing up, and I'll let you know as soon as we have something going."

After he had finished talking to Major Owens, Eric turned to Trent.

"Did Merlin say anything about clearing the finger out there?"

"You know he didn't, sir."

"Watch things a minute."

Holloway climbed out of the hole.

"I'm going up to George Company to find him."

Eric walked almost casually up the ridgeline, thinking as he walked of how different it was to be walking alone. A man who is a little bit crippled, he mused, will always walk faster or take longer strides when anyone is following him—why? Then Eric remembered why he was walking, and he was ashamed. He thought of Sam Mann, limping down the path, and his pace quickened.

Merlin was supervising the policing of a squad area when Holloway found him. The men were moving around their holes, picking up food cans and pieces of paper, even cigarette butts.

Merlin ignored Holloway's presence until he had inspected the area, then he muttered a few words at the men and walked away from them.

One of the men threw his steel helmet into a foxhole and screamed "You son of a bitch!"

Merlin wheeled around, but he was too late. All four of the men stood by their holes, all four were bareheaded, all four were staring at Merlin with cold hatred in their eyes.

Holloway broke the awful silence.

"Colonel Hobbs wants you, sir."

Merlin didn't respond for a moment, then he shifted his sullen gaze from the men to Holloway.

"Colonel Hobbs?"

"Yes, sir. He has an order for you."

"You know what it is?"

"Major Owens outlined it to me."

"What is it?"

"Regiment wants us to clear the finger that leads into this area, sir. Platoon-size patrol. As soon as we can get one out there."

Merlin looked out at the finger. It was as mean as any in the Octopus' system, a razor-sharp ridge running north for about two-hundred yards, then hooking sharply to the northeast, then east. An enemy using that finger could move along it to a point within rifle range of the Second Battalion's line, then halt, then build up firepower to support an assault, then hit the peak itself. That firepower was the real threat, as the men in the foxholes knew from the long night before, when it had been applied broadside to their line.

"Hobbs is right," Merlin said. "But it'll be company-size. George Company."

Merlin looked back at the bareheaded soldiers.

"George Company!"

"Colonel Merlin, I wouldn't recommend that at all," Holloway said. "Use a platoon from Easy Company. They're at the end of the line. George ought to stay in place, here."

"Loyalty to your old outfit is fine, Lieutenant, in its proper place. But I said George Company and by God I mean George Company!"

"Very well, sir. Are you going to issue the orders, or shall I?"

"You will, of course."

Merlin turned and walked down the trail a few paces, then he stopped and turned around.

"I will command the patrol."

6

Eric sat down beside Fandango at George Company's command post foxhole.

"I have news for you," he said to Alex Schaefer. "You are now in 'Task Force Merlin.'"

Holloway watched the looks on the faces of his friends change from cordial to grave ones, and he regretted his flippant manner.

"Regiment wants the finger out yonder cleared. Merlin's given you the mission, but he's going along to command the patrol."

"How soon?" Alex asked.

"It's ten after nine, now. Can you be ready by nine-thirty?"

"Yes."

Schaefer looked upset.

"All right, nine-thirty, then," Eric said. "Everything okay?"

"Merlin was just over here giving me a hard time. Is this patrol idea legitimate, or is it pure peevishness?"

Holloway thought for a moment before he answered. Really, the answer was "both." But he knew that the operation would be difficult enough without his adding fuel to the feud.

"It's legitimate. Orders of Colonel Hobbs."

"You said Merlin threw the ball to George Company," Schaefer cut in.

"He's the battalion commander."

Jamison turned so that he faced Holloway squarely.

"Look, Eric. You know you can level with us. Why are you covering for the bastard?"

"Steve, I don't like this any more than you do. But the man's the law on this part of the mountain. What you or I may think is interesting, but that's all. It's Merlin's job, Merlin's mission. It's tough that he chose to do it this way, but we've seen worse, and if we live we'll see worse yet."

"You didn't answer my question, Sport."

"All right! I'm covering for the bastard because he happens to be right."

Suddenly Holloway realized that Merlin *was* right. This was the only way the finger could be cleared. A platoon from Easy Company might have been able to sweep the finger, but

288

it couldn't stay out there to make sure that the finger stayed clear. George Company's use in the mission would cause a temporary gap in the line, it was true. Still, by having Fox and Easy stretch toward the peak and tie in with each other, covering George Company's part of the line, George Company could stay out there on the finger to protect the rest of the battalion from attack for as long as it had to.

"Merlin happens to be exactly right, and I was wrong in trying to sell him a platoon out of Easy Company, because they couldn't have done this thing right."

"Are you going, Eric?" Schaefer asked.

"No. With Merlin gone, I have to stay up here and see after Fox and Easy, and keep regiment pacified."

Fandango got up and walked away.

Schaefer began calling his platoons.

Holloway gave Schaefer a little more information on the mission, then he got up and left.

7

Eric Holloway moved the battalion command post up to the ridgeline as soon as George Company and the battalion commander jumped off on their mission. Easy and Fox Companies had stretched along the line and were tied in near the large foxhole Eric and Trent were using. The ground fog had burned off by nine-thirty, so visibility was perfect from the new command post.

Warfare, Eric thought, is always mean—but it is especially mean when a man can't see, when a man can't find his enemy. Thank God for this good weather.

Trent had been dozing in the warm sunshine. If it hadn't been for the patrol, Eric might have dozed off, too. As things were, he felt he had to keep an eye on the progress of the operation. So far, all had been quiet.

George Company had jumped off at nine-thirty sharp. A heavy artillery preparation, ordered by Merlin, had lasted until the last second before jump-off time. Holloway recalled that Merlin had been well pleased with the beginning of the operation. If all went well, Merlin might—

"Phone, sir," Trent said. "Regiment."

"Lieutenant Holloway speaking, sir."

"This is Colonel Hobbs, Holloway. I just heard that Merlin sent a whole company out on that finger and went with it himself. Is that right?"

"Yes, sir. That's right."

"They run into anything yet?"

"No, sir."

"As soon as Colonel Merlin returns, tell him I want to see him."

"Very well, sir. Is there anything I could do?"

"No. Just be sure he gets down here as soon as this thing's over. You understand?"

Eric could tell that the colonel was so angry he could hardly speak.

"Yes, Colonel. I'll tell him."

Eric handed the phone to Trent, then he walked over to the forward edge of the hole and picked up a pair of field-glasses. He scanned the finger, looking for signs of the enemy or the company. Signs were surprisingly few. He might have given up his scanning, he might even have taken a short nap —but scattered firing broke out on the finger, much closer to the Octopus' peak than Eric believed possible.

"Oh, hell!" he said to Trent.

8

"Now!" Merlin shouted back to Schaefer. "Get that platoon back of you to maneuvering!"

Schaefer looked blankly at Fandango.

"Maneuvering? Where?"

"Is the man nuts?" Jamison asked.

Schaefer looked down the finger to the place where Merlin had been a moment before, but Merlin had already moved on.

"Lord, I do believe that fool has gone up to lead a squad!" Schaefer said.

Merlin ran past the men of the First Platoon toward the place the firing had come from.

"Come on! Let's go get 'em!" Merlin called as he ran past the crouching figures. "You'll never get 'em hiding behind a rock."

The men didn't move. Some of them shook their heads sadly.

Suddenly Merlin realized that he was all alone. None of the men had followed him, and he was far out ahead of the lead scouts.

A burst of machine gun fire from the enemy cracked over his head, then there were ricochets from a low rock on his left.

Merlin mistook the thumps he heard for the sound of Dolan's machine gun, which had not been fired all morning. He turned to tell Digger's gunner to stop shooting, but he couldn't see the gunner anywhere.

"Cease firing!" Merlin shouted up the finger. "Cease firing that machine gun!"

Another burst cracked over him, and suddenly the morning air was filled with laughter. Merlin ran a few feet, then he ducked behind a rock.

" 'Cease firing' " someone shouted mockingly, and the men laughed all the more.

9

"Can you tell anything about it, Lieutenant?" Trent asked.

"No, except that it's all enemy fire. Get a radio opened up on George Company's channel."

Trent called a radioman over to the new command post hole. A minute or two later, the set was in operation, and Trent placed the handset on the rim of the hole where Holloway could hear Schaefer's transmissions.

"I'll be damned glad when this caper's over," Trent said.

"So will I."

"That man's got no more business out there with that company than my Aunt Emma."

Eric didn't reply. He was getting tired of defending Merlin. Moreover, he disliked Trent's being so outspoken.

"Wonder why Schaefer's not shooting back?" Eric asked.

"It's not Lieutenant Schaefer's show any more than it's mine."

"Dammit, Sergeant," Eric said sharply, "cut that out."

10

Merlin crawled up the trail toward the rock where Schaefer and Fandango were taking cover from the machine gun fire. When the men grew tired of laughing they stopped, but every minute or two someone would shout "Cease firing!" and there would be more snickers from behind the large rocks that were scattered on both sides of the narrow trail.

When Merlin reached Schaefer's rock, he slid behind it and rested for a minute before he said anything. Finally, when enough breath had returned, he began shouting curses at Schaefer for not maneuvering the Third Platoon around the First, and for not coming to his aid.

"By God, Lieutenant, I'm going to have you tried for cowardice as well as inefficiency! First thing I'm going to do when we finish this is get you replaced. You're trying to get me killed, I know, so your friend Holloway will get the battalion. You'd like that, wouldn't you? Then he'd hand out Silver Stars to all of you!"

"No, sir, I'm not trying to get you killed," Schaefer replied. "Now, just what do you want done about that machine gun?"

"Wipe it the hell out!" Merlin screamed.

"Very well, sir."

Schaefer turned to Fandango.

"Can you squirt some hot stuff on that damned thing?"

"I think so. I've got to move to make sure. Wait a minute."

Fandango ran across the trail to the place where his artillery radio was set up. He was about to begin calling a fire mission when Merlin spoke again.

"No, Lieutenant Schaefer, I do not want artillery on that target. We can take care of it ourselves. Where are your mortars?"

"In the column, sir, but they take too much time to adjust, and after all that firing last night, we're low on ammunition."

"No excuses, Lieutenant."

"Sir, I'm—"

"I said put mortar fire on that gun."

Schaefer shrugged his shoulders.

"Hold off, Fandango," he said.

Schaefer called back on his radio to the leader of the company's mortar section, and ordered the mortars forward.

"I can get the fire faster and save you ammo, Colonel," Jamison yelled to Merlin.

"Will you people stop arguing with me?" Merlin answered. "I'm the commander of this task force, and by God you'll do as I say! As for you, Jamison, I'm reporting you to your battalion commander."

"You do that, Colonel, you do that."

Then Fandango turned to Schaefer again.

"You want I should help your boy shoot?"

Merlin cut in before Schaefer could answer.

"You stay out of this, Lieutenant Jamison. A rifle company has enough fire power to take care of itself. There's no sense in our carrying all of this hardware around if it isn't going to be used, is there?"

"But, Colonel, dammit, he's low on ammunition!"

"If he is, it's his own fault. He should have rationed its use last night."

"Like hell he—"

"Lieutenant! I gave you a direct order to quit arguing with me!"

"You won the argument a long time ago, Colonel."

11

Regiment called at ten.

"How's that patrol, Holloway?" Major Owens asked.

"Quiet at the moment, sir," Eric answered. "A machine gun cut loose on them about ten minutes ago, but since then it's been quiet out there."

"Merlin doing all right?"

"As far as I can tell from here, he is. He looked good when he left. Maybe he's catching on."

"He'd damned well better do this one right, or he's had it. Well, let me have progress reports every half-hour from now on, will you?"

"Yes, sir. I'll do that."

Eric handed the phone back to Trent.

"Hobbs going to get Merlin's scalp?" Trent asked.

It was the first time either of them had spoken in some time.

"If anything goes wrong, and Colonel Merlin's at fault, I imagine he will."

"Which means we may get us a new battalion commander."

"Have it your way."

12

Out on the finger, mortar rounds began chumping into the enemy's portion of the long ridge.

As soon as the first rounds landed, Merlin jumped out from behind the rock and gleefully shouted, "We've got 'em now! Get up, men, and follow me!"

But the enemy's machine gun opened up again. Merlin slid on his face in the mud, then rolled off the trail, scratching for cover.

Curiously, three men had stood up. But now they were down again.

Fandango slipped over to the mortar observer and helped him bring the rounds closer to the enemy gun. But even with Fandango's expert help, the adjustment was painfully slow, and took over half the company's supply of mortar ammunition.

"Fire for effect!" Merlin called.

The mortar F. O. looked at Schaefer as if to say, "Is that right?"

Schaefer nodded.

The observer called "Fire for effect" back to the gunners. Jamison threw his map on the ground in disgust.

Nine rounds crunched into the finger in volleys of three, then the finger was quiet once more.

"Rounds complete," the F. O. reported to Merlin. "And we're slap-dab clean out of ammo."

But Merlin didn't hear. He jumped up and ran down the trail, getting men on their feet and organizing them for an assault on the machine gun position.

"Colonel," Digger Dolan protested, "you shouldn't be up here. This here's my job."

"Never mind, Sergeant. Follow me!"

Merlin started toward the rock from which the machine gun fire had been coming. The men followed him, bayonets fixed. But behind them, up the ridge, enemy mortar fire began falling on the rest of George Company.

13

"This is Colonel Hobbs, Holloway," the voice on the phone roared. "Get Merlin back. We've got two flights of fighter planes to put on that finger, and I want him back and out of the way."

"Very well, sir. I'll pass the order along and I'll call you back when the finger is clear."

Holloway tried to get Merlin on the radio, but Schaefer answered and told Eric about the machine gun and Merlin's assault.

"It was a hell of a thing, Eric. You should have seen him. He ran up there, and he had Digger Dolan's people right with him. The enemy had pulled out, though. All Merlin got was one of those little carts they pull their heavy machine guns around on."

"Regiment wants you back up here so that they can put an air strike or two on that finger. Can you get word up to Merlin? Over."

"I'll sure as hell try. Out. Merlin's got us moving again—it'll be kinda hard. Out."

"You hear that?" Holloway asked Trent.

"I did. I got me a Bronze Star once for doing the same thing. Only, I *had* to do it. Only four of us were left, and we had to shoot our way out. We weren't trying to impress anybody."

14

As soon as the hot steel splinters and shattered rocks had stopped flying, Merlin called "Cease firing those mortars!" back to George Company's F. O.

"You're killing your own people!" Merlin yelled.

"He is nuts," the F. O. said to Fandango. "Them's incoming rounds. I'm gettin' the hell out of here!"

The man jumped up and ran back to the mortar section.

Jamison picked up the microphone to his radio.

"Fandango Seven, this is Fandango Five-Seven. Fire mission!"

"It's down there, Steve," Schaefer shouted, pointing down to the left. "All the way down at the bottom. I can hear the damned mortar firing!"

"Are you sure?"

"Hell yes, I'm sure!"

"Then I can't get it—not even with high-angle fire."

Fandango was bitterly disappointed. All of the precision and skill that artillerymen had developed in two thousand years could not help George Company now, because of a sharp finger that dropped off so abruptly that rounds could not clear the ridge to get at the enemy's mortars at the base of that finger.

"And we haven't got any mortar rounds of our own," Schaefer said bitterly. "We've got to get out from under this stuff, though."

"Can't Holloway put some of How Company's mortars on this thing?" Fandango asked.

"He's got word from regiment that we're supposed to back up and let the damned airplanes shoot this place up. There isn't time for him to do anything, now."

"I don't care! I'll shoot over your radio—I'll do the adjusting, and you can go ahead and get out of here. But we've got to do something—"

Tears streamed down Fandango's face.

Rounds from the enemy mortars were crashing into George Company at a steady rate. Several men were already hit: the fire was coming in all over the finger.

"Pack up and go, Fandango," Schaefer yelled. "Now!"

Schaefer turned and gave orders for some of the company command group to get the wounded men out. That done, he passed the word for the men behind him to start backing out. Then he sent word forward to Merlin.

"Tell Colonel Merlin the withdrawal's by order of Colonel Hobbs. He won't come unless you tell him that," Schaefer told the messenger. "Move!"

15

"I'm sorry, Lieutenant," Trent said. "I shouldn't have shot my mouth off like that."

"Forget it."

"That mortar fire out there sounds mighty bad to me, sir."

"Give Lieutenant Schaefer a call on the radio. I'm going to put something out there, if he's clear."

A moment later, Trent handed the officer the handset.

"This is Gasoline Three. What's new out there?"

"Eric, it's bad. I'm afraid Gasoline Six and at least one squad are going to be cut off. I can't get them to pull back, but I've got everybody else turned around. Wounded are on the way out to you now. Over."

"How many wounded?"

"Too damned many, Eric. I can't get that bastard Merlin to bring the squad back—he's 'way ahead, and I've already lost two men trying to get word to him. Over."

Schaefer's voice was strained. Holloway could tell that Alex was about to crack.

"Alex. Listen carefully. Do you know where the enemy mortar is? Over."

"Hell yes I do, but Fandango can't hit it for the ridge. We're out of sixty-mortar rounds. Over."

"All right. I'll get Fox and How set up to shoot for you. They're up here by me. I want you to come back up here—the planes may get here any minute. Now, hurry! Over."

"What about my squad down there? Do we just kiss 'em off?"

Schaefer was furious. And Eric couldn't blame him.

Trent pulled Holloway's arm.

"Regiment is on the phone, sir. Owens says the planes are on the way. The controller is at Blue's observation post and will run the air strike from there. They want clearance, and they want all artillery and mortar fire turned off until further notice."

"Tell regiment to wait a minute."

Then Holloway spoke into the radio again.

"Alex. The damned planes are almost here. Is there any way on God's green earth to get those people out? Over."

Schaefer did not answer for nearly a minute. Holloway was about to throw down the radio and go see for himself when Alex Schaefer's heartbroken voice came back on the radio.

"No. There isn't any way to get them out—ever. Merlin's taken that squad down to the bottom of the finger to get the guy's mortars!"

16

Dolan yelled at the battalion commander, but he knew it wouldn't do any good.

"Colonel! Them mortars ain't ours. They're shootin' from down yonder."

Digger pointed to the low ground beyond the north slope of the ridge.

Merlin fell to the ground, exhausted from the strain of being shot at—and laughed at. He hugged the ground, wishing that he could escape into it, wishing that he had not come with the company, wishing that he were not Lieutenant Colonel Merlin, but—

Merlin heard Dolan yelling something at the men.

"Get up, Bad Eye, and let's us go down yonder and get that damn thing."

Merlin realized he couldn't let Dolan take command like that. He saw in a flash that if he didn't do something positive, the men would follow Dolan down to attack the mortar position and leave him belly-down in the mud right where he was.

I can't stay here, Merlin thought. I've got to get up and do something.

Merlin stood up.

A burst of machine gun fire ripped through the air over his head and glanced off rocks that lined the trail back up the finger. My God, Merlin thought. We're cut off from the rest of the company!

He dropped to the ground again.

"Cease firing!" he heard someone mock, and another man snickered.

"Come on, men!" Merlin yelled, rising to a crouch and scrambling down the slope toward the enemy mortar position. "Come on!" he yelled back over his shoulder. "Let's go!"

"You heered the Colonel," Digger Dolan said to a man near him. "Move!"

Digger and the seven men who had already followed Merlin too far got up and ran down the rocky hillside, behind their battalion commander.

When Merlin reached the bottom, an enemy rifleman began pumping one shot after another at him.

Merlin ducked behind a tree. He glanced over his shoulder and saw the men behind him scurrying for cover. Merlin felt like shouting for joy: they *had* followed him!

Suddenly Merlin was slammed to the ground. He opened his eyes a moment later, but he couldn't breathe. Something had knocked the breath out of him, but he wasn't cut anywhere.

"Hand grenades!" he heard one of the men shout as another explosion deafened him.

I thought I'd been killed, Merlin thought. I thought I was dead!

The enemy rifleman opened up on the soldier who had yelled.

"I'm hit! I'm hit!" the man screamed.

"God damn it, shut up!" Digger shouted.

Another hand grenade bounced to within a few feet of the wounded man's body and exploded.

Again the man screamed.

Then he stood up.

"I'm getting the hell out of here," he whimpered. He turned and began scratching and clawing at the hillside in a pitiful attempt to climb back to the top.

Shots stabbed at him, and once or twice the soldier cried out, as though he were nicked.

The soldier called Bad Eye rose to follow the wounded man.

"Get down," Digger Dolan growled, "or I'll shoot you myself."

Bad Eye ducked just as a whole volley of rifle shots cracked around his head.

"Look on your left," someone shouted to Merlin.

An enemy soldier had moved around to get behind the attackers, and Merlin saw the enemy soldier clearly.

Merlin raised his pistol to fire, but panic hit him. He couldn't hold the gun steady! The image of the enemy danced over the sights. Merlin watched, horrified. The target raised his rifle to his shoulder—then the target screamed and fell dead.

"Nice goin', Digger," someone said.

Digger and Bad Eye got up and moved toward the mortar position once more, and the others followed. Merlin took longer dashes than the others, for he was trying to catch up with Digger and Bad Eye. He couldn't let them lead him!

When they were only a few yards from the mortar, Merlin realized that the time had come.

"Let's rush 'em!" he shouted. "Go! *Now!*"

The men rose with him and began firing at the enemy soldiers who were protecting the mortar. Merlin saw one of the enemy soldiers drop, horribly wounded. Another had a machine gun that had jammed, but suddenly the gun began firing and someone behind Merlin screamed.

Then something hot tore through Merlin's stomach. His throat filled with blood, and his knees crumpled under him.

When Merlin opened his eyes, he saw an enemy soldier kicking Digger Dolan's body. Merlin rose on one elbow and reached out to grab the soldier's boot, but he missed, and fell dead.

Eighteen

George Company moved back up the finger slowly, sadly. No one knew exactly what had happened to Colonel Merlin or to Digger Dolan and the men from his platoon who had gone down with Merlin, but everyone in the column knew that Merlin and the others were being left behind.

Holloway went down the finger to meet Alex Schaefer when the company command group neared the top.

"Any word about Merlin?" he asked.

Schaefer didn't answer, but kept slogging up the muddy path, ignoring Holloway.

"Alex. Where's Merlin?"

"Go get him yourself."

"What?"

Schaefer stopped and faced Holloway.

"Look. You and Merlin sent us down that God damned thing to clear it. We got half-way out, and you said come back. Well, here we are—what's left of us. I don't know how many people I've lost, but Digger Dolan is gone and so is most of his platoon. You thought this thing up—now you figure it out. I can't."

"Alex—" Eric began, but he decided it would be better to leave explanations until later. "I'm sorry to hear about Digger and his men. I really am. Put your company into a rest area behind the ridgeline and take it easy for a while. And I wish you'd come to the battalion C. P. when you can."

Schaefer walked on and left Holloway standing beside the path.

As the men walked by Eric they glanced at him momentarily, then looked on ahead. They looked at him as though he were a stranger—a dangerous stranger.

When the last of George Company's men had passed, Eric walked back to the battalion C. P. hole.

"Hear anything about the battalion commander, sir?" Sergeant Trent asked.

"No. He's missing. So is Digger Dolan, and a lot of his people aren't back, either."

"Oh."

Four jets flashed over the Octopus, then pulled up into a tight turn and began circling the peak.

Eric called Blue and told the Tactical Air Controller there that the finger was clear. When he had finished the call he told one of the men near the hole to get some air panels out to mark the battalion's line, then he sat down.

The flight of jets made two laps around the peak, then flew away to the north.

Trent and Holloway watched them until they were out of sight, miles deep in enemy country.

"What the hell goes on here?" Eric said, grabbing the phone and turning the crank angrily.

Colonel Hobbs took the call at Blue.

"What's the trouble, Holloway?" Hobbs asked.

"Colonel, how come the planes didn't hit the finger? We're clear, and they damned well know we are."

"They were low on fuel, Holloway. They had to go up to the bomb line and unload their armament. The other flight that we had been expecting was pulled off and given to another target—they couldn't wait for George Company to get back up there."

"I see."

Holloway was sick at the thought of all that wasted effort —all that danger, all that loss. And for what?

"What do you hear from Merlin? He back there yet?"

"No sir, he's missing. George Company took some pretty

bad losses out there. They even had to leave men behind. Now it looks as though it was all for nothing."

"Well, that's too bad. I want you to send another patrol out there to try to recover Merlin and to finish the mission, but hold up on it for a while. Owens told me that Sam Mann turned up back here a few minutes ago. I think I'm gonna send him back up there to take command of that battalion."

"Very well, sir."

"I'll get up there myself this afternoon if I can. By the way, you did a mighty good job up there last night."

Trent took the phone from Holloway's limp hand.

"Okay if I go down to George Company for a few minutes, sir?"

Holloway nodded. "Yeah, go ahead."

2

Fandango slid into the hole beside Holloway.

"Friend," he said, "you look like hell."

Holloway looked up and said, "That fits."

"Fill me in."

"The Goddam planes were low on bugjuice, or whatever it is they burn. Had to go up to the bomb line because we were too slow getting out of their way. We lost the other flight for the same reason. Now Hobbs wants us to go back down there."

"Bad."

"But one good thing happened. Hobbs says he may send Mann up here to take command of the battalion."

"That's good."

Holloway heard someone coming up the path, so he turned to see who it was. It was Alex Schaefer.

Schaefer sat down on the floor by Fandango. He didn't speak to either officer, but Eric broke the awkward silence.

"Alex, go ahead and blame me if you want to."

"I don't blame anybody."

304

"It was regiment's—" Fandango began, but Schaefer interrupted him.

"I know. Trent told us the whole story."

Eric was glad of that.

"You know what some of the men are doing back there now?"

"No."

"Shaving."

3

Sam Mann arrived at the battalion C. P. about two hours later. Eric and Trent saw him coming up the path and walked down to meet him.

"If I didn't know what I do know, I'd say welcome back," Eric said.

Mann grinned and held out his hand.

"Did the colonel call while I was on the way up?"

"Yes, he did," Eric replied. "He wants us to finish the job he had Merlin start."

A grave look came over Mann's face.

"Well, we ought to get the bodies back, anyway. What have you got up here on this damned thing in the way of soldiers—besides George Company?"

"Not a hell of a lot."

"I guess I've got to get used to being proud of these here other companies, now. Never thought it'd come to that."

"Fox is still edgy. Easy's in good shape. I've got How Company in better positions, and they're all set to support anything you want to try out there on that finger. Also, George is resupplied with all kinds of ammo. We're shy a lot of men, and the medical supplies are just about gone. No litters at all left."

Mann walked up to the ridge and looked down at the finger, studying it, thinking about the men who had died out there a few hours before.

"You've got Fox and Easy dug in, haven't you?" Mann asked Eric.

"Yes, sir."

"George back of the ridgeline?"

"Resting up."

Eric thought he knew what Mann was worrying about. Mann knew that the men of George Company would want to go back out there to finish their mission and retrieve their dead, but he didn't want to expose them to more danger—especially now. And yet if he sent another company—

"Eric, get hold of Lieutenant Schaefer. Ask him to come up here for a minute, please."

"Very well, sir."

A moment after Eric left, Mann turned and looked at Trent.

"Trent, maybe you ain't got enough to do. You're kinda like a first sergeant up here, aren't you?"

"Yes, sir," Trent answered, "except I haven't got anything to yell at but a couple of telephones."

"Well, I reckon you could find a man a little drinkin' whiskey, couldn't you?"

"I think so."

Mann jerked his thumb in the direction of the old C. P. hole, and Trent left to get the bottle Mann had left with him.

When Eric returned a minute or two later, Mann motioned for him to come over and sit down.

"Look, Eric," the older man said. "I heered a little gossip while I was hidin' down there at regiment. I know they think pretty highly of you back there—they like the way you backed up Colonel Merlin even though . . . well, you know. Anyway, Owens is tryin' to talk the colonel into getting you for his assistant."

Eric was surprised at that.

"Now, I can see why you'd want to take 'em up on that. You've had more than your share of troubles up here, and it'd be good for you to put in some time at a big headquarters like regiment."

Mann stood up and took off his steel helmet and scratched his head.

"But I'd sure like to have you stay around here a little while longer to kinda keep an eye on me. I'll tell you somethin'. I'm 'way out of my league, commandin' a battalion. I'm gonna need all the help I can get. Hell, I don't want any of these braves gettin' kilt 'cause I don't know the artillery's phone number, or somethin'."

Eric smiled and bowed his head. Funny, he thought. A few days ago—just a few days ago, this man and I sat on a hill over yonder watching other men fight and die, and I was the one who felt weak and ignorant and confused. Lord knows I still am, but if I've learned anything, if I've grown at all, if I really am able to help this man—good God, what a wonderful thing. He's a born commander, and before long he'll realize that a battalion is just an overgrown rifle company—and maybe he really won't need me. But if he should —if I can help him, just for a little while, even—if I can do any damned thing at all, I don't care what—then everything that's happened to me will have been worthwhile, because those experiences will have gotten me ready to help him try to get these men through this war alive. To be needed here, now—

"You know damned well I'll stay here, sir."

Mann grinned and put his steel back on.

"I can't promise you'll get promotions and medals and stuff like that there, like you'd prob'ly get back at regiment."

"Those things don't matter to me any more."

"They will if you're gonna stay in the army after this damned thing's over."

"Sir, you let me do what I can here. I'll worry about the rest when that time comes."

Eric was thinking about what Mann had said the other

day as they sat watching Blue trying to move up Rhino: "It's just a matter of getting one man around one rock. If he don't make it, nobody else can, either." Eric knew—now—how true that was, and he knew that the dirty, frightened man in the point of the attack is the most important man on the face of the whole earth, and would be, until there were no more rocks that had to be gotten around. What could possibly equal the glory of simply having the duty of helping Sam Mann, of all people, get these great men around the rocks ahead?

"Well, I 'spect we'd better get on with this here finger. Schaefer and Fandangle are on the way up here?"

"Yes, sir."

"Then I guess we'd better have one of them five-paragraph field orders ready for 'em—Pentagon style."

Eric grinned.

"Think we'd better go take one more look, sir?"

"Yep, I reckon we better."

Eric stood up and waited until Sam Mann had crawled out of the foxhole, then he jumped out and followed Mann to look at the finger.